Praise j

A HISTORY OI

[REVIEWS TO COME]

A

HISTORY

OF

SILENCE

BOOK ONE OF THE
HEARTLAND TRILOGY

A

HISTORY

OF

A NOVEL

Cynthia J. Bogard

atmosphere press

A History of Silence

Copyright © 2023 by Cynthia J. Bogard

ISBN 978-1-63988-633-3

Published by Atmosphere Press

Cover design by Kevin Stone
Interior design by Cassandra Felten

This is a work of fiction. Names, characters, places, and incidents are used fictitiously. Any resemblance to actual persons, living or dead, business establishments, events or locales is entirely a product of the author's imagination, or, in the case of Madison, a fictionalized remembrance of treasured places and institutions.

atmospherepress.com

For Sylvia,
and all those determined to survive

PROLOGUE

MADDIE

Professor Johnny Wharton the Fifth had finally found the ultimate way to keep us all talking about him. He'd gotten himself murdered, bled out all over the expensive Persian rug that graced the floor of his spacious office. Stabbed to death with the office scissors, I'd heard from our department secretary, Maria, her voice hushed and excited. He had kept, stupidly, some early Roman-era antiquities and coins in his office. No one knew what had happened to them.

Even in death, the man had a huge ego. His funeral had to be held in an architecturally interesting, historically important church built circa 1855. The oldest Southern Baptist church in Pine Hill Station, built by pioneers. Or possibly slaves. Johnny wasn't religious as far as I knew, but then, I'd gone out of my way not to know him. Johnny's last gift to the living was to make the outsized crowd sit for way too long on straight-backed, cushionless, pine pews, sweating in the un-air-conditioned humidity of an unseasonably hot late March in southern Texas. The church still had its tiny original windows, which barely opened. I guess electric fans would have violated historic preservation protocols because there sure weren't any running. I was wearing a black wool dress with mid-length sleeves. It was the only dress I owned in black, and I'd be damned if I was going to buy something new for *this*.

I waved the printed funeral program in front of my face to create a tiny breeze. We weren't even halfway through it yet. Prayer followed eulogy followed prayer followed eulogy. Had every single historian of the Roman Empire in the entire nation (aging white men, paunchy and bespectacled all) been invited to wax poetic about Johnny's intellect and academic conquests? On they droned and on and on. How his books had changed the scholarly interpretation of the Roman Empire. What a dynamic presenter he'd been at conferences. What a wry sense of humor. What a great colleague. What a shame, what a shame. In the prime of his career.

It was hard to square these hagiographies with the man I would have characterized a few months ago as a good ol' boy backslapper type, from whom any self-respecting woman would recoil. Not that he had ever paid me, the lone woman in the department for the first five years of my internment here, the least bit of attention. I'd been hired the year he'd been on leave, he said to me once, not too subtly. He hadn't opposed granting me tenure, though, I'll give him that. He wasn't the only one who could write a paradigm-changing scholarly work on an important era. My *Rethinking the American Century*, published in my third year here, still sells well — for an academic book. The book had made it impossible to deny me tenure. So here I was, stuck in this God-fearing-vestige-of-a-bygone-era of a town, where even our decent-sized university didn't offer insulation from a culture both alien and distasteful to me. I had acted rashly in consenting to come here. But then, love often makes for intemperate decision making.

I noticed Roz's black, straightened, shoulder-length hair a few rows ahead of me, distinctive in the sea of blond bobs and male-pattern baldness. She still made my heart clench, even though the price I paid to be her love was exorbitant. After tenure, I was ready to declare myself and my love, to come out of that smothering closet that makes liars out of all of us. And I told Roz so.

"I'm *from* here, Maddie," she had gasped. "My mama would ... and you're *white*," she finished, as if envisioning the racial consequences of our relationship for the first time. End of discussion.

Even now we kept up the pretense of being only vaguely aware of each other, just two colleagues in different departments in a faculty that numbered in the hundreds. Never sitting together, never really living together, and certainly no public displays of affection. The feminist movement had been in full swing a decade ago in northern university towns, like Madison, where we'd both earned our doctorates, our lesbian professors (the tenured ones, at least) coming out with an audacity that had been impossible only a few years before. Not so in Pine Hill Station. Here, we still wore pearls and low heels, shoulder-length hair, and dresses. Yuck. That tiny, unresolved conversation had left Roz so scared she'd run from me. Or at least, that's what I thought then. I shook my head to clear it of the memories of those terrible months.

I'm sure many wondered why I didn't search for a more suitable environment in which to pursue the rest of my academic career. With my broad-voweled Midwestern accent and left-of-center politics, it was more than obvious I didn't fit in here. But I couldn't leave her, and she couldn't leave this place. So here I was, sweltering in black wool, pretending to honor a man I had thoroughly disliked a few months ago and now loathed. Academics in the same department are joined together in something of an old-fashioned marriage — 'til death do us part. And not even then, when it came to Johnny and me. A rivulet of sweat ran down the side of my neck.

The coffin lid clicked as it closed for the final time. Why anyone would make their family and friends endure an open casket was beyond me, but Johnny always had an outsized opinion of his tanned and square-jawed good looks. Now the coffin proceeded down the aisle, the bearers, members of our university football team with huge shoulders bursting out of their black suits. Then came Johnny's family: his wife Liz, whom I knew slightly from university functions over the years, and their one daughter, Jenny, in her late teens. Liz looked ethereal and serene in her black Chanel skirt and jacket; her silver-blond hair perfectly coifed in this heat.

Jenny's head bowed, and her blond shoulder-length hair swept in front of her face as she and Liz followed the casket down the aisle. Someone dropped their car keys across the aisle from me with a clang and Jenny's head snapped up as if it had been gunshot. I gasped as I saw her face. The memories of last fall began to overwhelm me ... again.

CHAPTER 1

UNIVERSITY OF WISCONSIN, MADISON, WISCONSIN

LATE AUGUST 1985

JENNY

"Hey, y'all, I'm your new roommate," I called out, brushing my knuckles against the half-open door without looking inside. My Walkman headphones hung around my neck, and I could hear Cyndi Lauper singing, *Girls just want to have fu-un*. I still had on my Vuarnet shades, and I kept them on. I knew how I'd look to the roommate I'd been assigned: my straw-colored hair tied in spiked ponytails all over my head and a red streak sprayed down the middle of one side; black nail polish, black leather stud bracelets, a belted "Fuck You Frankie" T-shirt over a black fake-leather mini, and black Roman sandals on my feet. I chewed my gum noisily and knocked again. I wanted to get this over with. If I played it cool and mean, whoever they stuck me with this, my sophomore year, would take one look and ask to get moved like last year's model had. Or at least leave me alone the rest of the semester. For confidence, I'd downed a couple of Valiums a half-hour before. I would be low-key but tough, real tough. I'd have this girl running scared.

No response from inside the room so I sauntered in. "Hey, y'all, it's me, your new roomie."

What I saw stopped me cold. They'd put me with a Black girl. In all the time I spent imagining what kind of dormmate I'd wind up with this fall at UW-Madison, I never once thought it might be a Black girl. UW mostly was a sea of white faces. At my Christian Academy high school, there had been exactly one Black girl, and she was two years older than me, so I'd never spoken to her. In fact, beyond store clerks and waitresses, I'd never spoken to a Black girl my age in my life.

She looked up slowly from a textbook she'd been paging through.

"What'd you say, girl?" she asked, unfolding her legs and sitting up a bit. I glanced at the number on the door to make sure I had the right room. Yeah, 207, that was the number all right.

"I said, I'm your new roommate." This time, it didn't come out so cool.

"You did not. You said, *Hey, y'all*. You wouldn't be from Texas, would you?" She was standing now, a good five inches taller than me. She had on bright pink shorts that set off her long, deep brown legs. This wasn't going as I had planned at all.

"So what if I am?"

She started laughing and shook her head. "I don't believe it. I just don't believe it. You aren't one of those John Bircher debutante types, are you?"

"You think a debutante would go to a school like this?" The University of Wisconsin at Madison was a top state school, but it sure wouldn't be where the upper crust in Dallas would send their daughters. "Besides, do I look like a debutante?" I hurled the words at her, ending my question with a snarl. All the work I'd put into my tough London street look and she asks me if I'm a debutante.

"How am I supposed to know what a debutante looks like? You think they let someone like me go to their parties and parade around in one of those frilly chiffon dresses, drinking tea with my little finger stuck out? I just think it's funny that you're from Texas."

"What's so funny about that?"

"Cuz, girl, I'm from Texas too! They put both us foreigners in the same room! Sort of like a quarantine so we won't infect their Yankee accents. They put us in the same room cuz they thought we'd have something in common, both being from Texas and all."

She looked me over from head to toe and put on an exaggerated Texas drawl. "Yep, we looks like we got lots in common, we do. Near to being identical twins, shore nuff." She could imitate a good ol' boy accent with the best of them. "Now ain't that 'bout the funniest thing you ever heard, girl?" she continued in the same accent and looked down at me, waiting to hear what I did think.

Here's my chance. We probably did have nothing in common but Texas. Fling that at her in a smartass way and maybe she'll ask to be moved. Strangely though, I found myself wondering what she was like.

Mostly because I couldn't figure out my next move, I walked around her like she had me. I looked her up and down. She was nice looking. Slim and muscular, her hair was cut in a close-cropped Afro which emphasized her high cheekbones and strong chin. Her large, dark eyes were fringed with thick lashes, and she had the kind of mouth I guess you'd call sensuous. She was staring back at me. Her eyes looked amused.

"Well," I said finally, in my best Texan accent, "we're not even close to being i-dentical twins. You're a hell of a lot *taller* than me. Maybe those housing office people think all Texans are the same *height*."

"You want to tell them they're mistaken?" she asked in her normal voice.

"Do you?" My question came out a bit quavery. Surprisingly, I cared what she thought.

"Hmmm." She looked down at me and my spiked hair. "It's hard for me to tell one way or the other, seeing how we haven't been properly introduced yet. You want to try a take two on this?"

My plan fizzled. I headed for the door. I shut it behind me and knocked.

"Please do come in," she said in polite Texan, opening the door and inviting me inside with a sweep of her slender arm.

"Good afternoon, miss," I replied in my best Texan drawl. "I do believe you're my new roommate."

"How de do," she said, laying it on thick. "If this ain't a pleasant surprise. Come in, come in. My name's LeeAnn Campbell, but folks 'round here call me Lena. I'd be mighty pleased if you'd do the same."

I shook her offered hand vigorously. "The pleasure is all mine, Miss Lena. My name's Jen Wharton and I *shore* am happy to meet you."

"You don't look like a Texan," Lena said, dropping the exaggerated accent all at once. Then her face cracked a smile and we both started giggling.

"Let's get you unpacked and then we can work on our décor," Lena said, regarding my pile of junk still outside the door. "We'll show 'em what two Texans can do."

So much for my mean girl act.

CHAPTER 2

PINE HILL STATION, TEXAS

AUGUST 1985

MADDIE

Damn kid. I pointed out that plant particularly. "Ronnie," I'd said, "whatever you do, don't forget to water the miniature rose bush at the edge of the patio." Now, look at it, dried and shriveled, brown leaves blowing around the parched skeleton. Dead as the rest of this place at the end of August.

Three weeks away, and I'd forgotten Texas in August. Dust scurried around the legs of the patio furniture in changing patterns of interlocking circles. It clung to the windows in a grimy film in which the kid had etched graffiti: the names of punk rock groups or slang I hadn't yet heard. Drifts of dust lined the edge of the driveway and piled against the house, making it look abandoned. How quickly this part of the world forgets its inhabitants.

I'd taken the usual route from the airport, the highway cutting through an endless plain of scorched grass, scraggly junipers, and endless dust. The wind blew a summer blizzard across the blacktop, and I gripped the wheel to keep the car on course. The car was sealed against the heat and dust, but I could hardly breathe. These winds, this dust could swallow me in an instant.

The city came upon me like an oasis, the glimpses of green a receding mirage the closer I drew. Dun-colored shacks struggling to stand out from the gray-brown landscape warned how tough life is on the edge of the plains. In the distance, a deserted factory built from rusty corrugated sheet metal flapped in the hot wind. The gravel side roads, straight arrows to the horizon, gave way to paved ones lined by small concrete houses with patches of parched grass in front. Finally, I came upon the manicured, green lawns of the more fortunate, of whom I am one. Green grass in August, an indication of one's ability to pay costly water bills in a dry land, is how wealth is measured in these parts.

After a half-dozen years, I knew each sweeping live oak that lined my street, I could anticipate each bump in the road, I could have found the place by the smell of the jasmine and honeysuckle that grew alongside the front porch railing. Yet, for a moment, I didn't recognize the house. I couldn't claim it for mine. It still looked the same. But it didn't seem like a place I knew. Had I once been happy here?

I parked in the carport and cautiously walked up the back sidewalk to the red brick patio. It was then that I saw our poor, dead rose bush.

I kicked it tentatively and a few more dried leaves fluttered to the ground. I'll forgive the neighbor kid, Ronnie. The rest of the garden looks watered, and I can see the cats rubbing against the kitchen bay window in anticipation of my homecoming.

It was easy to miss, being planted in the back corner of the patio. The kid's only thirteen. What would a kid that age care about the sentimental value of a white rose bush planted by a couple of romantic fools? It had been a housewarming gift we'd given each other to celebrate our new jobs, our new life, and the new house we would sort of inhabit together. Perhaps we'd been afraid to plant the bush right out front where it would be noticed if it died. It hadn't though, and through the years it brightened our Saturday morning breakfast table with clusters of tiny white roses. When we'd planted it, it had seemed a kind of marriage ritual, a promise for the future. Or maybe I've made it into that now that it's gone, too.

The old frame house, its burnt-sienna-red shuttered windows accenting the white board siding, seemed larger than I remembered. The lock on the red back door was loose and I struggled to turn the key. Finally, the door creaked open like in an old, haunted house and I inhaled the stale, musty air with a whiff of cat fur. Does this smell like home?

Ah, friendly faces at last, feline though they are. Cat cacophony and small furry bodies rubbing up against my bare legs. Look at me, tears streaming down my cheeks for Sam and Frieda. Nah. It's because that caramel-colored sweater with the oversized pockets is no longer hanging on its customary hook in the entranceway. It's because that floppy red hat you used to wear when you were out in the back watering the plants has gone missing.

The living room looks the same, but for the empty feel of it. Brick fireplace, soft, inviting sofas accentuated with earth-toned pillows. Shadows of us whiling away the late evening hours on our matching rockers, or tucked into the sofas, talking over the day's happenings, sipping wine, reading in companionable silence as the weavings on the walls took on otherworldly shapes in the fire's flicker. The kitchen, too — where once we spent so much time concocting meals both complex and delicious — seems cheerless now, the yellow walls trying too hard to look sunny.

I thought Madison would do me good. Get away during the worst part of the summer; the hot, dry spell when I've got nothing to teach and too much time on my hands. I thought it would help to reenact a pleasant ritual, the journey I've made every year since I've been here. It did feel good. The rejuvenating moisture, filling my lungs with fresh lake air, feasting my eyes on the profusion of green, feeling so warm and alive in the company of dear friends who have known me since my bohemian days. A luxury, being with friends who knew the whole of me. I was nearly my old self again. Cracking jokes and laughing like the old Maddie I'd lost these past months. Giving advice and listening to other people's troubles for a change. Going out again. Feeling loved and wanted again.

The mistake was coming back here. Here to this always-alien culture, to this sea of dead grass and heat and dust, to this house full of suddenly sad memories. Even tenure feels like a prison sentence in this too-small town, where too many know me. Most will wonder why I'm glum. It's the few we weren't closeted to I fear seeing most. I think how their faces will register pity, how their voices will show a touch too much concern. Right now, running into one of our mutual friends is more than I can bear.

Hell, it hurts. Surprising how bruised, how wounded I am, like the slightest touch would produce searing pain all the way in. Nope. Can't face my local gay friends — my family — when I feel like this. Can't face Lorraine, the red-haired artist, whose entrancing weavings decorate my walls. Can't face Barb and her partner Lefty who, as teachers at the local middle school, are even more closeted than Roz and me. Can't face Adrianne, who wears pearls and has her nails done by day but owns and operates the best (and only) gay bar in town by night.

Family. An odd word to describe such a haphazard collection of women, but it fits. We have bonds stronger than biology. We're tied by circumstances, ostracism, and love.

We're each other's preferred social group, the circle from which we choose our friends and lovers. We need each other to survive the load the world dumps on us, to feel we fit somewhere.

For us, when she says she doesn't want you, it's a family matter. She's in the family too, it can't help but be that way. But it can't help but hurt more.

"I'll change," I said desperately, at the end. "I'll be whoever you want me to be."

"Hon, you can't change being white," she whispered, gently taking my pale hand in her amber brown one. "You can't change that."

It was the last thing she ever said to me.

CHAPTER 3

PINE HILL STATION, TEXAS

LATE AUGUST 1985

JANE

Johnny frightened me when I first met him. Tall and lean, with eyes the cold gray of polished steel, my hand went to ice when he lightly shook it. When he glanced at my face, he drew in his breath sharply and quickly looked down at some folders he had placed in front of him — as if I'd shocked him. But what had he seen?

A moment later, he had composed his face into a pleasant smile and was introducing himself in a friendly Texan drawl. My fear vanished. I was taken in by his velvety voice, so unlike my own flat Iowa accent. For a moment, I was too embarrassed by the sound of my own voice to return the introduction. He was Professor Jonathan Wharton the Fifth, specialty, early Roman Christianity, and he would be my graduate school advisor, he informed me, adding what a pleasure it'd be advising such a pretty, young woman. I flushed. Then I caught his gaze on me again and flushed a deeper shade.

His irises were ringed with black, and an odd gleam lit the pupils. He looked as if a brilliant and satisfying idea had just come to him. So strong was the impression, I half expected him to share it with me.

Instead, he said with Southern smoothness, "You're Jane, Jane Meyer? Mind if I call you Janey?" He had then turned and left the room without waiting for an answer.

It was the first Monday of classes and the new graduate students in the history department had gathered in the grad office at 4:00 p.m. There were ten of us — three girls, six guys, and me. Scarred wood tables were scattered about the room, dented gray metal filing cabinets lined the walls, and the rickety chairs were a bit too short for the tables they pushed up against. The room's windows looked out on a brown, brick, four-story dormitory and a fluorescent light buzzed overhead. I could tell I'd spend little time in this dreary room.

The grad office had the building's leftover furniture, I discovered later. Many of the professors' offices were beautifully furnished with aged pecan desks and bookshelves. Even some of the classrooms had wooden seats and writing tables for the students. The buildings, too, were mostly from another century, some heavily whitewashed and shingled, others red brick. The grounds were covered with stately live oaks, dripping with Spanish moss, branches arching over small outbuildings and shading the grass. The campus was pretty and pleasant, in a way that fit my imaginings of the South.

It was what went on here — the learning, the students — I thought second rate. Besides the star Roman historian I had come to study with, the university seemed provincial, typical, as did the town itself. It was not a school that attracted top scholars, and its grad students, I guessed, were equally second rate. In the back of my mind, I knew I had formed this impression because this was the university that had accepted me.

While waiting for the meeting to begin, I studied the college newspaper, avoiding glances that could lead to conversation. I felt odd and gawky — nothing new there. I imagined everyone was looking at me or no one was. Southern cadences drifted around me as the students chatted hesitantly with one another, waiting for the professors to show. My cohorts were mostly locals, I believed, had gone to undergrad here, knew their way around, perhaps even recognized one another. I was the interloper, with my Midwestern accent, my casual clothes, my unstyled hair. Panic crept up on me, prickling the space between my eyes, whispering, "You'll be alone here too. Only the streets and the weather have changed. Not you, never you."

I turned the pages of my newspaper noisily to distract myself from my gloomy predictions and looked up to see the man I would come to know as Johnny re-enter the room and brusquely announce, "Jane Meyer, Bill Sanderson, and Justin Lee Collins, you're with me. Over here, please." Two young men hurried toward the older man as if afraid he might decide he didn't want them after all. He made appointments with them, dismissed them perfunctorily, and turned to me, his eyes locking onto mine. When he looked away to write our appointment down in his notebook, an appointment I forgot as soon as it was made, his eyes stayed in mine like the pink spot left by a photographer's flash. A feeling of powerlessness overwhelmed me, and I sank into a chair, my breath escaping in a long, defeated sigh.

I was examining the evidence of aging, his graying temples, the lines in his forehead and around his eyes, guessing he was forty-five, when he looked up and broke the silence, I assumed to dismiss me. I stood, backed up a few feet, ready to bolt, when he asked, "Interested in some coffee? I'll give you a head start on the reading for Maddie's class." He gestured at a diminutive woman on the other side of the room, with shoulder-length curly hair that was walnut-colored and even less arranged than mine. She was talking to one of the female grad students. "Professor Madeline Haystead, I mean," he expanded her name in a derisive drawl. He seemed about to tell me something confidential about her, then thought better of it. "Dining hall's this way," he informed me over his shoulder, "and I'd be pleased if you'd call me Johnny."

"Cream and sugar?" he pulled on the tap of the steel percolator, filling two Styrofoam cups with a thick looking brew.

"Just cream, please." The carpet was orange, indoor/outdoor tweed. Comfortable, brown-cushioned chairs and matching wood tables were scattered in cozy arrangements. Down the center of the room ran a row of wooden booths, with pew benches covered with orange canvas. It was to one of these Johnny led me after paying the cashier with a crisp dollar he'd taken out of a slim black wallet in his back pocket.

His gray slacks were neatly pressed, and his shirt was a lighter gray cotton. He wore it with rolled sleeves and an open neck. Even his loafers were gray. He managed to look elegant and relaxed at the same time, a feat I'd never manage no matter how long I tried. My drab blond longish hair hung on each side of my face, and I had to brush it aside repeatedly, even to see clearly. My school uniform was a loose T-shirt and rumpled jeans, a size too big. I had on my only pair of sandals, which were dark brown and flat soled, functional, not fashionable.

He motioned me into one end of the booth and slid easily into the facing seat.

"I'm afraid you'll have to get used to this sludge they call coffee, Janey, it's all they serve on campus. They did a good job of redecorating, though," he continued, looking around. "Before this past summer, the walls were institutional green, and the furniture was surplus from the second world war." He drew a packet of cigarettes from his shirt pocket and removed the last one, pulling a black plastic ashtray toward him.

"It's nice. I'm sure I'll study here sometimes." I had never been good at small talk. This was excruciating already. Why had I agreed to have coffee with him?

"Oh, please forgive me, do you smoke?" he asked, offering me the cigarette and when I shook my head no, he continued, "Good for you. Filthy habit. Do you mind if I indulge?"

"Oh no," I said quickly, though of course, I did mind. I've never been able to say so, though. Who was I to deny someone something they needed?

"You certainly are attractive," Johnny said, suddenly leaning toward me as though he were nearsighted and needed a closer look.

I flushed. Not being used to compliments on my looks from men, I didn't know how to respond. I knew in the abstract that I wasn't *bad* looking, average height, slim body, blond hair. My features were regular, my eyes blue, my skin pale. My looks were ordinary. Johnny, however, seemed to think otherwise.

While I fumbled for something to say, Johnny rescued me by demanding, "Tell me about yourself. You're not from around here, I hear. Where are you from?"

"Iowa," I answered humbly, expecting a laugh, perhaps.

After all, Johnny was a Texan, a breed of American I'd heard believed itself a cut above mere citizens of the inferior forty-nine. Instead, he prompted me, "Where in Iowa?"

"Hutton, a small town near Cedar Rapids. Well, actually, I grew up in the country."

"Ha, a farm girl, I knew it. Fresh and unspoiled like the fertile cropland of our fair Midwest."

I smiled with some effort. Right.

"I spent childhood on the land myself. On my grandfather's acres, not far from here. Not quite the same as a Midwestern farm, I'll admit, but country living all the same. What does your old man grow?"

"He's dead. He died about six years ago." I hated talking about this. "Ma — I mean — my mother and I still live in the house, but all we keep now are some chickens."

"I'm sorry about your dad. Are you an only child?"

I nodded.

"Me too. We have a lot in common, Janey. Tell me, what have you done with your life up there in corn country?"

"Studied mostly. There's not much else to do except listen to the corn grow." He laughed at the old Midwestern expression.

"Where'd you go for undergrad?" he asked next, although he must have known the answer if he'd hired me to be his research assistant. I supposed he was just making conversation.

"University of Iowa in Iowa City, where all the farm kids go." I grimaced.

"But you came all the way to Texas to go to graduate school. How come?"

"Because this was the only school that offered me a job and waived my tuition. I already have debts from Iowa," I told him, way too honestly. "And of course, I was interested in studying Roman history with you," I finished, too late.

"Of course." He squinted at me. Abruptly, he rose from the booth. "Excuse me a moment, Janey." He crumpled the empty pack of cigarettes he'd tossed on the table a few minutes ago. "I'm out of smokes." He headed towards the vending machines in a hall on the far side of the room.

He seemed nice enough. But I found his looks oddly disturbing. I'd imagined, even wanted, Jonathan Wharton to be a kindly older gentleman, a man of wisdom, perhaps a bit disorganized. Someone who'd treat me like a granddaughter, and whom I could treat as a mentor. Johnny didn't look the part. His charisma was impossible to ignore. I was afraid of him.

"Let me tell you about the work you'll be doing for me this semester, Janey," he said, to my relief, as he sat back down across the table from me. I noticed how neatly combed his black hair was.

He launched into an animated summary of the research project he had just gotten a small grant for and how I could be invaluable to him by searching for research materials, reading, and taking notes on other work done in the area, poring over first-hand sources, typing inquiry letters to other scholars and so forth. It did sound interesting to me, this first taste of what I thought would become my life's work. His enthusiasm was contagious and before long, I found myself offering suggestions. He might not fit my stereotype of a kindly old professor, but he was obviously a serious scholar who enjoyed his work.

He finished outlining the project and my responsibilities and glanced down at his watch.

"I'm sorry, Janey, I have another appointment in a few minutes, so I've got to be off. Let's get together on ..." he looked up the appointment we'd made earlier, and I listened, so I'd remember this time, "... Wednesday, at three o'clock in my office and talk about what you'd like to accomplish for yourself this year. We can arrange your work schedule then too, all right?"

I nodded.

He reached out to shake my hand goodbye. "Until next time, Janey," he said with a smile, and I answered faintly. In a moment, he was out of view.

He never did tell me what to read for Professor Haystead's class.

CHAPTER 4

PINE HILL STATION, TEXAS

LATE AUGUST 1985

LIZ

"My God," I swore softly, staring down at the half-smoked cigarette I hadn't even realized I'd lit. Johnny's mostly empty pack sat next to the telephone on my desk. Ashes were scattered over the catalogs I'd been meaning to sort through. I looked at the trembling hand holding the cigarette in detached disgust. It couldn't be, but this thin hand, shaking neurotically and holding proof I'd started smoking again, was mine. I reached across to Johnny's ashtray and ground the butt into it until it crumbled, leaving bits of tobacco on my fingers. In my mind, the phone still rang persistently, uselessly.

I had the dream again last night. The one where I'm driving through pea soup fog, unable to see two feet in front of the windshield. Oddly, my side window is rolled down and the thick fog is starting to fill the inside of the car. I had rolled it down in the dream because I had to be sure of what I'd heard in the murk outside. My daughter, calling frantically, "Mom! Mom!" But I can't see anything, not even the road, in this thickness. Never mind Jenny out there in the impenetrable mist. But she's calling me, I know she is. "Mom! Mom!" Then I wake up, terror sweat clinging to my skin. As soon as I can after the dream, I try to reach her.

Wednesday evening. Johnny at some meeting until late, he said. A perfect night for what's become a ridiculous ritual. Tonight, I had tried at six and then again at nine. I let the phone ring twenty, thirty times. No answer. I hang up. No answer. There's never any answer. Well, what do I expect? Why do I pretend, each time, she might pick up the phone and say, "Hi Mom, how are you?" after all these years of silence? Six years, since she was thirteen, that long since we've talked mother to daughter. Why go on pretending?

It's the same with the mail. I leaf frantically through the ads and the bills, the donation letters and catalogs, the academic journals and magazines, the infrequent personal letters, searching for the backhand scrawl with my name, with Johnny's. Nothing. Of course, there's nothing.

The dream haunts me. I have it so frequently lately it has become frightening. When I wake up, I'm so sure something has happened to her I've got the phone off the hook, ready to call the campus police up at the University of Wisconsin and have them break down her dormitory door. But in the seconds before I dial, my rational mind clicks in. I put the phone back in its cradle; I'm flushed red and ashamed. I've got to let her go. She's turned her back on her family, but she could be having a great time a thousand miles north of here in Madison. Maybe she's forgotten her father and I exist. I must stop dwelling on this. I feel hysteria coming on the moment Jenny's image flashes across my brain. As it does way too often.

The day after she got her high school diploma in the mail — almost a year-and-a-half ago now — she announced that she'd gotten a summer job in Wisconsin and that she would be on a flight up to Madison in two days' time.

"Where will you live, Jenny? How will you pay for everything to get started?" I said, the color draining from my face. "Your father and I were planning to drive you north in August." I'd done it wrong, been too emotional about it. Her voice, in contrast, was as cold and hard as ice.

"Old Johnny gave me money for graduation," she said, referring to her great-grandfather, "not that it's any business of yours. I'll be *fine*. Go to hell — and take him with you," she said, indicating the photo of my absent husband. She turned on her heel, strode down the hall to her room, and slammed the door behind her. She was as good as her word and left two days later, even calling herself a cab to get to the airport. All she took with her was a battered suitcase she'd scrounged from the basement and the large black canvass tote bag she used as a purse. We didn't hear from her until late August when a postcard with a university building on it arrived from Madison. On the back it said, "In case Old Johnny croaks," and a phone number in her distinctive script followed. No signature. Nothing else. This August, a similar card arrived — just a phone number with Madison's area code. The number I've been calling to no avail.

It had all started that January when I agreed to help my boss, George, expand his hours for tax season at the accounting firm at which I've worked for the past fifteen years. Jenny, a bright and mature thirteen-year-old then, had insisted she'd have no problem staying by herself if Johnny couldn't be home. Johnny said most Tuesdays and Thursdays, he'd work in his office at home and watch to see that Jenny did her homework.

That spring, Jenny changed. I started to come home to a sullen teenager locked in her room. Girls always go through this, I reminded myself. Hating your mother for a few years was normal for teenaged girls. I had fought with my own mother on occasion, despite the silencing pressure of Southern gentility. But Jenny didn't fight with me; she ignored me. If she looked at me at all, it was with daggers in her eyes. I felt guilty for taking the extra work. I would never have agreed to do it had I known how Jenny would react. Johnny kept insisting that Jenny's behavior had nothing to do with me taking on evening hours. It was just a phase she was going through, he said, a typical teenaged phase. She'd outgrow it one of these days, he claimed.

Her relations with her father seemed close enough. She didn't give *him* the silent treatment. I began to pester Johnny about her. As soon as the door to our large bedroom had closed for the night, ensuring privacy, I'd start in with my questions.

"Did she say anything about me to you tonight?" I'd ask, after returning home from my night of doing tax preparations for the anxious middle class.

"No, should she have?" he'd answer in a voice calculated to irritate me.

"Don't pretend you don't know what I'm talking about. Jenny has decided she hates me. She won't talk to me. You say she talks to you. What does she say?"

"Well, she doesn't say anything to me about you, and that's a fact."

"What does she talk to you about, then? Does she tell you secrets that she doesn't want me to know?" My voice quivered on the edge of tears.

"Come on, what secrets could a thirteen-year-old have?"

"Johnny, something is wrong with that girl."

"You're right, and I know just what it is. Puberty, plain and simple. Now forget it and come to bed. She'll grow out of it. You take your kid too seriously. This is nothing but normal adolescent behavior. You told me you felt the same way about your mother when you were Jenny's age." Johnny yawned from the bed and patted the other side. "Now come on and crawl in here. Tell me how work went tonight. There's nothing to do for our daughter but to quit worrying about her so much. She'll be okay in a couple of years, once her female hormones settle down." He grinned, and then, seeing my face, reached over and gave me a little pat.

"Just be patient and things will right themselves."

I found myself spending the evenings I didn't work making unnecessary trips past Jenny's room, listening for some small sound that might slip from under my daughter's door. I'm not sure what I expected to hear. Maybe I thought she sobbed alone those many evenings she spent cloistered in her room. But when she emerged, there was never a sign she'd been crying. Her face was calm and cold; her words, if she spoke at all, were cutting and cruel. Our Sunday ritual of church attendance also ceased that spring. She simply refused to leave her room, so I became the only member of the family to practice my faith. I spent so many hours praying that first year, but my faith, my God, my hours of spiritual contemplation were of no use to me whatsoever. I even talked to the minister once briefly, but as Johnny had done, he counseled patience and nothing more.

I had to get out of that stifling house. Jenny's behavior obsessed me. So, when tax season ended, I started volunteering evenings at the local animal shelter. Johnny was allergic to dogs — or, at least, that's what he told me — but I've always loved them. It was easy to love the work. Unlike my daughter, the dogs were so appreciative of the attention I gave them. And the other volunteers were big-hearted women. I soon found a niche for myself there. I started by being a volunteer evening dog walker, which I still do, but now, after six years of regular shifts there, I keep the books for the place and give adopters a two-hour course on how to care for their new dog. Time spent there has been a godsend. Accounting has not proven to be an all-consuming profession. Placing a dog in a good adoptive home or saving one from being euthanized — that was work I could feel proud to do.

By the time Jenny turned fifteen, I'd read all the adolescent psych books I could find. I knew kids were supposed to rebel against their parents at that age. But Jenny had also turned her back on the rest of the world. Her friends, kids from the neighborhood she'd played with for years, gradually stopped coming to the house.

One night, I told Johnny I thought Jenny should see a therapist. He wouldn't hear of it.

"Nonsense. There is nothing wrong with that girl that time won't cure," he decreed as soon as I suggested it.

"But she sits in that room all day and night and doesn't seem to have a friend in the world. Her grades are slipping this year and she won't say a civil word to anyone but you, it seems." As soon as the words were out of my mouth, I knew I'd made a mistake.

"Do I detect a note of jealousy in your voice?" Johnny demanded. "Well, do I?" he chided, as I looked at him helplessly.

"I'd have to be a heartless mother not to care if my daughter talks to me or not. Sure, I wished she did. Wouldn't you if our places were reversed? What does she tell you in these long heart-to-hearts you two supposedly have, anyway? At least you could tell me. I have a right to know. God, I'm her mother!"

Johnny motioned me to sit down. "Quiet, the neighbors will hear. Okay, listen. Jenny made me promise not to tell, but if you don't let on, I will anyway. You're right. You have a right to know. Jenny has a boyfriend," he continued conspiratorially. "He seems like a nice boy, from what she tells me. I think she spends most of her time at school with him, and moons about him in her room at night. Nothing more serious than that."

"Johnny," I sobbed, the tears suddenly flowing in rivers down my cheeks, "why doesn't my own daughter tell me what's going on in her life? Why does she only tell you?" I collapsed wearily on the bed, loud sobs escaping as I gasped for breath.

Johnny sat beside me and held me close, one hand caressing my hair. In his embrace, I gave into my tears and cried my heart out, letting my emotions win out for once.

"There, there, honey." Johnny patted my back and comforted me as though I were a two-year-old who'd just lost a toy.

"You know," Johnny said later, after I'd dried my tears, "I think Jenny has never forgiven you for that first spring you worked evenings during tax season. I think she felt you abandoned her. You know how kids are. They can be mean sometimes when they feel they've been wronged. They can hold grudges. But she'll get over it. She just needs to grow up a bit."

I turned towards him hopefully. "Did she say that? About me working nights that spring?"

"Naw, it's just my theory of why she's mad at you. But it will pass, it will. Jenny's certainly no case for an analyst's couch. It will only stigmatize the kid. You know how things get around in a town like this. Now, settle down so you can get some sleep for a change. You've been tossing and turning something awful these last couple nights."

I soon dismissed Johnny's story about a boyfriend as a well-intentioned lie. He didn't want me to worry so much. How I wanted to believe my daughter had quit loving me because I'd deserted her for tax season work, but I couldn't. I still can't.

Oh God, why do I torture myself with these useless memories? Why can't I learn to cope with this? All I've managed to do is become emotionally overwrought on those rare occasions when there's some contact from her and a hopeless insomniac in her absence. Eighteen months she's been gone. I still can't accept her hatred of us and her terrible silence. I pray on it every night but have found no comfort, no peace.

Jenny's college, the University of Wisconsin at Madison, met her only two criteria: it had accepted her despite her mediocre grades, and it was a thousand miles away from here. As suddenly as Jenny turned from me that spring of her thirteenth year, she turned on Johnny after getting accepted at Madison, in April of her senior year. Poor Johnny. He looked beaten, slinking around the house like a whipped dog, pretending all the while that things between them were as they should be. During those final months that Jenny lived with us, I tried hard to divert Johnny's attention from her. He seemed to sit and brood over his loss until I grew afraid of what was happening to him. We were both relieved when she left for Wisconsin. Since then, only silence and two postcards.

Johnny suffered a lot that first year she was gone. He must have come to some inner peace about Jenny though; this year he seems happier. But I still sit up nights wondering about her and making useless phone calls.

CHAPTER 5

PINE HILL STATION, TEXAS

SEPTEMBER 1985

MADDIE

I hated those rows of fresh young faces eagerly taking down every word I said. I know they're my salvation, part of that great diversion called work, that will save me from sinking into the murky waters of my grief. But today, I hated them for taking up my attention. I hated their innocence, their faces so bland and lineless with inexperience that they were barely distinguishable from one another. I hated their pretense, their trendy-magazine-inspired shallow sophistication. I hated their presumption that the cloistered life of the white middle class was all there was.

All the predictable questions were asked. How were grades determined, how many papers, how long, due when, was there a six-week exam, a midterm, a final? Multiple choice or essay, a combination? Was it okay to tape lectures, etc., until I felt myself gearing up for a long, maniacal scream.

I tried to concentrate on those who stood out. There weren't many. In my "The Great Depression and World War II" class, there was a Black woman who asked if we'd be studying all the ways Franklin Roosevelt prevented Black people from accessing aid during the Depression.

"Of course," I answered, and made a note to myself to reread a scholarly paper on that topic that I'd grazed recently. A huge redneck type fell asleep in the back and dropped his books with a crack that made everyone but him jump — he slept on. A handsome Guatemalan refugee made a point of telling me after class how happy he was to go to college in America and to have me for an instructor, stumbling over his words and apologizing for his heavily accented English.

In my grad historical research methods seminar, there was a pale, blond woman named Jane whose discomfort seemed to hover about her, a palpable shadow. Unbearably shy, she flushed as the small group of graduate students in the seminar each introduced themselves and shared a bit about their past. But when the discussion became more impersonal, she had no difficulty contributing — even hazarding an opinion that she knew would sound unusual and threatening to some of her more conservative classmates. I suppose she stood out because she's a stranger to Texas like I was. She doesn't dress right for school in the South (where was her permed big hair, her shoulder-padded blouse, her color-coordinated pumps?). She speaks with Midwestern vowels, and she seems very bright — a cut above the students we usually get here. She won't fit in and knows it, like I knew it when I first arrived fresh out of the feminist wilds of Madison. To me, Texas was cowboy hats and gun racks and repressive Christianity, but this is where Roz *had* to be, she told me. The university had jobs for both of us, so here was where our hard-won PhDs had gotten us.

During the time Roz was the center of my universe, this

place proved tolerable enough. Now I wondered how I could have wasted my talents at this third-rate institution, with its legions of half-literate students warming a seat in my class to complete their history requirement. Most of the students here are business majors or future CPAs, bound for management jobs in some chain store or cookie-cutter accounting firm. All but empty minds, embarking on empty, insipid lives.

Ah, Maddie, you're such a purist. Longing for those bygone days of social ferment and hope, when students were interested in ideas, in changing themselves and the world, when money was incidental and easily shared and upward mobility was thought a base, unworthy goal for a life.

It was the eighties, this decade of greed and selfishness I was chafing against. Not this place, exactly. The school is nowhere close to being Ivy League, not even close to the top, large public research schools like Madison. But it's adequate and this department is verging on good. My colleagues are respectable, if not always likeable. I have that most coveted of academic commodities — tenure — and all that comes with it. A choice schedule, interesting research projects, paid trips to conferences, an occasional sabbatical, decent pay (though probably less than my male counterparts). I was lucky to find a job at the same university in the same year as Roz got her job, lucky to have survived the pre-tenure years of posturing and politicking, damn lucky they didn't investigate my private life. All in all, a lot to be thankful for.

Can't feel it at the moment, though.

I always looked forward to the first day of classes, a new beginning every year, a seasonal cycle like the earth's, both familiar and comforting. This year, so much resentment flooded me, I almost couldn't finish my grad seminar and I didn't, I couldn't, stay and chat with the new grad students as in other years. I couldn't stop by the department office and talk to Maria, our longtime secretary. I couldn't find refuge in my own comfortably furnished office. Instead, as soon as class was over, I went for a walk to cool down, a ridiculous idea in this September heat. But as I was making my way past the drab, modern engineering building, I spotted an inviting garden that I'd never bothered to explore before. It proved a respite of well-watered shrubs and flowers, with trellised vines forming cozy alcoves in which oak benches with wrought iron armrests had been placed. I gratefully slumped into a bench, sat back in its shadowy cool, and let my mind drift. Nearby, there was a small pond with cattails and lily pads. Orange koi skimmed the surface from time to time. Citrus trees added their shade and color to the little square and warblers twittered in the branches. I had barely settled into my reverie and taken a few deep breaths, trying to let out the day's disappointments when I heard footsteps on the stone path at the other end of the garden.

I shrank into the alcove hoping the intruder was just passing through. It was Johnny Wharton, one of my department colleagues, and he looked pale and shaken — very odd in a man who was usually cocky and jovial in that Texas-man way I'd never get used to. He didn't see me hidden away in the vines. Just as well. I never know what to say to that man. He paced up and down the walk, his hand stroking his chin, sighing deeply, shaking his head from side to side. It was all very strange, coming from my arrogant senior colleague.

I never liked Johnny much. Maybe I resented how his masculine good looks, Texan-style charm and maleness always served him so much better than my over-serious workaholism ever served me. There's a falseness about him, something flickering behind that charm of his — something not so likeable. I have never tried to get to know him much — or anyone else in the department either — because I don't want them asking inconvenient personal questions about me. It's a shame how isolated I am from all of them, but there's nothing

I can do about it. Roz's fear made me be afraid to be out. She's probably right. Dykes are just not acceptable in this town, in this part of the country.

In a couple of minutes, Johnny stopped pacing and strode out of the garden, looking a little better, like he had decided what to do about something. I found myself wondering if he was having marital problems. I was probably projecting. He was more likely trying to figure out a way to reduce his class load or some similarly pedestrian concern.

I felt like going home, kicking off my shoes and having a glass of wine or three on the patio. The first few weeks after Roz told me it was over, that's exactly what I'd done. One evening when I was weaving my way to the fridge after consuming a bottle of wine myself, I slammed poor Frieda's tail in the screen door, sending her running for safety to the back of the walk-in closet in the bedroom upstairs. She wouldn't come out for a day and a half and when she did, her tail was sprained and swollen. That shocked me out of it. I know the statistics all too well. In my social group, one in three of us has a drinking problem. I don't want to be one of them. Now, I have a glass of iced tea when I get home and sort through my junk mail in the living room. I try not to think about how it used to be.

Chapter 6

PINE HILL STATION, TEXAS

SEPTEMBER 1985

JANE

It was Wednesday, five to three, and I sat shivering in a chair outside Johnny's office. It wasn't the air conditioning making my teeth chatter. I was nervous about this interview, as nervous as I used to get before the annual Christmas play my childhood teachers forced me to be in. My hands were cold and sweaty. I rubbed the right one against my jeans, not wanting Johnny to shake a damp palm. His door was closed and the office secretary's desk vacant. I looked at the door, deciding whether to hazard a knock. If I did, I might disturb a meeting with another student. I'm loath to knock on closed doors or make unsolicited telephone calls. No matter what the eventual welcome, there's always that moment when I feel certain I will only be an unwanted intruder. I decided to wait. I was a little early. Surely, he'd eventually come out to see if I was here.

I flipped disinterestedly through a college course catalog

lying on a Formica table next to the metal military surplus chair I'd sat down on and tried a couple of deep breaths. No good. I wasn't breathing out again.

Why was I so nervous about this interview? It was a job interview, natural to be a little nervous about that. But as is usual with situations like this, I was overreacting to it. I sat here shaking, shivering, breathing funny, a sinking feeling in the pit of my stomach. All over finding out what I'll be doing for work this semester and telling my professor what I'd like to concentrate on in my studies? It was Johnny, I had to admit, making me feel this way. He didn't look like a professor, that was the problem. Professors were a sedentary bunch, weren't they? Shouldn't Johnny have a bit of a paunch? He should look distracted, fatherly, wear glasses, have a receding hairline. I wasn't sure if my undergrad professors fit this description — I couldn't remember looking at any of them. They were disembodied voices at the front of the room, propounding theories and dispensing judgment. Johnny was too vital, too good looking, to be one of them. He didn't fit my stereotype of what a professor should be, that was it. Having him as an advisor would take some getting used to.

I jumped as the door opened and Johnny walked briskly toward me.

"Why, here you are, right on time." He took my sweat-scrubbed hand and then ushered me into his office.

"Come in. Let me get your file and I'll be right with you," he continued in his smooth voice, unlocked a file cabinet in the front office, and located my file. He'd been sitting alone in his office with the door closed. I entered and sat down on a comfortable dark leather chair facing the huge wooden desk that was angled to get the best light in the room. It was a corner office with two large windows on each outer wall. There were three ferns in Roman-style urns on pedestals placed in the room and a sumptuous Persian rug covered most of the dark wood floor. The floor-to-ceiling bookcases that lined the two inner walls were filled with thick volumes interspersed with Roman figurines and marble heads of classical-era Romans. The ivory walls set off the dark wood trim and furniture nicely. In a corner, a small wood table with a secretary swivel chair under it was covered by a desktop computer, its large gray box topped by a small TV, green cursor blinking. In front of it was a keyboard and, to the side of it were several boxes of file cards.

Johnny had joined me in staring around the room. "Do you like it? You'll be spending a lot of time working in the corner there." He closed the door. I nodded emphatically and put what I hoped was an enthusiastic smile on my face.

"Got this the last time I was in Rome," he said, pointing to a delicate glass vase on an iron tripod. "First Century AD."

"How beautiful," I mumbled in a weak voice. The room seemed suddenly claustrophobic and hot despite the windows and air conditioning. I was afraid I was going to faint.

"Feel free to peruse my bookshelves and borrow books whenever you'd like. Just let me know which ones you take."

I nodded. "Okay, thanks," somehow came out of my mouth. This was terrible. I could feel myself taking rapid, shallow breaths; my fingers were already starting to get numb.

"Janey, you look a little pale, if you don't mind my saying so." Johnny squinted his eyes in concern. "It's the heat. It's hot enough to fry eggs on the sidewalk today. Here, let me get you some water," he continued and took a glass out of a small cabinet and made for the hallway, where the water fountain was. I started to protest but then let him get me the water. Better that he thinks I'm unused to the heat. I accepted the glass gratefully and found it did calm me a little. Doing something external, even something as simple as drinking water, helps me relax and forget the crazy things my body is doing.

"There, that's better. You've got a little color back," Johnny looked kindly at me. I blushed in embarrassment. Why do I behave so childishly sometimes? But Johnny didn't seem to think there was anything odd about me. He had settled into the padded leather desk chair and leaned back, his clasped palms behind his head.

"I'm afraid I'm a bit old fashioned," he drawled. His eyes glanced over at the computer on the corner table. "You know how to work one of these things?" he said, leaning forward to look at me. I nodded. "Good. Part of what you'll be doing this semester is putting those file cards of citations for my next book into the computer. That'll be a big help. Then you can teach me how to use the damnable thing."

"Sure, I-I'd be glad to." I cursed myself for failing to get even a short comment out of my mouth without error.

He felt for the cigarettes in his breast pocket and hunted in the desk drawer for a lighter. "Mind if I smoke?" he asked automatically as he lit it and I shook my head no, though I was stifling a cough. Today he wore a white shirt open at the neck, revealing a nice tan. He had dark hair flecked with gray on his chest I couldn't help noticing. I immediately felt myself blush. Johnny took a long drag on his cigarette and stared off into space.

"Janey," he started, "I've been wondering ..." He looked at me and took a deep breath. "Well, never mind about that just now." He looked flustered and bent down to where his briefcase leaned against the desk. "What times would you be able to work?" He drew a daily planner bound in black leather out of his case and I rummaged through my backpack for my own cardboard covered schedule. Johnny walked around his desk and stood behind me, looking over my shoulder. I could smell his aftershave, a dark, woodsy scent, and the acrid odor of stale smoke. He was so close my skin could almost feel him. The back of my neck tightened into a rigid band. I was flushing furiously and grateful that he couldn't see my face from where he stood. I was sure he could sense my discomfort, so palpable was it to me, but all he said was, "How organized you are, Janey, writing your schedule out so neatly." He glanced back into his own book, then pointed to a bare spot on the schedule I held in my lap, brushing my bare arm with his. My hand jerked involuntarily away. He pretended not to notice. Goose flesh crept up my arm to where he had touched it.

"Here's a good amount of time — Monday afternoons, yes, I'm free then, too. Hmmm, how would you feel about evening hours? — looks like you have plenty of time after six. Now, feel free to refuse, Janey. I don't want to eat into your study time or social life."

"That's okay," I said, in a tiny voice. Why couldn't I get control over my voice? "Evenings would be fine. Whatever would be best for you."

"All right then, how about Tuesday and Thursday evenings and Monday afternoons? Why don't you start Thursday? That will give me time to prioritize what I want from you."

I nodded and Johnny returned to his desk chair. I breathed a silent sigh of relief and tried to hide my violently shaking hands.

"Now then, tell me what you're here to study." Johnny rested his elbows on the desk, folded his hands and rested his chin on them, staring right at me with those silver eyes. I cleared my throat and launched into the speech I'd prepared. I was gratified to hear my voice grow steady as it found itself in familiar territory. My heart was still wildly thumping in my chest. I imagined Johnny's eyes could see right through to it. He listened to my ideas quietly, and when I was finished, slowly took out another cigarette and lit it before he spoke.

"Very interesting proposal. I like it." He nodded as he said it and I let out a long breath. He went on to make some comments and suggested courses I might take next semester that would tie in. He had listened to me carefully, repeating some of the points I'd made verbatim, before suggesting a slight change in approach or making a compliment. He was bright, I decided, receptive to my somewhat offbeat ideas. He would be a helpful, flexible advisor. If I could just forget his physical presence, working with him would be enjoyable. I'd learn a lot. Possibly I'd get used to being around him, as unlikely as that seemed. I've never felt comfortable around men, and Johnny's geniality and good looks made that idea even more improbable. He was summing up his commentary. I'd only been half listening.

"I have high hopes for us working together. I admire a girl — I should say woman, eh Janey? — who combines brains and beauty. It'll be a pleasure to work with you. I'm looking forward to getting to know you better. Welcome to the department," he added, and offered his hand for me to shake. Instead of shaking mine when I placed it in his, he raised it and pressed it lightly to his lips. "At your service, Miss Janey." He smiled at me. I suppose I looked shocked, for he added, "There's a trace of Rhett Butler in every man from the South — no offense meant, of course."

I wasn't sure what my face was doing as I focused on the hot sensation running up my arm from the spot on my hand where he'd kissed it. Half of me was desperately trying to extricate myself from his hand — he still held mine — the other half was admonishing me to remember my manners and to whom I was speaking. I surprised us both by rejoining in Scarlet's voice, "Why Rhett, what a gentleman you are." We both laughed, and he let go of my hand, and suddenly everything felt all right.

"See you later." I smiled and hurried out the door before my rare moment of composure cracked. I had made it through the interview.

Across the quad from the history building, a small circle of benches surrounded a huge live oak tree. I sat on an empty bench facing away from the building, trying to calm myself. I found myself replaying the scene in my mind. What he'd said. How he'd looked. What I'd said. It wasn't like me to be able to deflect difficulty with humor. My face was still hot; the hand he had kissed still tingled. With a start I realized what my racing pulse had been trying to tell me for the past twenty minutes. This had never happened to me. Johnny was twice my age! He was my academic superior and advisor, my boss. He was probably married, perhaps with children — grown children. Yet I had fallen into what all the novels I read had taught me was a fatal trap. I had let myself be charmed by Johnny Wharton.

CHAPTER 7

MADISON, WISCONSIN

SEPTEMBER 1985

JENNY

"Babe, this is the life, ain't it?" Lena grinned over at me from across the table. She was stretched out on one of the decorative metal chairs that peppered the Union Terrace, a large outdoor café overlooking Lake Mendota that was the outside space of UW's student union. Everyone who was anyone hung out at the Union and outside on the terrace when it was the least bit nice out.

I smiled my agreement. It was a perfect late summer day with an almost warm breeze rustling through the yellowing leaves on the elm branches overhead. Out on the lake, a small regatta of sunfish sailboats practiced maneuvers. Now and then, a couple of kayaks or a crew boat filled with jocks rowing in unison would glide by.

Most of the tables were filled with students, some laughing and drinking, others studying or just taking in the sun as we were. The earthy odor of autumn leaves, the green smell of the lake, and the student smells of beer and fries made me want to breathe in deep and long. When I could turn off my brain, life was okay sometimes.

"You want a soda or something, Lena?" I asked, feeling generous. "It's on me."

"Well, in that case, I'll have a bottle of fine French champagne, but if they don't have that, I'll take a Dr. Pepper."

The outside order window was open, but I went into the dark, cool building and ordered from the bar. The Union, and particularly the low-slung contours of The Rathskeller, felt homey and I came here often, to sit, smoke a cigarette and listen to the snatches of conversation swirl around me. I liked the old, run-down feel of it; the fading German beer hall paintings on walls that glowed soft amber; the solid, deep brown oak tables, some with decades of initials carved in haphazardly; the massive arches that made the place feel like a cozy cave. Seeing the older, not so preppy students who met here to play chess and talk politics and philosophy made me feel like this was what college was all about: reading, hanging out, having bizarre conversations with people who didn't get their opinions from TV. I had to put up with hordes of plastic dormies in my classes, but they didn't come here much. I think they were scared of the place.

I placed my order, paid the student bartender, and took the two red plastic cups of soda back out to where Lena was still sitting with her head back, face up to the sun.

"Thanks, Jen, you're a pal." Lena sat upright and took a sip. "You know what this day reminds me of?"

"What?"

"Church picnics, especially this one my daddy would always have about this time of year — he and Mama and some of the church ladies would pack wicker baskets full of cold chicken and potato salad and everybody'd bring a dish to share. This old guy, Mr. Arland, would bring jugs of his homemade elderberry wine — he called it juice, but everyone knew it had a bit of alcohol in it — and we'd all drive out to this place by the river and have a picnic under the live oaks that grew on the banks. We always called it the 'cold picnic' because it was only one in the year that didn't have barbequing involved. But Daddy liked going there because it was such a beautiful and peaceful place. Mama had a couple of white and yellow-checkered tablecloths that she spread on the ground, and we had sit-upons — remember those Jen? We used to make them in Bible Camp."

I shook my head, having never been to Bible Camp.

"Well, you took a few feet of oilcloth and punched holes around the edges. Then you took a stack of old newspapers and put them on one side, folded over the other side and ran some string or yarn through the holes to make a cushion. I must have made a hundred for church activities." Lena looked out at the water; her gaze unfocused as she remembered. "We kids would go wading in the river while the ladies set up. Once they had a bit of that elderberry wine, they forgot all about hollering at us for getting the bottoms of our clothes wet!" Lena chuckled. "Daddy would give a nice little sermon about the beauty of nature or the precious jewel of community. Then we would sit around the picnic cloths on our sit-upons, the older folks in those folding lawn chairs, pass the food around and just eat and eat and talk and talk. And laugh and laugh and sing some of the old songs until the moon came up and the little ones had fallen asleep on the grass."

Lena's eyes got dreamy, and her voice spoke in a soft drawl. "I miss that kind of thing. Northern folks don't know how to have a good time. Even the few Black folks here are all closed-up and tight-lipped. They just don't know how to *relax*," she concluded, pronouncing the word in exaggerated Texan. "We Southerners might get on with things a bit more slowly than some up here would like us to, but we *shore* do know how to have a good time. What did y'all do on a day like this in your part of Texas?"

I'd been seeing checkered yellow picnic cloths, wicker picnic baskets, and kids splashing in the river like it was happening in front of my eyes. "Huh?" I said, to gain some time. I raced through my early memories, trying to come up with something.

"Did your folks ever go on church picnics? I don't even know if folks go on picnics in white churches."

"My grandfather on my dad's side was a Baptist minister, I think. But my father hated his guts, so only my mother and I went to church. Can't say I still believe in all that stuff."

"Why did your dad hate his ol' man?"

"I'm not sure. I think it had something to do with him being too strict with him as a boy, but nobody ever told me." My own drawl was creeping back into the conversations as I heard Lena's familiar cadences. I'd worked hard at erasing it from my everyday speech. I wanted to forget I was ever from Texas. But with Lena, it felt good to be speaking in my natural tones. A warning light flashed in my head. I ignored it.

"Whew, would my daddy shit if he knew I was rooming with a heathen!" Lena smiled. "He'd be up here in a minute trying to convert you to Jesus, white or not."

"What about if he knew what his own daughter is doing outside the bonds of holy matrimony?"

"I think he already suspects me of that sin. But so long as I'm a good girl and don't get caught, he's not going to say anything. You know, deep down beneath that preacher façade, I think he's shy!" We both giggled at that thought because Lena's father, whom I'd met two weeks before when he'd come up to visit, was an outgoing, burly guy with a musical, booming voice. Not the type you'd think of as shy.

"But anyways, what did you do when you were a kid on a

nice Sunday afternoon in autumn back in Texas?"

"Well, when I was little, he used to take me fishing some-times." In my mind, I always thought of him as a pronoun. "My father, I mean. There's this big reservoir about a half-hour drive from our house, where there was good fishing right from the shore. The fish were tiny, but it was fun to catch them anyways. I used to bait my own hook. We hardly ever caught any big enough to keep so mostly, we'd just throw them back. Dad would sit there and smoke while I did the fishing. Mom hated worms, so she never came along."

With a start, I clicked back into the present. I hadn't meant to say any of that and tried to shrug off other memories as they filtered into my brain. Both of them taking me horseback riding on Princess out at Wharton Hall, my mom reading me a story while I snuggled next to her in the big bed.

I shook my head, trying to clear out all that useless crap. "My family's boring," I said, when Lena looked over at me with questions in her eyes.

"Yeah, how so?"

"Well ... you know ... I stumbled, trying to come up with something. "They're so predictably middle class. Boring house. Boring neighborhood. Dad's always away working. Mom's mostly doing other people's taxes or taking care of dogs at this adoption shelter she volunteers at."

My guts were starting to churn. Too much of this acidic Coke.

"Come on, they can't be all that boring. What are your parents like?"

"I told you, they're boring," I replied, in what was on the verge of becoming a nasty tone.

But Lena wouldn't let it drop. "What do you mean, boring?"

"Listen, I don't want to talk about them, okay?" I snapped, momentarily too caught up in my memories to keep my mouth under control.

"Sorry. I didn't know it was tough for you to talk about them." Lena gave my hand a little pat.

"They're just not my favorite subject, that's all." Apologies were never my strong suit, and I hoped Lena knew I wasn't mad and was sorry I lashed out at her.

"Forget it. Let's take a walk on the lakeshore path and stretch our legs on this fine day."

I followed Lena down to the waterfront and we crossed the parking lot that led to the Lakeshore Path. Lena tried to get my spirits up by telling me about the first time she saw her boyfriend, Harry, a year ago on this very day, but I barely heard her.

The perfect day we'd started out having had been ruined by THEM. When would they leave me alone? Would they always be hovering near my conscious mind like some dark cloud waiting for a nice moment in my life to open up and start raining down, drenching me with unwanted memories?

If Madison wasn't far enough, where could I run to be rid of them?

CHAPTER 8

PINE HILL STATION, TEXAS

SEPTEMBER 1985

JANE

I tried to concentrate on the file card in front of me, but my fingers stumbled on the letters as I attempted to punch them into the computer. Johnny was only inches away looking for another card in the file box and I thought I could see his hands tremble too. My face felt alternately flushed and hot or drained and cold. My breath came in shallow gasps. The room appeared to be shrinking, and Johnny's presence loomed to fill it. My heart was thumping at a dangerous speed. I fought the urge to bolt for the door.

It was no good. I'd thought two weeks working in his office would have made it easier to be with him. Instead, it had grown harder. This was torture, feeling this way about another human being. It was humiliating to have failed, after so many days, to get a grip on my ill-equipped emotions. It was terrifying to think something so illusory could cause such a lack of control in my life. But what frightened me most was the suspicion that Johnny felt some attraction to me, too. Here, so close we almost touched, an electric current passed between us. I half-hated him for making me feel so alive. I half wanted to hear him say he desired me so I could rudely reject him. I wanted him to disappear altogether so I could continue my previous calm existence and forget there are feelings like this to be had.

Yet, there was something so compelling it seemed in the genes, that made me want to find out more, to see if I, too, could make it work like others did. I wanted to feel normal. To have a lover and a love life, to fulfill what was a birthright for all, save the odd few in whose company I placed myself. I wanted an end to the awful waiting. I wanted my feelings to subside. I wanted him to start something with me. I was terrified he would.

Abruptly, Johnny pushed the file box away, strode over to his desk, and sat down behind it. He cleared his throat several times in the thick silence that hung between us.

"Janey, could I interrupt you for a minute, please?" he said so harshly I thought I'd made some terrible error in my work. But his face, as I furtively glanced at it while making my way to my customary chair opposite his desk, was a mask of agony. He put one hand over it, pressing his temples with thumb and forefinger as if to massage some throbbing headache.

My stomach sank with fear as he looked at me. Even in my ignorance, there could be no mistaking that look.

"Sit down, Janey, please," he said in a weary voice. "It's high time we had a little talk."

"Yes," I answered weakly, half question, half admission.

"Ah Janey, I wanted to avoid saying what I'm going to say, but it's becoming increasingly clear that I just cannot do it. I feel it. I can't seem to stop myself from feeling it, and I might as well tell you."

He looked at me for encouragement, but I was caught up in taming the violent reactions my body was experiencing in anticipation of his words. I could only look at him blankly and wait for the words I knew were coming.

He paused to light a cigarette and then leaned over the desk and looked at me. "I don't want you to think I'm the type of man who does this sort of thing regularly or even occasionally. Frankly, I don't think it's right to put a young lady in a position like this. But there's something very compelling about you, Janey, and I find myself being drawn to you in a way I'm not sure I can control. I'd like to ask you ... if ... ah ... you'd consider seeing me ... ah ... on a social basis." He looked at me, his face agitated and flushed. This had been difficult for him. He sought some indication of my reaction. But my face was as still as stone. I was shaking badly, and a cold chill washed over me. He had asked and I was scared beyond reason.

"Listen now," he said quickly, after looking into my impassive face, "I know what you're thinking. It's almost like blackmail, me asking you something like this, with me being your advisor and all. You're thinking you can't refuse me if you want to be a successful student here. But Janey," he said, intensity making his voice quiver, "you could slap my face and leave me cold right now and I promise, your work here would not be affected in the least. I could never do that to you or any student. It would betray everything I believe in. If you want, you could be assigned to someone else, anything that would make you feel secure in your work here. What we do in our private lives would be totally separate from our academic lives. You have my word!

"Well, that's about all. Ah, I have to run these over to the admin building," he said, indicating a stack of folders on his desk. "I'll be back in ten minutes." He turned from me and walked briskly out the door.

With his departure, the awful implications of his words hit me with full force. I denied it for a moment. Not me. This had never happened. I had never let it happen. Not with men my own age, certainly not with older men. I had never talked much with men. I rewarded their efforts to engage me in conversation with stony stares and silences. I put them off by covering most of my face with my hair and with the baggy, shapeless clothes that were my uniform. In my world, men were creatures guided by unknowable, occasionally violent emotions. Like tigers, their freedom and power interested me without tempting me to get too close. Now, I had wandered into the jungle and must make friends with the beast or suffer the consequences.

A dark and fearful noise welled up inside my head. It was there, as it had always been, a senseless, raging torrent that drowned my voice, choked my throat closed. A fear that kept my life the closed room, safe and known, I had made it. I took several deep breaths and quickly rose from the chair. I paced the length of the room, hoping this would calm me, help me think.

Reject him, the larger part of me screamed. You don't need this awkward liaison between teacher and student, one generation and another, mature, experienced man, and gawky, scarred girl. He'll hurt you, the voice warned, and what will you have gained?

But there was another voice, a quiet reasoning voice that gathered its strength from somewhere deep inside me and spoke with an urgency as strong as survival itself. It was to this voice I finally listened. Johnny had reached out to me, had found some reason to look behind my veneer of silence. He offered me the chance to try on the part of a normal young woman, a woman who shared her conversation and affection, her bed, and her body, with a man. No matter that our relationship would be covert, hurried, and part time. Within the shelter of his company, maybe I could stop feeling so afraid. Although he did not know it, Johnny was offering me hope — hope of the limited, pitiful kind mistresses have always lived on. It was a gift I might be able to accept. To say yes to this was to stop dying, to try to shed my past. I would try it then, I decided. He would sleep with me, and I'd let him touch me in ways I once vowed no one would again. I'd keep quiet about it for the sake of the woman on the other side of the wedding band he wore. He had chosen me, and I would choose hope.

I sat down again, relieved, but still shaking from the decision I'd made.

Johnny returned a few minutes later, his face still flushed, his features still contorted. Perhaps he'd changed his mind? But no. His eyes conveyed everything he'd said earlier and more.

"I believe you," I said in a quavering voice, "about my work not being affected. It's okay though. I mean yes."

"You're sure? You've thought it over already? Have I been so transparent these past weeks?"

When I nodded, he laughed. "And I took you for a little innocent!"

He'll never realize how wrong he was.

CHAPTER 9

MADISON, WISCONSIN

SEPTEMBER 1985

JENNY

"What's new, Lou?" I smiled at the lanky, dark-haired guy behind the bar at the Esquire Inn. Shaking the rain out of my umbrella, I collapsed it into the bucket next to the door and hung up my coat on one of those hangers that won't come off the clothes rod. The Esquire Inn tried to pass itself off as a classy hotel, but operated like a sleaze pad where customers would try to steal everything that wasn't bolted down. It was a businessman's wet dream of a hotel, with X-rated movies and easy pickup, ask-no-questions fucks. I probably wasn't the only girl augmenting her income with the grateful dollars of its balding, rotund clients. Lou, the poorly paid bartender, ran the show from his bar stool perch. I didn't like to think of him in such crass terms, but Lou was my pimp.

I'd come across this opportunity, if you could call it that, about a year ago on a similarly rainy autumn evening. I'd been out shopping at the East Towne Mall when I'd noticed the "Every Room Equipped with X-Rated Videos" sign outside the Esquire and something prompted me to hop off the bus at the next stop. Something. Hell, I knew exactly what. I guess in normal people, you might call the feeling that comes over me lust. In my case, it's a twisted, evil compulsion to get fucked by some stranger. An anonymous ten-minute fuck to release the tension that builds up. I disgusted myself every time I did it, but it was an addiction I couldn't break, a need to purge myself — a sort of sexual bulimia.

When I'd opened the heavy dark wood door of the bar and checked out the interior, I knew I'd hit the jackpot. The dark paneled walls and stained red carpeting under cozy Formica tables and cushy black Naugahyde loveseats was made for the kind of scummy customers I was looking for. And there they were, perhaps two dozen, forty- to sixty-year-old men, most going to fat, smoking up the room and downing drinks, telling dirty jokes, and laughing ribaldly and too loud. I took up a place at the bar and decided to order a gin gimlet, an appropriately lady-like drink. I was one of three females in the place and the two others were work-worn heavyset women pushing fifty, having a beer together at one of the Formica tables.

"What'll it be?" said the bartender, who I later found out was named Lou, in the tone of voice that suggested he knew exactly what I'd come here for. My drink had barely arrived when a paunchy, red-faced, fifty-year-old with a too wide tie and a suit that looked like he'd slept in it sidled up to me.

"Let me buy you that drink, baby," he said with a smile that looked a bit too much like a leer.

"Why not?"

The bartender mixed the fat guy a drink and discreetly moved to the other end of the bar — a short enough distance away that he could still hear every word that passed between us.

My john — or whatever he was — and I had the usual conversation, most of it lies. I think I told him I was an off-duty stewardess or something equally loose sounding. I was relieved when we finished our drinks and he asked if I'd like to come up to his room for a nightcap. The bartender gave me a knowing and not-too-friendly glance as we donned our coats and left the bar. By the time we'd gotten to Fatso's second-floor room, charging for my services had come to mind. I'd never considered it before, though I was hardly experienced at this sort of blind screw either. I'd done it a few times early in last fall's semester and only when I was high on Valium. I was cool when he shut the door and copped a feel of my ass as he passed.

"It'll cost ya," I said nonchalantly and gave him what I hoped was a seductive glance.

"So I figured," he sighed a bit. He was pretty drunk. "How much?"

"Forty will do," I surprised myself with how easily it came out, like I said it all the time.

"Not a bad bargain for such a firm young ass." This time, he leered openly, got out his wallet and laid two twenties on the nightstand.

"Come on then, girly, I got a 7:00 a.m. meeting tomorrow." He began to take off his tie. And so, I discovered how simple it was to make money out of my disgusting compulsion. Forty bucks! It was all I could do to keep my attention on what was at hand. My eyes kept wandering to the money and my mind imagined the new shoes I'd buy.

It had become a regular thing. At first, I went just once a week, on Thursday nights, when most college students went out for an end-to-the-school-week pitcher of beer with their friends at the bars around campus. About the fourth time, my john turned out to be a rotund local pharmacist who'd come to the bar looking for an arrangement. He wasn't a bad sort of person, really. About forty and a first-class nerd, he was the type of guy who couldn't ask a girl out if he was the last man on earth. The first time I went with him, he took me to this little room he had fixed up behind the pharmacy he owned, just a couple of blocks from the hotel. I was a bit nervous, afraid he'd be a weirdo. Turned out he was just shy — and tentative — not the usual experience at all. By then, I'd raised my price to $50. But, when it came time to pay, the poor guy turned all shades of red and admitted he only had thirty-five bucks on him. Could give me the rest in an IOU or something since I knew where he worked?

Like a bold of lightning, a better idea came to me.

"How about the rest in pills?" I asked quietly, a little shocked at myself. I'd scammed Valiums a few times from a girl down the hall when I'd first come to Madison and liked the calm feeling they gave me.

"That's against the law, you know," he stammered.

I laughed. "So's what we just did, Al."

He nodded miserably. He was such a pitiful character, I felt sorry for him.

"How about this then?" he said stroking his chin. "Mmmmmmaybe you could come here once a week and I'll pay you part in cash, part whatever else you want?" He was petrified of what he'd said and looked like a deer just before your car bashed into it.

"Al, I wouldn't tell on you, no matter what," I said, to soothe him and because it was true. "You're a good guy, Al, and I'm not out to get anybody in trouble. I think once a week would be fine. Every Thursday, just like tonight, huh? And it would be nice to get a few Valiums then. I have trouble sleeping sometimes," I added to make him feel like he was doing me a medical service.

"Okay, tttthat'd be just great, JJJJenny," he said, hurrying to pull on his pants. "Okay if I bring them next time?" he asked, his voice quivering, and I nodded. So that's how I got on a regular downer supply line. It came in handy, too.

Just two weeks later, Lou, the bartender at the Esquire Inn, approached me during a lull in both our businesses.

"Listen, babe, I don't want to step on your toes but, you know, it could be dangerous working here like you do," he whispered close to my face. The way my eyes flashed must have given me away, but I tried playing dumb anyways. "I don't work here. I work up at the mall and I like to come in here for a drink after work," I insisted, unconvincingly.

"Well, maybe you need help fending off the uglies that frequent this joint, heh?" He tried to sound brotherly. "I just want to be your friend, you know. I don't want to see a young girl like you getting into any trouble. I thought we could make some kind of arrangement, for your own benefit, of course."

He didn't go on to tell me what would happen if I refused his offer, but I got the picture. I thought about it, but not for long. I told myself it was because of the good money I made here, but I knew that wasn't it. I was a perv sex addict; I needed to get my fuck fix, and this was a good place for it. I decided to play his game.

"Hmmm ... well, there are some unsavory types that might bother me sometimes. You think you could keep them away from me, huh?" I said sweetly, with a touch of Texan in my voice.

"Yeah, and more than that, I could make sure only the nice guys bought you drinks and such, the upper crust of the businessmen staying here." I could see the dollar signs in his eyes now. When I looked closer, I saw something else in his big hollow blue eyes, a kind of glazed look that was not the look of a drinker. I decided to take a chance.

"Working in a place like this, I bet it's hard to relax after work. You get home so late. I bet you need a couple of drinks just to mellow out," I laid on the Southern belle act.

"I don't drink."

"Then maybe you'd be interested in some other kind of relaxers."

"I might be. Like what?"

"Valium?"

"Girl, that's for kids like you. What about these?" He took two pills out of his front jeans pocket, let me scan them and quickly put them away. "Now, percs, that's a man's after-work medicine. Can you get those?"

"How many?" I asked, sensing a deal was about to be struck.

"Ten of the ones I showed you — a week."

"Hmmm," I acted unconvinced, knowing the ball was in my court. "And what do I get for it?"

"Listen," he replied, almost drooling, "we start this week. I line up some rich bastards for you whenever you want. I keep track of where you are and make sure you're okay. If you like what happens, then you pay in percs. You can get them?"

"Yeah, I can get them," I lied. Possibly I could. I'd have to press Al on Thursday. "Okay, we'll give it a week. I'll work Tuesdays and Thursdays, two dates a night."

Al didn't want me at his little room until 11:30, so I thought I could do three that night.

"Fifty a throw. No weirdos. Only guys from the hotel. If you do what you say, I'll get you what you want starting next week. These things take time to arrange."

"Fifty?" Lou said, incredulously. "You could get $70, and I'll take a tenner and the pills. You still make out better than now, and with protection, too. Deal?"

"Deal." Lou smiled and we shook on it, giggling a bit.

"Let me buy you a drink," said my drug-addict, bar-tending pimp. "Gin gimlet, ain't it?"

"You know it," I smiled. This was going to be all right.

So here we were, contented business partners with a

year's good earnings under our belts. Sometimes, Lou's was the only friendly face I'd see for weeks, and until Lena, I guess he was my only friend here. If you could call our odd relationship a friendship. After so many months of partnership, we knew precious little about one another. I knew he had an "old lady," as he called her, and a four-year-old son. Both Lou and his girlfriend, Lisa, who occasionally came to the bar, seemed to be high all the time.

It was Tuesday, the start of my work week. Lou had my drink mixed by the time I'd hung up my jacket and changed into the green dress in the bar bathroom. He had tonight's business all lined up. The mark was waiting in the usual corner chair to check me out. If he liked me (they always did), he'd walk by and up to number 211, his room. I was to follow in ten minutes, the typical setup. I sipped my drink and talked to Lou about the lousy weather, the sale at TV Lenny's on stereos, and the films we'd seen the past week. Movies was one subject Lou and I could connect on. We each saw a film or two a week — we both liked the escape they offered, I guess. I barely glanced at the middle-aged man as he nodded his approval to Lou and left the bar. I took a couple of gulps to polish off my drink and added a Valium just to mellow me out a bit before the night's work.

Lou hadn't found anyone for the second round yet and I told him to forget it. I had an exam the next day and thought I should at least crack the books enough to keep from flunking the test. I told him goodnight and left the percs and the ten I owed him for this one in the interior pocket of the navy surplus pea coat hanging on the coat rack out front. Then I took the back stairs up to room 211.

The man on the other side of the door cleared his throat at my knock.

"Come in," he said gruffly.

I did. He was barefoot and wore a silky maroon robe. He was smoking a small cigar and stood by the room's mirror as if he'd just finished combing his hair. A lot of them tried to impress me, as if they couldn't accept how little I cared.

He appraised me like a hunk of meat in a shop window. I stared downward demurely. They usually liked me to act a bit shy.

"Well then, take your coat off and let me have a better look at you." I complied. I was wearing my polyester emerald work dress, one of two I'd bought after realizing my preferred punk styles were not going to get me far in the flesh market. This one had a provocatively scooped neck, short sleeves gathered at the shoulder and a slit up the side that went almost to my crotch. I hated the sleazy thing, but these assholes sure didn't. When I wore it with black spike-heeled sling-backs, it did flatter my figure in a cheap, barroom sort of way. I always brought my outfit and shoes with me, changed in the bar bathroom before going into the bar and put my normal street clothes on before heading back to campus. That made me feel like I was two different people, Jenny here, Jen back on campus.

Jowly, as I mentally baptized this one, looked me over.

"Pretty young, aren't you?"

"Old enough, I guess, suh," I put on the Southern accent thick, which they all really liked.

"Yes, indeed, you certainly are. Take off the dress, honey."

I undid the zipper and stripped to the black slip and gartered stockings I wore beneath. I figured for seventy bucks they might as well have something to see. They were all so alike; these semi-naughty clothes brought gasps of delight to their tobacco-stained lips. Jowly was no exception.

"Let me get a feel of those nice stockings, sweetheart. You know how to please a man, don't you? I bet you do. Why don't you tell me about how I'm going to do it to you?"

Oh yuck, I groaned silently. Not one of these. I much preferred the silent, three-minute, heavy-breathing humpers, but I did have a little speech I used for requests like this. I started whispering it in a honeyed voice in his ear, and he stroked my legs and gave me an admiring glance when he discovered I wasn't wearing any panties. I could feel his cock get stiff as I went into detail about all the delights it would soon be experiencing. I prayed he wouldn't make me go down on him. My outfit and my little speech were designed precisely to entice these jerks into quick entry and orgasm. He was inexpertly squeezing my tits now, twice the size they were before I'd gone on the pill last year. Nice, full young breasts, a peach-shaped ass, a pair of shapely legs, a pretty, blue-eyed face and ripe wheat-colored hair. I was a first-class whore all right — they all told me that in so many words.

Jowly had maneuvered me to the bed by this time and was undoing the sash of his robe. I always kept my eyes droopy lidded in what I hoped was a seductive way when my johns undressed. Actually, I did it so I wouldn't have to see what manner of pudgy, flat-assed, pimply flesh was about to penetrate mine.

"Just spread 'em and lay still." Jowly ordered me and he played with my slinky slip and tweaked my crotch a bit as he fumbled in the pocket of his suit coat hanging on a chair next to the bed. He got out his wallet and took a crisp fifty and a twenty out of it. The twenty he put on my coat, draped over the room's one armchair. The fifty he stuck down the front of my slip. "I've been saving this bill for a sweet little cunt like you," he whispered in what he possibly thought was a sexy voice. It amazed me how many of these guys liked money to play a role in their little fantasies. I hoped the bill was in there securely.

"I'm telling ya now, keep still!" He tried to growl the words furiously and half-giggled at his attempt. I stole a glance at his prick and breathed a silent sigh of relief. It was stiff. Hopefully, this wouldn't take too long.

As he came at me, I turned away and turned on my heavy-breathing act. It was all so automatic. But this guy's orders for stillness unsettled me. I thought about the psych test I had tomorrow and tried to mentally recite the half-hearted notes I'd taken, all the while breathing heavy and moaning a bit. I was tight tonight, not like me. This stillness he wanted was making me nervous.

"Keep still, you little bitch," Jowly hissed in my ear as I wiggled under him, almost uncontrollably. I wasn't faking the heavy breathing now. I could feel myself starting to hyperventilate. I tried to concentrate on not moving, but I could feel my chest tightening. No, no, I willed myself to shut down. God, finish, you bastard, Skinner, operant conditioning, Freud, the id, ego and super ego, Jung, oh hell, what was his thing?

But in the silenced place inside me, the terrible words rang out; keep still, keep still, keep still!

Jowly came in an expulsion of foul breath and wetness. He got off me immediately and growled, "Get out of here, you lousy cunt." I grabbed for my clothes and caught a glimpse of my own reflection in the mirror. I was astonished to discover my face was wet with tears. I hurriedly wiped my face with my dress, put it on, made sure my money was secure, took my coat and left without a backward glance.

In the bathroom downstairs off the bar, I changed to my black stretch pants and baggy fluorescent pink sweater, belted it, and slipped on my Peter Pan boots. I put on my black raincoat, grabbed my umbrella, and stuffed the dress, the spike heels, and the stockings in the large black canvass bag I brought to these occasions. Combing my hair in front of the small, age-speckled mirror, the ghostly reflection staring back at me made facing what had happened unavoidable. I had almost lost control back there; how close I'd come I didn't want to think about. I thought I had buried all that in the far reaches of my brain. But tonight, it all had burst into my mind unsummoned, just because this lousy john had repeated those horrible nightmare words — keep still! As I saw the girl that I'd been in my mind's eye, two more wet drops slid down my cheeks. I turned from the mirror and ran out the door into the wet night as if I could outrun all that had happened, as if the cold autumn rain could wash it away for good.

CHAPTER 10

MADISON, WISCONSIN

JANUARY 1978

MADDIE

"You love me something awful, don't you, hon?" Roz asked and grasped my right hand. My left was occupied with a glass of red wine I'd been about to raise in a toast. We had reserved a window table at Madison's revolutionary gathering place, Lysistrata, for drinks and dinner. It was early evening on a bitterly cold January 13th, the fifth anniversary of the day we met.

My love's big baby browns had lost their twinkle. Usually, Roz looked like she had just finished laughing or was about to. When she did laugh, which was often, it started as a high-pitched tee-hee, then dropped an octave to the most heartfelt belly laugh I'd ever heard. It was her laugh, more than anything, that hooked me that first night we met. Now, though, her face was serious.

"You glorious woman, you're the love of my life. You know

that perfectly well, so what's up?"

"Let's drink to us first, huh?" Roz countered, without a hint of a smile. I let her divert me by the toast. I was not in a hurry to find out what was behind her grave demeanor. I knew I wasn't going to like it.

"To four magnificent years and the start to the fifth!" Roz raised her class, clinking mine. "You're the love of *my* life too, Maddie. You. Are." She said these last words slowly as if she had just realized it.

"To us, then!" I was bewildered at her definitively *not*-Roz behavior.

We sipped our red, a cabernet from Napa that cost significantly more than our usual bottle and tasted significantly better, too. Here we were, celebrating the beginning of our fifth year together at a restaurant where two lesbians could sit together at a window table, hold hands and no one noticed. Like it was normal.

Lysistrata had opened just over a year ago. We had attended the grand opening. No dark and seamy dyke bar on a bad side of town was this! It was all windows in the front, on Gorham Street, a busy Madison conduit. There were pots with ferns hanging from the ceiling, spacious dining tables covered with white linen tablecloths, and chairs comfy enough to sit in for hours, which we often did. The menu was innovative, mostly vegetarian, and the food was prepared and presented with care. It had a glorious crescent-moon shaped bar in the back that was stocked with everything from herbal tea and gourmet coffee to fine brandy. The casual wait staff, the collective that started it, and lots of the customers were women, most of them lesbians. It was like dykes had suddenly become first-class citizens. Oh, how we treasured this space as ours.

On off nights, womyn's organizations (increasingly, we spelled it with a "y" to banish any notion that our word for ourselves was a diminutive of their word for themselves) used Lysistrata as a meeting space. Sometimes, a lesbian poet or songster performed there. There was Scrabble, a chess board, and decks of cards with Greek Goddesses instead of jacks, queens, and kings. Roz and I loved going there for dinner and we did so as often as our puny graduate student budgets would allow. We were full-on *people* there and it felt absolutely liberating. We knew many of the customers and wait staff. Some of each appeared to know it was our anniversary because womyn kept coming over to congratulate us. That was Roz's doing. She was never shy about announcing our personal details to the womyn in our world and she did it in such a charming and humorous way that I never could get mad at her for it.

What with all the congratulatory interruptions, it wasn't until between the salad and the main course that we were able to return to my question. "What's up, Roz?" I repeated when we finally had a minute alone.

"I have news," she said, with not a hint of the sparkly eyes and about-to-grin lips that usually defined my Roz's face. I knew it wasn't good news.

"You got a job in Timbuktu and you're taking it?" I was only half kidding. Now that we were both on the verge of completing our doctorates, mine in history, hers in epidemiology, we'd talked often about the likelihood that there would not be a job for both of us at the same institution. It was not a conversation I relished. If we had it too many more times, that tight feeling in the pit of my stomach would become an ulcer.

"You could look at it that way." Roz was tearing up a bit, shaking her head and frowning. Misery was an expression so unusual for her that I wasn't sure I was interpreting it correctly. "But not that kind of job." She put her hand on her forehead and stared down at her wine.

I knew I really was not going to like this.

"It's Mama. Jerry called last night."

"What?" Alarm bells started ringing in my head. But Roz reached over and patted my hand.

"She's okay, though Jerry said her MS has taken a turn for the worse. She hasn't been out of her wheelchair for a month now. But it's Jerry this is about. He has held down the fort for so long ..." Her younger brother, Jerry, had decided to attend a mediocre university not far from where Roz's mama lived so he could help her with chores and shopping. "Jerry has been accepted to Howard Law School for fall. Not everybody gets a chance like that. He deserves to go, after all he's done for her. It's my turn now, that's what I'm saying."

"What does that mean? Are you giving up on your career before it even gets started?" It came out more desperate sounding than I had intended. "Are you moving back to *Texas*?" That came out as almost hysterical, and I clamped my mouth shut to prevent any further unhelpful utterances.

"Just hear me out." Roz reached across the table to take both my hands in hers. She held my gaze for a time. "It's not as bad as you're imagining. I do have a plan in mind."

Roz was the most methodical person I'd ever met, so I was sure she did have a plan. With dread, I said quietly, "Let's hear it, then."

Roz had done her research well. The mediocre university where Jerry had gone was hiring in both our fields. Moreover, the history department was looking for an Americanist specializing in the twentieth century. Damn. My dissertation was titled: "Rethinking the American Century: The Role of Economic Catastrophe and War in the Making of a Global Superpower." Why hadn't I studied Chinese Imperialism or some such thing? They were hiring in spring, not typical, but not unheard of. Probably, the person they had hired during the more typical fall hiring season had taken a job elsewhere, outside of Texas.

The job description for Roz's specialty was equally promising. The university wanted to hire someone with expertise in the impact of poverty on community disease profiles, just what Roz's dissertation had explored. In a flash, I knew that we both would be hired at the damn place. Texas! Not exactly heaven for an interracial dyke couple, that's for sure. Just as I was about to point that out, Roz continued. She had a plan for that, too.

"Texas doesn't exactly embrace lesbians," Roz admitted unnecessarily. She wasn't out to her very loving and accepting mama, never mind the white good ol' boy culture surrounding their neatly kept neighborhood in an older Black suburb of Houston.

I'd been there once. Roz wanted me to meet her family. But I had to stay in a hotel downtown. And when Roz brought me to meet Jerry and her mama at their modest brick ranch house, she'd introduced me as her friend from the university who was here for a conference and wasn't it great that I had an evening free and could come over for some authentic Southern cooking? I never did get to meet Roz's father, who had died suddenly the year before we met. He had a massive heart attack at the age of fifty-nine, after working at the sorting center of Houston's post office ever since he'd come back from service in World War II. Roz's mama had his pension, which enabled her to stay in their home, even after the MS got bad enough that she had to quit her job as an assistant at the local library.

Jerry was sweet but as serious as Roz was jovial. I had gotten into an interesting conversation with him over the delicious banana and pineapple concoction — hummingbird cake, Mama had called it — we had for dessert. Roz had obviously briefed him on my dissertation topic. He had asked if I'd considered how much enforcing Jim Crow in the South after the war had undermined America's ability to project itself to the rest of the world as a benevolent democratic superpower. It was a good question, and it gnawed at me so much that I changed a dissertation chapter to grapple with it. I was an instant fan of Jerry, who was careful in his thinking and whip smart. He'd make an excellent civil rights attorney, his lifelong dream. And now he'd gotten accepted at storied Howard University Law School. An impressive brother Roz had.

"So, if I could get a job like that one, I would move home to care for Mama and then Jerry could move to D.C. and go to Howard. It's an easy enough commute to the university from Mama's house." She'd even researched the commute! I was about to interrupt but Roz held up her finger to warn me she wasn't finished.

"You and I would buy a house in a neighborhood near the university, but not too near, if you know what I mean. I wouldn't be able to spend every night with you, but I could get some help for Mama for some days and nights, maybe a woman from Mama's church. On those days, we could be together, Maddie." She looked at me imploringly.

I knew better than to ask why this fictitious part-time helper couldn't be employed full time and Roz couldn't live with me. Roz's devotion to her mama would compel her to take on as much of Mama's care as she could. I half understood. Roz's mama, like Roz herself, was full of laughter and life, despite her encroaching disease. She was generous and utterly committed to the well-being of her children. So unlike my own uptight parents, both of whom rejected me thoroughly and with finality when I inadvisably decided to come out to them during my undergrad days. I *liked* Roz's family — I wanted to be part of that family, because that was the family that had produced this gem of a woman. But why couldn't Roz's family live somewhere else?

"Damn you, my sweet. If that's the only way to make you

happy, then let's get going on our applications. Tomorrow, though. Tonight, let's celebrate our love!" I raised my glass, and the sound it made when it contacted Roz's was as pure a tone as fine crystal glasses could deliver. Our love would have to be just that pure if we were to survive the throwback environment that Roz was proposing we relocate to.

That night, our lovemaking was breathtakingly passionate, our bodies committing to a future together that my mind was having trouble imagining or accepting. I'd try to follow my body's wisdom, then, I decided the next morning. I had to have Roz in whatever ways she'd let me. All the rest was negotiable.

CHAPTER 11

MADISON, WISCONSIN

SEPTEMBER 1985

JENNY

"Hello?" Lena was in the bathroom down the hall, so I answered the phone.

"Hi Jen," Harry's mellow voice came over the line. "Lena around?"

"Hang on, Harry, she's in the john — I'll run and get her."

"Thanks, kid," Harry answered, and I ran down the hall into the dorm's communal bathroom.

Lena was brushing her teeth at one of the sinks.

"Lena, your man's on the phone," I yelled so everyone in the bathroom could hear.

"Which one?" Lena replied, in an innocent voice. She had eyes only for Harry and they'd been seeing each other for a year already.

"Oh darn, I forgot to ask," I continued in a loud voice. "But let's see: Matthew, Mark, Luke, and John already called, so it must be Tom, Dick, or Harry — yes, that's right, it's Harry."

Lena loved to make the other girls on the floor think she was hot gossip material. "White girls always think we Black girls are loose, so I might as well roll with it," she had told me a few weeks ago. She didn't care what our dormmates thought about her.

We hurried back to the room. Lena picked up the phone and laid back in her bed, ready for a long love chat with Harry. I gathered my bag and waved at her as I left to go sit in the lounge down the hall until she came to get me.

I never answered the phone unless Lena wasn't in the room. It was never for me, anyway. No one knew my number. The only person I'd passed a number to was my mother, and I'd given her the number of the storeroom in the basement of the dorm. It was always empty. I didn't want that bitch calling me, pretending she gave a damn so she could tell her friends it was all my fault we didn't speak to each other. I didn't want anyone calling me. I don't like people in general. I like being a loner. Except for Lena. Lena is okay.

When I left her, Lena had been snuggled on her bed in her long, pink terrycloth robe. Lena loved pink and she looked great in it. How had I gotten so lucky as to get her for a roommate? Lena was smart. She was majoring in linguistics, which I had never heard of before she explained it to me. She was interested in the development of Black American dialects, she'd told me. She spoke French fluently, and could get along in Creole, as two of her cousins in Florida were married to Haitians. She was studying Swahili as a minor and she had even found someone to tutor her in Wolof, the language of the people of Senegal. *My* language, she said, because most of my people were snatched from there originally. She meant both her actual family and all Black Americans, she said. I had to look Senegal up on a map in her *Geography of Africa* book when she wasn't in the room. She was going to be a diplomat in Africa someday, she told me. I believed her.

She could guess someone's birthplace by the sound of their voice almost as well as Professor Higgins in *My Fair Lady*. She dreamed of becoming a jazz singer. She never told me this, but I guessed it from the large poster of Lena Horne that hung over her bed and the way she hung around jazz musicians. After we'd known each other about a month, she'd admitted she'd sung a few sets last spring at a place on Park Street where Harry's jazz group had a regular gig. She had tried to act casual when she told me, like it didn't mean anything. But the way her eyes lit up, I knew it did. I think she thought it was bad luck to talk about it right out in the open. Like her dream bubble would burst and she'd be left with nothing but air. So, I acted nonchalant about it like she did. But I think she knew I knew it was her secret dream.

Every Friday night so far this semester, Lena would go listen to Harry and his friends play at the Park Street bar. She kept trying to get me to go with her.

"Come on Jen, it'll be fun," she'd say. "I'll introduce you to one of the guys in Harry's group. This guy Chuck — he's a little shy — but he's nice. You might like him."

"Who needs a boyfriend?" I said in what I hoped was a nasty voice. "Men are just assholes, anyway."

"Whew, is she cool! She don't need no one, no how. 'Course, you're 95 percent right about that — most of them are assholes," she agreed, but she gave me a curious look, as if she wanted to know why I thought so. She didn't ask, though.

Lena might have her suspicions about what I did with my evenings, but she was cool about it and never came out and asked me. I told Lena my parents sent me money but since they never called; I don't think she believed me. I didn't like lying to her, but it beat telling her the truth. That was one of the reasons she kept inviting me to go with her. She was trying to get me away from something she couldn't believe I did in the first place.

One night, after a month of her pestering me to go out and hear the band and me acting disinterested, she upped the ante.

"Hey, you stick-in-the-mud." She came into the room and gave me a poke.

I looked up from my bed where I'd been reading some boring history assignment. "Hi, what's up?"

"You coming out with me tonight or what? You might miss something if you don't," she continued as she saw I was going to turn her down again.

"What, miss you snuggling with Harry in the corner of the bar between sets?" I teased her. She'd told me all about that.

"I'll be snuggling with him all right, but not in the corner." She looked at me and I could see she was excited. "I'll be right there in the center of the stage with him."

"Lena, what are you talking about? Hey, you're not going to sing with the band, are you?" She grinned. "All right! That's great!"

"If you have it, flaunt it, I always say." Her face was all smiles now. "So, girl, you coming to watch your roomie make a fool of herself or what?" I could tell she wanted me to come, and I'd been dying to hear Lena sing.

"Who could pass up an opportunity like that? I'll be sitting in the front row, just waiting to laugh when you trip on the mic cord!" I looked over at her to be sure she knew I was kidding. She did.

"About time I fix you up with Chuck, that guy in the band I keep telling you about. You need a man in your life. That's what you need."

"Hold on, Miss Matchmaker. I never said I was in the market for one. Besides, I'm very fussy when it comes to men. Maybe I won't like what you've got picked out for me." Fussy, ha, I hated every last one of them. But I wasn't about to tell Lena that.

"Oh, you'll like him all right., Just you wait. He's just your type. Good looking, laid back. I don't know him that well, I guess, but he seems like a nice guy. Why don't you come early with me? Then you'll have a chance to meet him before the show."

I wouldn't like him, I told myself. I said I'd go because I knew Lena wanted me to hear her sing. But my stomach tightened when I agreed to the plan.

I washed my hair in the group bathroom and blow-dried it in front of the mirror. Back in the room, I put on a pair of tight black pants and the blood red sweater Lena had picked out for me when we'd gone shopping a couple of weekends ago. Over that, I wore a black-and-white patterned vest and a thick black belt with a huge buckle.

Lena was busy putting mascara on her already long, thick lashes. She rarely wore makeup, but tonight she had put on blusher, eye shadow, the works. Her close-cropped hair had just a bit of gel in it to make it shine, and she wore a large gold drop earring in one ear and two gold studs in the other. She'd bought an old tuxedo at a second-hand shop and had altered it to make it fit just right. When she took off the jacket, you could see the saturated pink satin ruffled shirt under the tux jacket was a halter like what Jennifer Beal wore in *Flashdance*. She looked fabulous. I told her so.

"Wow, you look like you could be on your way to Carnegie Hall!" I said, standing behind her as she put on lipstick in front of the dresser-top mirror.

"Oh, go on." She turned away from her reflection. "I guess I do look pretty good." She beamed shyly at me. "You ready to go?"

"Hey, where's the limo?" I pretended to look around for it as we walked over the hill from our dorm, Liz Waters, to Park

Street, where the bar was. Lena had on yellow jogging shoes and carried her black heels in one gloved hand. I hurried to keep up with her long strides. The wind howled around us, and storm clouds gathered in the dark sky. We'd have snow tonight.

The band was already there setting up equipment when we arrived. I got in without paying the cover charge because Lena explained we were with the band. Harry came over and gave Lena a long whistle of appreciation. "Who's this fancy lady you got with you, Jen? Looks like Lena Campbell all grown up. Hey sexy lady, you Lena's older sister from Chi-town? Wanna do something with the lead horn player of this band after the show, ma'am?" Lena gave him a playful whop across the butt. I could see she was happy and excited. God, let her do good, I prayed to no one in particular.

"You shut up, you two-timer, you," she teased him back. "I wouldn't let no sister of mine go out with a man of your low character."

"Ooh, she's feisty tonight," Harry said, giving Lena a little squeeze. "You're gonna wow 'em, Lena." He smiled at her. You could see how much he liked her. Harry was as tall and handsome as his namesake, Harry Belafonte, with an aquiline nose and a high forehead. Though his singing voice didn't live up to the famous Belafonte's, Lena told me, "He could blow a trumpet 'bout as good as Miles Davis. Or at least half as good!" She grinned. Harry, like most of the members of the band, was a grad student studying jazz at Madison's famed jazz program, headed by the legendary Richard Davis, a world-famous jazz bassist. I didn't know jazz from a hole in the ground, but that's what Lena told me, proudly.

"Glad you could make it, Jen," Harry said, turning to me. "You look great, too! Come on over here and I'll introduce you to my men." He indicated the corner where three guys were testing instruments and turning dials. "Hey guys, this here's a friend of Lena's. Name's Jen. That's Jimmy there messing around with the drums." A small, very dark guy waved a drumstick in salute. "Fred, here." A kind of pudgy white guy with a businessman's haircut and glasses tuning his guitar paused to reach over and shake my hand. "There's Rupert, our bass player," he indicated a lanky Black guy with a longish Afro who turned from tuning his glossy stand-up bass to say hi. "Richard Davis is his mentor," Harry said in an awe-filled voice. "That's cool," I managed and was glad that Lena had filled me in on who Richard David was. "And that's Chuck," Harry finished, pointing to a guy with longish light-brown hair coming through the door of the bar with a rolled-up extension cord slung over his shoulder.

"Chuck plays keyboard," Lena explained, indicating the baby grand taking up a good part of the low platform they used for a stage. Then she jabbed me in the ribs with her elbow. "Him," she whispered.

Chuck steadfastly ignored me when he came up to where Lena, Harry and I were standing, looking at the stage. "Harry, I think this will do it," he said about the cord. "Let's try 'er out. Hi Lena," he said over his shoulder as Harry and he went over to Rupert and started discussing how to work out the wiring.

"He's a little shy. Nice though, you'll see. Let me go over and see if I can push him in your direction a bit."

"Lena, don't you dare," I whispered back urgently. "Shouldn't you be singing scales or something?"

"Yeah, I guess you're right. I'm so nervous I don't know what I'm doing. Don't tell Harry. He thinks I have nerves of steel." She winked and went over to the piano.

I looked over at where the guys were trying out the mixer or tuner or whatever it was. He was good looking, I decided about Chuck. Not too tall. Lena was probably taller, but he was three or four inches taller than me. He had nice thick hair that didn't follow any particular style, preppy or punk. And there was something about his face that looked kind. He was older than me, too. I think Lena said he was getting his masters in piano performance, so he was twenty-three or twenty-four?

I pulled back from these considerations with a start. What was I thinking? I didn't want a boyfriend. I didn't need the hassle.

People had slowly started filtering into the bar. A few older Black men that looked like regulars were sitting on stools against the bar, chatting with the two college-aged white guys mixing drinks behind the counter. A group of guys were playing pool in the corner farthest from the stage and the front tables were filling up with couples and small groups. The band members were mixing with the crowd now. It looked like a lot of people were regulars or friends of the band. Chuck wasn't talking to anyone, though; he was running through a couple of bars on the piano. Lena motioned for me to sit with her at the band's table to the right of the platform.

"When are you on?"

"Second set, if I don't die during the first. Feel my hand." She put her slender hand in mine. It was icy. "I'm scared silly."

"Don't be crazy, Lena, you've got this. Remember how often you soloed at your dad's church when you were in high school? You told me you liked being the soloist." But Lena looked scared now. I guess jazz was more important to her than soloing in the gospel choir as a teenager.

"Why don't you have some tea? Here, I'll get it." I jumped up and went to the bar. Suddenly, there were quite a few people wanting drinks, and no one paid any attention to me.

"Hey, what do you want? I'll get it for you." I turned and saw Chuck standing behind me.

"I was hoping to get some tea for Lena," I mumbled.

Chuck yelled over the heads of the crowd. "Hey, Nick, a tea, and a Miller for the band, will ya?" He turned back to me. "What are you drinking?"

I hadn't thought about it. Except at the Esquire, I didn't usually drink, but I'd forgotten to pop a couple Valiums and my hands were shaky. "Uh, white wine?"

"And a glass of house white, Nick," Chuck yelled again, and Nick grinned.

"Coming right up, my man."

I got out some money, but Chuck waved it away. "Drinks for the band are on the house. Friends of the band, too. Hey, what's your name again — I didn't catch it before. Preoccupied, I guess." He gave me a wan smile.

"Jenny — ah, Jen," I said.

"Yeah. Well, hi. I'm Chuck. You're Lena's roommate, right? She talks about you all the time."

"She does?" I asked and flushed.

"Don't worry, it's all good," Chuck assured me with a smile. "She likes you so much I think Harry gets jealous sometimes."

"I've never heard her sing before. I can't wait."

"You're in for a treat. She's great. Here's your wine and the tea. Wish Lena luck for me." Chuck took his beer and headed back to the stage.

"Thanks, Jen," Lena warmed her hands on the cup of tea. "Hey, who was that I saw you talking to?"

"Oh, shut up," I said, blushing ridiculously. "He's just got pull with the bartender, that's all."

"Sure," Lena agreed with a smile. "Just used him to get our drinks, huh?"

They started to play then. I sipped my wine and listened. They were good, I could tell, even though I knew nothing at all about jazz and never thought I liked it. But something in what they were doing involved me. Lena sat next to me humming low in her throat to the songs, all of which she knew. I looked at Chuck, his brow furrowed with concentration. He had a solo then and the audience clapped. The first half-hour zipped by.

Then it was Lena's turn.

"Shit, I'm going to blow it," she said suddenly, and her eyes were scared.

"You are not. You didn't drag me out here to watch you blow it, did you? I'm going to kill you if you blow it now. I spent good money on this new sweater that you made me buy," I said, guessing that she had plotted all along to bring me tonight.

"Busted," she said, and her face relaxed a bit. "But how can you say I'm not going to blow it?" She looked at me seriously like I would have a cure for her stage fright. And then I did.

"Cuz your name is Lena, that's why. And you're going to do it like *the* Lena, just like her."

"Yeah," she said, her eyes sparkling again. "I am."

She did.

By the time she'd finished half of her first number, the entire place was quiet, everyone listening to her. Her voice was confident and smooth as honey. Her voice gave me goose bumps all over. She was doing it. Nobody clapped harder than I did when the band took an intermission.

When the night's music was over, a small crowd gathered around Lena and the band. I noticed it included the older Black guys who had been there from the first — fellow jazz musicians, I figured. She was all smiles, her eyes brimming with tears she was so happy. She caught my eye and I smiled at her. I was so proud, even though she was just my friend, and I wasn't sure I had the right to be. I noticed Chuck wasn't talking to the group of people gathered on the stage. He was busy putting away equipment. I noticed him because I'd felt someone's eyes on me and looked up to see Chuck staring at me. But as soon as I noticed him, he turned his gaze back to what he'd been doing. Lena would go home with Harry and by the look of things, I wouldn't get close enough to say goodbye. So, I left the bar into the snow-flurried night and headed home alone. But I noticed Chuck stared after me.

CHAPTER 12

PINE HILL STATION, TEXAS

SEPTEMBER 1985

JANE

By anyone's standards, a strange first date. Not just the first date with Johnny; it was a milestone I celebrated tonight. My first date ever, with anyone. Strange then, what I would have to remember from it. Not the child-becoming-woman shy pageantry of a prom or homecoming dance, nor the nervous tension and tentative fondles of a teenage movie date. Instead, Johnny picked me up in his gray sedan on a prearranged corner some distance from my studio apartment and from the university. We drove thirty miles to another middle-sized town and parked in front of a chain hotel with a bar and restaurant attached. Johnny checked us in as Mr. and Mrs. Justin Lee Collins, a name that made me smile behind my hand as I recognized it as the name of one of Johnny's other grad students. He had even brought an overnight bag to make it look legitimate, a detail that made me wonder if he'd done this before. Johnny seemed to be enjoying himself and the deception we were trying to create.

We took a quick glance at our room and deposited the small suitcase there. My stomach clenched in fear at the sight of the matching double beds with their gold bedspreads. Would I be able to survive this? Could I feign passion enough to convince a man experienced in these things? As doubts about my acting abilities infiltrated my brain, I became convinced that I'd made a horrible mistake. Why had I let myself drift so far out of my depth? As I groped frantically for some context to put this in, some way to make sense of it, so I would know what to say, how to be with this man, Johnny touched my arm gently. I jumped.

"Don't worry about a thing," he said, smiling down at me. "It's not so bad as going to the dentist now, is it?" I smiled and shook my head. "Johnny'll take care of you. No need for the jitters at all." I looked up at him in terror — pale, slack-jawed and staring.

"Janey, I don't like seeing a face like that on a pretty, young girl. Am I all that terrible?" But when I tried to answer — to tell him that no, of course not, it was how I might act, not him, that terrified me — he interrupted.

"No, no, I don't need you to tell me a thing. How about having a little drink at the bar? You'll feel more relaxed." He guided me out the door, his hand at my elbow. At the restaurant, after choosing a quiet booth in the far corner of the place, Johnny encouraged me to order a drink. To help calm myself, he said. At first, I refused him, asking for tea instead. I rarely drank and did not want my head swimming later when I would need all the wits I possessed. But he insisted, and when the tired-looking middle-aged waitress came to take our order, he ordered a double bourbon and a rum and Coke for "the little lady," as he put it to the waitress. When the drinks came, Johnny concertedly started talking about work, how my computer entries were helping him to organize his project better, what various graduate students he'd worked with in the past were doing now — safe neutral topics that did for a time distract me from the two double beds in the room upstairs.

We lingered over our drinks a bit longer than necessary. Perhaps Johnny, too, was nervous? Possibly he *hadn't* done this before? Or possibly, it was because I was the new one, and he wanted to savor the moments before he took me to bed. As I was sitting across from him, in the booth with black vinyl covered benches next to a window overlooking the highway, I thought about how Johnny had never asked me if the terms he'd set for our relationship were all right with me. The clandestine meeting, the drive to a more anonymous town, the fumblings in an impersonal motel room that were sure to follow. Until just that moment, it had never occurred to me to question the arrangements he'd made. Would I have made other plans for our first meeting, vetoed these, had I been asked?

No. As a novice in romance, illicit or otherwise, I lacked the confidence to initiate suggestions, to like or dislike arrangements. Like a foreigner in a strange country, who was I to question the customs, the behavior of the inhabitants? It was altogether out of my realm. Did Johnny sense this about me? Is that what he meant by calling me a little innocent? Is that why he didn't bother to consult me about these plans? Or did he want to surprise me, impress me with his willingness to spring for a motel room? Or perhaps it was some old-fashioned sense of chivalry. It was the man's place to plan the evening twenty-five years ago when he was my age dating college girls. Or maybe he just didn't care if I liked his plans or not, didn't care how I felt, just wanted to use me for some self-congratulatory reasons of his own. But I didn't, I couldn't, dwell on that thought for long. I was at his mercy, after all. It was best to think well of him.

Finally, he called the waitress and paid our bill, left some coins on the table for a tip and herded me toward the wing where our room was. He fumbled with the key a bit before it would turn and open the door. Was he nervous too? I couldn't tell. Once inside, he excused himself and went into the bathroom, leaving me to stare at the homogenized décor. With nothing to read but the restaurant menu, I pretended interest in the breakfast offerings and perched on the edge of one of the beds, more ready for flight than for lust or romance, whatever this would turn out to be.

When Johnny came out of the bathroom, he drew the curtains, cutting off most of the light from the hotel sign in the parking lot. Then he came over to where I was, gently gave my hair a stroke and sat beside me on the bed. Well, here goes, I thought. I felt like I was going into surgery.

He didn't say anything at all, and I found it better that way. My first real kiss, I thought ruefully as he bent down to give me one. It was all right, this kiss, gentle and not too serious, no excess of passion or longing or even lust. It was controlled, this kiss, and that was fine by me. But with it went my last illusion of selfhood. It was his game now. He controlled me as utterly as if marionette strings were attached to my limbs and head. He didn't seem surprised at my lack of initiative, my shyness. In fact, he seemed to like me that way. He murmured my name over and over into my hair in his still-strange accent as he carefully undid my denim shirt buttons. The near darkness enfolded me like a protective shield. I relaxed a bit, knowing I didn't have to control my expressions or my eyes, only my actions and breathing, a feat I thought I could manage. It wasn't so scary after all. He went slowly, caressing me in places that, had I been less afraid, might have felt good. Then he entered me roughly, painfully, and came quickly and very quietly, as if he was afraid of feeling too much.

Afterwards, he shed a few quiet tears. I could feel them wet against my shoulder as he lay on top of me for a few more moments. They touched me, these unadmitted, unexplained tears. Was he, too, trying to find some solace here? Did this little act give him a respite, insulate him from a reality he lived in at other times? Or were they, my cynical side conjectured, just a continuance of the nameless emotional release he'd found in the depths of my unprotesting flesh?

He was mumbling something into my nape, words I couldn't quite believe. But I'm sure I heard them right. "I'm sorry," he said into the hollow of my neck, "Janey, I'm so sorry." Though I had no idea why he should apologize for what had happened, the pathos in his voice turned me to ice.

Suddenly, he was gone from the bed and had switched on the bedside lamp. His back was turned. I could hear him adjusting his slacks.

"That was real sweet, Janey," he said in what I supposed was a sexy voice, a voice with no trace of the anguish of only moments earlier.

"Well, look at the time," he continued, glancing at his watch. "I'm sorry but we can't dally. It's quite late, I'm afraid." He smiled over at me, and I obediently rearranged my clothes, made a quick trip to the toilet, and hastily pulled on my jacket.

We drove back to the corner near my apartment, a distant, almost cold silence between us. Johnny seemed distracted — by guilt, possibly? Possibly this secret life would be too much for him; maybe he had regrets already? I steeled myself for words of "Well, it's been nice, but ..." as we came to the outskirts of town. Instead, as he pulled up to the dimly lit corner where he'd picked me up a few hours earlier, he leaned over and stroked my hand.

"Can we meet on Thursday?" he asked, not quite meeting my gaze. Could even a man like Johnny fear rejection?

"Yes, of course," I said, sealing my promise with a grasp of his hand. Then I stood there on the dark, still corner and watched the taillights of the car as it sped away, taking my lover home to his wife.

CHAPTER 13

PINE HILL STATION, TEXAS

SEPTEMBER 1985

LIZ

Johnny's car pulled into the driveway. I glanced up from my reading chair and my glass of sherry to the clock on the mantle. It was nearly eleven: quite a bit later than usual for Johnny. A new research grant proposal had to be written in a hurry, he'd said, and a history department committee that Johnny headed was cranking it out as quickly as it could. Still, he thought the work for it would take all semester.

I hadn't been home long myself. I closed the shelter on Tuesdays and Thursdays, so didn't get home until nearly ten. In past years, we'd spent more evenings together, talked more about our jobs, the house, the news. Now, time seems compressed, things left unsaid. Or had it always been that way and I've just thought about it more since Jenny left? The thought made me shiver and I quickly brushed it aside.

"How were the pooches tonight?" Johnny peeked in at me

with his briefcase under his arm.

"Oh, they were great, as usual. We found a home for a middle-aged Doberman, so that felt good."

"That's nice," Johnny said absently. It was clear he wasn't listening. "Give me a minute to change and I'll be down for a nightcap." He disappeared up the steps and I could hear him walking down the hall toward our bedroom. In a minute, I could hear the shower drumming. Johnny had always had fastidious grooming habits. He often took two showers a day and his hair and attire were impeccably neat, his closet and bureau drawers, too.

In a few minutes, he appeared in the entranceway to the living room wrapped in the burgundy silk robe I'd given him years ago. Even after all these years, I felt a rush of pleasure at the sight of him. He'd aged so well — nearly fifty and still so handsome. Maturity seemed to suit him. His graying temples made him look wise and distinguished, the lines around his eyes softened them. He'd kept his figure trim, too, with twice weekly games of handball with a colleague from physics and a careful, lean diet. He was opening the liquor cabinet, getting out his customary drink, bourbon, and pouring himself a couple of fingers. "Top off your sherry?"

"No thanks, I have an early meeting tomorrow," I replied. "How'd the grant writing go tonight?"

"It was a planning meeting. We need to do a lot of research before we start writing." He replied, his back to me. I could hear the bourbon splash into the glass. "But it will receive special consideration, because I'll be the first author." Johnny crossed the room, beamed at me, and we clinked glasses.

"Oh, Mister Modest, what other wonderful accomplishments are you taking credit for today?"

"Well, we're finally getting those file cards I told you about on computer. But I can't take credit for that. The department gave me a decent research assistant for once. This girl, Jane, knows what she's doing around a computer. She's working out well. Should have me pecking away at the damn thing before too long."

"That's good. About time you entered the modern world." At the accounting firm I worked at, we had the most advanced computers and had transferred all our records onto them a while back.

"How'd work go for you today, Lizzy?"

"Johnny, you know I hate that name." I wrinkled my nose, "It makes me feel reptilian."

"I beg your pardon, ma'am." He smiled. Then he drained his glass, set it on the end table between our chairs, led me over to the sage green sofa and started caressing me.

I usually liked these little intimate moments with Johnny, especially this year when they were infrequent. But my heart wasn't in it tonight. My mind wouldn't quiet, and it ground mercilessly on like some machine out of control, thinking about a phone, endlessly ringing. He was a thoughtful, forgiving man, I thought, momentarily flashing back twenty years to right after Jenny's birth, to the massive hemorrhaging, the emergency hysterectomy. To Johnny holding my hand at the hospital bedside and telling me it didn't matter that we'd never have any more children, never have a son to carry on the family name. That as long as his wife and our new daughter were safe, that was good enough for him. He was bright, an able professional, a good companion most of the time, I thought, as he kissed and fondled me. He was perhaps a bit full of himself, a little fussy. He made sure his shirts were starched and his pants well pressed, insisting I stop weekly at the cleaners to ensure that was so. He dressed in front of our full-length mirror, checking his musculature, his waistline, combing through his hair to make sure it was all still there. Once dressed, he turned to check that his shirt was tucked in neatly, that he hadn't missed a belt loop, that his matching gray loafers were polished and buffed to a gleam. I'd always considered this ritual narcissistic and girlishly vain. But lately, I had wondered if, instead of gloating over his cool good looks, he'd been worrying about them.

And what about his bragging to me of journal publication decisions that had gone his way, of the students who revered him, of the games of handball he'd won against a man half his age? Could it be that Johnny's show of bravado, his continual claim of being on top of the world, perhaps even his gentlemanly demeanor, were all acts, all part of an image of a successful man that he was trying to project to all around him? I had always thought his confidence and charisma were inherent characteristics of the Wharton men — Old Johnny was much the same. But since Jenny left, since I've seen him immobilized with grief, I've begun to wonder. Was Johnny putting on an act, even in front of me? If it was an act, who was Johnny? Did I even know my own husband? I found these thoughts profoundly disturbing.

As if he read my mind, Johnny stopped nuzzling me and sat up.

"Please say you're mine forever, Liz," he said strangely. "I couldn't bear to lose you, too."

"Lose me, too?" I queried. But I knew what he meant. Who he meant.

"I was thinking of Jenny," he said quietly. "How I — how we lost Jenny." There was a real note of sadness in his voice.

"You miss her a lot too, don't you?" I said, as I put my arms around him.

"Yeah, I do," he admitted hoarsely.

"Honey, isn't there some way we can reach her?" My failed phone call started reverberating in my ear again. "Don't you think we've got to make a try?" I pulled away and looked at him.

"There's nothing we can do. She's gone. We've lost her."

He said the words with finality.

"Don't blame yourself, honey. Please don't. It won't help us to blame ourselves." I held him by both arms and shook him a bit, for he looked so stricken it frightened me.

But all he said was, "I'm tired, Liz. Let's go to bed."

The subject of Jenny was closed for tonight. I followed him to our room, and an image of a ten-year-old smiling Jenny filled my mind. A daughter who had long since been replaced by a surly stranger, one who said she hated us.

Chapter 14

PINE HILL STATION, TEXAS

OCTOBER 1985

MADDIE

I saw her today. I was expecting it, fearing it, longing for it, all mixed up together in my aching heart. I'd dragged myself to one of our favorite restaurants for a solitary lunch. Was I trying to move on and reclaim the space for myself or just being masochistic? The place evoked some lovely memories, and when I'd entered, they appeared as ghosts of our former selves. Our January 13th anniversaries, the publication of my book and its favorable reviews, her early tenure (such a prodigious writer she was, her department let her come up a year early), the next year, my tenure. All celebrated here at Chez Nous, all celebrated in the same cozy nook, at "our table." I should not have come. I had turned to leave when the pretty, blond lunchtime hostess politely inquired, "Table for one?"

I nodded, my throat too tight to answer, my legs too weak to run. I was grateful that she took me to a small central table on the other side of the room from our special spot. I had just given the waitress my order when there was a slight commotion from the hallway to the private dining room at the back of the restaurant. We professors dined here frequently as the sophisticated menu let us show off our French and the wine list was replete with complex and expensive vintages from Bordeaux, Loire, and the Rhone Valley. Someone had probably gotten promoted or published a book, I surmised, as a cluster of folks unmistakably of the professoriate emerged from the back room and made their noisy way to the front exit. Roz was second from the end, chatting in her animated, all-in way with a colleague I vaguely recognized from other times when our two departments had been at the same events.

I was not prepared for the sudden, painful clenching of my heart, and I had to steady myself by gripping the table edge with both hands.

Fortunately, because when Roz interacts with a person, she gives them her complete attention, she failed to notice a solitary, pitiful-looking woman (me), grasping her table for two for dear life. Not ready to launch, Maddie, I remonstrated. Big mistake, this.

Abruptly, like the lights had gone out and scenes from a treasured classic film had appeared in front of me, my mind conjured a vivid memory of that first night we met. A frigid Thursday night when I would have been better off cozying up to the radiator in my tiny apartment off the end of Langdon Street, fifty feet from Lake Mendota. Lake Mendota, so lovely in late summer when I'd agreed to the lease, now an icy plain with Siberian winds whipping off it, right through the cracks around my apartment's few windows. Still though, better next to my radiator on a night like this than trying to wend my way down the avenue of fraternities over to an old house on Lake Street that housed WTA, the Women's Transit Authority.

I had given myself a semester to settle into graduate

school. Once I had successfully wrapped my arms around the outrageous workload of that first semester, I knew the next stop would be to find out what kind of lesbians lived in Madison, Wisconsin. I wasn't averse to seeking out the dyke bar that I was sure existed somewhere in town. But before I'd even managed to figure out where it was, I saw a poster for WTA on the ubiquitous kiosks that advertised all manner of entertainment and services on the huge campus. The logo on the WTA poster — a raised fist inside the circle with the plus sign under it that had become, in recent years, a feminist trope, told me that WTA would be a women's movement group, hopefully with a smattering of dykes. The Women's Transit Authority, the poster informed me, was a free taxi service for women only, to make sure we got home safe after a night out drinking or studying or doing whatever the hell else we wanted to do. "Dispatcher and driver volunteers always welcome," it said below the phone number. So, I had called and said I'd be happy to learn how to be a dispatcher one night a week and the friendly woman on the other end of the phone suggested I come down the next night and she'd train me herself.

As soon as I saw the dispatcher, I thought, "Bingo!" She wore her hair short, and her solid frame sported the leather jacket and jeans look common to feminist lesbians in the 1970s. Her name was Thorpe and she quickly taught me how to use the dispatcher radio that was connected to the WTA's one "taxi." The WTA had just started that fall of 1973, Thorpe informed me, "after a good night of hard drinking at Lily's, a dyke bar that closed down almost as soon as it opened, sadly." She looked at me meaningfully.

"Here's to dyke bars staying open," I replied, and lifted an imaginary drink. I was in.

"We have to use our own cars and scrounge our own gas money, too," Thorpe said. "Though lots of women give us tips, even though we don't charge and, so far, that's the gas money. However," she continued in a professional voice, "the university recognizes what a crucial service we offer. They did get us this dispatch radio equipment and a desk here at the Campus Assistance Center," she concluded, indicating the old house we were in. The place was obviously functioning as some kind of service center, with its inviting front entrance, open-plan rooms, and desks with phones on them and file drawers next to them. "If we keep increasing the number of rides we provide, the university said they'd give us a grant for gas, insurance, and someday, even vans."

At precisely 10:00 p.m. (after which bus service became less frequent in our college town), a battered blue station wagon from the early 1960s pulled into to the driveway adjacent to the old house in which the WTA was housed. It may not look like much, Thorpe said, but it was big, and could take five or even six women at a time in a pinch. "And it has an excellent heater. Let me introduce you to our most reliable driver," she said, walking out into the bitter cold in her sweatshirt with me trailing behind her, trying to wrap my hastily grabbed coat around me to ward off the icy wind. "Maddie, this is Roz," Thorpe said, after Roz had struggled with, and then managed, to roll down the window of the old station wagon. "Roz, Maddie's going to be doing Thursday night dispatch starting next week."

"Welcome to the WTA, Maddie," Roz said out the window and turned her beautiful smile on me. "We make sure women get home safely no matter how stupid drunk they get!"

Thorpe rolled her eyes. "If they can slur their address at us well enough to understand it, we get 'em home," she agreed.

"Seriously, we give lots of women who work late a ride home too, waitresses especially, but hotel workers, late-night shop clerks, even librarians. And we're a great group, aren't we, Thorpe?"

"You betcha," Thorpe replied, in pure Wisconsin.

"Maddie, let's get out of this cold. Almost forgot, Roz, you've a got a fare, corner of Broom and Dayton. Shirley, she said her name was. And two friends, back to Liz Waters," she told her, referring to one of the undergrad dorms.

"Great to meet you, Maddie," beamed Roz. "You'll be my dispatcher next week. See you then."

And that was it, that first night. A brown face in a bright orange knit cap with a beautiful smile. It wasn't until the next Thursday, when I was the solo dispatcher for the first time, that I heard Roz's laugh. She started calling me on the dispatch radio between fares and asking me about myself. She would tell me about herself too, in self-deprecating, humorous detail, her Texas accent creeping into her stories the more personal they got. On the third Thursday we worked together, Roz said over the scratchy radio as she dropped off her last fare around 2:00 a.m., "Maddie, wanna come to my place for a nightcap? I'll give you a ride home for free!" She laughed at her little joke, that laugh I was already finding irresistibly charming.

I never did make it home that night and by the time Roz served me coffee in bed the next morning, I was hooked.

And still am, I noted ruefully as I paid my check and left Chez Nous. Scratch this place off the list. Anywhere this good at triggering these painful reveries would have to go. Not sure any place in this damn town would be left if I used that criterion. Roz had been my life here. Roz! I mentally sighed. Roz! I screamed in my mind as anguish washed over me.

But the silence as I walked back to campus was as big as the Texas sky.

CHAPTER 15

MADISON, WISCONSIN

OCTOBER 1985

JENNY

Next week! I stared down at the syllabus in disbelief. Damn, why hadn't I dropped this class? But that wasn't an option. I was only taking thirteen credits this semester. If I dropped this class, I'd be less than a full-time student. And I had to be full time to stay in the dorm.

What had possessed me to take this class anyhow? But I knew the answer to that one, too. It met at 9:55 Tuesdays and Thursdays and had fit neatly into my mornings-only class schedule. I could always use another psych course (they were easy), and I hadn't even looked at the subject, much less the syllabus. Adolescent Psychology. Probably wouldn't have changed my mind about taking it had I known the title. It had turned out to be taught by one of those '60s types, a guy much too passionate for the bored corporate executive wannabes and clueless sorority girls sitting in front of him in the huge lecture hall. And like the classic, he wore old jeans and T-shirts and had a drooping mustache and long, scraggly hair, even though he had a receding hairline, for Christ sakes. It was like he was still trying to hold on to adolescence himself. And worse, he was into this passé encounter group stuff. Had he taken a minute to look around him he'd have seen that no one was in the least interested.

Fortunately, the class was too large to involve everyone in gut spilling. I'd managed to keep a low profile and merely squirm as I watched my pitiful or narcissistic classmates reveal the intimacies of their adolescence. I hadn't actually forgotten the paper was due at six weeks. I had conveniently put off thinking about it until now. And now, here it was: "Using data from your own adolescence, explore how you resolved one of the basic conflicts of the teen years. Be sure to illustrate your points with specific examples of you as an adolescent in conflict/crisis and contextualize your own experience using the theories of adolescence studied in the course." A list of topics and names of various guys we'd studied so far followed. I looked over the list one last time, hoping to find a neutral subject I could bullshit about. Nothing. I thought about making up a fictitious adolescence. But what kind of model would I use? *Jane Eyre*? *Little Women*? Something from *Happy Days*? I couldn't even imagine what a modern normal adolescence might be like.

There was no way I could do this paper. But I couldn't fail the course. I was already on probation from last semester. Damn, why hadn't I worked a bit harder, then? I'd have to go talk to the hippie, Gorenson.

I glanced back at the syllabus and saw that he held office hours Tuesdays and Thursdays from 3:30 to 5:00 p.m. If I left now, I could still catch him.

I pulled on some clothes and ran out of my room.

Liz Waters, the quiet study dorm I'd chosen to live in

hoping to find solitude, was the best dorm on campus. It was away from the other complexes and had its own cafeteria. And it was an all-women's dorm, a big factor in my book. It was also only a couple of minutes to the Social Science building that housed Gorenson's office and many of my classes. I hiked up Campus Drive, the shortest route to my destination, promising myself a leisurely walk on the lakeshore path after I'd taken care of this nagging business.

With my cigarette lungs and in a hurry, I was winded by the time I climbed the short hill to the Social Science building. The music-student-staffed carillon tower in front of the building inexpertly chimed a complex classical piece on its many bells. The building itself was squat and modern in an ugly, institutional way, one of the ugliest buildings on campus. But it did have a nice view of the lake in some of its back rooms. I scouted for Gorenson's office in the underground warren of professor offices built into the side of the hill that made up the lower regions of the building. It was strangely quiet in the halls. Since I usually tried to avoid anything to do with studying or school, I rarely found myself in class buildings after my morning classes were over. I followed the office numbers down to the end of a corridor and saw Gorenson's door was slightly ajar. Good, he was still in.

I knocked tentatively and tried to look embarrassed. I'd decided even hippies might fall for the Southern belle routine, so I'd dressed in some out-of-date slacks and a cowl-necked sweater with penny loafers I hadn't touched since arriving from Texas over a year ago now.

"Mr. Gorenson, suh?" I peeked around the corner of his office door. "Do you have a spare minute?"

"Huh?" He looked up absently from his desk and failed to recognize me. I wasn't surprised, I usually sat way in the back. "Yes, sure, come on in."

"I'm Jenny Wharton, in your adolescent psych class," I said

in my best Texas drawl.

"Of course, Jenny." He pretended to place me. "What can I do for you?"

"Well, suh, I'm afraid I'm having an awful lot of trouble on that six-weeks paper assignment. I just can't seem to come up with anything worthy of mention in my own adolescence and I was wondering, well, if I might do a paper on something else for y'all." I glanced up to see if he was falling for my honeyed accent, but his face was impassive, and I couldn't tell.

"Jenny, the paper's due next week. Why haven't you come in before?"

"Well, suh, I thought I could think of something. But I've been racking my brains for days now and I just can't think of a thing in my life that would apply." He began to look doubtful. "My adolescence was pretty boring, I guess."

"Come now, Jenny. I can't believe you haven't experienced any friction, any self-confidence crisis, any periods of rebellion against authority figures, any sibling rivalry?"

I shook my head — a bit too quickly. "No suh, nothing like that." He looked over at me, exasperated.

"You never wanted to stay out later than your parents would let you? Never had friends they didn't approve of? Never wanted something they wouldn't let you have?"

I shook my head no, but I could feel my face reddening.

"No one ever snubbed you at school? You never felt dumb or ugly or weird or shy around your peers?"

All these flashes of memory started beating down on the closed door in my brain then. I began to feel claustrophobic. I had to get out of here quick, but he hadn't let me off the hook yet.

"Can't say that I did." Shit. My words had come out curt and defensive, not the sweet damsel in distress at all. My act was crumbling.

"Everything in your late childhood years was picture perfect, huh?"

"You might say that." I had dropped my act completely now and gave him a cold, mean stare, daring him to push the issue further.

"Listen. I can see you don't want to do this assignment, so I'll let you choose one of these topics instead." He rose from his desk, burrowed in his file cabinet, and handed me a mimeographed sheet. I glanced at the topics, dry, boring, but impersonal choices, such as comparing Freud's psychosexual theory of adolescent development with Erikson's psychosocial theory or Piaget with Kohlberg. I would have to crack the books to turn in something on time, but it was better than the alternative; that was for sure.

"Thanks," I mumbled, and turned to go.

"Just a minute." He went back to his files and ruffled through some folders at the back. While he looked, he said into the files, "I've had other students who haven't been able to do this assignment — for one reason or another," he added in a meaningful voice I tried to ignore. "No one, Jenny, goes through adolescence with no conflict whatsoever, except those who've put off dealing with adolescent issues until they're older. Many times, these are people who've had a traumatic time of their teenage years. When students refuse to do this paper, I've found it's usually for this reason: They just can't bear yet to analyze the pain of their adolescence. Sooner or later, this brochure becomes useful to many of them." He pulled a light green leaflet from a folder in the back of the cabinet and handed it to me.

The lettering on the outside said, "We're Here for You: The University Counseling Center."

I felt the blood drain from my face. Who did this jerk think he was, a pseudo-psychiatrist? And what did he think he knew about me?

"I ... I ... I can't see what this has to do with me." I automatically put on a thick Texas accent again as I backed toward the door.

"Save it. There's pain written all over your face."

My mind suddenly seemed to have lost control over my body. Horrified, I stood there and heard the terrible sound of my lungs audibly gasping for breath in what sounded like an imminent sob. My brain went on red alert. I was breaking out in a sweat. I had just seconds to get out before I lost it completely in front of this know-it-all asshole and his armchair psychology.

"I don't need this," I heard myself practically shouting at him. "You keep it for somebody who really has problems." I threw the brochure on his desk, turned, and fled the room.

But the echo of my words followed me. The words might have been those of an angry young woman whose privacy has been violated. But the tone was that of a desperate and terrified girl. Me.

CHAPTER 16

PINE HILL STATION, TEXAS

OCTOBER 1985

LIZ

My lips were set in a sentimental half-smile, the kind reserved for babies and puppies and weddings. Suddenly finding myself back in the real world, I shoved the novel I'd been reading under some magazines on the coffee table in front of me. Novel, huh. I was certainly debasing that word by calling the predictable and overly melodramatic trash I'd just finished reading a novel. It was my not-so-secret pleasure, though, reading romance novels. I enjoyed every minute of the escape they provided, never mind that the plots were so similar they faded from memory as soon as the last page was turned. I didn't indulge in these often. But every three months or so, I'd find myself with the urge to escape to a fantasy land of old-fashioned romance, where marriage was the end, not the beginning — a girl's main goal in life. Once accomplished, there was no point in continuing the story as the rest wasn't half so interesting, nor did it have much to offer in the romance department.

These depressing musings were also part of my ritual. First, I'd stop at the public library and select a title from the shelves reserved for just such insipid writing. I'd go home, make supper for Johnny and get him settled into his evening of reading and writing. Then I'd place a glass of sherry on the end table, curl up on my favorite chair, a sink-into-it, pillowed armchair in burgundy, and disappear into the well-worn plot.

She's young, beautiful, and innocent, but knows what she wants. He's older, handsome, and invariably rich. They meet by mysterious design, or she's employed by him as a secretary. He might seem cold or distant or is otherwise involved. It seems hopeless. But finally, somehow — often by him saving her from a physical danger — the barriers break down. They each discover the other has loved them all along. They exchange words of love, commitment, a kiss or two and suggestions of more. Imminent marriage is implied. You never stop to think until after the book's been finished that they have absolutely nothing in common but attraction to each other's good looks. But then, romantic love is a myth after all; why spoil it by being realistic?

When I'm sated with my fraudulent romance story for the night, I should go to bed. Then the cozy dream world of the story would hang on until morning. But instead, I sit and think about all the ways my marriage hasn't lived up to the happily ever after I'd been led to expect since I started reading these in ninth grade.

One memory, though, made me believe for a time that the tales I read as a girl could come true. Like romance novels, the first night we met was an illusion. But I didn't accept that for a long while. Thus, my nostalgic smile.

I had attended the private university where wealthy Texans sent their children and where my not-so-wealthy parents insisted I go to get my M-R-S degree, as everyone called it. College for middle-class Texan daughters of my generation had little to do with furthering one's education or improving one's mind. Making a favorable match during one's "blossoming years" as my mother termed them, was the only reason parents bothered. Since a college degree had increasingly become obligatory for ambitious young men in the years after the war, the university was the site of the great husband hunt in the early 1960s.

Until I met my Prince Charming, I would major in something practical, my parents told me. As my father was an accountant, why not that? Tax returns could be prepared part time, in case a young and growing family needed a bit of extra "pin money." I could do other people's taxes in moments free from my real life's work — homemaker and mother.

I suppose I agreed with this plan for my life. It was what my parents wanted for my life. It was what my high school friends from Southern Christian Academy wanted for their lives. It was what girls like me did. "You're a pretty one, Liz," my mother kept saying to me, "and it's as easy to fall in love with a rich man as with a poor man, if you catch my meaning." I did. My romance books backed her up on this point.

With a student body brimming with the Texan upper crust, he'd likely be wealthy, they thought, and what more could one desire for a daughter of the South? I was petite, blond, blue-eyed with regular features. People other than my parents called me pretty. Pretty girls in the South, in the early '60s were expected to learn and to practice techniques to ensnare "Mr. Right." Though I was naturally reserved and a bit shy and never saw myself as being as good looking as the feedback I received, I did what I was encouraged to do. I became that girl who devoted herself to doing whatever it took to lure the wealthy husband who, everyone assured me, would be my crowning glory and complete my life.

On that romance novel evening, in my junior year, a few fraternities on campus had gotten together to invite a few sororities to a Halloween costume party. I went as a princess, resurrecting a prom dress my older sister had worn a few years prior, one of those off the shoulder things with a crinoline skirt. The dress was ice blue, a color that has always suited me. I had borrowed the tiara my sister had worn as homecoming queen and had even found golden slippers to match. Unlike most girls in my class, my conservative mother hadn't allowed me to cut my hair chin-length or wear it in a fashionable bouffant. That night, I realized she had been right to refuse to let me cut it. "It's your crowning glory," she always said. I did have a beautiful head of hair, thick, a bit wavy and honey colored. My princess look would not have come off so well had I cut it short. As it was, my hair hung down my back in loose ringlets, crowned by my sister's tiara. I'd taken care with my makeup and looked altogether regal, a Cinderella dressed for the ball.

I'd been nervous for this event, constantly asking friends if I looked okay, shivering under my gown. I was rarely altogether comfortable in social situations though I could never put my finger on just why. Even in my shyness, I'd never been without boyfriends. Besides my regular features, I had a nice smile, which was all many boys wanted in a girlfriend, it seemed. My mother's supervision of her two daughters' manners and wardrobe ensured we'd always exude the decorum that made us appropriate to take home to meet a boy's parents, in case it came to that. I'd fallen silently in love with each of the half-dozen boyfriends I'd had. But I'd never said any words of love to them, never encouraged them, never showed much emotion at all, or much personality either. I was constantly afraid of doing or saying the wrong thing, and thus ruining my chances of catching a better, bigger fish, a fear that paralyzed me into silent acquiescence.

I went to the costume party with Laura, my roommate, who had dressed as a bawdy barroom maid from the Wild West. She was an outgoing girl who was miraculously able to come up with witty small talk and keep boys who approached us interested. I hoped her ease would rub off on me if I hung around her long enough.

The fraternity house was one of the old, stately mansions that lined certain neighborhoods near campus. Inside, there were high-ceilinged rooms with white walls outlined by dark wood. An early cold snap had made the air crisp and cool and there seemed an elusive anticipation to the night. The house was decorated beautifully with cornstalks and jack-o'-lanterns and orange and black streamers suspended from the ceiling. We mingled, talking mostly with the other girls at first, or floated around in the comfort of big groups of clowns and witches, scarecrows and hoboes. I stood in the background across the room from the front door, where, as Laura suggested, we'd have the best views of new arrivals. We'd been at the party for about an hour, and I'd danced with one boy in a werewolf mask who'd taken it off for the occasion and another dressed as an old-time film director with a beret and a painted-on mustache. Neither could be defined as "dreamy," and I hadn't encouraged either of them by accepting second dance invitations. So, I was chatting with Laura when I saw the front door begin to open to the sound of an oboe playing some Middle Eastern-sounding wail accompanied by cymbals. As the door opened wide, the oboe player stopped long enough to shout, "Make way for His Highness the Sheik," and then started up his song again. I recognized the oboe player as someone from my theater class the year before, which I'd taken in a fruitless attempt to become more outgoing. I recognized his costume too: it was one in the collection we'd used to put on a children's production of *1001 Nights*. He had a gold cloth wrapped around his head with a feather sticking out of the top, a rich red vest with strips of embroidered cloth sewn around the edges, and billowing red Turkish pants drawn tight at the ankle. His feet were bare and around his neck hung a rope with a basket attached to it with a fake cobra's head coming out of the top. Someone had stopped the record player and most of the students in the large front hall had turned to watch this procession. The oboist twirled into the room and sat cross-legged in a bare space the crowd had gathered around, put the fake snake basket in front of him, and continued to play a tune in a minor key that suggested caravans and camels. Two women, in harem costumes from the same production, danced in next, clanging finger cymbals and rotating their bare bellies to the applause of the many who had gathered to watch. They knelt in mock homage, their faces pressed to the floor and arms outstretched toward the empty doorway. They were followed by two men dressed in Arabian Nights costumes as the first had been, but carrying large palm fronds, which they waved in exaggerated deference at the figure about to come through the door. Suddenly, there appeared a stunning man, tall and well-muscled, with a chiseled jaw — a sheik dressed in long, flowing white robes, topped with a crimson velvet cape that created a bride's train behind him. His head was covered in a black-and-white checkered scarf held on by a black braided rope. He gave a mysterious Eastern smile and looked as darkly handsome as any actual sheik.

I felt my heart leap in my chest. He was so good looking and enigmatic, never once stepping from the role of important visiting royalty from another place, another time. I learned his name from the impressed girls whispering around me: Johnny Wharton, yes, of *those* Whartons, a wealthy planter family west of here, the ones the town is named after, they said. He walked in a dignified fashion to the center of the crowd, bowed deeply and raised his arms for silence. "My loyal subjects," he said to the room in general in an accent I interpreted as Middle Eastern. "I command you to enjoy yourselves. Let the celebration commence!" At that, the oboe and women cymbal players sprang into action, the women belly dancing, the man accompanying them on his exotic instrument. Everyone began to clap and cheer, and the dancers started to work the crowd. One of the frond-bearing servants went over to the record player and started up the party once again by putting on Elvis's "Little Sister," and people began mingling and dancing again.

Out of the corner of my eye, I saw His Highness the Sheik approaching. My heart was pounding in my ears, as if for a moment I'd forgotten that he was only a normal college boy and I a normal girl. With the regal air of an actual sheik, he walked over and stopped a few feet in front of where I was standing. There were other people talking nearby, but everyone stopped and listened as he came up to me.

"My lovely maiden," he bowed, still in character. "It is the custom in my country to greet a beautiful woman with a kiss," he said, his eyes locking onto mine.

I drew back in surprise. This was not gentlemanly behavior for a Texas fraternity man in 1960, no matter what his pretensions were. But before I could react further, his arm came up from his side and with a little flourish, he opened his hand in front of me and presented me with a kiss, a Hershey's chocolate kiss, that little droplet of chocolate wrapped in silver with a white flag sticking out of its top. I took it out of his hand, smiling in delight and relief and as I did so, he stayed my hand a moment and pressed his lips to it. "Dance, lovely maiden?" he asked, and magically (or arranged by his friend as he admitted many years later), a romantic slow song came on, astonishingly titled, "Johnny Angel." He was an accomplished dancer, and by the end of the song, he had completely captivated me. What girl could ask for a more romantic start to a relationship? It was a scene cut from the novels I had been reading for years by then.

He kept up the role for the entire evening and I, too, found myself pretending to be a princess who had found her prince. For that one night, that wonderful first night, I was Cinderella at the ball. He was my prince, my knight on a white horse, my fairytale lover. For a long while after, the power of that first night cast a glamor on our relationship. After an hour in which he danced only with me, he bade me farewell in his Middle Eastern accent and left the party complete with the dancing girls, the oboe player and the two palm-frond waving servants, as ceremoniously as he had arrived, and without even asking my name.

I spent the night replaying that magical hour over and over in my mind and despairing, as young women will, that that was all, that it was a dream, that I'd never see him again. Two days later, he showed up at my door, asked my roommate if "her highness the princess was in" and with a smile and a courtly bow, presented me with a bouquet of pink roses. I blushed furiously when he appraised me with his steel-gray eyes and declared that I was as lovely in the light of day as I had been on that romantic night.

He charmed me with little surprises like that all the while we were dating and for a time after we were married, too. He always had something sweet to say to me and made me laugh with funny anecdotes about his professors and fraternity brothers. I discovered that he was ambitious, with plans to be a historian, to get a PhD. He was bright, entertaining, handsome, *and* he came from a prominent Texas family. All the attributes of a "good catch" that a shy, middle-class but supposedly pretty girl like me could have ever hoped for.

He didn't tell me much about his background at first and I didn't ask. I suppose I was afraid of bursting the bubble. His father, he told me finally, had been a Baptist minister but he and his father had "parted ways," as Johnny had put it, "upon my coming of age." That same year, his father had been killed in a one-car accident. At this news, I tried to express sympathy for his loss, as anyone would. Johnny cut me short. "I hope he's rotting in hell," was his reply. "Not that I believe in hell." This was quite shocking to me, a normal Southern Baptist girl, raised in the faith, surrounded by friends and neighbors who all believed in the same Christian tradition. But I said nothing. Old Johnny, my Johnny said, his grandfather, now he was a good man. "He's anxious to meet you," he said. "He wants to host the wedding," he said with a grin. He hadn't asked me yet.

Johnny chose a late May wedding day for us the year I graduated from college. He had insisted I finish my degree. Many girls didn't bother once they'd secured a husband. "The wife of a famous historian has to have a BA behind her name," he decreed, before he'd even applied to graduate school. So, we "went steady" for the year-and-a-half it took me to graduate. Johnny would pick me up in the classic Plymouth and off we'd go for an evening of shows or dancing, parties at friends' homes, sailing in the summer, and riding in the winter. We did our share of "making out" as all young couples did, but there was never a moment I felt like he would take it further. As many young women still thought then, the taking of my virginity was meant for a marriage bed. On the single occasion we obliquely discussed it, Johnny told me he agreed wholeheartedly with my wishes. For some reason that seems wholly irrelevant now, virginity in a wife was important to the higher class of men as much as keeping it was to young women who wanted to marry a reputable man. Unlike other men I'd heard about and even a couple I had dated, it was never a constant struggle to hold him off. He was a complete gentleman in every way. I was proud to be his girl. If he had a darker side, I never saw it, never suspected it. I never found out about any of his secrets until after our marriage. And even then, it was Old Johnny, not my husband, who hinted at the dreadful legacy shared by Wharton men.

CHAPTER 17

PINE HILL STATION, TEXAS

OCTOBER 1985

MADDIE

This makes the second time in as many department meetings Johnny's late and I'm irritated. Not over the fact he's late again as over the reason, which I know full well. He's having an affair with Jane Meyer, that shy, blond grad student who seems to be hanging around his office a lot more than she needs to, even given she's his research assistant. I'll be damned if I'm going to waste my time waiting for that dick to wrap up his pawing and drooling session with a woman too young to know better, apparently. Why, Johnny has a daughter almost her age!

I worry about Jane. She seems so vulnerable and alone. I know she doesn't have a friend in this department. She seems so withdrawn. I, Maddie, the great conversationalist, can hardly get a peep out of her. When he dumps her, she's going to fall hard.

Jane's never done this before. I can tell by the way she flushes every time he enters a room. The poor kid was probably a virgin until he got his grimy mitts on her. I don't know why I say that. She must be at least twenty-three and is pretty. These days, I can't imagine many young women get that far without having some sexual experiences. But she seems younger than her years, and raw too, like touching her would cause her pain.

Come to think of it, I've never noticed Johnny having one of these sorts of unsavory flings before. I might have been too busy chasing tenure. Maybe Jane's extreme vulnerability and his total power over her future makes her irresistible to him. Or maybe I'm just over-analyzing a straightforward modern-day case of "I'll scratch your back if you scratch mine." What do I know? I haven't been on the prowl for love for years. And I shudder to think what it might be like to put myself out there again. Since Roz, I haven't had eyes for anyone else.

I can imagine a bit of what Johnny feels. Having some adoring female in the blush of youth telling you you're God's gift to the world. It could make you forget for a while that you're over the hill in this teenage-worshipping world. But what kind of reality is a relationship like that? I don't want to be somebody's idol. It's equality I'm after, or would be if I could bear to think about dating at all.

Ooooh. I cannot bear to think of moving on yet. Hurts. Too. Much.

There he is, finally. The three other men wrap up their football discussion and nod curtly. They're tired of his tardiness, too. I close the journal that I'd pretended to read as Johnny sits down heavily across from me, mumbling a greeting. He opens his briefcase and hauls out a stack of papers and a legal pad, trying to make up for his lateness by a show of seriousness. While he studies the sheets before him, I glance at his face. Not bad for a man pushing fifty. Chiseled features, a firm mouth, a neat, clean-shaven, well-groomed look even at this late afternoon hour. Unusual eyes, and not just the metallic gray color, either. Something hard about those eyes. If I looked at them more often, the man might come to scare me.

Johnny compensates for the ice in his eyes by smiling frequently. He's got a surprisingly genuine-seeming smile, even if he's putting it on to gain advantage.

He's not looking himself today though. There are dark circles under his eyes and his forehead is riddled with worry lines. It's not easy managing your job, participating in a family, and having an affair all at once. Perhaps Liz suspects. Damn him. Why does he have to do this? Why does it have to be so obvious he's doing it?

Poor Jane. I'll stop by the grad office tomorrow and ask her how her work's going. I'll invite her over for dinner — as a fellow Midwesterner. When I get to know her a bit better, I'm sure I could think of some other grad students she might like in the department; introduce her to a group where she'll meet men her own age and make some women friends.

Why this impulse to take care of her, to save her from a bad start here? I want her to have an easier time adjusting than I did when I was the raw recruit from the North. Possibly, she reminds me of my younger self more than I'd like to admit. Or maybe she's the one person around here who's lonelier than I am.

CHAPTER 18

MADISON, WISCONSIN

OCTOBER 1985

JENNY

"Hurry up, Lena," I said as she waltzed down the hall towards our room with the keys jingling in her coat pocket, "the phone's ringing."

She broke into a run and stuck the key in the lock, turning the door handle and opening it all in the same motion. She threw her book bag on the bed and made it to the phone on the fourth ring.

"Hello? Oh, hi. How are you doing? That's good. How's the arrangement of that Ellington song coming? Yeah, the Ella tempo — real slow — works great for me. You and I should get together and run over it a couple of times before Friday. Yeah, Wednesday morning would be okay with me." Lena listened into the phone for a couple of moments, then broke into a grin. "Sure thing." She motioned for me, her hand over the mouthpiece. "It's for you."

"What?"

"For you, Jen. It's Chuck." She grinned wickedly. "Maybe's he's not as shy as I thought!"

Lena wrapped my limp hand around the phone. "Here, talk to him."

"Uh...hi, Chuck."

"Hi Jen. I wanted to see if you were planning on coming to hear us on Friday. Lena's worked up some new numbers and I know she's too modest to tell you how great she sings them, so I thought I'd call and tell you. You've got to hear her."

"I was planning on coming for part of the show. I wouldn't miss hearing Lena sing for anything." Lena beamed over at me. I had planned to come a little late and leave before the last number so I wouldn't have to stand around feeling stupid like last time.

Then Chuck said, "We're going to go out to eat at Denny's after the show. I hope you'll come with us."

"Oh, who's all going?" I asked, stalling for time. Was this a low-key pickup, or was he just a nice guy trying to include me because I was a friend of Lena's?

"The guys in the band and Lena, Ginny, that's Rupert's wife, Nick, the guy behind the bar, and you, if you'll come."

Lena poked me from behind. "Say yes," she mouthed at me silently.

"Sure, yeah, I'll come." I tried to act like it was nothing. Lena was making a champ sign, fists clenched over her head, across the room. I rolled my eyes and looked away before I started to giggle.

"Great," Chuck was saying. "Guess I'll be seeing you Friday, then."

"Yeah, see you then, bye." I hung up quickly.

"Yahoo, my roomie's got a date!" Lena was howling.

"Will you cut it out? He just invited me because I'm your friend."

"He did not, girl. He asked you out. Believe me, that's how the shy ones operate. They ask you out on a group date first, so they don't have to do all the talking. That was a date. I knew it. I knew you two would go for each other. Too bad he took so long to get his nerve up. I hope he doesn't take that long to get his whatsit up!" she giggled.

"Why Lena Campbell, how could you even think a dirty thought like that?" I asked in a Texas debutante voice. I sure didn't want to think about that. I didn't like the idea of going to bed with somebody I knew. I probably wouldn't have to, I reasoned. Probably nothing will come of this. Anyway, I can handle it, I told myself. No sweat. But Friday came sooner than I wanted it to.

Seemed like everyone in Madison was there to hear Lena sing. I was lucky I knew her and got to sit at the table reserved for friends of the band. Rupert's wife, Ginny, sat next to me. A slight Black woman in her late twenties, she smiled and said she'd heard all about me. Lena sat there too, in the same tux she'd worn every time, looking radiant and a bit nervous. But she came alive on stage. She had been working on her stage presence and I noticed the difference. She was more at ease than she'd been a month earlier and better involved the audience in her songs. The audience, which had more older people than college students in it tonight, clapped enthusiastically when her set was over. I was ecstatic. For Lena. For a minute. Then I started thinking about what was ahead.

Besides a perfunctory "hi" when we'd first come in, Chuck had paid me no attention all evening. It was as I'd thought, then, he had invited me out of some sense of politeness. I didn't need it. I'd be damned if I'd let Lena's friends treat me like some fat, ugly sister they'd drag along because they felt sorry for me. Hanging around with Lena, I'd all but forgotten who I really was. Lena had an energy that wouldn't quit. No matter how resistant I'd been, she always managed to convince me to be involved in a life that was foreign to me. Maybe she was like Chuck, and felt pity for poor, lonely Jenny. But it was my fault too. I'd gotten myself into this situation. I'd let her and the band get too close and now they were making a fool out of me. It had been comforting to forget myself, my life, my past, and live in Lena's world for a while. Comforting, even fun, at times. But it wasn't real life. It wasn't *my* life. Not that I wanted my life. I thought of it as a slimy hump, perpetually stuck to my back. Lena had made me forget about it for a time and I'd wanted to believe I could. This phony invitation was just the shock I needed to slam me back to reality. Lena pitied me. The more I thought about it, the more certain I was. And Chuck was just well brought up and had an overactive sense of politeness. Or maybe he was horny and wanted me for an easy lay. Who needed them? They talked about me behind my back. I knew they did from what Ginny said when we were introduced. She'd heard all about me. I wonder what. I couldn't even begin to guess what they said. That I was stuck up? Shy? Bold and bitchy? Timid and mousy? I didn't know how I had acted with them. I couldn't remember.

My usual act with people who aren't fucking me is cold, aloof, and disdainful: like, "I'm so much better than you I'm not even going to bother talking to you." That kind of act. It works like a charm to keep people at arm's length, which is exactly where I like them. When I was with Lena, I'd forgotten that. Which scared me. I'd forgotten to put on my act. What did they see when they talked to me? Obviously, it was some pitiful creature who had to be brought along to their parties to make them feel noble. But pity soon turns to contempt. And I wasn't going to wait around for that to happen. I decided to leave.

I didn't want to be obvious about it, so I thought I'd slip on my coat and go to the bathroom first, then cross over to where the door was, out of sight of the band. So, during a lively number Lena was singing during her next set, I slipped out of my chair, mumbled something about using the john to Ginny, and headed for it.

There was a girl puking in the other stall. How anyone could let themselves get so out of control that they ended up doing something like that in public I could not understand. I heard a crash then and hurried out of my stall to see the girl lying on the floor in the other one. All that was visible was her arm sticking out from under the door. I wanted to get out of there. Something about her laying there in a public toilet really shook me. It was none of my business. She was a stupid fool for drinking so much. Somebody else will come in and find her or she'll wake up, I told myself as I washed my hands and dried them. But I couldn't leave. I had to see if she was all right. There was a chair in a corner of the bathroom. I hauled it over to the stall, stood on it and looked over the top of the door. I couldn't see her face; her hair was covering it. All I could see was her slack mouth, which didn't reassure me. I reached down over the door and flipped up the latch so I could get inside the stall. I pushed her hair away from her face and looked at her. She was out cold. But she was breathing. I remembered hearing about how you could choke on your own vomit and die. That scared me.

I'd tell Nick, the bartender who was friends with the band. I sighed, relieved at my decision. He'd know what to do.

The band had finished their set and people were crowding around the bar trying to order drinks. I tried flagging down Nick. No luck. So, I went around to his side of the bar.

"Hey, you can't come on this side, lady," Nick started to say and then he recognized me. "Wait, you're Lena's friend, right? What's your name again?"

"Jen." I said quickly, "But I came back here to tell you

there's a girl passed out in the john, and she doesn't look good. I thought you'd want to do something about it."

"Shit. Yeah, thanks for telling me. I better go in and have a look at her," Nick said. "Will you come, too, in case I need help?"

I nodded and went with him. I could always leave after the next set started, I thought. And something about leaving the girl now, before I knew if she'd be okay, didn't seem right. I was involved.

"Guy coming in!" Nick yelled as we pushed through the bathroom door. A couple of girls were looking down at the one passed out. She hadn't moved since I'd left her.

"You girls know her?" They shook their heads. One started giggling. They were drunk, too.

"You done in here?" Nick asked in a nasty tone. They left.

Nick knelt on the bathroom floor next to her and pulled back one of the girl's eyelids. There was no response. He listened to her breathing. "Too shallow." He threw me her purse. "Will you look for her ID and find out if she's with anybody here? But first call an ambulance, will you? Use the phone behind the bar. The number's on the wall right next to it."

I walked out into the bar and went behind to where the phone was. The other bartender came up and asked where Nick was. I told him what was happening. "Wow, too bad," he said and went back to fielding orders from the crowd gathered around the bar. I called the ambulance and told them where to come and what was wrong. Then I dug through the girl's purse and found her ID. Mona Winkler, it said. I headed toward the stage where the microphone was, but I didn't have the guts to have all eyes on me. Chuck was adjusting some knobs on the sound equipment, and I approached him with my request.

"Chuck, there's a girl passed out in the bathroom. Nick

sent for an ambulance, but he wanted to send one of her friends with her to the hospital. Could you announce her name and ask her friends to come over to the bar?"

"Jeez, I'm not so good at being at the front mic, but since you asked me, sure." He smiled at me, then noted my expression. "Hey, don't worry, she'll be all right," he said about the girl and went to make the announcement. He quieted the crowd and announced her name twice. But nobody came to say she was their friend. She had been here all alone.

I watched as the ambulance arrived and a couple of guys took her out of the bathroom on a stretcher. Chuck came over and stood next to me. "Nick said you found her. That was nice, what you did. A lot of people would have just left her there." He looked over at me just as she went by on the stretcher looking very pale and very quiet. To my surprise, a tear escaped my eyelid and rolled down my cheek.

Chuck saw it. "When you get involved with someone like that, it's like you know them, even if you've never seen them before, isn't it?"

"Yeah," I said. I didn't trust my voice. For some reason, I was all choked up.

"Hey," Chuck said. "I got an idea. After we're through here, I'll drive you over to the hospital and we can see how she is. We'll do it on the way to Denny's. It's too bad none of her friends were here when it happened, so nobody knows where she is."

"Maybe she doesn't have any friends."

"Well, if you want, we can stop in. That'll make her feel better. If she's awake by then."

"Thanks. Yeah, I'd like that." I looked at him, surprised. "That's a nice thing to think of doing."

"I could see you were upset about her." Chuck shrugged it off. "We've only got one more set tonight. Then we'll go."

"Okay, that'd be great. Thanks," I heard myself saying. I

tried to forget about what I'd been thinking earlier. Chuck was a nice guy.

We parted at the stage and the band began the last set.

But I didn't hear it. I was thinking about that girl. I hoped we got to the hospital before she woke up. I didn't want her to think nobody cared. But I wondered if she had any friends.

Or did she, too, find it easier to go it alone?

CHAPTER 19

PINE HILL STATION, TEXAS

OCTOBER 1985

MADDIE

It feels good, cooking for someone besides myself again. It's been so long since I've had someone over for a meal, I'd quite forgotten the thrill I get preparing food for a guest. I can't decide if Jane is the type who can appreciate a fine meal. Usually, I can spot it in a person right away, that certain hedonistic willingness to abandon one's inhibitions in front of a plate. But Jane seems an odd confusion of traits. Most of the time, she is so reserved she seems embarrassed to be merely taking up space. But when she is intellectually stimulated, she loses herself in the idea of the moment and becomes articulate, forthright, commanding attention with her solid grasp of an idea.

She relishes these moments of self-confidence, I can tell. It's as if she is willing herself to have more of them, to come out her shell. She seems a woman with a desire to remake herself from the core out.

I play it safe, sautéed chicken breasts with white wine, garlic, and mushrooms, a rice pilaf, a Waldorf salad, and one of my sumptuous lemon cheesecakes for dessert.

I can't recall ever doing anything like this in my life, inviting a stranger over for dinner — at least one I'm not interested in as a lover. But this is the year for doing things differently. I've got nothing to lose but my depressing self-absorption.

A knock at the door. Suddenly, I'm nervous. What do I have to say to her after all? Can we find any common ground? I'm out of practice at meeting new people. Why did I invite her, anyway? She'll wonder too — and if she's already heard rumors about me, my offer of friendship will already be suspect. Just a pretext for a pickup, she'll think.

Oh Maddie, don't be so paranoid. She came, didn't she? Just because Roz rejected you doesn't mean the rest of the world will follow suit. Just be yourself. You used to be able to talk to anyone, remember? That person you used to be — just a few months ago — is still lurking around somewhere. Haul her out for the occasion. Be sociable.

"Jane, hi. Glad you could make it. And mums, how nice. They're my favorite fall flowers. Come right in." Her obvious nervousness gave me more confidence. Why should I be nervous? I was orchestrating this evening. It was at my house. Make the poor thing feel comfortable, Maddie. You're good at that, remember? Jane hadn't managed so much as a word yet. I took that as a challenge to draw her out.

Sam and Frieda came running at the sound of the door opening and started wrapping themselves around Jane's ankles, purring loudly. She bent to pet them. The house was too empty for them, too.

She walked into the living room. There had been an autumn chill in the air the last couple of days and I'd lit a small fire that was flickering cheerfully and warming up the room. Jane noticed it at once.

"Oh, you have a fireplace!" She walked over to it and put her hands up to the warmth. She wore the same clothes tonight that she seemed to wear every day: a pair of faded and baggy jeans, some nondescript flannel shirt, a bulky brown cardigan sweater. Even I knew this outfit was hopelessly out of style. The other graduate students probably talked behind her back about her. Half of them came dressed for a job interview to attend class. Jane wore clothes that made her sexless, that detracted from her good looks. I wondered why.

"It reminds me of our potbellied stove in Iowa on the farm."

"You lived on a farm, then?" The clothes made more sense knowing this, but still, farms were not isolated bastions of the rugged life anymore.

"Yes. I was raised on a farm, just a small one," she said with some embarrassment, as if she had talked too much about herself.

"I'm from the Midwest, too," I said, to take the spotlight off her. "I was raised in small-town Wisconsin and went to undergrad at UW-Eau Claire and graduate school at UW-Madison. It sounds crazy, but even after all these years in Texas, I still miss living up north. What's even crazier, the weather's one of the things I miss most."

"You do? I thought I was the only one. I can't believe how people could live their whole lives without seeing fall colors like we have in Iowa."

"Texas is a strange place. It took me years to adjust and sometimes I'm still not so sure I have."

"I guess it's too early for me to judge, but I am a little homesick." She studied the floor, and I saw tears glistening behind her lashes.

"Sit down, Jane, make yourself comfortable. What can I get

you to drink? I bought some apple cider at the health food store today. I thought that would be nice warmed up with a cinnamon stick. Or there's wine, soda, beer, whatever you'd like." I indicated a well-stocked liquor cabinet, filled with leftovers from the days when we had entertained our small circle of friends regularly. My God, was that only a few months ago?

"The cider sounds wonderful, thank you." Jane smiled tentatively.

I went to the kitchen and returned with two mugs of warmed cider.

"Professor Haystead, this is a lovely room. These weavings are wonderful." She indicated the glorious three-dimensional wall weavings made by Lorraine, an artist friend of Roz's and mine.

The room did seem cozy suddenly, with the fire crackling and cider perfume permeating the air. It was the first time in months I felt an attachment to this place.

"Please call me Maddie, Jane. That's short for Madeline. Don't ever call me that!" I smiled. "Way too snooty for the likes of me."

"Okay ... Maddie. I love your class, you know. I never thought about how much methodology shapes historical interpretation before."

"I'm glad you like it. Where did you study before coming here?" I hoped to turn the discussion in a more personal direction. I got all the academic talk I needed from a full day on campus. I wanted human warmth, companionship. I wanted a friend that wasn't related to my old life with Roz, though Jane seemed an odd choice for that. I suppose I wanted someone to need me. Jane, being new and shy, fit that category, at least.

I listened to her rather over-detailed explanations of what she studied at the University of Iowa in Iowa City. Her studies were familiar turf, and she talked about them enthusiastically. "Did you enjoy living in Iowa City after growing up on a farm?" I tried again, angling for a few personal details. Surely Jane must be someone other than merely a student.

"Oh," she said, a bit flustered. "I never lived there. I commuted from Hutton. Well, the farm is near Hutton. Hutton's a tiny town, just a couple hundred people."

"Did you want to commute? Or did you do it to save money or something?"

"Well, yes, to save money. And there's Ma ... my mother, I mean. I didn't want to leave her alone so soon. So soon after my father died, I mean." She flushed deeply as she said this.

"He died when you were in high school?" She nodded. "How terrible that must have been for you. What did he die of?"

"They said it was a heart attack," she said woodenly, as if she had gone back the distance of the years and had just heard the news.

"But you thought it was something else?" I pictured a mysterious hospital death or work accident.

She shook her head to clear it, it seemed, of bad thoughts. "No, no, it was just a heart attack. Of course, it was. Just as they said. Just a heart attack."

"You're an only child, then?" I thought it best not to pursue that subject any longer. Her father's death obviously still upset her greatly, though it must have been five or six years ago by now.

"Yes, there's just me. My mother had to work a lot, so she didn't have time for any more children. She's a nurse's aide at an old age home. She's a wonderful person. So kind to all the old people at the home. We're very close."

"How nice. You don't see closeness between mothers and daughters much anymore." I flashed for a moment on my own mother's terminal judgmentalness. Put that one away, Maddie. "How old is she?"

"Um. She'll be forty-three this spring."

"Think she'll ever remarry?"

"My mother? Oh, she wouldn't ... oh no, no. She wouldn't do that." Jane seemed taken aback at the thought, as if it had never occurred to her before.

I decided not to pursue that line of conversation either. If you're twenty-three and close to your mother, the thought of her getting married to some stranger might be threatening. Still, it seemed an attitude more likely found in someone half Jane's age.

"Excuse me, Jane, I must check on the rice. Choose a tape if you'd like." I pointed at the stereo and tape collection. Jane selected a Segovia tape I hadn't heard in a while, a Sunday morning favorite of Roz's. I caught my breath as the music sent a wave of nostalgia sweeping over me, leaving a hole in my chest and my heart thudding quickly, uselessly, against my ribs. The tape, the friendly fire, the smell of good food cooking in our well-appointed kitchen, all evoked those many cozy evenings spent in Roz's company. But there was no Roz. In her place, a pale blond woman, a stranger, fidgeted uncomfortably on the sofa.

The rice was done. The chicken looked scrumptious flanked by mushrooms and covered in a rich white wine gravy. I brought out the salads and utensils, napkins, salt and pepper, plated the main course, and invited Jane to have a seat in the dining area.

We'd remodeled part of the too-large living room into a dining area about three years ago. It was a corner area right off the kitchen and it had two large windows looking out on the patio and garden and a view of the fireplace on the other side of the room. Our square wooden dining table for four had wooden chairs with comfortable cushions. There were Japanese bamboo place mats at the four settings and our china, too, was of a simple Asian design in a light gray.

Japanese prints of cranes and calligraphy hung between the windows. A white paper globe cast a diffused light over the table. Roz had been the decorator in the family and because her mark was so indelibly cast onto this area, I hadn't used it in the months since she'd left. It was a lovely corner of the house, though. I vowed to make myself eat and grade papers at the table again. As if she could read my thoughts, Jane asked as we seated ourselves, "You live here all alone?"

"Yes, I do now. I used to have a roommate, but she moved out a few months ago." A roommate. The word was so juvenile, so diminishing, so wrong. The love of my life, years of companionship, reduced to a collegiate-sounding, rent-sharing arrangement. It was humiliating to have to resort to such lies to preserve one's livelihood, to secure a measure of protection from narrow-minded malice. It was necessary, it was imperative, for a woman in my position in Texas to live a life of lies. But God, how it hurt sometimes.

"But you like it here, now? Texas, I mean?" Jane asked hesitantly, as if she was unused to asking questions and was afraid she'd strayed over the line of propriety.

Dangerous question. I hate it here, I felt like screaming. It's horrible. The people are so different, so alien somehow, and nice as they are, I don't know any of them, not really. My violent internal reaction surprised me. And of course, it wasn't true. Roz, after all, was a true-blue Texan and many of our friends here are, too. It was just now, now that they'd all deserted me, or that I'd deserted them, that I felt such a stranger here and so desperately lonely. Just what she needs to hear. I tried to put a smile on my face.

"Most of the years I've lived here, I've enjoyed it," I said truthfully in what I hoped was a convincing tone of voice. "It's my home now." I lied. "I've lived here almost seven years," I finished noncommittally. It had taken me a moment to compose my answer, and Jane seemed relieved that I'd finally spoken.

"And before that you lived in Madison?" she asked in a tone that indicated she'd like to hear about my life there. So, over dinner, I told her.

I told her the edited version of course, the one where mostly everything but the ideas that we believed in gets left out. I told her about my work with the Women's Transit Authority, my participation in Take Back the Night Marches, my contributions to the local feminist magazine, and our favorite hangout, Lysistrata. About all the discussions of a new history, a history of forgotten voices, which was a growing perspective during the time I was studying there. About the winter break I lived in a stick hut overlooking the ocean in the hippie colony of Zipolite, Mexico, where the local kids would go diving in the sea for our dinners of scallops and abalone that their mothers cooked into all kinds of wonderful on open wood fires on the beach.

Jane enjoyed my little stories. Her eyes lit with an excitement I saw in her only occasionally in class, when I'd drawn a conclusion or made an observation she hadn't considered before.

"What a wonderful graduate school experience you had! I wish I could have a life like that." The sentence must have slipped out unintentionally, for upon hearing herself, she bowed her head, pursed her lips, and toyed with her fork uncomfortably.

"Oh, I almost forgot the cheesecake," I lied, to break the tension and jumped up to get it.

When I returned with her piece of cheesecake in one hand, a pot of coffee in the other, I said, "Jane, you're young yet. You've got lots of great experiences ahead of you. Sometimes, you've just got to get out there and make them happen." Inwardly, I groaned. Jane probably didn't need to hear that half as much as I did of late. But she seemed to contemplate my advice seriously.

"Of course, Of course, you're right. That's why I came here, to have good experiences ... I mean, more of them." She seemed afraid I might believe she hadn't had anything nice happen to her before.

We polished off the last of the coffee and I wrapped two pieces of cheesecake for her, insisting she was doing my hips a favor by taking them home. The conversation, inevitably, returned to school.

"How do you like working for Johnny Wharton?" I asked, finally, in an innocent voice.

She kept her eyes on her plate. "Oh, it's great," she mumbled, not at all at ease. "He's a very bright man. I mean, I have a lot of respect for him." She was quite uncomfortable with this line of talk.

I was curious but I couldn't continue torturing the poor thing. "I'm glad you get along with him, though most people do, it seems."

"I must be going," Jane said suddenly, rising from the table. "I've got a ton of reading to do. It was a wonderful dinner, though. Thanks so much for inviting me."

And in a flurry of half-embarrassed thanks and compliments, she was gone.

I took my mug with a few dregs of coffee left in it and retreated to the rocker closest to the fireplace. With my free hand, I poked the fire a bit with the wrought iron poker, part of an antique set Roz had picked up at an auction when we first got here. Damn, did everything have to remind me of her? Must every thought be permeated with Roz's memory?

Don't go there, Maddie. Think about Jane instead. The evening had gone well enough. Jane seemed to enjoy herself, though with her it was hard to tell. She seemed so young in some ways, and it was more than the decade difference in our ages. I supposed it was her lack of worldly experience. What a sheltered life she seemed to have led, a quiet country upbringing, living with her family until this year. It sounded so wholesome. Yet, that description didn't fit Jane's character at all. Her face belied what she'd told me of her past. There was an aged, worn look in her eyes, like what I imagine war survivors look like. Her mouth was set with a seriousness unnatural to someone so young. She had the flat, colorless personality of the deeply depressed.

I snorted. How much of my assessment of Jane's character was projection onto Jane of my own loneliness and depression? Probably, she's just who she said she is. An overprotected only child from a rural home with not much in the way of experience. The death of her father had obviously scarred her. She's probably looking for her lost father in Johnny. I smiled. I was quite certain that having an affair in which Johnny played a substitute father figure was the last role he'd choose for himself.

With that mischievous thought, I headed up to bed. I slept better than I had in a long time. That was triumph enough for one night.

CHAPTER 20

MADISON, WISCONSIN

OCTOBER 1985

JENNY

"Hey, girl, what are you doing here already?" Lena yelled across the near-empty restaurant and motioned for Chuck and me to come over and join them. The gang was gathered in a large circular vinyl booth at Denny's, one of those twenty-four-hour places that specialize in fluorescent lights, hideous Muzak, and fake-looking custard pies. This one was on East Washington Ave., uncomfortably close to the Esquire Inn. Ginny, Nick, and Rupert were poring over the plastic-coated menu, and Fred and Harry were winding up a conversation about some technical aspect of stereophonic sound. Lena was smiling and animated, still high from her night's success.

"Yeah, what happened at the hospital?" Nick asked as we slid in next to Lena.

"They wouldn't let us in. It's after visiting hours, you understand," Chuck said in a Big Nurse voice.

"Ginny, can I bum a smoke?" I was dying for a cigarette. I gratefully took one and a light from Ginny, then took a deep drag. I hoped it would calm my nerves. I felt shaky, like I'd had too much coffee.

"So d'ja find out how she was at least?" Nick was really concerned about this girl. That made me feel better. I was, too.

"The nurse said they'd pumped her stomach, given her medication and that she was resting peacefully," I told him. "But something about the way she said it didn't sound right."

"Yeah," Chuck said. "She said they'd contacted her parents. But that sounded fishy to us, didn't it, Jen?"

"Uh huh." I felt an odd twinge in my ribcage at the way he'd spoken, like we had been long familiar to each other. Like we were friends.

Chuck continued. "Why would they contact her parents in the middle of the night if she was resting peacefully?"

"You're right," Nick agreed. "The nurse was lying, I'll bet. I'm pretty sure they pump you full of amphetamines if you OD on booze. No way would you be peacefully resting with speed running through your veins. Jeez, I don't like the sound of this."

"Well, we can check again in the morning during regular visiting hours," Chuck said.

"I'm sure she'll be all right," I added, because at that moment I knew she wouldn't. I sat back in the booth and hoped no one saw me shiver.

"You know," Nick said about a half-hour later, after we'd praised Lena for the great job she'd done, ordered our pseudo-food, and were munching on fries and onion rings washed down with Cokes, "I've seen her in the bar before. Pretty often, in fact. And now that I think about it, I've never seen her come in with anybody. Think she's a hooker or something?"

"Maybe's she's just lonely and likes jazz," I put in quickly.

"And drinks too much," finished Chuck.

Chuck, Nick, and I felt like a team tonight. The poor, drunk girl, Mona, had pushed us into a sort of instant intimacy, the way crises do. They seemed like buddies, friends, though I hardly knew them. Just an illusion, I warned myself.

I guess I didn't feel *that* comfortable with them — I still had to excuse myself and pop a couple of Valiums in the john. And I was smoking like a chimney all through dinner until Lena chided me.

"Trying to catch cancer all in one night, Jen?" She hated it when people she liked smoked.

"Upset about that girl, I guess." Well, that was partially true. The other part of me was thinking about what came next. The ride home in the car with Chuck. The expectation I'd ask him up to our room. He knew Lena would go home with Harry and we'd have the room to ourselves. I wasn't exactly sure why I dreaded this. I was hardly a virgin, after all. It was different though, different than fucking strangers, or even that fat slob of a pharmacist who kept me and Lou in pills. I wondered if it would be different, sleeping with someone you could respect. I didn't know what it was like to sleep with a decent human being. I was afraid to find out. What if it was just like all the others?

"Dollar for your thoughts," Lena leaned over and whispered. The rest of the group was discussing a new club that was opening on Regent Street.

"A dollar, huh? You must think I've got pretty racy thoughts." I could feel Chuck tuning in next to me while he pretended to be interested in the other conversation.

"You know it, girl. Bet you got the raciest thoughts in this place at least." She looked around at the smattering of old truck drivers and half-drunk students occupying a few other tables in the place.

"Sorry to disappoint, but I was just thinking how I'll have to buckle down this weekend and study if I want to avoid flunking my midterm exams."

"Uh huh, just like I was plotting the best way to break into Fort Knox. The girl's like a clam, she is. Won't open up to no one, no how." Lena pursed her lips, sucked in her cheeks, and stared at me.

"Your clam imitation?" I tried to keep a straight face.

"Pretty good, huh?" Lena giggled and I snorted. Leave it to Lena to make a weird situation feel all right.

"Anybody need a lift home?" Chuck said later as we chipped in for the bill. "Besides you Jen, I mean."

"Could you drop me?" I heard Nick say and was surprised to find myself only half-relieved. The other half might have been disappointed. After saying goodbye to the others, the three of us set out towards the lit-up dome of the Capitol in Chuck's old beater, the same car he'd had since high school, he told me proudly. It was late and only one or two cars waited with us at the stoplights. Sure enough, a few flurries were spattering against the windshield.

"Your first Wisconsin winter, Jen?" Chuck asked.

"Second."

"You ski or skate or anything?"

"Nope. I'm not the jock type."

"You should try something this year. Getting into it is the only way to enjoy winter. Nick and I go cross-country skiing in the Arboretum or up in Black Earth every chance we get, don't we, Nick?"

"Yeah, sure." By the way he said it, I could tell he hadn't been listening. "I never saw one that bad," he mumbled from the back seat.

"What's that?" Chuck asked, glancing at him in the rear-view mirror.

"Uh, I was just thinking. I've seen my share of drunk kids passing out, but I've never seen one that scared me like this girl."

We were all quiet for a few blocks. Then Chuck turned the car onto a side street on the Near East Side. Nick lived just off East Washington Street in a two-flat that used to be a big one-family house.

"'Night, you guys," he said when he got out of the car. "Hey, thanks for helping with that girl," he added.

I could tell he was still thinking about it, and I shrunk into my black wool coat as a cold gust of air blew into the car as he closed the car door. Chuck and I drove on through the deserted streets. We passed the Capitol and headed toward University Avenue and the campus.

"You like going to school here?" Chuck asked as we started passing university buildings.

"All right, I guess. I've never gone to another school, so I can't compare. I'm not into school that much."

"What are you into then?" Chuck asked innocently, but to me it sounded like a threat. I lit a cigarette from the pack I'd bought in the lobby of Denny's.

"Oh, sex, drugs, rock and roll," I answered glibly and hoped he didn't believe me. "The usual." Especially about the sex part.

"You are elusive, aren't you?" Chuck glanced in my direction, betraying that he had eavesdropped on my words with Lena a bit earlier.

"I want to retain an air of mystery. That's every Southern girl's prerogative." I batted my eyelids in mock flirtation as we paused at a red light.

"Hmmm, you're pitting yourself against Sherlock the Second, I hope you realize. Give me a few weeks and I'll have you all figured out."

"I'm tougher than I look." I wondered what he meant by that last crack. Was he trying to say he wanted to go out with me?

"Now, that I'll believe. But your 'cold as a stone' act doesn't fool me one bit." Chuck had parked the car in front of my dorm. I turned my head away from him and looked out the window. The way he had spoken, with his voice low and gentle, sent a wave of some odd emotion through me. I was scared out of my mind. I had to put an end to this now. He probably just wants to screw me, I thought, and felt relieved. I just didn't understand the lingo.

"Well, wanna come in?" The way I said it, the implications were clear.

"Jeez, Jen, that's not what I meant ... you said that on purpose, didn't you?"

I kept my eyes on the cigarette in my hand. I didn't trust my voice or what I might say if I opened my mouth. I just wanted out. Well, only part of me did. Otherwise, I would have opened the car door and bolted into the wet falling snow.

He took my silence for assent. I suppose he was right.

"Look," he said into a silence muffled by the snow, which had turned into a cascade of big, wet flakes spattering on the windshield. "Are you trying to get rid of me?"

Was I? Another me came up to the surface and silently screamed No! with blood-curdling urgency. But Chuck hadn't heard her, and I pushed her back under the protective weight of my icy persona.

"I don't know," I mumbled, knowing I was being rude, possibly mean, and not quite honest.

"Let me put it another way," Chuck said, with some emotion. "If I called you up again, would you go out with me — just the two of us?"

I took a deep breath. "It probably wouldn't be worth it," I said, and then amended it, realizing how he might interpret it. "I mean, from your point of view, it would be a waste."

"What do you mean, from my point of view? You have another boyfriend? You think I'm a jerk, or what?" I could see this conversation was rough on him. Why was I prolonging the agony? He shouldn't have to go through this.

"No, neither of those. I mean *I'm* not worth it — this mystery stuff, it's all bull. Look behind the mask and there's nobody home."

"Jen, that's a crock. I know you better than that already. I know you're a good friend to Lena and I know how you felt about that girl tonight. I betcha beneath all the frost, there's a warm human heart beating. Are you going to give me the chance to thaw it out a little or not?"

"Go to hell," I muttered, got out of the car, and slammed the door. I wanted to say, yeah, call me, please call, sure, I'd love to. But I was too damned scared. So, I got out of the car and started up the walk to the dorm entrance. I heard the motor shut off and footsteps that I tried to ignore.

Then he grabbed my coat sleeve from behind and swung me around to face him.

"Was that a yes or a no?" he demanded, looking straight into my eyes.

"You asshole," I hissed. His face was about a foot away from mine. "That was a yes," I finished desperately, forcing down the fear just long enough to get out the words.

"That's what I thought," he said with a wry smile. Then he gave me a long look, let go of my coat, turned, and walked back to his car.

It was only after the car was out of sight and I turned towards the door of the dorm that I realized he'd also kissed my cheek.

The next morning, I called the hospital. They told me the girl had died during the night.

CHAPTER 21

PINE HILL STATION, TEXAS

OCTOBER 1985

JANE

"You had dinner at Haystead's?" Johnny asked me incredulously. "Don't you know she's a dyke?" He said the word with a mixture of disgust and horror, as if being a lesbian was equivalent to being an axe murderer or rapist.

"How do you know I'm not one, too?" I said, challenging him with a smile.

"That's almost funny, Janey." He looked at me a bit upset, then finished a last forkful of cheesecake. "I guess even *lesbians* can make a good cheesecake. This is excellent, I must admit. You watch out with her, Janey. A pretty, young girl like you, and new in town, too. You're perfect dyke bait."

I almost said that I was perfect older-married-man bait too, but thought better of it and just said, "I'll do that Johnny, don't you worry."

I was irritated with Johnny tonight, and that surprised me.

Was I really growing so confident of his affection that I could afford such a chancy emotion? For once felt, didn't irritation erode respect, threaten the good feelings I was trying so hard to cultivate, to believe in? Scary thoughts. I needed to believe that Johnny was a good man, despite the doubt our illicit relationship cast on that belief. But he was my hope, my foray into relationships with men. I needed to believe that there was goodness in it. Please don't let me down, I prayed to Johnny silently.

He'd suggested that we meet at my tiny apartment going forward and that I could make him dinner. I supposed he had noticed that the entrance to my second-floor studio was in a dark alley, so it would be unlikely he'd be seen or identified. Meeting here instead of making the drive out of town would shorten the time he spent with me on these evenings, too, perhaps helping him keep up whatever lie he told his wife. So here is where we would meet now.

After he was done with me — in my own bed for the first time — he left down the dark backstairs that had been the servants' conduit back when the huge house had been inhabited by a wealthy family. Curled up now in the room's one easy chair, my mind wandered back to Maddie, the dinner we'd shared, and what Johnny had said.

For I hadn't known. It hadn't even entered my mind as a possibility that Maddie was a lesbian. It was more picturesque to think of her as a spinster, a woman who turned down suitors when she was my age to devote herself to a chaste life of study and teaching. A secular nun. A model for my own life, if I found the travails of normal womanhood too much for me. I'd half-consciously drawn hope from the mere existence of Maddie Haystead, hope that a full life, an interesting future might await me even if I must forego the intimate pleasures that life offered. To find out differently, to realize that Maddie too, like the rest of the world, had pursued love and intimacy and lost it, perhaps, somehow made my back-up plan of a life of scholarly, solitary reflection less possible. Of course, Johnny might have been making it up, trying to disparage her in the worst way he could think of. I knew she threatened him. She had quite a mind and no doubt was not afraid to speak it. She'd probably put Johnny in his place a few times. Possibly, he was afraid of her. What better way to put an enemy you feared on a level below yourself than by calling them a pervert, a creature given to unnatural predilections? It was simple, time-tested war psychology.

Although Johnny apparently had reasons of his own to flail at Maddie with so much venom, the gist of his accusation fit. It was probably true. She was a lesbian. If Johnny hadn't spoken, I might have known Maddie for years without ever suspecting. In part it would be because of ignorance; it would not have occurred to me. A single woman is never asked about her personal life once she reaches a certain age. If she's not married, or recently divorced, it's assumed she doesn't have a love life. She becomes a shameful thing, an unwanted woman, an old maid. Her personality, her very self, is suspect. She's too brassy, too bossy, cold-hearted, or mean. Or ugly. Or she was too fussy when it came to accepting a man for her husband and so it serves her right to be unwanted, to have to live what married women call "half a life."

Maddie could easily lead a double life with impunity. If she didn't flaunt it, no one would notice. No one thought an old maid had a love life. It intrigued me, the double life of Maddie Haystead. Yes, I was sure of it, she must be a lesbian. In graduate school, she had been inclined toward the radical, the feminist. She had lived in a place where rules were tested and broken, where a new order, a more humane order, was being forged. I envied her life. I was greedy for it. How I wanted to live as she had, bravely trying out new ideas, living a life full of surprises, breaking the barriers of propriety. Not looking back. Especially that. Not hedonism, not indulging in base whims, but flexing the boundaries of the allowable, trying out new ways of living.

I was living the antithesis of Maddie's life. My straying from the standard and acceptable was nothing more than a sordid, sneaky, and common affair — an embarrassment next to the groundbreaking life Maddie had led. My seamy attempt at healing. We all must start from somewhere, I suppose. Could I ever raise myself from my base beginnings and live the brave life of the confident?

It didn't disgust me, thinking of Maddie as a lesbian, the way it was supposed to. It didn't seem unnatural. With my perverse sense of what is normal, two women loving each other seemed an easier thing to grasp than a fair and decent relationship between man and woman. It seemed to hold more promise for intimacy. Couldn't two women know each other much better than partners of the opposite sex, coming as they did from such separate places, from psychology and cultures so different as to be almost aliens to one another? Women loving each other initially seemed so much less threatening, at least in my romanticized idea of it. For two women started out on equal footing with each other. It would be different from the relationship men and women started with, he with all the power, she with only her feminine wiles and charms.

How close a woman could come to another one, though, frightened me to my very core. With Johnny, probably with any man, it was so easy to put on a face, an act, to pretend to be pleased, pretend to feel pleasure, create a persona to display for them, and keep yourself, the real you, intact, safe, not even suspected of existing. My experience of relating with men was almost non-existent and yet even I found it so easy to put up a front, be who he imagined me to be. It was as if it were an instinctual ability, a protection for a woman's soul in times of danger.

But could you hide yourself from a woman lover? Wouldn't she sense the illusion? Call your bluff? And what would happen then, your very soul spinning out of control, subject to betrayal? Not only the betrayal of a lifestyle that was so abhorred by "normal" society that it could lose you a job, turn colleagues against you, maybe even make you want to run from your life. Much worse, a woman lover could see, and therefore, could expose, your deepest, most vital core. She had the power to betray your true self to the heartless world. How could anyone survive that? I couldn't. Yet, there were women who did expose themselves like that; Maddie was one of them. She was an attractive, kind woman. She could have married and had a family had she wanted to. She hadn't turned to women as something second best, better than nobody. No, I was sure she embraced being a lesbian freely and happily.

Maddie said that a roommate had recently moved out. I imagined a lover leaving, exposing her to the betrayal of her deepest secrets, taking part of her soul with her when she left. But Maddie had survived. Perhaps the soul replenishes itself, like skin when it's cut.

I was not as brave as Maddie. It was safer to try to make a life with men. But I could wonder how it would feel to be loved by a woman, or by anyone at all.

CHAPTER 22

WHARTON HALL, TEXAS

1962

LIZ

Old Johnny wanted to host the wedding, Johnny said to me, just a few months into our romance. That was after my father told me that Fred Barnes, the CEO of the middle-sized accounting firm my father worked at, had informed him of a call from John Wharton III, the man I knew of as Old Johnny. Old Johnny, whom I hadn't yet met, had called my father's firm to ask Fred for a character reference for my father. Was he of good character? What role did he play at the firm, and did he earn a decent income? Was my father a solid family man who raised his children right? It was only then that Old Johnny had asked about me, particularly, whether he knew me and knew of any "unsavory gossip" about me, as Fred had laughingly told my father. Fred had known me since childhood, he had assured the old man, and Liz had been raised with the best of Southern Christian values. "I gave you my highest rating," Fred told my father with a smile in his voice, "and your daughter, too."

My parents were thrilled with this news, especially Mother, who saw her aspirations for a wealthy marriage for her daughter on the verge of coming true. "But," she asked in a worried tone, "don't people of that caliber usually marry their own?" None of us had an answer for that, for I was a daughter of an accountant, solidly middle class but nothing more.

Planter family. That's how the whispering girls at the Halloween party had described the Whartons. Even a sheltered suburban Houston girl like me knew what that meant. The Whartons, apparently, had made their money in the traditional way in our part of the country. The mystery of it all finally overcame even my natural reticence. One evening, after a movie at the theater and an ice cream float at the drive-in root beer stand, I tentatively said from my side of the Plymouth, "I heard somewhere that the Whartons were a planter family?"

Johnny snorted derisively at the question. "Well, once upon a time we were. Right at the center of King Cotton, Texas style. One of the wealthiest families in this part of Texas. Town named after the family holdings, even. The first Johnny, my great-great-grandfather, the one who started it all, was the youngest son of a wealthy planter family in Virginia. His father gave him a sizable purse, so the story goes, and said, 'Go West, young man.' When he found a huge patch of sandy loam good for growing cotton not too far west of here, he put his roots down, invested in everything that was needed, and started the family business."

What the girls had whispered was true.

Johnny continued, "My ancestors made it through the war in style, though Old Johnny's father, the first Johnny's son — we always called him Gray Johnny for the uniform — did some fighting in Georgia for some months when he was a teenager. But he came back without a scratch. One of the few. We were lucky because the Union Army didn't fight much in Texas, never got much beyond the port towns. Afterwards, we transitioned to shares and Gray Johnny became a very wealthy man. But the weevils got us in the '20s, three crops lost in a row. Gray Johnny, who was in his seventies by then, sold off most of the land after that. Then he stupidly invested what he'd made on it in some stock market speculation right before the crash. Most of the fortune, gone in a matter of weeks."

I audibly gasped at this revelation and reached across the car's bench seat to put my hand on his. He looked over at me, shaking his head at the stupidity of it all.

"The family holdings were reduced to acreage enough to graze the horses on and a bit to grow horse feed for the six horses we kept then. The house and outbuildings, the grounds around the house, those are still there and in good shape, thanks to our longtime groundskeepers, who have two cottages behind the family home. We have someone who does the housekeeping for Old Johnny and the cooking and shopping, too. That's the only staff we have left on the place these days. I've been trying to convince Old Johnny to turn Wharton Hall into a tourist destination, but he's attached to the old place, and says he's not leaving except in a hearse. Nice place for a wedding, though!" He grinned at me, still not proposing.

"Not a sheik, then?"

"I am afraid not, lovely maiden," he said in the exotic accent he'd used on that first night and drew my hand to his lips as he'd done that night. "I suppose that means Old Johnny has made 'the call' then? He told me he had to investigate your family to make sure you were worthy of me." He laughed an ironic ha, ha and patted my hand. "He's hopelessly old fashioned."

I nodded mutely, still trying to absorb what he had told

me. Reputation from the old days then, but no money in the present. Mother would be disappointed, but I was relieved. It all made sense now. Johnny's career plans, his pursuit of a mere accountant's daughter. We'd be comfortable enough, I thought, though I had no idea what professors of history made. But no grand parties to host, no pretenses to keep up, no haute couture to select and replenish each season, no aristocratic manners to learn. If indeed, that's what the wealthy wives of the planter class occupied their time with. I looked up appreciatively from the other end of the wide car's gray leather bench seat. I loved him more for his lost wealth than I could have managed if he had been a member of the current Southern aristocracy.

"I hope you're up for a Southern belle wedding, Liz," Johnny said, looking at me in mock seriousness, "I'm afraid Old Johnny will insist. We'll get married in classic Southern style, in front of the big house, as soon as school's out next May," he told me. "Okay with you, Lizzie?"

I nodded and that was it. He never did ask me to marry him.

We had the Antebellum wedding Old Johnny had craved. I had three bridesmaids — Laura, my roommate from college; my older sister, Anne; and Johnny's cousin Violet; blonds all, just like me. We all wore somewhat toned-down period dresses. I had insisted that hoop skirts were just too uncomfortable and eventually a compromise was reached. My dress resembled the one Jackie Kennedy had worn a decade earlier, which, as everyone knew by this point, had been designed by the granddaughter of a Negro domestic servant who had designed classic dresses for her mistress and other Antebellum belles in Alabama. It was a full-skirted, lustrous pearl-white taffeta with an off-the-shoulder look and embroidered bodice but, unlike Jackie's, with a lace front that better hid my small bosom. I wore Old Johnny's departed wife's veil, as Jackie had worn her grandmother's. It trailed behind me gloriously, as did the train of the dress. My bridesmaids wore ice blue taffeta dresses like I had worn the night Johnny and I had met and big-brimmed bonnets like Scarlet's. We managed to evoke Southern heritage without the trouble of wearing hoops.

The Baptist minister from our church married us in the garden in front of Wharton Hall in a simple ceremony on the most beautiful of late May days. I was grateful that Johnny hadn't made a fuss over my request that my family's minister marry us — but he said Old Johnny wanted it done up proper and, in his book, that meant the bride's family preacher.

It was a storybook wedding. Wharton Hall was a classic planter house, with a huge veranda bolstered by white Grecian columns. A quartet played the wedding march. I walked down the steps of the porch and out to the garden, to a flowered trellis where the minister stood. My proud father beamed as he "gave me away" to my handsome husband-to-be. After the proper words had been said, Johnny put the ring on my finger and kissed me to applause as Reverend Thomson pronounced us "man and wife." Later, the quartet played songs of the South, as we mingled with the guests, mostly relatives of the Whartons and friends of Johnny's. Wharton Hall's well-kept grounds, one section partially shaded by elegant and old live oaks, was the site of the cocktail and appetizer buffet that followed the ceremony. The spread was full of intricate tidbits, artistically arranged on white linen-covered tables. Bouquets of yellow roses were interspersed with the dishes. Fruity cocktails and a peach champagne punch had been prepared and served with stylish efficiency by hired Negro servants dressed in long-tailed butler wear for the men and long black dresses, white aprons, and headscarves for the women. It was all a bride could want.

Eventually though, I had to use the restroom, a daunting

project in my complicated outfit. Laura helped me with my crinoline slips and then went back to the party, leaving me to do the final adjustments to my skirts and fix my lipstick in the gilded bathroom mirror. As I left the tiled, first-floor restroom and entered the timbered-ceiling hallway heading to the house's front entrance, I could hear two men talking on the veranda. Johnny and Old Johnny, I recognized their voices.

"Look over yonder, Johnny my boy, over by the punch bowl. Ain't that the sweetest pickaninny you laid your eyes on in a month of Sundays? Look at those nubile titties, would you? Hard to keep from drooling in my bourbon. She's a fine little Negress trollop, and that's a fact. Just like the good ol' days, huh, Johnny? Dammit, my pecker's just not what it once was, Johnny my boy, so's all I can do is go down memory lane. Too bad there ain't no 'croppers on the old place anymore. Them girls never gave us no trouble a' tall, none a' tall," he said in the exaggerated accent Old Johnny adopted when he'd had a couple of bourbons.

"Well, Old Johnny," said my new husband, "I ..."

And then, my wide skirt somehow managed to knock a small white and blue china bowl off the hall side table and it shattered into a thousand pieces.

CHAPTER 23

MADISON, WISCONSIN

JUNE 19, 1974

MADDIE

"So, white lady historian," Roz said as she handed me a mug, set hers down on the night table and crawled back into my double bed. I'd plumped the pillows and we could look into the treetops while we sipped our Ethiopian coffee, with a dollop of half and half in it. A breeze rustled the maple leaves outside our second-story window and the sky was summer blue. It was promising to be a fine June day.

"Do you know what day it is?" Roz finished, looking over at me, eyebrows raised. "If you want to hang with a Black babe from Texas, you've got to know what day this is."

I thought about it. Flag Day had been the 14th, Roz's birthday was last month. I couldn't think of any other holidays, personal, political, or otherwise. "I'm stumped," I admitted. "Tell me, my Texan, what day is it?"

"Ever heard of Juneteenth? That's today, Juneteenth, June 19th."

"Juneteenth? No, should I have?" I took a sip of the delicious brew Roz brought me in bed every morning, early riser that she was. It was one of my favorite rituals, developed with tentative caring these past six months of bliss.

"I'm not surprised, even though you are supposed to be an Americanist historian. How many Black professors are there in the department?"

"One," I said, feeling guilty, though it wasn't my fault. "And his specialty is the history of higher education. Tell me what Juneteenth is, Roz, besides today."

"You tell me, would-be historian, when did we end slavery in these here not too U-nited States?"

"Well, September 22, 1862, was when Lincoln first signed off on the Emancipation Proclamation, but it was just a warning to the Confederate States that they had to end their rebellion by January 1, 1863, or all their slaves would be freed. They didn't, so Lincoln did free the slaves in the South on that day. But of course, January 31, 1865, was the day that Congress passed the 13th Amendment, and even though it didn't get ratified by enough states until December 6th of that year, that's the day slavery effectively ended in the entire country. How am I doing?" I smiled over at her, confident of these facts.

"Wrong, wrong, wrong! Slavery didn't end in my Southern home state until June 19th, 1865, not too far from where my people are from. In Texas, slavery ended in Galveston, on Juneteenth, 1865."

"Explain," I said, intrigued. Roz was gearing up for a story and oh, how the historian in me loved to hear Roz tell stories.

"Juneteenth was the day that all the slaves in my part of America finally *heard* that they were free. A change like that only matters if the people affected actually know about it."

I couldn't disagree.

"The slaves in Galveston never knew they were free until General Order Number Three came their way. They were still working the Texas cotton fields as slaves for over two years after they were supposedly emancipated! And that happened when Major General Gordon Granger of the Union Army arrived in Galveston to announce General Order Number Three on June 19, 1865. You want to hear what he said?"

"I do." I looked up at her as Roz got out of bed in her oversized T-shirt and silk boxer shorts. She stood at attention as if reciting something for elementary school. I couldn't help but notice her athletic, but very womanly build and sighed at the beauty of her. How had I gotten so lucky?

Indeed, as if she were in her old elementary school classroom, when she spoke, it was in a little girl's voice, reciting a paragraph that she had learned by heart decades ago.

"General Order Number Three

The people of Texas are informed that in accordance with a Proclamation from the Executive of the United States, all slaves are free. This involves an absolute equality of rights and rights of property between former masters and slaves, and the connection heretofore existing between them becomes that between employer and hired laborer."

"He read it to a group of slaves and free people in Galveston. It was only then that the slaves of Texas, some of whom were possibly my foremothers and fathers, found out that they had been freed by Presidential Proclamation over two years earlier!"

"What? I never heard of this before!" said the white, small-town Midwesterner that I am. "Why didn't the Union Army announce this earlier?"

"Well," said Roz, bumping me over a bit so she could slide back into bed beside me. I put my head on her glorious bosom and she started to stroke my hair as she talked. "Some say the messenger that was supposed to tell Texan slaves that they were free got murdered on his way there. I like that version of the story best because it's so dramatic. But the more realistic, and likely, story is that both the slaveholders and the Union Army delayed mentioning it so the plantation owners could get in a few more seasons of free cotton picking before they had to close the whole slave economy down."

"Wow, I'm embarrassed I didn't know about this. And I call myself a historian!"

"I forgive you, my sweet," Roz said and lifted my chin with her free hand so she could kiss me more easily. Damn, could Roz kiss. Six months in and I practically swooned every time our lips touched.

"So, what do the descendants do to commemorate the day the long bondage finally ended, you ask?" Roz said into my hair.

"Yes, tell me, my goddess."

"It varies. But in my clan, it's like this. First, everyone wears their Sunday best. It's said that this is done to remind us of how there were laws against slaves wearing fine clothes. When the slaves found out they were free people, they went into the big houses that were abandoned by that point in the war and put on the finery of their former masters. So, we dress up to demonstrate that aspect of freedom and to honor the day. It was the only day of the year Mama didn't have to argue to get me to wear a dress!" Roz, an unrepentant tomboy, laughed.

"Then we all pile into our cars. Most of my cousins on my dad's side live in South Union — that's a suburb of Houston — same as my mom and brother. We convoy down to Galveston, where they have a big ol' parade with floats and marching bands from the Black high schools, folks in kente cloth and Black cowboys on horses. And all manner of dancing. Anyone can march in it, which I always did when I was a kid. The parade is both fun and symbolic; our marching represents all the former slaves that left their plantations after emancipation and headed north or to find long-lost relatives.

"Around dinner time, we have a barbeque on the beach, heavy on the pork and beef, because slaves rarely got to eat meat. Before we sit down to eat, someone recites the Emancipation Proclamation and General Order Number Three and then everyone stands up as a chorus and sings the Black National Anthem, which is...."

"Lift Every Voice and Sing," I replied, only because I had learned this from Roz in one of her previous stories. She'd sung the beautiful song in her mellow alto.

"Later, we roast marshmallows over the coals and sing spirituals and songs from the civil rights movement. Usually, someone gives a speech or a sermon about freedom and how precious it is and don't squander yours and voting and how necessary to racial uplift that is and stuff like that. It's my favorite holiday, better than Christmas!"

"That does sound wonderful. Is there something happening here for Juneteenth?"

"Not in Madison, near as I can tell. I did hear from that guy in my history of medicine class that there is a celebration in Milwaukee. I've got to work in the lab this afternoon though, so that's out. Would you mind if I celebrated Juneteenth with my favorite white person — a person from a bona fide, non-slave-owning background?" Roz smiled down at me, and I lifted my head to look up at her.

"What kind of celebration did you have in mind?" I asked in my most sultry voice. A delicious interlude followed, a celebration of exquisite love and egregious miscegenation.

Later, though, her words troubled me. I could not believe how much Black history I didn't know; how much was missing from my graduate education. Even Howard Zinn, who had been one of the biggest influences on my decision to study history, on my perception of what the study of history could accomplish, had never mentioned Juneteenth as far as I could recall. It was like the mural of American history had a section that had never been painted in. What else was I missing?

That evening, we dressed in what passed for dyke graduate student finery and had our own two-person parade down State Street to an understated French bistro tucked into the second floor of an old Victorian. Over our tarte Tatin and snifters of Courvoisier, I tried to fill in more blanks.

"Tell me what you know about your people — where they were from in Africa, where they were enslaved in America, what they did. That would be a way to honor your day, wouldn't it?"

Roz looked at me with love. I'd somehow managed to say just what she needed to hear.

"We don't know that much about the ancestors. We know — or we think we do — that our father's ancestors were captured in what is today Senegal — because some of the words that came down to us were Wolof, the language spoken there. *Yaay*, mother, *baay*, father, and *mba*, thank you; *metit* — the word Gran used when her arthritis was bothering her. I knew the words, but I didn't know what language they were from until I happened to go to a lecture on the state of medicine in West Africa by a man from Senegal when I was an undergraduate. I practically keeled over when he referred to his mother as his *Yaay* during his talk. I rushed up to him afterwards, and he graciously confirmed that the handful of words I knew in his native language were indeed Wolof. I was weeping by the time we finished our conversation and I remember he looked so sorry for me, a girl with no ancestors, and gave me a huge hug." Roz looked over at me with uncharacteristic sadness.

"There was a male relative — maybe it was my great-great-great-grandfather on my mother's side — who was a runaway slave. He made it to Maryland but then he was captured. His original master didn't want such a troublesome slave back, the story goes, so he sold him. George Henry, his name was, and we were never sure if Henry was a last name or if he had two first names. A lot of recaptured runaway slaves were sold to Texas plantations as a punishment. It was in the middle of nowhere, the weather was extreme compared to Virginia where he was originally enslaved, and the work — picking and baling cotton — was brutal. Our family story gets a bit sketchy after that for a while. Remember, my ancestors were forbidden to read and there were no photos, no memorabilia in some trunk in the attic, nothing like that. Just stories passed down through the years. Lots got lost and lots got garbled over the generations. We know we had some ancestors working on a cotton plantation in Texas, descendants of George Henry, we think, when the first Juneteenth took place, but we don't know what plantation. I guess in the years after emancipation some ancestor on my mother's side gave themselves a new last name because none of the slave-owning families in the area had my mother's maiden name. That happened a lot after emancipation, which was ..." she paused slyly.

"Juneteenth, 1865!" I smiled sheepishly. I still could not believe I had never heard of this before. "To the ancestors and their courage!" I said, lifting my snifter. By this time, I knew that part of the appeal of this particular white girl with ancestors who had been peasants in the middle of Europe to this particular Black girl from Texas who had ancestors who had been enslaved was my sincere fascination with the history of America as Roz knew it. She was changing what I thought I knew, which authors I thought I should read, what I thought about the books I was reading, what kind of historian I was becoming. Up until Roz, I thought I had a decent understanding of American history. Now I felt an entire second story ran in some shadowy parallel to what I thought I knew, much of it still not an official part of American history's canon at this fine graduate school I was attending. I knew practically nothing of the history that was meaningful to Roz, that had shaped her life and the lives of everyone she was close to. She was a patient tutor but the gulf between our worlds was as wide as the difference between the steamer full of poor immigrants that had brought my ancestors here in the late nineteenth century and the horrors of the slave ships of the Middle Passage that had brought hers a century earlier. We had only the Atlantic and our love in common. It seemed such a tenuous connection, full of unexpected currents and dangerous shoals.

CHAPTER 24

PINE HILL STATION, TEXAS

HALLOWEEN 1985

JANE

My eye caught a glimpse of a huge, angry face reflected in the window. I jumped, almost dropping the dish I'd been drying. I had thought I'd carved a smiling face in the night's traditional jack-o'-lantern. I went to the balcony door, opened it, reached for the pumpkin I'd placed on the half-wall perpendicular to the door, and turned it a bit to face me fully. Two rows of bared teeth confronted me, not the toothy smile I thought I'd carved. The eyes I had tried to make crinkle with laughter looked hard and mean-squinting instead. I sighed and turned it back fully toward the street, re-entered the room, and shut the balcony door. Too late now, Halloween was underway. But the face bothered me when I saw its flickering reflection in the glass. Dimming to a glimmer at times from impurities in the candle set inside, and then raging until it seemed an inferno burned within the orange head, the pumpkin took on a life of its own like some Frankenstein's monster. I tried to concentrate on the scene outside.

There was a big campus costume party tonight and students were making their way to the student center from the surrounding neighborhoods. Ghosts, witches, and goblins passed by on the street below me mixed with princesses and pirates, Romans in togas and face-painted clowns.

I turned from the glass balcony door and my horrible pumpkin face and went to sit on my tiny sofa where I couldn't see the awful reflection. A wave of homesickness washed over me. Memories of childhood Halloween nights paraded by in my mind like the otherworldly creatures I'd just observed. Ma's warm hand holding mine when she took me around to the houses in town to trick or treat. Feeling brave in my witch costume, a character I portrayed year after year without tiring of it. After the night's ritual was complete and we'd driven back to the farm, Ma would make me wait on the porch to see if he was "in his cups" as she called it, enough that he was snoring on the worn brown leather La-Z-Boy, and it was safe to come in. Ma and I would sneak into the kitchen and dump out the brown paper bag I'd used for the treats I had collected from the town ladies onto the chrome-legged, gray-Formica-topped kitchen table. Then we'd sort the night's takings, dividing the haul into fourteen small piles, one for each day of the following two weeks. Ma and I carefully put each pile into a baggie and then Ma would stow the candy up high in the kitchen cabinets. She would give me the day's ration after the bus dropped me off from school and she had gotten home from her shift as a nurse's aide at the old folks' home and he was still out in the barn finishing the evening milking. I remember the delicious secretiveness of it — that witch-conjured candy that only Ma and I knew about. She even let me have a jawbreaker or a twist of Smarties before dinner. The rest I could have when he was on his chair watching the game, first drinking beer in a can followed by swigging generous sloshes of Black Velvet Canadian Whiskey from the bottle he kept on the floor next to his chair. On a good night, he ignored us.

We spent most of our evenings during those years, Ma and I, at the kitchen table, I religiously disappearing into my homework, she, keeping the milk records for the farm or reading one of the outdated magazines the other women at work had given her. I could see our tiny farmhouse, the dreary kitchen with its 1950s table and chairs, the sparsely furnished living room with only a sofa, a La-Z-Boy, and a TV, so clearly in my mind, it half surprised me to open my eyes and find myself in my new accommodations instead.

I live now in a corner of what was once a grand Southern mansion. My room is spacious and sunny when the weather's nice, but I think it will be cold and damp when the rainy season starts. There are thick, worn green curtains on the windows and the bed folds out from a closet like an old-fashioned ironing board. My cheap pine kitchen table is stained dark and has two straight-backed carved chairs that I pretend were part of the original mansion furnishings. In a corner sits a rickety desk someone painted black with a metal chair that doesn't quite fit under it. Next to the desk is the green vinyl loveseat I'm sitting on and across from it is a gray tweed overstuffed chair — the room's only decent piece of furniture — that I curl up on in the evenings when I do my grad school reading. Aside from that, there is a small, battered end table that also serves as a night table when the bed is pulled down, a stand-up lamp with a stained silk shade that used to be white, and brick and board shelves that I bought for my books and my two cactus plants. In one wall is a small fireplace that's been converted to a gas space heater. To the right of the front door is the bathroom with a claw-foot white cast-iron tub, like the one we have back home.

The kitchen is a niche in the room's only dark corner. It's furnished simply with a sink, a two-burner hot plate, a black iron skillet, a saucepan, a pan big enough to cook noodles in and a battered tin tea kettle. For dishes, I bought the rummage sale remnants of an elegant white china service decorated with blue morning glories. There are four large plates, two soup bowls, a half-dozen dessert dishes and a serving dish left from the original set. But the best part is the creamer and sugar bowl that somehow survived the years intact. They're small and delicate and remind me of the set Ma kept in a cabinet over the stove and brought out only to use with her morning coffee, long after he'd left to do the morning milking. Then she'd clean them and put them back in their hiding place until the next morning. Having these two fragile pieces of china on my kitchen table feels like a small act of courage, of independence.

Although there have been many frosty evenings back home by now, the weather here hasn't gotten cold. The trees are turning brown and beginning to drop their leaves, never showing brilliant colors as they do up North. Each day, the town grows a little more colorless. Here, fall is just a dreary waning of the warm weather.

My life passes in a quiet routine of classes, work, and study, punctuated only by the one or two evenings a week I spend with Johnny. The years I've spent in internal exile, shying away from tentative offers of friendship, have left me caught up in solitary habits, convinced in advance of the futility of engaging anyone further. The world moves in front of me as flat as a TV screen and as involving. I could no sooner touch those people who pass before me in life than I could reach through the glass to the characters laughing and living and loving on the other side of the screen.

When Johnny visits and takes over the gray tweed chair, I don't say much. He fills our evenings with talk of his work, interesting research he's read about, complaints about colleagues. I take it in like one more lecture. At times, I have a crazy compulsion to take notes.

He talks of the subjects that interest him through the glass of wine we drink before dinner, through the simple meal I serve him, and while Johnny smokes a cigarette and I stack the dishes into the sink to be done after he's left down the dark back stairs leading to the alleyway.

His words have become a comforting background for me, like old, familiar songs on the radio. I like to listen to his voice with its slow, friendly tones, still foreign and exotic sounding to my Northern ears. He talks almost exclusively about his work life, and we know little more about each other's pasts or personal lives than we learned in the first few days of the semester. His wife's name is Liz. She's an accountant. They own a brick house in a shady, older suburb. If they have children, he's never mentioned them. He seems a man who lives for his work. And now, in some strange way, he lives for his visits to me. I know this the way I first knew he wanted me.

Sometimes, I catch his eyes on me and find them filled with an adoration more appropriate to one of the great goddesses in the books on pre-Christian Rome I have borrowed from him. It's confusing, as I am quite certain I am undeserving of such a sentiment. Perhaps I am, like a prostitute, a repository for the guilt of a half-failed marriage.

That doesn't disturb me much. My womanhood cannot be further devalued, and I have my own reasons for holding on to this awkward relationship. I thaw as slowly as a glacier, but Johnny is gradually melting the wall of ice that surrounds my emotions. I have come to anticipate his arrival. He is making me care for another human being besides Ma, and a man at that. It is a feeling rusty with disuse.

I have found I can endure the physical aspect of our

relationship. He demands little of me but submission. Over the weeks we've been together, his sexual routine has not varied. I no longer fear his touch. Another small triumph. If there is little pleasure in it for me, well, I expected none. He seems to find a satisfaction in these repetitive evenings that has not diminished over these past two months. I am learning facts that help me in my studies and ways to receive human warmth. We both are gaining something we lack during these few hours we spend together. That is justification enough for me.

Something was burning. I jumped up and rushed to the window, where my jack-o'-lantern was smoking on the balcony wall. I had set the candle too close to the front and as it had melted, the candle flame had licked the outside skin, charring the already ugly face. I grabbed the thing, threw it into the sink, and ran water over it. The skin had burned deeply: layers came off into the sink. It stared up at me with dead, angry eyes. I turned the face away in disgust and threw the slimy, wet thing into the lidded wastebasket. But the face came back to haunt my dreams.

CHAPTER 25

MADISON, WISCONSIN

OCTOBER 1985

JENNY

She was dead. Though I hadn't known her, the news shook me. All I could think about was how she'd been at that bar getting drunk all alone, with nobody to go with her to the hospital. I wanted to bolt out of this puny cubicle of a dorm room and go somewhere; a place like the Union where there would be people around who seemed friendly so that even if you were alone, you could almost feel like you weren't. Maybe that's why Mona had gone to the bar, just to be around somebody. That thought made me shiver.

I frantically pulled on some clothes and was headed out the door when I realized I should call Chuck and tell him the terrible news. He and Nick had been involved too; it was only right that they be told. I knew it wasn't my Southern manners, though, that made me put down my shoulder bag and dial the number from the list Lena had pasted up next to the phone. I was half hoping Chuck could take the kick out of this almost desperate loneliness that rushed through me when I thought about Mona. Only death could be lonelier.

"Chuck, this is Jen." In my nervousness, my Southern accent was coming through.

"Jen, hi there," he said in a voice so warm I stopped shivering.

"Ah ... I called the hospital this morning and they told me Mona ... well, she's ... she's dead." I heard the frightened quiver in my voice and stopped speaking.

"Jesus, that's terrible. Poor, lonely kid. Does Nick know?"

"I don't think so. I didn't have his phone number. But I'll call him right now if you'll give it to me." I felt more confident now that this was turning into a business call.

"Yeah, sure," Chuck replied, and gave me Nick's number.

"Thanks." I hesitated, not knowing what else to say. "Well, I'll see ya around." I was about to hang up when Chuck's voice held me back.

"Wait. Ah ... maybe you don't feel like doing anything tonight cuz of what's happened but, well, there's this good Bogart-Bacall flick playing on campus, and I thought, well, maybe it would help you take your mind off it ..." His voice trailed off and I realized he was nervous, too.

"*To Have and Have Not* you mean? I saw it advertised on the kiosks," I said, stalling for time. "Where is it playing?"

"The Commerce Building. At seven. Can you make it?"

Panic voices were buzzing around in my brain. Cut it off now, girl, while you're still in control. He doesn't know who you are, that's the only reason he's bothering. Once he sees what's in your eyes, he'll drop you fast. Besides, you don't need the complications. You're doing just fine as it is. All he wants is some ass. I felt myself teetering on the edge of a black hole.

"Hey, you still there?" Chuck broke what must have been an embarrassingly long silence.

"Ah ... yeah," I said, stupidly.

"If you'd rather not go ..." Doubt was beginning to cloud the softness of his voice.

My heart started hammering against my ribcage, and that scared me. I was getting too into this. It was no big deal, I told myself, if I went out with this guy or not. It was just a goddamn date, nothing to get bent out of shape over. Lena'd like it if I went, I knew. I could go out with the guy a couple of times, play it cool, and he'd get the message and leave me alone. I could tell Lena he was just not my type and no hard feelings. You can handle this, kid, I coached myself. You've had plenty of practice. You know how to socialize with men. So, he's a bit less sleazy than most. In the end, what they want from you is all the same.

"Sorry. I was in the ozone there for a minute, thinking about Mona. Yeah, let's do that, go to the movies." My old cool confidence act was back. "I'll meet you right inside the door to Commerce about ten to, okay?"

"Great, see ya then." He seemed about to add something but then didn't and just hung up.

I decided not to think about any of this stuff 'til I had to. I downed a couple of Valium fives and headed out for a coffee at the Union before my first class.

I'd been right about one thing: Lena was ecstatic when I told her what was up for the evening. I could tell she thought the outfit I'd decided on was a little outrageous, but that was the idea. I wanted to impress Chuck with how tough I was and how weird. Not the type of girl you'd bring home to mother. So, I went for long maroon nails with lipstick to match, lots of blue and pink eye makeup, and I gelled my hair into some wild spikes. Then I dressed in my black stretch tights and Peter Pan boots, long, black sweater jacket over it all. I thought I'd created just the right look — one Chuck, a longtime resident of super casual Madison probably wouldn't like. And that was fine by me.

I got to the lecture hall where the film was being shown and bought a ticket. I didn't want him buying me one and figured if he stood me up, I'd just go in and see the film anyways. The john was right near the entrance. I made a pit stop to check out my face and pop a couple of more pills. I'd been high all day and saw no reason to quit now. Out in the hall, I leaned up against a wall across from the door, lit up a smoke and practiced my Garbo imitation. I felt calm now. Dealing with Chuck would be a cinch.

The clock on the wall was just about to hit seven when Chuck strode in the door, bringing a gust of wet October wind with him.

"Sorry I'm late. I couldn't find a place to park. We'd better go right in, huh," he said, stopping at the ticket window to pay. I held up my ticket so he could see I already had one. He followed me through the lecture hall door, and I chose a seat toward the front. Chuck sat down next to me. I could feel his eyes checking me out, but he didn't say anything.

"How are you doing?" he asked instead. For some reason it didn't seem like one of those automatic questions people ask out of a sense of politeness.

"It felt pretty weird," I heard myself admitting, "finding out she was dead. I feel like I should have done something — been her friend or something."

"Yeah, I know what you mean. You never realize how lonely people are and then it's too late."

The film started just then, the distinctive whir of the reel drawing our eyes to the white screen in front of us. I tried to put Mona and Chuck, all of it, out of my mind. It's easy for me to get lost in a film. In movies like this old favorite, the characters were like comfortable old shoes. I knew their peculiarities, their problems. In a voyeuristic sort of way, they were almost friends.

During the break, I went back to the john and stayed out in the hall to smoke a cigarette. I didn't even want one that much, but I didn't want to have to spend the whole time making small talk with Chuck. I was better at entrances and especially, exits. It was the in between stuff I didn't like. People always wanted you to expose yourself or listen to them talk about their private lives. It was embarrassing and I couldn't understand why people did that. I sure wasn't going to.

"You hungry, Jen? I thought maybe we could stop for a pizza or something," Chuck asked after the end of the film was slap, slap, slapping around the projector, giving us notice that the night's diversion was over. "I had to leave my car near Gino's — maybe we could go there."

"Sure, why not?" I was starving. I can handle it, I reminded myself as we started walking down Bascom Hill to State Street. The dome of the Capitol building, lights ablaze, was visible in the distance, above the trees that lined the iconic street.

Talking to Chuck wasn't that tough. He shared my interest in old films and we discussed our favorites as we walked up the wet sidewalk the couple of blocks to Gino's. Once ensconced in one of their cozy wood booths with red leather covered benches and classic red and white checked tablecloths, we talked about what we liked to eat here and how good the food was. A plump older woman with her black hair pulled back in a severe bun, who everyone called Mama Gino, always perched on a bar stool near the front door so she could make sure the waitresses delivered food and the check with Gino's customary speed. Lena had insisted I come here with her a few weeks ago, so I was able to act like Gino's was an old favorite of mine. We gobbled our pizza, and I couldn't refuse it when Chuck asked if we should have vanilla panna cotta and coffee for dessert.

Then I made the mistake of asking him how he'd come to be interested in music.

"My mom forced me to take piano lessons when I was a kid. I really hated it at first. I tried to keep it a secret from all the guys in the neighborhood cuz a boy who took piano lessons wasn't thought of as the most macho kid on the block. I played a lot of sports I wasn't that interested in, just to prove myself around the other guys. During eighth grade, though, I started to change my mind about it. All those years of struggling to play some stupid song right had finally gelled, and I found myself being able to actually pick up a piece of sheet music and play it by sight."

I couldn't help thinking about how my parents encouraged me to take the flute in sixth grade, but when I complained about the spit, they just let me stop. I wonder what would have happened if ... But Chuck was continuing his tale.

"About the same time, my sister was rummaging around in the attic one day and found all these 78 records in some forgotten box in a corner. They turned out to be old jazz recordings: Billie Holiday, Ella Fitzgerald, Duke Ellington, even some Dixieland. The collection had belonged to this eccentric great-aunt who died when I was a baby. Judging by the number of records featuring him, my aunt had been a big fan of Teddy Wilson, who had played piano with both Louis Armstrong and Benny Goodman. I'd never heard music like that before. My folks were strictly the *My Fair Lady* and *South Pacific* types. I really got off on those old recordings and began trying to bang out those songs on our old upright. I started spending the money I earned cutting grass and shoveling snow on piano music of jazz classics. Then I discovered the music teacher in high school was a jazz lover and she turned me on to all these great sounds from the '50s and '60s, especially Art Tatum, Thelonious Monk, Bill Evans, Beegie Adair, Red Garland, folks like that. She also found me a piano teacher who showed me what improvisation was all about. Hey, am I boring you with all this? Jeez, I really got going there ..."

"I'll tell you when I'm bored," I said in a voice that I hoped sounded experienced at putting men in their place. "How'd you meet up with Harry and the rest of the band?"

Despite myself, I was finding all this interesting. It wasn't often I heard about anyone else's life except Lena's.

"When I was a junior, I'd gone out to this place over on the East Side with Nick — it's a sandwich shop now but it used to be a sleazy jazz and blues place — and Rupert, Jimmy, Harry, and this other guy, who plays guitar, were playing a gig. They really impressed me, especially Harry's trumpet blowing.

"I'd never heard anyone local who'd had half his class. So, when the show was over, I went up to tell them how much I enjoyed it. 'Thanks, man,' Harry said, 'But what this outfit needs is a keyboard player.'

"Would you mind if he's white? I asked him. 'Man,' Harry said, 'If he can lay out some good riffs, he can be green if he wants. You know somebody?'

"'When can I audition?' I asked, just like that. Jen, you wouldn't believe how scared I was. I was shaking. I couldn't believe I'd had the balls to even suggest it. I mean I'd never played with a band, didn't know the first thing about it. I was just some lousy honky who liked to fool around on a piano. I didn't even know how to use an electronic keyboard. I'd just been playing an old upright all my life.

"But Harry and the other guys were real cool. They had an old piano right there, and the owner agreed to let us stay late so I could show them my stuff. I could have kicked myself for saying anything. I was so damned nervous my hands were sweating. I think they knew I was inexperienced, though when I talked to Harry and Jimmy about it once, they both swore that they thought I'd had years of performing under my belt.

So anyways, the five of us messed around for an hour or so. I could hardly believe it. I stayed with them pretty well. They always did old classics about half the show and those at least, I knew. I guess my ear was good enough to fake it on the rest. Anyways, they said I could give it a go, and that's how I got with the band. The original guitar player, Robert, moved down to Atlanta last year, and we got Fred to replace him. But the rest of us have been playing together for more than two years now and we're getting pretty tight." Chuck paused for a breath and a sip of coffee.

"I don't know anything about music, but even I can tell you can practically read each other's thoughts."

Chuck smiled at my compliment and then continued, in a tone that indicated he was telling me something confidential, "I used to be satisfied playing as a hobby or a part-time thing. But lately, I got this dream in my head that maybe we could make it, cut an album, play in the cities that know what jazz is all about. It's stupid, cuz the market for jazz is so damn small and there are plenty of great groups out there already. But still, this idea, it won't let me alone. Harry and Rupert — who both are a year ahead of me — convinced me to apply to the graduate program and dammit if I didn't get in. But shit, I've been droning on about myself all night. What about you? You got a dream — you know, something you stay awake thinking about at night?"

I had begun to relax when he'd come out with that. Maybe it was the lateness of the hour or the Valiums, but I had been feeling mellow, almost comfortable. But when he asked me that question, the old alarms started ringing in my head, the adrenalin started pumping through my veins and my temporary good feelings vanished. I tried playing it cool.

"Nah, I'm just one of those 'live for the moment' type of girls." I smiled and shrugged in what I hoped passed for nonchalance and took a long drag on the cigarette I'd just lit.

"Come on, Jen, be straight with me. What makes you tick? I can't figure you out. You've got beauty, brains — but it's like you don't want anyone to get to know you."

"Hey, man, maybe it's just you," I snapped.

"Sorry, I didn't mean anything bad. I'm curious. I want to get to know you, find out who you are," Chuck hesitated, as if he'd just digested what I'd said. "But maybe you've had enough of me already, huh? Talking all night, boring the shit out of you ..." Chuck looked into his coffee, waiting for the axe to fall.

Here was my chance to dump him. But when it came right to it, I couldn't. I guess I didn't want to. He was a sensitive guy, afraid of getting hurt. We had that in common, I realized suddenly. Maybe it was enough to build a friendship on? Half of me was screaming in the background: You don't want friends. You don't need anybody. What are you getting yourself into? But for once, I didn't listen to that other voice. Maybe I didn't want to hurt Chuck's feelings. He'll get turned off soon enough and drop me. Meanwhile, why be mean?

"Chuck, I didn't mean that. I ... well ... I get nervous talking about personal stuff," I managed, truthfully enough.

"Hurt in love before, huh?" He asked. I gave a nod of consent. I guess you could call it that.

"I can relate to that." Chuck sighed. "Let's get out of here. How 'bout I drive you back to campus and we can take a walk on the lakeshore path?"

"That sounds nice," I said, suddenly exhausted and willing to be compliant.

The night was damp but not cold. There was a half-moon trying to burn through the hazy midnight sky. The leaves smelled earthy and fresh as we crushed them under our boots. For a few footsteps, we seemed to walk to the same rhythm, Chuck and me. It was an eerie feeling.

After a while, Chuck reached out and took my hand and I

let him hold it as we walked in silence. When we came to the path up to my dorm, Liz Waters, Chuck stopped half under the light that marked the path up to my building and turned me to look at him. "I don't know what it is about you, but you're not like the other girls I've gone out with."

No kidding, I thought cynically. That's putting it mildly. I'm a goddamn freak. Just wait until you find out.

"You intrigue me." Chuck went on. "Something about you." He took my shoulders in his hands and turned my face into the light. "Something in your eyes ..."

I drew in my breath in a horrified gasp. What did he mean, something in my eyes? Could he see what was behind the façade, into the dark secrets I thought I'd buried too deeply for anyone to find? I broke his grasp and turned away. I started to run.

"Jen, wait. Please." Chuck easily caught up to me and called behind me. He didn't try to touch me. "Please." He repeated. I stopped, my back to him. I didn't know what to say. How could I explain what his words had made me feel? He'd never understand, even if I tried.

"Listen, I don't want to scare you away. Maybe you had some bad experiences in the past — I don't know — and you don't have to tell me about them, either. But this is now. Maybe it won't be so bad for you this time. All I'm asking is for you to give me a chance. Okay? I won't bite." He half smiled at me as I turned around to look at him. "I won't make you do anything — or say anything — you don't want to. Is it a deal?" He stuck out his hand like we should shake on it.

"What's in it for you? I asked defensively, folding my arms across my chest.

He paused to consider it for a moment. "Despite the fact that you're so goddamn belligerent, that you pick a fight with me at every opportunity, and run the rest of the time," Chuck said in a voice full of smiles, "I like you. Is that a good enough reason? Huh? Well, is it?"

I stared at him like a dummy. "Well ... maybe," was all that wisecracking mouth of mine could mumble.

"Maybe? Is it a deal or not?" Chuck took a couple of steps closer and stuck out his hand again.

"Oh .... okay. Yeah, I guess so." I found myself smiling as I returned his shake. Suddenly, a giggle escaped me. Here we were, making a business deal about going out with each other. It was so ridiculous. I started snorting, then finally laughing as Chuck pulled me close and started tickling me. I got him back and soon we were both laughing our heads off. I couldn't stop for about five minutes until I was weak and wheezing convulsively.

"Do you know how gorgeous you look when you laugh?" Chuck whispered into my ear. Then I let him hold me and finally kiss me.

It was a kiss like no other I've ever had — a kiss filled with goodness and liking, not revulsion like with those men at the Esquire ... Then I stopped thinking and let Chuck kiss me.

It wasn't until the next morning when I woke up with aching ribs that I realized how many years it had been since I'd laughed.

CHAPTER 26

PINE HILL STATION, TEXAS

1962 – 1974

LIZ

I had only a very sketchy idea of what to expect on my wedding night, which seems odd now but was quite typical for a girl raised in the 1950s in a conservative Christian family in Texas. Of the young women I knew well enough to ask, only my older sister Anne, who had married two years before, had any real experience of what went on in a marriage bed. "Just do what he says," she advised, "and pretend you like it, no matter what. Well, within reason." Not very reassuring advice, but Anne, who was even more straitlaced than my parents, would not go into any details. "It's usually over in just a few minutes," she comforted me. I didn't feel comforted.

We had kissed and necked in the classic Plymouth with the big bench front seat. I guess that felt good, though there was always a fear in the back of my mind that he'd want to go further, so I never gave our touching my full attention. But no attempted touch ever happened below my belted dresses or skirt waist bands, and I had never let the boyfriends of my younger years have access to my privates either, so I had no idea what to expect of "down there." In truth, I was nervous because I am so petite — just five feet tall — with small hips and hardly any bosom. Johnny was so tall and broad in comparison. I think I was afraid he would hurt me. In this, he did not disappoint on our wedding night. I had no idea about hymens, no idea that he would be "breaking my cherry," as it was put euphemistically. I never learned about such things until much later.

Our "congress" that first wedding night, as the romance novels might call it, was far from the blissful fulfillment those books had implied. Johnny was a little drunk, but not so much as to be out of control. Indeed, it was control he seemed to desire above all else. "Keep still!" he whispered harshly, as he pinned my wrists above my head with one of his hands while I lay on the soft mattress of the brass bed in the bedroom closest to the back door in Wharton Hall. Then he parted my legs with his other hand and thrust his rigid penis into me deeper than I thought my small body could accommodate. As Anne advised, I tried to do what he wanted, lying still, biting my cheek to keep from crying out in pain as he penetrated me, as he ruptured me, that first time he thrust inside me. I was so focused on keeping still and not gasping in pain that I cannot remember how long he kept thrusting into me. But suddenly, it was over as he moaned and exited as quickly as he'd entered. "Just what I needed from my bride," he mumbled into my ear. A few moments later, he fell asleep.

And that's how it was. When we had our clothes on, he would kiss and caress me like he had before we were married. But once we had undressed, once we were in bed, he liked me to lie still in the dark, dressed in a white knee-length slip he had bought for me. He liked to pin my wrists above my head.

And he liked to say in a whispered snarl, "Keep still!" right before he shoved the slip up around my waist, parted my legs with his free hand and penetrated me quickly and deeply. It became less painful, in time, as I learned to anticipate and relax myself before he entered, though I continued to feel not big enough inside for him. He thankfully didn't want me every night. "I like to wait until it builds up in me," he said to me once.

It went on like that in our bedroom for two years before I missed my period and discovered I was pregnant.

Jenny was a disappointment to him, he told me weeks after her birth, when I finally started feeling myself again, when I finally started to be able to care for her myself and let my mother go back to her home across the city.

"Of course, I was hoping for a son," he said, looking down at the beautiful daughter I held in my arms, a daughter I had nearly died giving birth to. "Someone to carry on the family name. And now ..." He hadn't needed to say more. I knew full well what he meant. Now there would be no John Wharton VI because the woman who was supposed to give birth to that person had to have an emergency hysterectomy after almost bleeding to death in the aftermath of Jenny's birth. I would be having no more children at all.

We started going our separate ways, in a fashion, from that moment onward. While Jenny was little, she was my whole life, aside from my wifely housekeeping duties. She was bright and curious and hated to be shown how to do anything — she wanted to figure it out for herself. I caught her reading one of her baby books to herself when she was just three. She was my treasure, as is the only child of most mothers, I suppose.

Johnny dove into his work. His PhD program, undertaken at the same prestigious university we had attended as undergraduates, was daunting and absorbing. Most nights, he stayed at school late, "away from the chaos of childhood," as he put it. He did warm up to her though, even if she wasn't a son, and would buy her little gifts and take her on walks in the neighborhood now and again.

We led separate lives, but that was typical of all the couples we knew. I had coffee with other new mothers while our children played together in someone's living room. Johnny played poker a couple times a month with graduate school friends. We ate together as a family the nights Johnny didn't work late.

Johnny finished his PhD the summer before Jenny was to enter first grade. He decided to take a job in Pine Hill Station at the decent but not noteworthy university there because it was close to Wharton Hall and Old Johnny. He was devoted to his grandfather, and I respected him for that. We moved to an acceptable house in a nice neighborhood near the university. We met other couples like us, a husband who was a professor in some department or other and a wife who was typically a homemaker and mother and occasionally had a job. We had bridge dates with them and summer barbeques now and again. We were just like everyone else, except that I had only one child, an anomaly in a world where most had three or four children.

After Jenny started school full time, I asked Johnny if it would be okay to try to find a job. Except for a few summer jobs during college and high school babysitting, I had never worked in my life. He was surprisingly obliging. "We could use the money, Liz," he admitted. I didn't know anything about our household finances even though I was the one with the accounting degree. He earned everything, paid for everything, and gave me a small "allowance" for groceries and items Jenny and I needed.

I found a job, first, as a receptionist, at a small accounting firm. When it became obvious that I could keep books, they promoted me to a junior assistant accounting position. It was all a woman could ask for in those days, more than most achieved.

As time went on, the women's magazines I occasionally perused became more explicit about what could happen between a woman and her husband in bed. A few even gave rather specific advice. I tried initiating activities I'd read about a few times, but Johnny would always stop me. "I'm an old-fashioned man," he'd say, as if talking to a child. "And I like what I like." So, the line between our clothes-on kissing and cuddling and our less frequent bedroom doings, which were rough and quick and came to feel so impersonal to me, continued.

I concentrated on trying not to feel resentful and prayed for patience and tolerance. He was a good provider, within the bounds of his career. There was never any trouble over money. He let me work, and though my checks went to the bank account he controlled, he'd always been generous with Jenny and me. He took us on his conference trips at least once a year, and we often went to see Old Johnny at Wharton Hall, where Jenny and I, occasionally joined by Johnny, would go riding on the quiet country lanes. Sometimes, Johnny would stay with the old man for a few days while the two of us went back to town. We went to the beach near Galveston in the summer, though typically, that was with just Jenny and other mothers and their children. It was a placid, predictable lifestyle, entirely in concert with other marriages I knew of, except that possibly, other couples had a more interesting sex life. It was a small price to pay. He even let me send Jenny to a similar Christian Academy to the one I had attended as a girl. And the two of us, though never Johnny, went to church on Sundays. I had even concocted a line to explain Johnny's absence on Sundays, which was occasionally asked about. "Oh, you know how historians can be," I'd say with a smile and a shrug, and that usually put an end to the inquiries.

He was a bit rigid generally, I realized, when I thought on the matter of our bedroom life, which wasn't that often and mostly coincided with my cribbed reading of romance novels. He had to have his clothes and shoes and hair and dresser drawers just so. Maybe his habits in the bedroom were all part of the same personality quirk.

Once, when we were out at Wharton Hall for the day, when Jenny was nine or thereabouts, she came out to the barn, where we were saddling up the mares and her pony for an afternoon ride, wearing a black felt cowboy hat that was worn along the brim and many sizes too big for her. The band had a small hawk feather in it and Jenny was grinning from under the huge hat, her eyes twinkling. "Can I wear it riding, Mommy?" she asked.

"It's a little big on you, honey, but go show your daddy how cute you look in it. Watch for Belle," I added automatically, referring to the big bay mare Johnny liked to ride. Jenny obediently went around to the other stall, where Johnny was saddling his horse.

"Get that off your fool head immediately!" I heard Johnny roar and saw the hat come flying over the top of the stall, where it landed in a pile of manure that Elton hadn't taken care of yet.

Jenny was howling. "My hat, it's ruined!" she said, as she came out of the stall and saw where it had landed. "Why did you do that to my hat?"

"That is not your goddamned hat!" Johnny was still in the stall, trying to control Belle, who had understandably become scared at Johnny's yelling. As we all had. Johnny never yelled. "That is that goddamned son of a bitch of a father of mine's hat! And you are never to touch it or any of his things again. Is that understood?"

Jenny was sobbing. After calming my own horse, Babe, I

tied her to a barn post and went to my daughter. I pulled her up from the pile she had crumpled into in the straw near the manure pile and held her close. "I don't know what's gotten into your father," I said loud enough for him to hear.

"That traitor! He betrayed our traditions! He betrayed me! And then tried to use the threat of eternal damnation to take our family down! I don't want to ever see that hat or anything else to remind me of that bastard ever again! Is that clear?"

Jenny continued sobbing loudly in my arms.

"No," I heard myself saying with a deadly calm in my voice. "It is not clear. It has never been clear. And you are terrorizing our child for no reason. She didn't even know it was his hat, for heaven's sake." I had never, up to that point, spoken back to my husband.

Johnny turned on his heel, mounted the still agitated Belle, and left the barn at a canter.

I stood in the straw, held my daughter, and stroked her hair, trying to calm her. At that moment, I decided I would go to Old Johnny and demand answers I had never been able to get from my husband. We both deserved no less.

CHAPTER 27

PINE HILL STATION, TEXAS

NOVEMBER 1985

JANE

Sometimes memories ease their way into my mind like early winter snowstorms. Images begin to drift through my reveries that, with the winter wind to stir them and the cold to freeze them out of the clouds, turn into a blizzard, obscuring the road and threatening safety.

One night after Johnny left my bed and quietly slipped through the unlocked door and down the backstairs to the alleyway and to his wife, I lay wrapped in the old patchwork quilt that had been on my bed on the farm since I was little. I slowly found myself in Iowa the summer I turned twelve. There was a day in late August that marked the end of my already terrorized childhood and launched me without warning into a life of pain, lies, and secrets that haunt me even here, a thousand miles away.

When Ma was away at work and I didn't have to stick close

to protect her, or try to, I often took solace in nature. I had been walking through the corn rows that pristine early morning of what promised to be a hot and humid day. The leafy stalks towered over me and enclosed me in a private, jungly world that the blue Midwest sky had no part of. I crept along with stealth, hoping to cross the path of a field mouse or rabbit or even a raccoon. The ground was damp beneath me; the dark earth perfume permeated each breath. Here, under the corn leaf canopy, it was cool, and the swelter of summer was somewhere else. In the distance, I could hear the purr of my father's tractor as he cut alfalfa from a field across the road. In a moment, it stopped and only birds and insects broke the silence. He was headed for the house, I figured, as he often forgot his chewing tobacco and didn't realize it until the day's work had begun.

It was wise to know where he was at any given time, but my father's sporadic states of rage rarely were aimed at me unless I got in the way. Otherwise, he mostly ignored me or called on me to bring him a beer. Ma had learned to stay out of his way as much as possible, but there were unavoidable triggers to his outbursts, such as if Ma would get home late from work or fail to get dinner on the table precisely at 5:00 p.m. Or if we ran out of beer. There was a ritual quality to these events. He would start by getting up off his recliner in front of the TV and come into what I thought of as "our space," the kitchen. When I was little, I hid under the table when I heard his footsteps. Ma cowered in the corner; her arms ready to protect her face. "Please, Frank," she would plead, "I didn't mean to. Frank, think about your daughter."

"You lousy cunt!" was his usual phrase for these moments. He used to grab her by the hair next, but one morning, she came down to breakfast with it cut close to her head and she kept it that way. She got a punch in the stomach for her efforts, but I suppose she thought it was an investment, disabling his favorite hurtful act permanently. He shifted tactics then and would grab her wrist — twice, he broke it, and she had to go to the emergency room and tell them she had fallen. After he removed her from the corner, he usually pushed her to the floor. Sometimes he would just stand over her and berate her while she tried to make herself small. Sometimes, his harsh words were followed by spitting on her face. Sometimes, he would kick her, his farmer's work boots making a dull thud into her kidneys. Sometimes, he dragged her to her feet and punched her, mostly in the stomach. He never hit her in the head, I suppose, to keep neighbors and coworkers from noticing. Once, that I know of, she miscarried shortly after one of these incidences and years later she told me that she also had lost another earlier pregnancy to his fists. I had a front-row seat to it all from my hiding place under the table. When I was little, I prayed to God each night, not for him to stop, because that seemed as hopeless as praying away the thunderstorms that rolled across our part of Iowa with flashes of lightning and crashes of thunder. I prayed to grow bigger faster so I could protect Ma.

For an Iowa farm girl, I had comparatively few chores. Most of the older kids in my school spent the summer and parts of the spring and fall out in the fields, planting, irrigating, spraying, and harvesting alongside their folks. The younger ones had lengthy early morning and evening chores feeding animals, cleaning stalls, or helping with the milking. Besides feeding our dozen chickens and collecting eggs in the morning, I had only household duties like dishes, ironing, and scrubbing floors on the weekends. Though I felt fortunate about that, I knew the reason was one that brought my father much shame. He had lost the farm when I was seven and now worked as a hired hand for the neighbor who had bought him out. At twelve, I was a bit fuzzy about why the farm had failed but later I learned it was a combination of low milk prices and debt my father had piled up from speculating on grain markets, gambles that hadn't paid off for several years in a row. The loan officer at the local bank, who was a cousin of the neighbor who now owned the farm, had convinced my father that the only way to make good on his debts was to sell out. So, he had to work for the neighbor as a hired hand on the land he once had proudly called his own. Ma had to find a job full time and since she had always figured on being a farm wife, the only job she was qualified for was as a nursing assistant at the old folks' home in town. She worked the day shift so she could see me off for school in the morning. She got home an hour or so after the school bus dropped me off, a time when I sat at the table and did my homework. During the summers, Ma had dropped me off at the neighbors' house as she drove our old Chevy to the nursing home early in the morning. The summer I turned twelve though, she had decided I was old enough to stay by myself though I still went over to the neighbors' farm on my bike several times a week for company.

On that day, I had no plans to see the kids down the road. Ma had left a big pile of ironing and set up the board in front of the black-and-white TV we had in the sparsely furnished living room, a room Ma and I used only when my father wasn't around. I had planned to do the ironing right after lunch, while I watched *Days of Our Lives* and *One Life to Live*. Watching the soap operas while I ironed made me feel like a grown-up woman.

The small and shabby farmhouse, its white paint peeling in places, was about all we had left of the farm, just the house and the equally weathered barn and the yard around it. On the side of the barn, we had a chicken coop and next to that was the garden Ma used to keep before she had to go back to work. It was nothing but weeds now, with the wind-worn remnants of the scarecrow we'd made four or five summers ago to keep the blackbirds away, poking forlornly above the mess of useless green the garden had become.

My father would soon be in to eat his slice of ham and potato salad, prepared by Ma before she went to work, and left in the fridge. He would eat at the table in the kitchen. I would eat my sandwich, as I usually did in the summer, on the back steps. Even though the tractor's silence probably meant my father was heading back to the house, I was thirsty. So, I retraced my steps through the corn field that once had belonged to my father, back to the house to get a drink from the pitcher of lemonade that Ma made fresh each day and kept in the fridge the entire summer because that's what my father wanted to drink when he was driving the tractor. Ma said we should be grateful he didn't drink while driving the tractor. I guess she was right.

He wasn't back at the house when I got there for my drink. But I was just taking my first sips from the green glass that I liked to drink from when I heard the screen door slam and his heavy boots stomp through the entryway that led to the kitchen where I was standing next to the fridge.

I recognized immediately that something was wrong. His breath smelled of liquor, his eyes were bloodshot, and his face was angry and surprised.

"What are ya doin' here, girl?" he growled. "Can't a man have any privacy even in his own house?"

"I ... was ... just ..." I could see he was well beyond reason.

"You lazy girl, get outta my way!" He stumbled toward me.

I made to move aside, thinking he was headed toward the fridge, but it was the living room entrance he'd been aiming for, just what I was inadvertently blocking.

"You little cunt, yer just like your mother!" He grabbed my wrist and backed me into the living room. I thought he would hit me. But his big hands grabbed my shoulders and he pulled me to him and kissed me hard on the mouth instead. A brutal, bruising kiss. It was that kiss, more than anything that followed, that irrevocably ripped apart my girl-child hazy understanding of what could happen between a man and a woman. For in that moment, I learned that intimacy could be hurtful and dirty, that the comfort, care, and trust of love could be turned in an instant into their opposites.

In my shock, I went quite limp. With no trouble at all, he threw me on the worn hardwood floor. I did not struggle as he fumbled with my shorts. I lay as still as death my eyes shut tight. I prayed to God to let me die right then. But he didn't hear me.

I knew something about sex. I had grown up on a farm and had seen mating animals. I'd listened to the sixth-grade gossip, which, though erroneous about most things, had been graphically correct in describing the act that defined that most taboo of four-letter words. I vaguely knew this impossible sounding thing was going to happen to me momentarily. But nothing in the lurid insinuations of my peers had prepared me for the pain that shot through me like hot metal as he thrust inside me.

When he got to his feet again, in one motion, he removed his belt from his still-unzipped pants, turned me over from where I still lay motionless on the floor, and whipped me twice with it on my bare backside. Suddenly, that was all, and he turned me to face him. What I saw in his eyes then was something I was not expecting. Fear. Fear had sobered him some and his voice was flat as he said, "You go clean yourself up now. If you breathe a word of this to your mother, I swear I'll kill her." His threat was precisely calibrated to cause me maximum fear. Then he walked the few steps to the kitchen and washed briefly in the sink. I heard the screen door slam.

There was a wrenching pain in my left shoulder, though whether it was caused by him first grabbing me or forcing me to the floor I couldn't say. Panic made me bolt into the bathroom once I realized the wet goo between my legs was mostly my own blood. My underpants were soiled, and no amount of scrubbing took out the stain. My stomach cramped and for a minute I thought I would vomit. A hot burning sensation eased only a little when I put a cool washcloth where I was sure he had ripped a hole through me. I looked down at the washcloth and saw that it, too, now had blood on it. What would I tell Ma? What would she say about ruining my underpants and now the washrag? Then, I had an inspiration. I decided to tell her I'd gotten my period. She had told me all about it last summer and had even bought a pack of sanitary pads for me and put them in the cabinet under the sink in case I got my first one when she wasn't home. Gratefully, I rummaged through the bottles and rags and found the box hidden away in a back corner. I finished washing the blood off myself, scrubbed the washcloth and my underwear as clean as I could and hung them over the old claw-footed tub to dry. I struggled with the elastic waist band the box called a "sanitary belt" and how to attach the pad to it, but I finally got it to fit well enough. I put my shorts back on over the loathsome thing. I tottered back to my little room under the eaves, suddenly overcome with exhaustion. Once under the covers, I fell into a deep, desperate sleep, as if unconsciousness could wipe the day from my waking memory.

The next thing I remember is hearing the screen door slam and Ma's musical voice calling me. "Up here, Ma," I croaked, my throat parched with thirst.

"Jane, you didn't even touch that ironing ... honey, are you sick?" she said, her tone changing as she rounded the corner of the second-floor landing and saw me in bed.

"I got my period." This lie made me want to cry more than what had happened before.

"Oh honey, congratulations. You're a real woman, now." Ma smiled back and then, noticing my expression added, "Did you get cramps?" I nodded miserably and a few tears escaped and rolled down my cheeks. How I hated him for making me lie to Ma! She gave me a little hug and said, "Cheer up, honey, the cramps only last for one day at the most. I'll get you a couple of aspirins and you'll feel fine in a few hours. Why don't you come down and help me get supper started? Maybe that will help you get your mind off it."

Ma had to ring the dinner bell mounted on the outside wall of the house next to the back door to get him to come in for supper that night. We waited at the table while he changed out of his work clothes and washed up. Ma told me about a new resident at the home that was the grandma of somebody in my class at school. When he came into the room, Ma beamed.

"Frank, Jane has something to tell you."

I blushed to the roots of my hair in shame more than embarrassment and whispered, "You tell him, Ma."

"Our girl got her period today, her first one."

He looked at me with something like gratitude. "That's nice," he mumbled. "Pass the potatoes, Helen." Ma talked on about her day at work, oblivious to our silence. I toyed with my food. A lump of fear in my throat made eating impossible, but Ma chalked it up to period symptoms.

"Helen, there's something come up at work today I have to talk to you about," he said after he'd cleaned his plate of pot roast and mashed potatoes and gravy.

"You feel up to doing the dishes tonight, honey?"

"Yeah, Ma, I can do it." I tried to make my voice sound normal.

I was afraid for a moment that he was going to tell Ma what had happened and that was the reason why he wanted to talk to her alone. It occurred to me then that even if he hadn't threatened me with Ma's death if I told, I would have kept my mouth shut. I knew there was something dirty and shameful about what he had done, of course. But more than that, I wanted to protect Ma. As if it was some kind of disease and I could keep her from being contaminated if I kept the awful truth of it to myself. Our perverse conspiracy of silence started from that mealtime. It was to last almost four years before events took a turn that ended our secret relations.

By the time the evening's dishes were drying on the rack next to the sink, another wave of drowsiness washed over me. I crawled upstairs, changed the blood-stained pad, and fell instantly into a dreamless sleep.

The next day, Ma told me that the neighbors had sold the farm to a corporation and my father would no longer be employed there. For the next six months he moped around the house, doing odd jobs occasionally and drinking heavily. At first, he came to me nearly every day Ma worked, and repeated what he'd done. Later, when he found a job working evenings as a janitor, it dwindled to twice a week, never less. In time, I trained my body not to reject his intrusion and the pain subsided. But what he did created an emotional vortex in me, and every feeling was sucked in and lost in that dark inner abyss. I never did get my period for real until he was gone for good.

CHAPTER 28

MADISON, WISCONSIN

NOVEMBER 1985

JENNY

"Are you still in bed, girl?" I heard Lena's voice from a deep fog, as the door to our dorm room opened, letting in a blinding patch of light from the window across the hall.

"Turn off the light," I moaned, knowing in the back of my mind that it was daylight she'd let in and not early morning daylight, either.

"Do you know it's practically afternoon already? If you think you're going to roll over for a few more winks, forget it," Lena said in a near shout as I turned my face to the wall. "It's eleven thirty, and I got out of a nice warm bed with a nice warm man in it on a Saturday morning just to hightail it home to hear all. So, turn toward the light, pry open those baby blues and let it spill." Lena grinned into my face and pulled off the covers.

"Lena, you asshole," I said sleepily. "Just a few more

minutes. Give me a break, huh?"

"Nothing doing. You're getting up and talking. Now. Here, I even brought some coffee from Mickey Dee's to bribe you with."

"Ah, I knew that would work!" she continued, too loudly, as I stumbled out of bed and grabbed my red terrycloth bathrobe from where I'd dropped it on the floor.

"Coffee, I need coffee. Jeez, I feel terrible." I didn't usually get hangovers, but I sure had one this morning. "Got any aspirin handy? I must have smoked a pack and a half last night. I can hardly breathe." I broke into a coughing jag.

"Serves you right, messing around with them stinky things. I have no sympathy for you whatsoever." Lena handed me a couple of aspirins and a nice big Styrofoam cup of coffee.

"Thanks, pal." I smiled sleepily up at her. "If it weren't for you, I'd still be in that nice warm bed, fast asleep."

Lena was peering under the beds and snooping cautiously in the closets.

"What, exactly, are you doing?" I yawned.

"Looking for Chuck, of course." Lena grinned wickedly over at me. "Where did you hide that man, sugar?" she asked in an exaggerated accent.

"I suspect *he's* still in bed, seeing how he doesn't have an obnoxious roommate waking him up and snooping around."

"You mean I came all the way back to campus for nothing?"

"I wouldn't call it nothing, exactly."

"Oh good," Lena purred. "Now tell me everything, play by play."

"You won't believe it, Lena, really." I broke into a huge grin. "I felt like Cinderella going to the ball. Chuck knows this guitarist who plays blues around town who has this old car, a '48 Buick Roadmaster. He'd vaguely mentioned working on it with this guy, Mark, his name is, a couple of weeks ago. I didn't pay much attention. Chuck said the guy knew a lot about putting cars together and that he loved restoring this old one. So, about six, I hear a knock on the door. Thank God I was ready cuz it was Chuck, fifteen minutes early. I open the door, and there he is, in a '40s suit and fedora that he'd rented from that costume store on the East Side. He had a dozen red roses in his arms for me. You know, no one has ever given me flowers before, never once," I said, thoughtfully, gazing at the flowers on the desk in a vase I'd borrowed from Lena. Then I clicked back into gear.

"You knew all about this, didn't you, Lena? That's why you made me buy that vintage dress from that store on State Street last weekend. You creep." I smiled at how long it had taken her to convince me to buy it. But it had fit like it was made for me and, secretly, I was thrilled with how different, how womanly, somehow, I'd looked in it.

"So, did he give you a birthday kiss right away?" Lena's eyes were sparkling.

"Yeah," I admitted, "a romantic one, too. In fact, I had to put on more lipstick before we even left the room!" We both laughed. "So, then we left." I paused and imagined Chuck in his fancy outfit in my mind. He had looked great — a grown-up, serious man.

"And when we got outside, I saw this classy green antique car, and I just knew he had borrowed it from Mark for the evening. He even opened the car door for me. What a car. I felt great riding in it, though Chuck was a little nervous cuz he didn't want to bang it up or anything. But there wasn't much traffic. He even had rented a '40s woman's hat for me, with hatpins to hold it in place and a piece of netting that went over the front. And it gets better. The car has a cassette player hidden behind the big old radio it has and Chuck had recorded all this big band music, so it was like that's what the radio was playing. It felt like we were time tripping. Chuck even started to talk about World War II and stuff like that like it had just happened. After a while, we were laughing too much to keep it up."

I realized I was talking more than I had in years, maybe in my whole life.

"And then?"

"And then, we got to this classy Italian restaurant somewhere in Milwaukee, with waiters in tuxedos who had Italian accents! Chuck had made reservations and the maître d' — I didn't even know that word until Chuck explained it — the maître d' came to lead 'Signore Chuck and the beautiful Signorina' as he called us, to our table like we were preferred customers. Lena, it was so great. Chuck ordered white wine and it came with one of those silver bottle holders filled with crushed ice. It was all so perfect." I was almost getting teary-eyed. "The food was just incredible. I let Chuck order everything — turns out he had talked it over with the chef beforehand! We had the best dishes — pumpkin tortellini and a salad course and a fish course and the best wine. And tiramisu for dessert — I never had that before! They had a small orchestra playing Italian songs and during dessert, the violinist came over to the table and played *Happy Birthday*. A couple of waiters came over and sang, too. Everyone was staring and at the end, the whole place clapped. I was so embarrassed, but I loved it, too." I paused for breath. It was so unlike me, going on like this.

"And then?"

"Then, he took me to a nightclub that once a month has a live big band orchestra, just like in the '40s. There were all these people there. Some were older folks who missed the music of their youth, and some were our age but liked to dance to those songs. But nobody, nobody, was as swank as we were, driving up in the Roadmaster and wearing our '40s outfits! I felt like a celebrity!"

"Hey," I said, a lightbulb going off in my cottony brain. "How long has Chuck been planning this, anyway? Did he put you up to dragging me to that ballroom dancing class at the Union?" Lena had talked me into taking the month-long class. I thought it was dumb at first, but I discovered, if I just forgot myself for a while, I could dance decently and have fun, too.

"Chuck didn't want to be stepped on when he wore those borrowed spiffy shoes. And he wanted to make sure you'd enjoy something like that. Not everyone would, you know. Did you?"

"We danced every dance and stayed until the place closed down. I never had such a good time in my life!" I said earnestly and honestly.

"So, then what happened?" Lena asked for the hundredth time.

"Well, we drove back to Madison. Chuck knew about this after-hours place, so we went there for an hour and had a couple of drinks. I guess I did most of the drinking. Chuck ordered me a couple of exotic drinks that I had never heard of before — who remembers, what now?" I said, searching my memory for that part of the night in vain. I remember seeking oblivion though, steeling myself against what was next.

"Maybe he was trying to loosen you up so he could take advantage of you later." Lena grinned.

"You can't seem to get off that subject, can you?"

"So, you left the bar ...."

"Okay, so I was a little drunk by the time we left the bar. Chuck hadn't been keeping up with me. He doesn't drink that much usually and, also, he wanted to stay sober for driving because a car like that would be stopped by the cops for sure. Anyway, you'll never believe what we did then."

"Do tell," Lena leaned forward.

"Well, we drove to this nice romantic spot — somewhere on the shore of Lake Monona that I'd never been to before —

and we went parking."

"All right. Finally, we're getting to the good stuff. So?"

"Well," here my enthusiasm to tell Lena everything dampened. I had a hard enough time doing anything physical with Chuck, much less talking about it. Basically, we had just kissed. But for the first time, I had felt a tingly sensation in my chest. I had even gotten a little damp between my legs. Real progress for me. It had partly been the booze. But it had felt good, so good, to be able to return the passion Chuck was feeling when he was kissing me.

"Really, Lena, it was nothing exciting. Nothing compared to what you and Harry do, I'm sure."

When Lena just stared at me, I continued. "We just necked. Chuck said he wouldn't try to compromise me — you know, good girls in the '40s always kept their legs together when parking."

"Oh you," Lena pretended exasperation with me, but I think she knew I had a hard time with this subject. "Good girls don't kiss and tell, huh?"

"Right you are, roomie, especially good Southern girls."

"But oh, if we talked, what we'd have to say, woo wee!"

Just then the phone rang. Lena picked it up. "Oh, you devil, you!" she said into the phone, and I laid back in the bed and cuddled up in the blankets, assuming it was Harry on the other end.

"It's for you." Lena grinned mischievously as she handed over the receiver. "Bet you can't guess who this is."

My Southern manners scolded me from the depths of my booze-fogged brain. I should have called Chuck this morning to thank him. It was the least I could have done after all the planning and money he'd put into making my birthday so wonderful. My face was hot with embarrassment as I took the phone from Lena and breathed a soft hello into it.

"Hi, Jen," Chuck answered in that sweet, low tone he had.

"Did I wake you up?"

"No, Lena took care of that," I yawned, uncontrollably. "Chuck," I pulled myself out of my stupor enough to remember to thank him. "I can't tell you how perfect it all was — the car, the dinner, the dancing, the roses — everything. It was the greatest, the best birthday I ever had ..." I trailed off, astonished to find myself misty-eyed over the idea that someone would go to so much trouble over me.

"Thanks. It did turn out all right, huh? Hey, did I tell you how fantastic you looked?"

"I think you might have mentioned it." I smiled. He'd told me at least twenty times how great I looked and by the end of the evening, he had me believing it.

"Well, I just called to say hi and make sure you were no worse for wear after those couple of late-night drinks you had. You are okay, aren't you, Jen?"

"Yeah, I'm great, really," I said with emphasis.

Whatever residual side effects I'd been experiencing from last night's drinking had suddenly disappeared.

"I had such a great time with you. It kind of scares me, you know what I mean?"

"Yeah, I know, believe me, I know," I half-whispered.

"But what's life worth if it doesn't scare the hell out of you now and then, huh?"

I couldn't say anything to that. Getting scared was what I'd been trying to avoid for years.

"So, can you handle getting even more scared?" Chuck asked gently.

"I don't know. I don't know," I answered truthfully before I thought better of it.

"You want to check it out in a couple of days, go out for Chinese or something?"

"Hey, I'm a tough kid," I rejoined, some of my familiar bravado finally surfacing. "But only on one condition."

"What's that?"

"I pay."

"You got it," Chuck agreed cheerfully. "Jen, have I told you recently that you're beautiful?" he asked, and then the line went dead.

I hung up the phone in a daze. Lena had discreetly disappeared, and I was alone in the still half-darkened room. Last night, this morning's phone call, in fact, a great deal of my life lately, seemed to be part of some dreamy fairy tale. Could it really have been me who was wined and dined for a twentieth birthday? Me, who had been given the bouquet of roses that were tangibly filling the room with their perfume? Me, who had just finished talking with a man whom I could truthfully call "my boyfriend?" It didn't seem possible. I did feel like Cinderella, just waiting for the chimes to strike twelve and expose my fraudulent image.

I was even dressing differently, and partly, I knew, it was to let my feminine side come out a little more. Oh, I still wore lots of stretch pants and big baggy sweaters, with wide big-buckled belts, but I often let my hair hang loose and toned down the wild makeup I used to wear to intimidate people. When I looked in the mirror now, I thought I looked more myself. That scared me because I wasn't sure that was who I wanted to be.

If I let my image slip, the act the others thought was the real me, and let this illusive, undefined, raw thing called self peek through, anything could happen. Half of me was urging me to try it, to go with these new experiences, new people, and let go. The other half saw me spinning off the edge into nothingness.

I shivered under my blankets. Just then, Lena stuck her head in the door. "Are you off the phone with lover-boy, yet?" When I nodded, she waltzed in and whisked back the curtains, throwing the room into a blinding light. "Well then, girl, get yourself out of bed cuz this day is too good to miss. I borrowed a bike for you from Harry's roommate and we're going for a ride in the Arboretum," Lena announced, referring to the huge and beautiful nature reserve on the other side of town. "I made a trip to the cafeteria and bought some sandwiches and stuff. We can have a picnic in the shelter on the lakeshore and see what's up at the zoo. C'mon you lazy bones, the day's a wasting."

I opened my mouth to protest, but then realized I didn't want to. Count on Lena to get me out of the morbid thoughts galloping around my head. Count on Lena. I did count on her, and that terrified me.

"Sounds like you planned a great day for us, Lena," I sighed and pulled myself out of bed and into the brave new world I'd let myself in for. I hoped it would be kind to me.

CHAPTER 29

PINE HILL STATION AND WHARTON HALL, TEXAS

1974

LIZ

"Hi, Old Johnny, what's up?" It was Thursday at 5:00 p.m., so of course, when the phone rang, I knew just who it would be.

"How'd you know it was me, Elizabeth?" Johnny's grandfather, at eighty-five, still spry and mentally sound, always asked me this when he called at precisely 5:00 p.m. on Thursdays.

"Oh, a little bird told me."

"I'll get that pigeon yet," Old Johnny threatened good-naturedly.

"How are you, Old Johnny?"

"Pretty chipper for an old character. And how is my favorite daughter-in-law?"

"The same as always," I replied, inaccurately. Since Johnny had lost his temper over his dead father's hat a few weeks before, I'd been obsessing over the need to know more about

Johnny's father and what had happened to produce the venom Johnny had for his deceased parent, a man that I'd heard called 'Reverend Johnny' the few times his name had come up.

"And how's that sweet Jenny of mine?" Old Johnny continued in the Southern gentleman's accent of another age.

"She's having a great summer of skating and swimming — and riding, thanks to you, Old Johnny. She's over at a friend's house for a pool party right now, or I'd put her on."

"And what about my favorite grandson?"

"Off in the city of brotherly love for his annual history conference. He won't be back until Sunday evening." Johnny had told the old man this before he left, and I was sure Old Johnny remembered. But there was no getting around the manners of Southern gentlemen, as I had learned long ago.

"Elizabeth, my girl, you must be lonely all by yourself over there. I would be delighted if you would join me for a light repast tomorrow afternoon. I can have Patty make up her famous sweet potato pie."

"What a nice coincidence, since I was about to ask you if I could come and ride Babe and then visit for a while. I surely couldn't pass up a piece of Patty's pie, now could I?" I said with an encouraging smile in my voice. Old Johnny's longtime housekeeper, cook, and now caregiver made the most delicious sweet potato pie I'd ever tasted. "How about if I come out for a ride at around four tomorrow and we can have dinner on the veranda afterwards?" I knew Old Johnny always had dinner on the veranda in the summer, no matter the heat. I had heard on the news last night that a front was moving through, and the weather would be cool and not so humid for a few days, unusual for Texas in August. I had asked for an early day at work so I could get the horses out, and now I had an invitation to dinner with Old Johnny as well. The time had come to ask him about his son, Reverend Johnny.

"I'll see you after my ride tomorrow, then, Old Johnny.

Thanks for the invitation. Bye now."

"Goodbye, Elizabeth, I am looking forward to our date on the morrow." The phone went dead. I could practically see him giving a little bow.

A frisson of something I couldn't quite identify ran through me as I replaced the receiver on my end. Was I excited to finally be about to learn my husband's secrets? Or was I afraid that his past would turn out to be more troubling than I wanted to know?

A cerulean sky, vivid blue to the horizon, backgrounded the stately white house as I pulled up to Wharton Hall the next afternoon. I saw Patty, a sturdy Black woman about my age, open the heavy wooden door, painted black to match the house's many shutters, and come out on the veranda to greet me. Patty was dressed neatly in a white blouse and dark skirt and her hair was held back by a wide black headband. I noticed her ankles were a bit swollen, making her sensible black oxfords look too tight for her.

"Good afternoon, Miz Wharton. Mr. Wharton tells me you'll be having dinner with him on the veranda this evening?"

"Yes, Patty. Dinner at 6:15, please. I'm going to exercise the horses first."

"Of course, Miz Wharton, I told Marvin that he needn't do that today because you'd be over to take them out." Her son, Marvin, a quiet, small wiry boy in his late teens, usually served as groomsman and exercised the horses when we didn't get out here to ride. When he wasn't cleaning out the stalls, feeding them, currying them, or exercising the two mares, Babe and her mother Belle, and Princess, the pony that Jenny would grow out of in a couple of years, Marvin was outside helping his father Elton with tending the grounds, a massive undertaking in itself.

"I hear your famous sweet potato pie is on the menu," I smiled up at her.

"Yes, ma'am."

"See you later, then." I walked over to the horse barn to saddle up my favorite, Babe, a red-brown quarter horse with three white socks and a wide white streak down her forehead. Babe nickered when she saw me, an honor I never failed to appreciate. After stroking her muzzle for a bit and feeding all three of them the carrot pieces in my riding vest pocket, I saddled up Babe and put halters on the two other mares, who would obediently follow behind us on a long rope when we took off at a trot down the empty dirt road that abutted the side of Old Johnny's property. We had a great gallop for a piece, cantered for a while and trotted and walked the remaining course that we usually took, ninety minutes on dirt roads that sliced through the wheat and alfalfa fields that now surrounded Old Johnny's shrunken estate. This had all once belonged to the Whartons. And in those days, it was cotton as far as the eye could see, not this sea of green. I was happy that it was regular farm crops now. I didn't want to think about how it used to be.

There was a light breeze wafting across the veranda and Patty had put out Wharton Hall's best china for Old Johnny and me, the same china that had been used for our evening-before-the-wedding dinner, Jenny's one-year-old celebration, and Johnny's tenure party. It was a bit busy for my taste, intertwined summer flowers in pink, gold, and blue in three places around the plates and an intricate gold fleur-de-lis pattern that rimmed each piece. But it gave me an idea about how to open the conversation I wanted to have.

Patty's dinner was just what an eighty-five-year-old man would want — chicken fried steak with sides of okra, and mashed potatoes and gravy. One of her homemade biscuits, running with butter and honey, sat on a small plate to the side. The plain food was cooked deliciously. Patty had served me often enough that she knew to give me, with my petite frame, a child's portion and skip the biscuit. I'd find two wrapped in wax paper on the passenger seat of my car, as she always did when we made these visits to Wharton Hall. Old Johnny ate every crumb and Patty whisked the dinner plates away, asked if I wanted coffee, tea, or sherry, and I asked for a tea. She returned shortly with the tea, the two dessert plates of sweet potato pie with whipped cream, and Old Johnny's modest measure of bourbon all balanced on a wooden serving tray. She set out the dessert things and then disappeared back into the house.

"Old Johnny, has this china pattern been in the family long? It's lovely," I lied.

"Not so long as the Wharton family history goes back, I reckon. It was my mother's wedding gift back in '70. It's more than one hundred years old now and only the creamer has been chipped. Service for twenty, too. My papa, Gray Johnny, we called him for the uniform he wore in the uprising, went all out for my mother, that he did. Not many were left standing after that cruel war, but Gray Johnny was a lucky son of a gun. Not in family matters, though. I'm the only surviving chile, the only one who didn't die before they were grown. And the only son, too, so I was named Johnny like my papa and my grandpapa before him."

"Oh, I didn't know there were others who passed on. I've never seen any photos of them on the walls of Wharton Hall."

"Yes ma'am, the eldest was Louisa Jean and three years after her, Beatrice Rose. Both died of the diphtheria within days of each other. Beatrice was just six months old when she passed. Near to broke my mother's heart, I heard tell. She destroyed all evidence of them, their clothes, their toys, all photos of them, all set to fire out in that bare area in front of where the 'croppers shacks used to be. She didn't want to have any more children after that, and it took my papa a long time to convince her otherwise. She had me a dozen years after the girls died. She was thirty-seven by that time, too old for bearing babies, and she never did recover fully. She just took to her bed and wasted away. Some say it was consumption, but my papa always maintained that she died of a broken heart, losing the girls and all. I was only three at the time she passed, so I don't recall much except going to visit her in her big bed. She used to stroke my hair and tell me to be a good boy. I remember that." He paused and I could see that he was in the past, thinking about his long-gone mother. We were silent for a while.

Then he spoke again. "She was one of those narrow-hipped, small-bosomed women we Wharton men tend to favor. That's why the minute I laid eyes on you, Elizabeth, I knew you were the one for Johnny, the perfect one." He looked over at me in what felt like a leer. He's just an old man, starting to lose his marbles a bit, I admonished myself. But still, this bit of information threw me. I was a *type*? That's what Johnny had seen in me, that first, most romantic night of my life, the night we met? But then, I had an idea. This might be the very way to get Old Johnny to talk about his son, the Reverend Johnny.

I asked, all innocence, "Did you marry a narrow-hipped woman, Old Johnny?"

"I did indeed, Elizabeth. Gray Johnny found the daughter of a fellow planter for me, and we were betrothed and married when we were both seventeen years of age. Alice May was just a slip of a thing, as tiny as you. One year later and we were parents of a big strapping boy that resembled the Wharton side of the family. She had two more sons for us after that, but both died when they were still babes in arms. One died of the croup and the other one got yellow fever or cholera or some such thing. You know, we were constantly getting infected by the 'croppers, who never did take to hygiene proper."

"How long did Alice May live? Was she able to raise your Johnny?" I asked, aware that I was now getting to the story I wanted to hear, but Old Johnny possibly didn't want to share.

"Alice May died in the Spanish Flu pandemic in 1918, when our son was ten years old." Old Johnny had that faraway look in his eye that he got more and more often these past few years. "I took to raising him after that. Tried and failed to raise him like a Wharton. Tried and failed mightily." The old man was shaking his head, maybe with regret. "In my defense, he was a self-righteous son of a gun, always thinking he was better than other folk. I had a right nice bride picked out for him too, but he was too good to take advice from his mere earthly father. He run away to the seminary, all the way to Louisville, Kentucky, and he never slept another night in Wharton Hall."

"Oh, I'm so sorry to hear that, Old Johnny," I said in my most sympathetic tones. "How old was he when he ran away?"

"He was fourteen, I believe, because it was just a month after ..."

"A month after?"

"Well, Elizabeth, we Wharton men have our initiation rites and rituals, as many of the planter families do. It was just after the *Reverend*'s initiation that he took off. Didn't want to be a Wharton, he tole me. A real ingrate, he was. Just run off and left me."

"So, he became a minister, then? Up in Louisville?"

"I don't rightly know what he did up there, Elizabeth," Old Johnny had his dander up now. His voice had grown harsh. "Except get a child on some Louisville woman, some no-count woman that he wed by the shotgun, if you know what I mean, cuz her daddy insisted on it. But she produced my only grandchile, my only grandson, and blood is blood, so when things went south, I took in the little near-to-bastard. Your Johnny's only half planter blood. Maybe you didn't know that. Not the way it's supposed to be a' tall, not a' tall. He ruined our lineage, that good-for-nothing son of mine did, ruined it for good and all." He paused to take another sip of his bourbon.

Thirteen years into our marriage and I had known none of this. Maybe Johnny had been ashamed of his mother.

"The *Reverend* Johnny and his bride did try to get a congregation going, somewhere north of Louisville, I believe. Jennifer Ellen could play the organ real well, her pappy told me on the telephone one of the few times we spoke. But my despicable son had trouble getting out of bed in the morning. Jennifer Ellen's pappy, Mr. Ernest Stapleton, said, even on a Sunday to do the services. And his sermons, when he did get up the gumption to deliver them, were peculiar, he said. All about ..." and here Old Johnny looked over his shoulder as if he were afraid of being overheard, "'loving the colored as yourself' and such like. Nobody wanted to hear nonsense like that in Kentucky, Mr. Stapleton told me. So, they were forced to move on."

"Where did they go?" I wondered why my husband had never spoken of this history. And the words "Jennifer Ellen" repeated themselves as a kind of prayer in the back of my mind.

"When your Johnny was five years old, that no-count mother of his ran off with some other man of the cloth and left Young Johnny with her folks, who didn't want him and could not care for him even if they did. His grandpappy, Mr. Stapleton, found out how to reach me, and wrote me to come up to fetch the youngster. But with the Great Depression and the Second World War goin' on and with the gas shortages and all, it was mighty difficult to arrange. Finally, Mr. Stapleton found a cousin in the trucking business who was making a run to Little Rock, and I was able to find gas enough to get that far so I filled the back of my 1939 Chevy pickup with gas cans and met the little feller at a gas station in Little Rock in the fall of 1942. That was quite the adventure, roads being what they were back in those days, quite the adventure."

All Johnny had told me was that he'd come to live with Old Johnny when he was five and that he didn't remember anything from before that. But it wasn't only that. Before I lost him, I had to ask one more question. "What happened to Reverend Johnny then, that he couldn't raise his son?"

"Don't rightly know, Elizabeth. He disappeared for near to ten years, then came back to Wharton Hall for one evening. Next morning, folks found a car had gone into the river right outside of town. It was him, drowned to death in his own car."

"Oh, I'm so sorry, Old Johnny. It's just that Johnny seems to hate him so, and I always wondered why." I wasn't sure what I didn't know and what I wanted to know.

"Johnny has his reasons, Elizabeth, of that I can assure you. We took an oath, your Johnny and I, to never speak of that night and I intend to keep it. I perhaps spoke too much as it is. But that's enough with your questions now, Elizabeth. I'm an old man and I suddenly feel a bout of exhaustion coming on." He picked up a small silver bell that went everywhere with him and rang it. Patty soon appeared.

"I believe I am ready to retire now," he said to his caregiver when she poked her head out the front door. "See Miz Wharton to her car first, though. It's getting mighty gloomy out there."

He was right. Dusk was falling quickly, and I hated driving home from Wharton Hall in the dark. "Thanks, Patty, but no need. You go ahead and get Old Johnny ready for bed. It's not that dark yet."

Patty nodded and retrieved Old Johnny's cane from where it was standing against the house.

I quickly went over to give Old Johnny a peck on the cheek. "Thank you for a lovely evening, Old Johnny. I hope I didn't upset you with all my questions."

"No matter, Elizabeth. You take care to drive safely now." Old Johnny stretched out his arm and Patty helped the old man to his feet and got the cane positioned underneath his hand.

"Thank you, too, Patty," I said, almost forgetting my manners in my need to get away so I could think about all I had learned. "That pie was a true delight."

"Thank you, Miz Wharton. Nice of you to say so. You take care, now," Patty replied, then turned to help Old Johnny step over the sill of the huge front door. They both disappeared into the big old house without another word.

I got into my white Ford Pinto wagon, noted the wax-paper-covered biscuits that Patty had left on the passenger side seat, and headed down the dirt road flanked on both sides by alfalfa to the paved one about a mile away. It was almost dusk, as Old Johnny had said, and I put the headlights on. But my mind was elsewhere. "Jennifer Ellen," he had called Johnny's mother, "Jennifer Ellen!" I could hardly breathe. My mind flashed back to the month before my daughter's birth in 1965. It had been hot that October and the pregnancy had become an uncomfortable weight on my small frame. I remember lying big belly up on the bed in the small bedroom we'd had in that rented apartment, a damp cloth on my forehead, waving a magazine as a makeshift fan in some futile effort to stop myself from sweating, when Johnny peeked into the room.

"Of course, you know what we'll name him, if it's a boy," he said, smiling in that confident way of his.

"Yes, I do, dear." There simply would be no choice in the matter.

"It'll probably be a boy. But if it's a girl, we'll name her Jennifer Ellen," he stated flatly. No room for what I might have to say in the matter.

"Why, that's a lovely name." I meant it. "Is it for someone in your family?"

"It is," Johnny said, and that was all he said. Then he turned on his heel and left the doorway of the bedroom. And that was that.

He named her after his mother! I thought triumphantly. A tiny mystery had been cleared up, at least. My mind was whirring. There had been sisters and brothers among the Whartons. And grief, lots of grief, among the Wharton women.

At the very last second, I saw a white flash out of the corner of my eye and instinctually slammed on my brakes. I'd come within a couple of feet of hitting the doe now looking into my headlights in terror. Only the white warning twitch of her tail had saved her life and that of the fawn shadowing her. I looked out at the doe, standing there, herself and her child, nearly victims of her own poor vision, and I broke into a sob.

CHAPTER 30

MADISON, WISCONSIN

NOVEMBER 1985

JENNY

Well, tonight's the night. A thick fog of dread had been hanging over me like a shroud since Chuck's invitation. It was too late to turn back. The bus I was riding had almost arrived at Chuck's stop. What was I so afraid of, anyways? I couldn't really understand it. Chuck had invited me over for dinner at the old Victorian turned duplex he shared with two roommates. The roommates had both gone away for the weekend and Chuck had wanted to celebrate having some privacy by having me over for a cozy romantic evening of wining and dining next to the fireplace on a Saturday night. The unspoken invitation to stay over that would surely follow this meal had clouded my mind since the invitation. We had been dating for almost two months now. Chuck had been very understanding of my fears without having talked about it at all. I'm sure he thinks I'm a virgin, scared of deflowerment and guilt. If he only knew his shy young thing was a cut-rate whore working out of a sleazy hotel bar.

Since I'd started seeing Chuck, my stints at the Esquire had become less frequent, though until recently I'd kept my weekly date with Al, the sweaty pharmacist, because Lou and I needed our fix, didn't we? At first, I told myself I was cutting back on my Esquire gigs because it was getting hard to juggle stories — Lena and Chuck might compare notes some day and I didn't want to get caught in the middle of the web of lies I'd woven to cover my tracks. But there was more to it than that. I began to feel I was "cheating" on Chuck — even though the flabby, aging flesh that screwed me surely was no competition for Chuck's well-muscled leanness. It disgusted me to think they were the same species. It wasn't so much my activities that made me feel disloyal; it was my debasement by engaging in them. Chuck seemed to care for me, he treated me like a human being and then I had to go out and prove I wasn't worth it by fucking old farts for money. I suppose I *didn't* feel I was worth it — maybe that's why I'd always done it. Yet, somehow, my behavior seemed to be a slap in the face to Chuck and he didn't deserve that. Even if he didn't know it, it rubbed me the wrong way to treat somebody Chuck treated so well — me — so shabbily. I'd thought about it a lot and that was the best I could do at figuring it out.

My honorable intentions, however, could not live up to reality. I'd gotten used to the money. Then there was Al and his pills. I'd tried to cut back on them too, really tried, but I found I couldn't get by without at least a few every day. A whore drug addict, that's the girlfriend Chuck really had. Besides, Lou the bartender had gotten used to my supply of percs coming in regular weekly installments and I felt I owed him. So, I was compromising; just going to the Esquire on Thursdays, for one early "date" (okay, sometimes two), and then over to Al's for my usual stint there. After paying off Lou,

I was still bringing home enough to keep me in smokes and shampoo plus chipping in for movies, drinks, and dinners when I went out with Chuck or Lena and the band. I wasn't above heisting mascara and other small items when I thought I could get away with it, either. But I thought I'd apply for a job on campus next semester. Then, maybe I could give up my life of crime — all but Al, anyway. I pushed the thought of Valium from my mind at the same time feeling for the little pill box in the inside breast pocket of the new black leather jacket I was wearing tonight, bought with my ill-gotten gains. It was there, filled with my old buddy, downers.

I almost forgot to press the bell that would tell the driver to leave me off at Chuck's stop, just off Johnson Street on the Near East Side. But at the last minute, I noticed the scenery and jumped off the bus into the frigid November air. Winter had arrived in Wisconsin, and again, I wondered why I'd ever decided to go to school this far north. At the time, it had seemed crucial to put as much distance between THEM and me as possible. But why hadn't I chosen California?

I ran up the front porch steps and pushed the buzzer. I still hadn't resolved what I'd do when he asked me to spend the night. It was stupid, I knew, to feel so afraid, when I'd been with so many, many men in my life. But the idea scared me silly. Maybe this intimate act, in my life always so degrading, would finally break the spell I'd been under ever since I'd started seeing Chuck. Cinderella's midnight was finally upon her, I grinned to myself ruefully. Back to the ashes, girl!

"What's so funny?" Chuck asked as he opened the door to let me in.

"Oh, just random thoughts jerking my facial muscles around," I lied weakly, and walked into the entranceway, with the stairs to the three bedrooms straight ahead and the usually drafty living room off to the left. "Wow, you cleaned and everything — I never knew you had a green carpet under all those precious relics." Usually, a collection of musical instruments and their cases, and speakers and mixers and sound boards and music stands littered the room. I noticed I was talking a little faster than normal in my nervousness.

"Cold weather makes you look great. Your cheeks get all rosy," Chuck looked at me smiling as he took my jacket.

"Yeah, and my nose." He kissed it and then gave me a long, sweet kiss on the mouth. Yeah, this is the night, I thought as I kissed him back.

He'd set up a small table next to the fireplace and put a red and white checked tablecloth and white linen napkins, wine glasses, and a carafe of red wine on it. In a bud vase at the table's center, was a single red rose.

"Wow, you really went all out, cloth napkins and everything."

"Well, it helps to have roommates who are waiters." He laughed a sort of funny way and I realized he was uptight, too. "Would you like some music with your wine, madam?" He went over to the stereo and made a little bow. "What's your pleasure?"

"How about John Klemmer's *Barefoot Ballet*?" I asked innocently.

"That is a great album, but unfortunately, it's not in the collection."

"It is now," I smiled and fished the album in its plastic wrapper out of the large black tote I constantly carried with me. I offered it to him.

"You didn't have to do that."

"I know, but I thought you might appreciate music more than flowers and I wanted to bring some sort of guest gift. You wouldn't believe how much research it took to pick it out — I had half the guys in the music store helping me."

Chuck smiled appreciatively. "Thanks. That's sweet and something I'll enjoy a lot longer than flowers." He came over and kissed me lightly on the lips. He put the record on and disappeared into the kitchen. Klemmer's saxophone came out of the speakers, somehow mellow and excited at the same time. I stood in front of the fireplace this place was lucky enough to have and warmed my hands in front of the nicely crackling fire.

Chuck returned with a plate of cheese and crackers arranged in a swirl. I looked up, surprised. He'd really worked at making everything nice. For me. Don't fuck it up, now, Jenny, I said to myself. But I didn't know what that meant. Up until recently, being a cold-hearted jerk had been my specialty, my best act.

He motioned me to have a seat at the table, put down the cheese plate and poured us each a glass of red wine. The wine and the snacks and the music gave us something to talk about and we both started drinking a bit too fast in our nervousness. Chuck had cooked a great meal which he served in courses like in a restaurant. First came a salad, a classic Caesar with croutons and parmesan. Then, he served a roasted Cornish game hen with gravy, one half for each of us, a half acorn squash with butter and spices and pecans, and green beans with almonds. Fortunately, I had learned to love interesting food and was taught good table manners as a child. It would come in handy when you're older, she had insisted. I put her out of my mind as soon as she'd slithered into it. With the food to tuck into and the fire lighting our faces with a flickering glow, our conversation became more natural, with Chuck sticking to topics like where I had shopped for the album and my new jacket and what Lena was up to, even though we had all spent the evening together just last night at their weekly gig. I asked him what he was working on for class — he was in a composition class this semester. With the wine and food, I was feeling relaxed. Maybe I could handle what was coming after all.

"Finished?" Chuck interrupted my thoughts and took my plate away. "I have dessert, of a sort, too." He came back to the living room in a few minutes with two mugs of hot chocolate, a plate of chocolate chip cookies and a small bottle of schnapps on a tray. He changed the album then and put the couch cushions on the floor next to the fire. "Come sit here." He handed me my mug when I'd gotten comfortable.

"Chuck, the meal was perfect. Thanks." He sat down next to me. I leaned over and kissed him briefly on the mouth. I had never done that before, been the one to start a kiss. It felt kind of nice. Chuck began to stroke my hair and told me how golden it looked in the firelight. He was good at being romantic, he had me falling for it. Soon I was kissing and being kissed, touching, and being touched and living right in the moment, forgetting my fears, my past, everything but the sweetness of his touch.

Although I could feel Chuck's hardness through his jeans and wondered if I should be doing something more for him, he'd made no effort to take off his pants, or mine, or direct my hand anywhere.

I wondered if he was waiting for me to make the first move and I had almost decided to unzip his pants when Chuck stopped kissing me and looked me in the eyes.

"Jen," he said, his voice warm and low, "will you stay with me tonight?"

I looked back at him incredulously. Then, to my astonishment, tears began to roll down my cheeks. I tried to cover it by pressing my face into Chuck's chest, but he'd seen them reflecting in the firelight and pulled me back to face him.

"What's wrong, sweet girl?" he asked and there wasn't a trace of impatience or meanness in his voice, only concern.

"Nobody ..." I started and found it hard to suppress the sobbing that was right there, ready to burst out. "Nobody ever *asked* before." I somehow got that out and then realized maybe he didn't understand what I meant. "They just did it." I whispered the confession into Chuck's neck and then he was holding me and rocking me like I was a baby.

"My poor Jen," he repeated over and over, stroking my hair and back, and just holding me.

"Chuck," I said quietly, calmly, when I finally got control over myself, "I'd love to spend the night with you."

He looked at me in that straightforward way of his. "You're sure now? You can say no. Don't be afraid to if you don't want to."

"I want to say yes," I told him and realized it was true.

"Let's put some wood on the fire and go up and get my mattress down from upstairs and sleep right down here where it's warm. We've got all night to be romantic," he added and pulled me to my feet, kissing the top of my head.

When we were up in his room, getting the bedding and mattress, Chuck opened a drawer and took out a packet of condoms. "Do I need to bring these along?" he asked, kind of embarrassed.

"I'm on the pill," I said in a guilty voice. The admission incriminated me, proved I was unfaithful to Chuck.

But Chuck said, "Great," and put the condoms back in the drawer.

We took the mattress, sheets, pillows, and blankets down to the living room and made up a cozy nest next to the warm fire. I excused myself to go to the bathroom, washed the tears from my face and thought about the Valiums in my jacket. I decided to skip them for now, figuring I could get them later if I needed to.

When I came back to the living room-made-bedroom, Chuck had undressed and was under the covers. He looked handsome with his hair a little messed up and his broad shoulders and somewhat hairy chest sticking out from the top of the blankets. I began to take my clothes off too, though it was weird undressing in front of Chuck. But Chuck stopped me.

"Come here, let me do it."

He reached for my hand and pulled me onto the bed. Then he began to kiss me slowly as he pulled off one layer after another. I started to fade into a dream. These sweet, caring acts weren't what I had been expecting at all. Until now, I hadn't believed they existed. My body began to respond to Chuck's gentle caresses. I found myself getting aroused in a way that was new to me. I was half terrified. Feeling this good would make me lose control. Part of me wanted to shut down, the way I always had when men had sex with me. But this was different. It was safe. No one would hurt me. It was Chuck and he was making me feel good. I should try and enjoy this for Chuck. Because he wanted me to. Because, by his words, by his actions, he was trying to make up for all those other times. The least I could do is let him.

Chuck stopped his caresses for a moment and looked up, sensing my wavering attention. "Is this okay for you?" he asked. He looked so sincere, I melted.

"More than okay. It's wonderful." It was the truth. Then I let him do everything he wanted and found myself wanting to do things back. I gave up trying to keep control and went with the warm wave of good feelings that was washing over me. If these deep but placid waters meant to drown me, they showed no signs of doing it tonight.

CHAPTER 31

PINE HILL STATION, TEXAS

1974

LIZ

I was a *type*. The Wharton men liked narrow-hipped, slip of a things, Old Johnny had told me, and in that sense, I'd been the perfect catch. I hugged myself in the empty bed, a bit before dawn the morning after that strange dinner, not sure what I was feeling except vulnerable. That happens a good deal, I supposed, that men in the same family learn to favor the same kind of women. Maybe it was a way they bonded with one another. Though I'd slept in the same bed with one for more than a decade now, men were still mostly a mystery to me, maybe the one I called husband most of all. How they thought, why they did what they did, why they kept the secrets they kept.

What had I learned besides that my daughter was named for her paternal grandmother? There had been a lot more Whartons than I had known about, two daughters and two sons I had never heard of before last night. The family had a much more complex and grief-filled history than I had realized, with disease, suicide, and dying from unrelenting mourning, all taking a toll on the family line.

Besides having the right body type to be a female member of the family, I fit right in on another dimension, too — the Wharton women had lots of trouble keeping their children alive. In my case, they would never even be conceived.

I hadn't learned as much as I'd hoped about Reverend Johnny, but what Old Johnny had been willing to reveal did go some distance to answering my questions about why my Johnny felt the way he did about him. No doubt there is a simmering resentment that any child might feel about a parent who abandoned him, and surely that was part of it. Johnny's antipathy towards his father, though, seemed to largely stem from one night, the last night of his father's life. What could have happened between father and son in such a short space of time to cause such lasting hatred? And why had the two surviving Johnnys made a pact never to speak about that night?

Over the next few days, while Johnny was still at his conference, I talked myself into being resigned to never knowing about that night of my husband's life. My Johnny was not going to speak of it, or I would have learned what happened by now. Old Johnny was not going to speak of it because he was a Southern gentleman and Southern gentlemen kept their pacts of silence.

Life went on. When Johnny came home from Philadelphia, he was full of enthusiasm for the ideas he had gleaned at the conference, ready to dive into a new project, glad to have caught up with colleagues and friends from around the country, happy with the reception his own paper had received. Our life together quickly resumed its typical patterns. I found a late summer day camp for Jenny to attend while I worked. I cooked for her and Johnny in the evenings. I made sure she was keeping up with her summer reading and all the other myriad details that go into caring for a girl who is almost, but not quite yet, able to care for herself.

I pushed that half revelatory, half infuriating night out of my mind. I perhaps admonished myself more if I was impatient or short with Johnny. The dinner with Old Johnny had revealed that Johnny had had a share of real pain in his life and though he didn't want to talk about it with me, his wife, he still had to cope with it. It was clear to me that he hadn't left it behind. At night I prayed for patience and understanding. During the day I tried to be more forgiving of his shortcomings, which were not that many in number, really.

The strange conversation with Old Johnny was never repeated.

And it wasn't until many years later that it occurred to me there might be another person in possession of the answers to the questions that still pressed on my heart.

CHAPTER 32

PINE HILL STATION, TEXAS

DECEMBER 1985

MADDIE

"Hello?" I said absently into the receiver. Probably another charity wanting a donation or a salesman trying to get me to buy something. Those are all the calls I get these days. My head was still in the middle of critiquing Jane's quite innovative methods paper, easily the most well-written and interesting in the class. It was grading season and I wasn't even halfway through tonight's stack, though it was nine in the evening.

"Oh, Maddie." It was Roz's rich alto on the other end of the line. "How are you, lady historian?"

How I had longed for this phone call, imagined it, waited for it, these six long months since Roz left. Now, here she was, really, truly, calling me. I couldn't think of a word to say for the longest minute. My heart was thumping, my hands broke out in a sweat, and I almost dropped the phone. After too many silent seconds, I replied, "Living in the past, when life was better and more interesting," a line I'd used on Roz many times before as a little historian joke in answer to this question. This time, it had a double meaning, I realized, just a second after it was already out of my mouth. Could I do nothing right when it came to Roz?

Now it was Roz's turn to not be able to find words. She was silent so long, I almost thought she had hung up. Then she said quietly, "Maddie, it's so good to hear your voice." Then she sniffled. Was she crying?

"Are you okay?" Was I hoping she *wasn't* okay and calling on me to help her feel better? Yeah, I was.

She sniffled into the phone again. She *was* crying.

"Roz, tell me, what is it?" Was there too much desperation in my voice? Probably.

"It's about ... history," she finally got out and the woman I had known as unrelentingly cheerful and sunny started sobbing into my ear. "Sorry, sorry," she said a bit later. I could tell she was trying to get a hold of herself. I could tell it wasn't working.

"Well, if it's about history, you've made the right call." I tried to keep the emotion out of my voice, but wasn't too successful at it. My voice sounded quavery and kind of whiny and possibly, I was on the verge of tears myself.

"Damn, damn, this is too hard." My former love had never sworn in my presence before in all the years I'd known her. I could hear her taking a deep breath, then another. "I'm not sure I can ..."

"Roz, what is it? What's the matter?" I did sound desperate. I was desperate. What was going on? This was not like Roz. Was it her Mama? Her job? Was she ill? "You can tell me anything, you know, anything. I'll listen, you know I will." Oh God. Said too much. Here I was, begging her. Blowing it. Again.

But she said, "I know. That's why I called." Then she

started sobbing again. Minutes, maybe hours went by. "Jerry ... then Mama ..." she finally said between gasps and sobs.

"You're scaring me! Has something happened to them? Are they okay?"

"Yes ... no ... oh, this is too hard ... I can't ..." Her voice was muffled by a Kleenex or maybe her hand was over the receiver. Then the line went dead.

I pressed that little silver button that the receiver sits on over and over. "Roz? Roz? ROZ?" I yelled, pointlessly, into the phone. There was no one on the other end of the line.

I put the receiver back in its cradle. I stared dully at the beige phone, sitting so innocently now in its place on the desk. Had I had hallucinated that? A flashback, maybe? But certainly, if I were making this up, I wouldn't have invented such a weird, disjointed script. I would have had Roz say she was so very sorry for leaving in that abrupt way, that she didn't mean it, and could I find it in my heart to forgive her? And I would say of course I could, and then she'd start crying in relief.

This call had been alarming because the Roz I knew was not the crying type. The Roz I knew was never at a loss for words. I reviewed what she had said. It seemed it was something to do with Jerry and Mama, but that they were okay. Or was I just trying to make her words fit that scenario? It's about history, she had said. But what was she talking about? The entire call made no sense. My historian's training kicked in. I asked myself, what are the facts of this conversation? Roz, who hadn't spoken to me since she ended our decade-long relationship, had called. Roz, who was an upbeat, I-can-handle-this type of person, had been upset to the point of sobbing. Roz, who was well-spoken and logical, was unable to tell me what was going on. Roz, who never swore, had said "damn" twice in the short time we'd been on the phone. The swearing got to me the most. It was so not like Roz.

I didn't know what to do. I did have Roz's mama's phone number, but she had specifically told me to never call after 8:00 p.m. because at that point in the evening Mama was trying to get her MS-ravaged body relaxed so she could sleep. I wasn't even sure that's where Roz was.

This was torture, feeling that Roz needed me, and I could do nothing about it.

Then the phone rang again. "Hello?" I croaked into the receiver.

"Maddie, can I come over?" said my love in a shaky voice full of fear and doubt. "Right now?"

CHAPTER 33

PINE HILL STATION, TEXAS

DECEMBER 1985

JANE

In the half-light of a bleak winter morning, I read Ma's letter again. Before going to bed, I had carefully returned the delicate sheets that she perfumed with lavender from the now-wild area that used to be our garden to their matching envelope and put the letter in my pillowcase like a charm to ward off the night's evil. But the smell had only reminded me of my life on the farm. My dreams had come in fast, frightening swirls, each scene somehow caused by the one before it. She had worn lavender oil that she'd made herself for as long as I can remember. In the way that sometimes the unconscious seeks to protect us from hurt, the scent of lavender also evokes pleasant memories of being read a story on Ma's lap, or the two of us taking a walk on the deserted county trunk road in May when spring wildflowers filled the ditches with color.

My father remains in my childhood memories as a hazy

presence, never quite stepping out of the shadow my mind has consigned him to. Despite the six years he's been gone and despite my efforts to move on, he creeps unbidden into my dreams and reveries from time to time. But he has been exorcized from my daily life like a wormed hook from the belly of a fish who had made the horrible mistake of swallowing it.

I dug my hand in the pillowcase, groping for the smooth feel of paper that represented the reality I sorely needed to shake off the night. My sheets were damp with the sweat of nightmares, so I took my patchwork quilt and huddled under it in the big gray chair. I fumbled with the envelope, ripping off a corner of one sheet in my haste to read it again. My cold, moist hands smeared the blue ink, obliterating the "Dear" in front of "Jane." The words were mundane and comforting. She told me first about the weather, how it had been a typical fall, October was nice and colorful, she'd said, and I imagined the crisp October mornings and the brilliant maple reds and oranges, the crunch of leaves as I trampled them underfoot and the sweet smell of dying foliage. November was wet and windy, she wrote, and I conjured images of the glistening black fields, tawny corn stubble parting the land as far as the gray and brooding horizon, and the borders of brown-leaved scrub oaks rattling as the wind tried to snatch their dead leaves from them. December had arrived with a cold snap, she went on, and my mind saw the picture window in our living room edged with crystal fairy paintings and snow lightly sifting into the field corners in a flurry of white.

When was I coming home for Christmas, she'd asked, and how were my studies going? Then, she filled me in on the latest marriages, divorces, and births of half-forgotten relatives and neighbors, told me of the social evenings she'd had and what bachelor or widower had been trying to snatch up Ma, the forty-two-year-old, eligible young widow. She laughed at the ludicrous matches her neighbors had pushed on her. Some of them, she wrote, "were so old I could have been interviewing them for admission to the old folks' home!" The letter closed urging me to call collect and tell her when the Greyhound would deposit me in Cedar Rapids, the closest the bus line got to our rural area. In two weeks, I'd somehow manage to complete my first semester's work, pack, and board a bus for the long ride to Iowa and home.

Ma's mentioning the old people's home made me think of death and part of the night's restless dreams came back to me. I had dreamed of murdering my father again, a dream that recurred in different variations every few months, even after all this time. Funny how all the ways I dreamed of killing him were utterly bloodless, deaths that were not far from the manner of his actual death. My dreams reminded me that, maybe, I was his murderer. I had prayed for his death every night for four years until I stopped believing anybody up there or anywhere else was listening. Only six months after my prayers had deteriorated into fervent first evening star wishes, I arrived home from school one late afternoon to find him stone cold dead on our worn living room couch. His face, the only face he had for me now, was angry and surprised in death, a death come too soon at forty.

The bloodless innocence of his death convinced me my sinister prayers had been granted. At sixteen, I still believed in a universe as purposeful as it was mysterious. God or the stars had answered my pleas, but like in *The Monkey's Paw*, a story we had studied in school, wishes were not granted without cost. He was dead at my request, but I would be haunted forever by the shock of touching that cold, dead arm and turning his body towards me to reveal a bluish, dead face staring. The anger in his face was directed specifically at me, of that I had been certain. In the six years he'd been dead, I had not been able to rid myself of that death mask in all its clarity. It would remain indelibly imprinted on my brain for life. I stared at that face for what seemed an eternity. He compelled me to memorize every line in his face, note every insinuation in his ice-blue, dead eyes. Even after I had called Ma, who in a voice shrill with emotion kept asking, "Jane, are you sure, are you sure he's dead?" and rushed home to make sure and told me it had been a heart attack and he'd probably gone fast, even after an autopsy confirmed Ma's pronouncement, I remained suspicious that I had murdered him.

Ma's life as his fearful victim was finally over. The pain and humiliation of his after-school visits to me were finally, finally, gone and with them, the fear that Ma would detect our shameful secret. Yet, I could not feel glad. Nor could I grieve for him. I felt nothing, not even relief. Family friends and relatives said I was in shock and perhaps they were right.

Like a prisoner freed after half a life behind bars, I no longer knew how to live as a normal human in the company of my peers. I stared, blinking at the life of dating and Friday night parties that my school mates lived, unable to conceive of myself as one of them.

If I could not obliterate my emptiness in the social life of our small rural high school, I could bury myself in study. This I did, and the mediocre grades I'd earned in the prior four years reverted to the mostly A's I had received as a child, transforming me from the Future Homemakers of America track to the ranks of the college-bound elite. Having never imagined a future for myself, I felt more comfortable with the impersonal and tangible past. When high school ended, I moved naturally toward a history major at the University of Iowa in Iowa City, a forty-five-minute commute from the farmhouse. I had no intention of leaving Ma, my only source of stability and love in a world I shrank from. I was convinced others would sense my vileness under the veneer of shy seriousness I had adopted over the years. Six years on, Ma urged me to fly the nest. I supposed she thought her daughter odd because she spent too much time with her mother. I acquiesced when I was awarded a research assistant's place, all tuition paid for, at this second-rate Texan school. So here I am.

All through my adolescent years, I believed my real self to be hidden somewhere deep inside me, waiting for a time when my father would disappear, and Ma and I would be safe. When his death did not bring about my glorious metamorphosis, I blamed it on the memories, always with me at the farm. Yet now that I have left it, probably forever, I find that in my own way, I cherish and cling to my past. It is the only one I have, after all, and all the minutes of his horror are entwined with Ma's love for me.

I came here half hoping that my teenage dreams of transformation might yet come true. I am not sure what this new me might be like. Relaxed? No longer fearful? Happy? Even the adjectives to describe my hidden self have not yet emerged. But she's in there somewhere. She's survived these years. Johnny's feelings for me are encouraging that secret self to wake from hibernation. Although I cannot yet give much of myself, I am slowly, tentatively reaching towards him. Johnny is a first step towards hope, a first glimpse of my future.

CHAPTER 34

PINE HILL STATION, TEXAS

DECEMBER 1985

MADDIE

It was the longest half-hour of my life. I spent most of it pacing, but then I thought to make some coffee. Roz! She was coming here. There was some emergency or maybe not, but whatever was behind her decision to come here, I resolved to offer what support I could. If it would help, I'd just pretend these last six months had never happened. Her abandonment of me had never happened. Roz needed me. I could feel sorry for myself later.

She rang the front doorbell — a sound I'd heard so infrequently I couldn't place it at first. She rang the doorbell of a house that I, that we, had so recently thought of as ours, despite our strange terms of cohabitation. I found myself afraid to open it. I checked my frizzy mass of hair in the front hall mirror — nothing I could do about that at this late date. Quit thinking about yourself, Maddie. It's Roz. She needs you.

Thus fortified, I turned the knob and opened the door.

"Maddie." She stood bedraggled on the porch in an orange shirt that was thoroughly soaked. Her hair was curling up onto itself and dripping onto her shoulders. It was raining quite hard. I hadn't noticed. Her eyes were red and swollen. She'd been crying, maybe the whole way here. How had I let her drive here in the dark, in the rain, in this condition?

"Roz, come in. I'll get you a towel," was all that I could think of to say, and I went to the downstairs linen closet and came back with a big sage-colored bath towel.

Roz dried her hair and put the towel around her neck. When she noticed her red high-top, Chuck Taylors were making squishing noises and leaving wet footprints on the entryway floor, she bent over to unlace them, take them off, and place them neatly on the inside welcome mat after she shut the front door behind her. She glanced into the front hall mirror herself and gave a little ironic chuckle. "Not exactly at my best ..." Then she turned to look at me and started to sob.

I could resist touching her no longer, but I was unsure if holding her in my arms, as I longed to do, would be welcome. So, I took her hand instead. "I'm going to get you a robe and some coffee. You come into the living room and sit by the fire." I rushed to get her one of the white, terry cloth guest robes we kept in the now unused guest room, realizing as I took the stairs two at a time, that I didn't want to give her a robe that had any memories of the two of us being together in this house attached to it. "Here, I'll be right back with the coffee." I handed her the robe. I went to pour us two large mugs of our still-favorite Ethiopian brew with a dollop of half and half. When I returned, she had taken off the soaked orange shirt and it and the towel were neatly folded on the rug next to the sofa. She was wrapped in the robe and had sat down on the love seat, which was closest to the fire. I sat on the sofa perpendicular to her, fearing to do the wrong thing by sitting too close. Take it slow, Maddie. Don't you dare mess this up.

Roz's sobs had subsided by this point, and she took a few sips of her coffee. "I'm sorry I came here so late, but I just couldn't ..." she began, and stopped, a tear escaping her right eye and rolling down her cheek. She took a deep breath. "I couldn't handle this by myself anymore." Then she stopped talking and we sat there, furtively glancing at each other from seats that seemed to be miles instead of feet away.

"You said something about history?" I finally managed, in a weak, quiet voice that didn't sound like my own at all.

"Okay, Roz," Roz admonished herself harshly. "You came over here to talk about it, so talk about it." She took a deep breath. "You know how my daddy died of a heart attack before you even had a chance to meet him?"

I nodded.

"He was such a good man, such a hardworking man, such a good father to me and Jerry," she broke off, uncertainly. "But I never knew just how good he was until a couple of days ago." She sighed. "I don't even know how to start ..."

Another pause while Roz collected herself. "When I was growing up, I played with lots of cousins, but they were all from Daddy's side of the family. When we went visiting for Christmas, it was always Daddy's sisters and brothers and their children, my cousins, we always spent time with. We went to the same church as some of my cousins and some of them lived in South Union, our neighborhood. But we never visited any of Mama's relatives. When I got old enough to ask about that, Mama always said, 'I come from a small family,' and that was all. Once, I asked Daddy about why we never visited any of Mama's relatives. 'If there comes a time your mama wants to talk about that subject, I'm sure she'll bring it up. Until that time, you best leave it alone, Rosalyn.' So, I left it alone, but there was always that mystery hanging around in the back of my head. She did tell us about that long-ago ancestor George Henry. Maybe you remember me talking about him when I first told you about Juneteenth."

I nodded. "I remember," I said. "The one who got sold to Texas as a punishment for running away."

"But she never said anything about her more recent ancestors. She implied she didn't know much about them. My mama is not the type of person to come out and lie, but she sure didn't want to talk about her side of our family. I got to wondering if Mama was an orphan, but after Daddy told me not to, I never dared to ask her." Then Roz started crying again and I got up to move the box of Kleenex close to her. It was a few minutes before she had enough control over herself to continue. "Maybe I never mentioned it, but Daddy was nine years older than Mama," she started again. "Mama always said that when you find a man as fine as Harold Gaines, you just hold on tight no matter what age he is. She also said that Daddy was in the army fighting Hitler when most young folks were finding love and starting families, so he got started late. They really loved each other." Roz stopped again.

I couldn't figure out where this was going. "How did they meet?" I asked, just to keep her talking.

"Funny you should ask," she replied in a voice that was deadly serious. "They met at a diner for Black folks in Houston on the other side of town from where we live now. My mama was working there as the waitress, and he came in for lunch. The third time he came in for lunch in the same week, he finally said something not strictly business to my mama. You want to hear what he used as a pickup line with my mama?"

I nodded.

"'Grace,'" he said, because that's the name it said on her uniform's name tag, 'you've sure got a right pretty girl in that cradle behind the counter there. What's her name?' And you'll never guess what she replied," Roz said, though I had a pretty good idea. "'My girl is named Rosalyn,' my mama said,

'Rosalyn Eleanor, for the first lady,' and that's how they got talking."

"You never knew that Harold wasn't your biological father? No one told you, even when you reached adulthood?"

"No. Not one word until two days ago. I was only a year old when they got married, so he's the only father I ever knew." Roz was weeping quietly again.

My historian training snapped in. "But what about when you got your first passport? You must have seen your birth certificate then."

"Yes, I did. It said Rosalyn Eleanor Gaines on it. I pointed that out, first thing, when Mama told me that Daddy wasn't my biological father. That's when Mama broke down. She'd been real calm telling me my birth story up until then. 'When you were born,' Mama told me, 'Jim Crow was still in full swing. So many Black ladies had their babies with a midwife at home, especially when they had special circumstances like I had. My midwife came only because the minister asked her to. She didn't want to be there, helping to birth an out-of-wedlock child. But thank the Lord, you were an easy birth, and the midwife didn't have to do much. She left as soon as she decently could.' Mama said that the midwife never offered to certify my birth, and she never thought to ask about it and the Reverend and his missus didn't think of it either. It wasn't until she and Daddy got wed and he wanted to adopt me that Mama realized I wasn't certified. Daddy got the Veterans Administration to help, and, though they weren't that keen on it, they had to have some kind of paperwork, so the VA minister married Mama and Daddy first and then the white man at the office made a birth certificate for me that put Grace Gaines and Harold Gaines as the lawful parents of Rosalyn Gaines. 'It was just a Negro baby, so what did they care if it was correct or not?' that's what Mama said."

"But Roz, you have always talked glowingly of your daddy.

You loved him. So, what does it matter that he wasn't your biological parent? He's the man who raised you. He's the man who loved you!" I said, with maybe a bit too much passion in my voice. "Your mama made a mistake. Lots of young women have done that throughout history. And who is this minister you mentioned? Did your mother go to a home for unwed mothers? Is that why a minister was involved in your birth?"

I had asked too many questions. Roz was rising from the sofa and throwing off the terry-cloth robe. She was trying to get her arms through the holes of her still-wet orange shirt. She was heading toward the door. "I knew I shouldn't have come. I knew you couldn't understand."

Roz, my Roz, the love of my life, was heading toward the door. I had messed up and I had no idea how. But I could not let her walk out of my life again. That I knew. No matter what.

I got to the front door while Roz was struggling to put on her red high-tops. She was so upset she couldn't even figure out which shoe to put on what foot. She had just decided to grab them and walk out the door barefoot into the rain when I got to it and stood in front of the door and her.

"No. No, you are not leaving. You are not accusing me of not understanding and taking off when you haven't even told me why this is upsetting you so much. I have known you for over a decade and I know just finding out your daddy — a daddy you adored — adopted you as a baby and your mom got pregnant before she was married, like lots of girls did before birth control, could not possibly ..."

"Get out of the way. I have to get out of here. You can't understand. You just can't." Roz was almost whimpering as she clutched her red sneakers to her chest and futilely tried to wave me away from the door.

"Why, Roz?" I grabbed her by the shoulders and stopped her progress, at least for a moment. She was a head taller than me and outweighed me by thirty pounds, so it wasn't much of a tactic, but it was all I had. "*Why* can't I understand?" It came out like a pitiful plea as indeed it was.

But she stopped and looked down at me, square in the eyes, hers puffy from crying for days, mine desperate with longing and love and anger and confusion.

"Because this is about history, Maddie, the history of slavery and the rape of my people."

And then, to my infinite surprise, she dropped her shoes, collapsed into me, and my arms closed around her.

CHAPTER 35

MADISON, WISCONSIN

DECEMBER 1985

JENNY

Something was up. Lena had called from the Union and caught me as I was about to leave for my last class of the day. She had stayed at Harry's the night before and I hadn't seen her all day. On the phone, she'd sounded excited but mysterious. She'd asked me to meet her at Sunprint Gallery, an upstairs coffee bar on State Street near the campus, just as soon as I had finished my last class.

"We have something important to tell you," she'd said, but wouldn't tell me who the other half of "we" was.

I couldn't imagine what her news would be. Was she marrying Harry? Dropping out of school? Did she win a lottery prize? All these ideas sounded extremely unlikely, but then, it was also odd for Lena to be so secretive. I tried to have patience and took some half-hearted notes at my sociology lecture. It scared me to think how much letting Lena, and then

Chuck, into my life had changed it from a safe and known, if dull, daily existence to this roller coaster ride of thrills and alarms. In a couple of months, all my patterns, the foundations of my life, had slipped away and been replaced by risky human substitutes — friends. Since I started seeing Chuck, I'd changed my habits at school, studying regularly now to improve my "pass by the skin of your teeth" grades. It was working, too. I thought I'd pull a couple of Bs this semester if I kept up with my classes.

It was cold and big wet flakes had just started to fall as I left the Social Science Building and headed down Bascom Hill towards State Street. Winter had come early this year and there was a dusting of white covering the dirty snow from last week. Strange how I hadn't minded winter's arrival this year. I'd had too much fun playing in it. Lena had dragged me to the Lakeshore dorms' annual snowball fight. Once I'd lost my inhibitions, I ended up having a blast hurling snowballs at whoever came into range. There were hundreds of people and thousands of snowballs flying and lots of laughing and yelling as people dodged and slipped, got hit and got revenge. The fight went on, the sides forming and reforming until all the snow had been scraped off the huge expanse of grass that had been the battlefield. Wet and shivering, but in great spirits, lots of the participants ended the evening at the dorm cafeteria singing Christmas carols and being silly until the place closed at midnight. In the snowball slinging, the shouting, and the laughter, I'd forgotten myself for a moment. I had become a part of the crowd, a normal frivolous college girl, out for a good time, no hidden agendas. And dammit, it had felt good just letting go, laughing for no reason, acting like a kid. I'd come back smiling, rosy-cheeked, and tired in a real good sort of way.

Chuck had tried his hand at getting some winter spirit into me, too. He and Nick had decided they were going to teach me to ice skate, whether I wanted to learn or not. It had been so cold so long already in Madison that the city had opened Tenney Park for skating a few weeks earlier than usual. Tenney was a beautiful, peaceful park of canals and wooded islands with arched bridges connecting them in the summer. In winter, the canals became a maze of premier skating ice. A closed-in pavilion with a fireplace served as the warming house. The pavilion rented skates and sold hot chocolate, coffee, and hot cider to drink at picnic tables that were arranged near an outdoor fireplace. Chuck and I had met Nick there the first day of December. I was supposedly going to sip coffee and watch the two guys skate for a while. But Nick had already rented skates for me and the two of them made it clear they weren't going to leave the pavilion without me. Chuck had even brought an extra pair of thick wool socks for me to wear, proving they'd planned it all along. Though I thought for sure I'd make a complete fool out of myself, I was kind of flattered that they'd decided to bother to teach me to skate.

It had been a perfect day for it, too. It was cold but sunny, not too much wind, and the ice was smooth from being newly sprayed with water. Chuck helped me strap on my skates and then, one nice-looking man on either side, I wobbled onto the ice. I would have wiped out first thing, but Chuck and Nick took hold of me and kept me on my feet. At first, all I thought about was how I'd fall and embarrass myself, but after a few spills, I started to relax and enjoy myself. It turned out I wasn't that bad at it. I had learned to roller skate on the sidewalks in our neighborhood in Texas when I was a kid and found skating on ice was not all that different, except for the balancing act you had to keep up on two thin blades of steel. After a few rounds, I was able to only hold their hands on either side of me, instead of grabbing on for dear life. Then, by some signal I didn't catch, Chuck and Nick launched me and let go. I skated forward and found I could take a few hesitant strokes by myself. The guys came up behind me, kidding me about how they'd forgotten to teach me how to stop.

"Well, I don't know, Nick. Should we show her? It would be pretty funny to just let her pile up into another skater or fall on that cute derrière of hers."

"Yeah, let's just show her how to go faster." Nick grinned and swung around behind me and gave me a little push.

"Help me, you creeps, or I'll aim myself right at you and take you both down with me." I smiled. Skating was sort of fun after all.

"Okay," Nick relented. "I sure don't want to look as ridiculous as you're going to when you wipe out. You've got figure skates so it's easier for you to stop than for these macho escorts you've got here. All you do is this." He demonstrated a little turn that looked impossibly hard. "Or with your skates, you can kind of dig the front end into the ice, but carefully or your momentum will bring you right down."

Chuck grabbed me from behind. "Okay now, just bring yourself around ... like this," he said and guided me into doing it right.

"I knew there'd be a catch to this." I groaned and tried to do it. It wasn't that hard, though, and after a few tries, and one spill, I sort of got it down, at least coming to a stop at the speeds I was going.

"Okay, I think you're ready for a little train, right, Chuck? I'll be in front," Nick continued, and squatted down in front of my feet, facing away from me. He grabbed the top of one of my skates in each hand and told me to bend over and put a hand on each of his knees. I did it, almost falling onto him in the process. Then Chuck started pushing and away we went. It was great flying down the ice and Nick even managed to keep us upright around the corners. Finally, we hit a chip in the ice and the three of us went sprawling, ending up in a laughing, tangled mass. "See, winter's not so bad, now is it?"

Chuck teased, as we were untangling ourselves.

"Hey, I never knew I'd have two gorgeous guys keeping me warm." Then we got into position and off we went again.

Later, Nick stopped to talk to a couple of guys he knew, and Chuck and I skated around by ourselves. Chuck grabbed my hands and swung around to face me. "Okay, you skate forward, and I'll go backwards," he said, and we started off that way. Chuck was graceful on the ice; his compact body seemed to be dancing.

"This reminds me of my birthday. You know, when we were dancing, and I was stepping all over you and you were stepping like Gene Kelly."

"Aw, you weren't too klutzy that night. In fact, you were pretty cute." Chuck smiled at me, and I felt this weird rush in my chest, sort of like I'd drunk too much coffee, only all at once. "In fact, very cute," he continued, and I found myself blushing at his intonation.

"Come on, let's go faster." Chuck pulled me along as he skated backwards like a pro. I was feeling great, like I was high, though I hadn't taken anything all day. It was wonderful, just skating around, forgetting everything.

I remembered I used to love to roller skate as a kid, too, something I hadn't thought about in years. I was smiling, I guess, because Chuck said, "You're gorgeous when you're having fun. Winter's not so bad on the ice, is it?"

"I'll have to listen to your advice more often." I smiled again. I couldn't help it. I was feeling good.

"You do that." He smiled back.

Then it happened. I tripped on a stick or my luck and went flying into Chuck. We were near the edge of the ice and we both went down onto the little bank of snow on the side of the rink. I fell right on top of Chuck.

"Mmmmm," he said, pulling me back towards him as I struggled to get up. "I've been waiting all day for this to happen." He pulled me close and gave me a little kiss. Then he held me at arm's length and just looked at me, looked right into my eyes.

"Know something?" he asked, and there wasn't a trace of humor in his face. "I love you, Jen."

I guess my mouth must have made some attempt at working cuz he put a gloved finger up to my lips. "Don't say anything, no need to." Then the moment was over, and he pulled himself to his feet and helped me get up.

"For Pete's sake, will you wipe that expression off your face? You look like I told you I have the clap." He looked toward the pavilion. "Hey, there's Nick." Chuck raced over to him, leaving me unsteadily trying to skate over to join them. I guess he felt embarrassed. I had reacted to his words in a really dumb way. But I'd been paralyzed by fear. I didn't know what to think about what he'd said. I felt shell-shocked. There were emotions, reactions to what had happened, somewhere inside me. There must be. But I couldn't even figure out where to look.

Afterwards, I began to figure myself out a little. Basically, it came down to this: If Chuck really knew me, would he have said those words? I doubted it. Chuck must love some illusion of who I was, not the real me at all. Of course, part of the reason he didn't know the real me was because I'd taken a lot of care to hide all those parts of myself that Chuck would find ugly, repellent. And those were the very things that made me, me. It was a problem with no solution, a circle of lies or losses. If Chuck knew the "real" me, he wouldn't love me, so why should I tell him? But if I didn't tell him, he'd be loving an apparition and that didn't seem right either. It wasn't as though I wanted anyone to know about all the ugliness of my life. In fact, I couldn't imagine telling Chuck about my past, or lots about my present, for that matter. But it bothered me that such a nice guy was being taken for a ride by me, the big fake.

After days of circling inside my head about it and getting nowhere, I used the usual Jenny technique for solving problems. I buried it. I pretended it hadn't happened, that none of my thoughts about it had happened. Most of the time, this method worked. And really, what else could I do but give up seeing Chuck for humanitarian reasons? In some ways, that would be easy enough for me — no more intense emotions, no more of the constant self-analysis I'd been doing since Chuck came into my life. But, in another more important, even desperate way, I wanted and needed this guy, this relationship. I didn't want to think about exactly why Chuck had become so crucial to me. Hard-assed Jen who didn't need no one, no how, as Lena had put it, suddenly found herself desperately clinging to a lifebuoy named Chuck, somehow believing he could save her from the dark waters of her own history. It was scary, almost crazy thinking, and so I shut down. I tried to forget about thinking and concentrated on doing the right things, saying the right things, and having fun with the two people most important to me in the world: Lena and Chuck.

CHAPTER 36

PINE HILL STATION, TEXAS

DECEMBER 1985

MADDIE

I walked her back to the living room. I took the wet orange shirt off her again and helped her on with the terry robe. Then I sat on the sofa and motioned Roz to sit beside me. She did, and I held her in my arms for precious moments I didn't think I'd ever have again. She even put her head on my shoulder.

"What aren't you telling me, Roz?" I asked, speaking softly into her damp hair. "You can tell me the rest. I'm on your side, always, always."

She was crying quietly in my arms now, but she wasn't withdrawing. Minutes passed, or maybe hours. Eventually, Roz said, "It's because of Jerry," mystifying me even more. "He's been on this research binge ever since he started working for the NAACP."

I knew much of this. Jerry had been hired by the lauded civil rights group in their legal division, right after graduating summa cum laude from Howard Law School three years ago. They had a long-term project on reparations, with the goal of getting some compensation for the centuries of bondage Black people have endured. But reparations started with being able to legally document that one's ancestors had been slaves and that meant a lot of digging through local records, which had been kept nightmarishly unevenly, varying from district to district, courthouse to courthouse. Jerry and I had a long discussion about this last year when we went to visit him in his new apartment in Washington, D.C. Roz had an infectious diseases conference in Washington and I went along, spending my days at the city's many fine history museums while she attended her conference sessions and presented a paper at one of them. We were able to share a room at the conference hotel for three whole days, my idea of bliss compared to the closeted lifestyle we had to endure in Texas. Baby brother Jerry had told Roz that he was "on to us" being a couple years ago already, and he'd said it with a hug and an 'I love you' to his big sister. It was a relief to be out to Jerry, as I really liked him. We loved to talk research methods together. All this flashed through my mind. I corrected myself. Jerry was Roz's half-brother, biologically, apparently. But in terms of love, he was as much a brother to her as anyone could hope for.

"Jerry decided to see if he could locate any records for a Virginian runaway slave named George Henry, the one name from Mama's side of the family we had. I thought it was a great idea at the time. I could never have imagined how wrong I was." Roz was on the verge of another spasm of weeping but this time she fought it down. "It took a while — more than a year — but he came up with something in Montross, the County Seat of Westmoreland County, where some of the early Virginia plantations were located. Many of their records were kept at the old courthouse. There was a record of the planta-tion owner who had held him in bondage — someone named

Samuel Tucker — and a bill advertising a reward for his recapture. Eventually, Jerry found a bill of sale after his recapture in 1839, when George Henry was sold, along with a young woman named Chrissie, to a plantation in Texas." Roz's voice was taking on more of its normal tone now that she was immersed in one of her stories about Black history, though this time, it was about recovering the lost history of her own family.

"Good for Jerry. That's great that he was able to find something definitive about your family's story."

She drew back from where her head had been resting on my shoulder and looked at me with such a mix of emotions that I didn't know how to interpret them. "No, Maddie, not good for Jerry. I wish to God he had never uncovered this story because it led to Mama feeling she finally had to reveal things that maybe were better left unsaid." Then she changed tack. "I don't think I ever told you what Mama's maiden name was, the name she was born with."

I shook my head, confirming this. As far as I could recall, it had never come up.

"It was Grace Harton. So of course, Jerry and I did some investigating of phone books and such over the years to see if there were any other Hartons in Houston. No luck. When Jerry was an undergrad, he went to some courthouses around here looking through plantation records, hoping to find a slave-owning family named Harton. He tried Hinton, Hartson, all kinds of that name, but he never found anything related to the purchase of a slave named George Henry. But after Jerry found the Virginia records, he realized that a letter had somehow gone missing from my mother's records. And when I questioned her about this yesterday, she said probably her people changed their name after the war, as so many Black families did. She knew her great-grandmother, who was born right after the war and lived until she was eighty-five. She used Harton, so that was the first generation to use the new name."

The historian in me started to feel the pit of my stomach drop. Then Roz confirmed it.

"On the bill of sale," Roz said, very slowly and deliberately, "it said that George Henry, a stable groom, age twenty-six, and a house slave named Chrissie, age twenty-one, of Tucker Manor, Tucker, Virginia, were sold for fifteen hundred dollars for the two of them to Jonathan Wharton, of Wharton Hall, Texas on September 13, 1839. Wharton, not Harton, was the name Jerry should have been looking for all this time. That would be your colleague's great-great-grandfather, I believe."

"What? What? You're telling me that Johnny Wharton's family owned *your* family?"

"Yes, that's right. The Whartons *owned* the Hartons, my mother's people. Who were no doubt also called Whartons until after the war."

"But," I said, valiantly trying to put a positive spin on all this mess, "you showed the Whartons — their former slaves' descendant has a PhD in epidemiology and is a tenured university professor. That's something to be proud of, Roz."

But Roz just sighed. "The first Johnny Wharton kept excellent records of the genealogy of the nearly one hundred slaves he kept in bondage, mostly to pick cotton. Jerry found the records at the Wharton County Courthouse. Remember that importing new slaves had been outlawed for thirty years prior to when the first Johnny Wharton started his plantation in Texas. So, they had to breed their own," Roz said with bitterness. "George Henry and Chrissie were apparently a breeding pair. Whether they cared for each other at all, or the master just thought they had good genes for his purposes, isn't known. They first had a son but under the name for their first daughter, Fanny, born in 1841, the descriptor said mulatto. You know what that means, huh, lady historian?"

"Yeah. It means Chrissie was raped, probably, by the first Johnny Wharton." After this many years of Roz's tutoring, I knew I was still grossly ignorant of the history of the "peculiar institution," but not that ignorant.

"Fanny had a daughter when she was fifteen. The girl's name was Addy, and she was also listed as mulatto. Now maybe that's just because Fanny was half white, but it could also mean ..."

"That Fanny was raped by him too when she was just a kid. Wow, that is terrible. What an awful history Jerry uncovered. I can see why ..."

"Shut up, Maddie," Roz said, but she said it with some fondness and familiarity in her voice. "I'm not done yet and I have to tell this now or I don't know if I will ever be able to."

I shut up and took Roz's hand in my mine. She didn't resist.

"After the war and Juneteenth, the people at the Wharton plantation, including my ancestors, mostly stayed on as sharecroppers. This is what Mama told me and she got it from her great-grandmother, Betty, who was Addy's daughter. Mama and Betty lived in the same house when Mama was a girl. The Whartons still owned all that land and grew all that cotton, so not much changed except that my folks were technically employees now, instead of slaves. Mostly, what changed is that there were no more records. That just stops after 1865."

"But sharecropping ends around ..." I butted in before realizing I was interrupting again.

"For us Hartons, sharecropping ended sometime in the 1920s. Mama was a bit hazy on this point, but she said her own mama Daisy told her they left the plantation when my grandmother was fifteen or sixteen. She was born in 1910, so the mid-twenties, I guess. But some cousins stayed on as the Whartons still needed servants and gardeners and such for the "big house,"'" she said, putting sarcastic air quotes around the old term for the plantation house.

"There was a cousin, Patty, who was just a year older than my mama and, when they could afford to, Mama's family and cousin Patty's family used to get together because their mothers, Suzy and Daisy, were close. Mama told me when she was a girl, she used to go stay with Patty's mama and daddy out in the cottages behind the Wharton mansion as a sort of summer vacation. There was another family too, and their son, Elton, who was also close to Patty and Mama in age. The three of them played together a lot in the summer on the old Wharton estate when they were kids. Patty's daddy was the stable man for the Whartons.

"So, one early evening on one of these summer visits, when my mama, Grace, was fourteen years old, one of the mares was giving birth and everyone was out in the barn to see. Grace had taken a break from the excitement because she had to use the outhouse. On her way back to the barn, she was intercepted by your Johnny Wharton, who asked her to come help him get some cloths and such to use for the foal's birth. She'd never been in the big house — all those years of going to visit and never once. Mama said she was eager to help because she wanted to see what the big house was like inside. But once she got inside the back door, which wasn't visible from the barn or the cottages, there was Old Mr. Wharton — Old Johnny, as he was called — the grandfather, who was around fifty then, and he said, 'Very nicely done, Young Johnny,' and then he grabbed Grace, who was just a girl — she'd only had her period twice and she was a puny thing, skinny as a rail, and tossed her into the bedroom and onto a bed nearest the back door. He held her there, then he handed her off to Young Johnny and he said, 'She's all yours. A right proper pickaninny, for your big day.' They were of an age, Grace, and Johnny — both fourteen, but Johnny probably outweighed her by fifty pounds. Johnny the younger, my mama said, held her wrists over her head in one hand and pinned her down with the other. 'Keep still! If you scream, you die, and all your Negro relations will be out on the street,' my mama told me he said. Only he didn't use the word Negro — he used the other word. Grace, my mama, had almost no idea about sex, she told me, the day before yesterday. And then he ..." Here Roz stopped still as death, like there was no breath left in her. Then she started again. "He pushed up her dress and slip, ripped off her panties and ..." Roz struggled to continue, "... raped her, while Old Johnny watched and egged him on from the doorway. When Johnny finally got off her, my mama distinctly remembers Old Johnny said, 'Congratulations, Young Johnny. Welcome to the club.'"

"Maddie." Roz looked at me with so much pain in her face that it was hard not to look away, hard not to caress her tear-stained face, hard not to grab her and hold her and somehow save her from this awful news. "When Mama told me this, and towards the end, her voice got flat and monotone like she was reciting a scene from someone else's life, I could not believe it, I could not accept it. I started screaming at her, something I had never done in all thirty-three years of my life. Screaming at my mama, my mama who had to take the bus back to Houston by herself after what happened to her; my mama, who was so ashamed that she ran away from home when her belly started to show; my mama, who had to go beg for help from the minister of her church; my mama, who had to give birth to me with no kin to help her; my mama, who had to raise me in the back of a diner owned by the minister's cousin while she worked every day to feed me and pay for that tiny shack of a room attached to the back of the diner that we lived in. That's the woman I screamed at. And all I could scream at her was, 'Who's my daddy, Mama? Who's my daddy?'

"My mama just sat in her wheelchair shaking and sobbing.

'I never wanted you to know, Rosalyn,' she said, real quiet when I finally stopped screaming. 'But your daddy is Professor Johnny Wharton who works up at the college, same as you.'"

I looked at Roz, my beautiful love, my only love, the love of my life and there was simply nothing I could say, nothing I could do to take this pain away. So, I just told her the only thing I knew to be the truth. "I love you, Roz," I said quietly, as tears rolled fast and heavy down my own cheeks.

"That isn't even all of it," she continued, as if she hadn't heard me. "Not only am I the product of the abominable actions of a son of the planter class, but I am also the product of generations of rape by the men of that same vile family. My foremothers, at least twice over and maybe more, were raped by the forefathers of my ... fa ..." she couldn't spit out the word, "my mother's rapist. Like Fanny and Addy before me, I, too, am a *mulatto*," Roz said with anguish in her voice, "in the fullest meaning of that word in this misbegotten culture. It's rape and incest, incest and rape for almost 150 years, we Whartons and Hartons. How could you possibly love a creature like me?"

CHAPTER 37

MADISON, WISCONSIN

DECEMBER 1985

JENNY

I came out of my reverie as I climbed the ugly stairs that led to Sunprint Gallery. I opened the door and there they were, Lena and Chuck, sitting together at a round, glass-topped table by the window, waiting for me. My heart skipped a beat when I saw them both together like that. For a stupid second, I wondered if they were having an affair, if that was the big news. Right. Lena was in love with Harry, and Chuck had mentioned that emotion in relation to me. Besides, would they be sitting there smiling and waving me over only to tell me they were lovers? Sometimes, I thought the craziest things. But what the hell did they want to tell me, the two of them together?

I walked over, pretending nonchalance. "Hi guys, what 'cha eating?" I looked over their food and decided to get something to eat myself. "Be back in a minute." I walked over to the counter to place my order. The Sunprint was a simple place, with gray carpeting, black wrought iron tables topped by glass, and matching chairs with spring green cushions, where you could while away the hours without getting harassed by the waitresses. They had great desserts, a half-dozen kinds of coffee, plus salads and sandwiches. My kind of place. After mulling over the coffee list, I decided on a cup of Viennese and a slice of flourless chocolate cake. On the way back to the table, I paused to check out the black-and-white photograph display on the interior wall, which featured trees in winter landscapes.

Lena and Chuck were almost jumping out of their chairs in anticipation, but I made small talk until the waitress brought me my food.

"Okay," I said, savoring the taste of the coffee, "what's up?"

"We got some news last night and Chuck and I couldn't decide which one of us should tell you, so we decided to do it together," Lena started. "The whole band was at Harry's last night practicing when the phone rang. It was Robert — oh, I forgot, you don't know him, do you? He's the guitarist that used to play with Harry, Rupert, and Jimmy way back when, before Chuck joined the band."

"I mentioned him before to you," Chuck broke in, and I nodded.

"He's the guy who moved to Atlanta, right?" I asked.

"Yeah, that's right," Lena continued. "Fred replaced him in the band. Anyway, Robert called from Atlanta last night. He and Harry had been working on something without letting the rest of us know, and last night, it finally came through."

"You tell her, Chuck," Lena stopped, beaming from ear to ear.

"Robert was working some pretty regular gigs at this nightclub in Atlanta that's the hottest thing for the integrated yuppie crowd down there," Chuck picked up the story. "They have live jazz four nights a week. It's become the in thing to be seen there so the place is jammed and the pay is good. Robert decided to take matters into his own hands and asked Harry to send him a tape of our recent stuff. He finally got to play it for the Black dude who owns the place and he really liked it. We've got a decent repertoire and can do one night of classics and another of modern stuff, so the guy thought we'd be flexible for his nightclub. Plus, he likes Robert a lot and respects his taste in music. So last night the decision came down. He signed us on for a three-night-a-week gig for two whole months!"

"Chuck, you didn't even tell her the best part. The club owner just started up a small record company, and Robert says, if things work out the way he's planned, we'll be doing a demo before the month is out. If he likes it, we'll sign on with his label and make ourselves an album!"

"Wow, that's great! I can't believe it. I'll know big recording artists soon. Can I have your autograph?" I teased and offered them my napkin. "No really, it couldn't have happened to a better band. When do you leave?" I was still calm. The news hadn't registered yet.

"Well, that's the catch," Chuck said in a more serious tone. "The guy wants us there for this Friday's show."

"What? It's Monday already. How could you possibly arrange everything, get off work — and Lena, it's the last week of classes! What are you going to do about finals?" I couldn't believe what I was hearing.

"I raced around to all my professors today and sweet-talked them into giving me incompletes or a take-home test. As it turned out, one of them said I could just skip the final as I was getting an A anyway, and Peterson in Linguistics is letting me do a take-home exam. Two are letting me do papers instead, so I only have one exam to make up when I get back up here."

"What about you, Chuck? What's Dave going to say?" Besides being a graduate student, Chuck worked as a car mechanic at Dave's Garage on the West Side.

"He said he'd try and keep a place open for me if I could let him know in a month or so whether I'm coming back or not. So that worked out. And my three classes are all over but the final projects. One is done and my other two can be finished up on the nights we don't play and put in the mail. So, I'm good. Since Harry, Rupert and I are all in the music department, all the professors know what's up. They're excited for us."

"How are you getting there?" I asked woodenly. The news and its implications for me were beginning to sink in.

"Some of us are going to drive in Rupert's van," Chuck said. "And we've rented a small truck from U-Haul to get all the equipment down there. It was unbelievable how fast everything came together. Ginny's staying up here to run the dry cleaning store, and Rupert's mom is going to help out with the store and their kid, Sammy." I already knew that Jimmy and Rupert had taken over an old dry cleaning store on the South Side from Jimmy's uncle, who had barely survived a heart attack. The two friends had turned it into a thriving dry cleaning and laundry business. "And Fred can work from anywhere." Fred, as I also knew, was a computer programmer and mostly worked freelance, debugging huge reams of programming text. "The professor he works for has gotten his friend at Emory to give him some mainframe time, in case he has to check to see if what he fixed works. It all worked out without too many hassles," Chuck concluded.

"And Jen," Lena broke in, "I hope my favorite fan is going to come down for at least some of my shows."

"Who, me? How exactly am I supposed to get to Atlanta? Some people have finals to take and can't pick up and go cruising whenever they feel like it." I tried to keep my voice light and humorous without much success. I was getting bummed about this.

"That's easy. You're going in Nick's car," Chuck told me authoritatively.

"That old beater of his is never going to make it all the way to Atlanta. And even if he's fool enough to try to drive it there in the middle of winter, I'm not dumb enough to go along. You're not going to catch me hitching on the interstate in December when the thing breaks down."

"Listen to Miz Negativity, here," Lena chided me. "Nope, she ain't going even if it's in a Cadillac, nope, she ain't going. No how, no way. She made up her mind already, Chuck." Lena put on one of her thick accents.

"Well then, I guess we shouldn't bother telling her that Nick is driving his parents' six-month-old Oldsmobile with brand new radials down to their winter home in Sarasota a few days before Christmas. He's agreed to make a special stop in Atlanta just to drop off our fair lady friend here." Chuck looked at Lena in mock seriousness.

"Naw, she has her mind made up. Guess she just doesn't want to be there to see her friends make the big time." Lena pointedly ignored me, adjusting her chair so that her back was to me. "We might as well say goodbye right now then, huh, Chuck?"

"Okay, okay," I cut in, trying to keep a disdainful look on my face. "If it's a chauffeured ride in a new car, I *may* consider it." Then I broke into a grin. "You mean it? Nick's really driving down there and I'm going with him?"

"We wanted to be sure there was someone in the audience applauding," Chuck said. "This is not a free ride, you know. We're not offering a vacation here. You're our groupie and you better act like one. In fact, if you want to tear off my shirt or anything, go right ahead." He offered me an arm and we all laughed.

I was going to Atlanta. The Novocain-like feeling that had been creeping up my arms toward my heart was inching its way back towards my fingertips. They hadn't forgotten about me in all their planning and excitement. These people cared about me enough to want me there with them when they got their big break. It was hard to wrap my head around that idea.

"You guys, this is great. You're fantastic, you know that?" I felt my voice getting quavery. There were, amazingly, tears coming to the corners of my eyes.

Lena and Chuck looked at me and then at each other.

"Yeah, we know," they said in unison, and we all broke up laughing.

"Shit, look at the time," Chuck said a few minutes later as we were talking about Atlanta and the good times we'd have there.

"I got tons to crate up yet to get this show on the road. I got to get over to Harry's and start getting the equipment together." He threw a ten on the table. "Settle the bill with that, will you ladies? Listen, Jen, I'll call you when I'm done and come pick you up. Okay?" I nodded, and he gave me a swift peck on the lips. "See ya later," he said as he turned and flipped his blue wool scarf over his shoulder and headed for the door.

I stared after him in a daze of conflicting emotions. Lena noticed my blank look and patted my arm.

"What a difference a day makes!" she quoted the old song. "We're all blown away by it. It's great, but scary too ..." She paused and followed my gaze out the window to where I could see Chuck crossing the street below.

"Kinda like you and Chuck." I glanced over at her appreciatively. Lena knew, without needing all the details, how it was for me. I loved her for that.

"Come on, Lena, I'll help you pack." I got up.

Snow was falling thick and fast, covering our jackets in a

numbing white blanket. So white and sparkling, so peaceful it looked, falling straight down on the bundled-up pedestrians, the streets trimmed with Christmas decorations, the craggy old Red Gym and Union buildings as we made our way back to campus. It all seemed so nice, like one of those paperweights you shake and watch the snow fall inside the glass bubble. Impossible to believe this same stuff could bury a person in an avalanche, make them snow blind, freeze them to death. Right now, it looked so perfect, so innocent. But I knew better than anyone how looks could be deceiving.

I shivered and ran a little to catch up with Lena's long strides. Then I just listened while she told me about the great time we'd have in Atlanta.

CHAPTER 38

PINE HILL STATION, TEXAS

DECEMBER 1985

LIZ

It took me a full minute to realize *she'd* done it. The envelope I'd sent to Jenny with a birthday card and a fifty-dollar check was there among the other pieces of mail. The address had been crossed out in red and an arrow pointing to my return address label indicated that the envelope was to be sent back here. But the words had thrown me, bold letters in red ink — "DECEASED, RETURN TO SENDER." My hands started to shake, and I sank weak-kneed into my desk chair, staring at the thing in shock for at least a minute before I realized what was so odd about it. The words had been written by "the deceased" herself. Once I had stopped shaking and examined the envelope, it was easy enough to recognize my daughter's distinctive script. And in red, the only color I'd seen Jenny write in since eighth grade. I'd taken a gamble that she was living in the same dormitory as her freshman year — Elizabeth

Waters — and sent the card there. So, she was still living there, apparently, and still very much alive.

The returned envelope seemed a premonition. My gut feeling that Jenny was in trouble was probably a perverse illusion — I wanted more than anything for Jenny to need me. If she was in trouble — and there was no proof of that at all, only my recurring nightmare about her calling out from the fog — she'd turn to her friends up there or Old Johnny, or maybe a perfect stranger before she'd turn to me or her father. That was the reality of it. Yet this morbid feeling that the letter was a warning would not leave me.

The envelope had been carefully opened and resealed. The card was still there completely untouched, with its ignored message of love and birthday wishes and offers of a beach Christmas vacation in Florida. The check, though, had been torn into little pieces and returned to the card. "I don't need you or your money either" might as well have been written out. It was plain enough. She did need us though. The University of Wisconsin-Madison was on the list of colleges that took college professors' children tuition-free, and we'd had to certify that Jenny was Johnny's child with UW-Madison each year to get that benefit. We'd also come up with a plan for paying for her room and board. Old Johnny had said he was paying, a gift that Jenny could accept. Johnny always paid his grandfather in advance for those dormitory fees. The only clues that our daughter was indeed alive, pretty much since she'd left a year-and-a-half ago now, were two terse, mass produced bills for room and board sent by the university at the end of August with her name on them, that one postcard last year, and now, this. Of the rest of her life in the cold Midwest, we knew nothing. Not what her course of study was, who she lived with, if she had friends, a job, what she did with her leisure time.

After he'd given Old Johnny the room and board check this

past August, Johnny had angrily justified sending her no spending money. "I know that girl. She'll want her nice clothes, her good times out, maybe even a car. The way I figure it, if I don't send her enough to live on, she'll have to go out and get a job. Teach her a bit of responsibility. She might learn to respect adults. Maybe the little ingrate will even learn not to bite the hand that feeds her. Sometimes, Liz, I want to cut her off completely, show her what can happen to unappreciative kids who want, want, want but give nothing, nothing in return." At this point, Johnny had almost been sobbing. He had choked it back and left the room for a few minutes. When he'd returned, he'd pointedly changed the subject.

I understood how he felt. It was hard to keep trying, hard to keep giving when silence and insults were your only rewards. It was hard to keep caring, a shameful thing to admit about your own flesh and blood, your only daughter, your only child. But when Johnny's sorrow could be heard in his voice, or times like this, when Jenny's contempt for me was written in red on a birthday card envelope, I found myself wishing I had had a son instead — or no children at all.

It was no wonder that women prayed for sons. Daughters were bound to be disappointments to their mothers, weren't they? I had been one to my mother, by marrying a man who wasn't wealthy, by working full time, by having only one child, and by making a mess of that. When Jenny started turning against me, my relationship with my mother disintegrated into long arguments over the phone filled with "I told you so's." I'd hang up filled with shame at my inadequacies as a mother, which my own felt it was her duty to remind me of, and frustration with my inability to ask her, "Mother, I'm at the end of my rope, won't you help me? Won't you be on my side?"

We'd managed an unspoken reconciliation since Jenny left, making mention of her a taboo subject in our monthly phone calls and infrequent visits. But I imagine I can hear the disappointment in her voice, feel the silent disapproval in her gaze, each time we speak or meet. It seems a legacy, this disappointment passed along from mother to daughter. Despite my guilt, I know my estrangement from Jenny is not all my doing. It is her fault also that she can't explain to me why she feels such animosity towards me, why she can't sit down with me and talk things out. I am disappointed in her immaturity, her aloofness, her silence, how she hurts Johnny. How she's destroyed this family. The list of the ways Jenny has disappointed me is endless.

Oh, it works both ways, for a time. The daughter is also disappointed in her mother, as she gains sophistication enough to see that her mother is only human after all. Perhaps she's not pretty enough, or has a harsh voice, is too fat, doesn't treat her husband the way the daughter thinks the man of the house should be treated. But we outgrow this period, we daughters do, when we become wives and mothers ourselves and realize how impossible it is to live up to the myths. We forgive our mothers for their humanness, don't we? But it is not so easy to forgive your daughter, your creation, a creation you hoped had somehow escaped the inadequacies that you yourself were burdened with. Does a mother ever really forgive her daughter for her flaws, some of them bearing an uncanny resemblance to her own? My mother hasn't forgiven mine, not yet, and I'm nearly fifty now, and she, seventy. Will I ever be able to forgive Jenny her flaws, let her be the merely human person she is and love her all the same? I'd like to think I could rise above all that and love Jenny unreservedly, a true mother's love. But I wonder.

Don't I half hate her for merely existing, for making me feel so inadequate, such a failure as a mother? It's hard to say just what I feel for Jenny. I'm not sure who she is anymore. A fading high school picture on the mantle? Fond memories of childhood birthday parties and mother-daughter dresses for the holidays?

One memory that sticks in my craw all these years later is the night when I came home exhausted from the evening tax preparation job that I had taken on that spring Jenny was in eighth grade. It was 10:00 p.m. and I had entered the kitchen just as Jenny was leaving it. "Hi kiddo, how'd your homework go tonight?" I asked.

She wheeled on me. "Oh, my *homework* is going really *well*, Mother. Just like you and Daddy planned." Her voice was dripping with sarcasm, even hate.

"What are you talking about, Jenny?" I said, completely surprised by this venom. "And do not use that tone with me," I stupidly, so stupidly added.

But Jenny was done with me, done with me maybe forever, as it has turned out. "Fine. That's it. You are dead to me, Mother." She turned on her heel, climbed the stairs, stomped down the hall and slammed her room door. It was about the last conversation we ever had. She had Johnny take her to the doctor or shopping or all the other places a mother might have taken her only daughter. When absolutely necessary, she talked to me as if I were a stranger. But mostly, she just gave me drop dead looks and left my presence as soon as she could. She took her meals in her room. And eventually, I gave up. I must admit that. I decided to pour my rejected mother's love into foundling mutts at the dog shelter.

I have no idea who my daughter is. I am clinging to memories of her childhood and to hope; all my feelings for Jenny are based on those two ephemeral elements. Not much to sustain love on, not when the feelings are mixed up with resentment, anger, and disappointment. Still, I glance wistfully at the few words on this returned envelope, hoping for a clue to my daughter's life, wishing for a letter in her bold red writing. For the hundredth time, I wondered why I never found the courage to grab her by the shoulders and demand she talk to me, tell me why she turned on me, and later, Johnny. Did I fear I couldn't take her truths about me? I wonder what I'd say to her now if I had the chance to see her, just us two, face to face. Would I have the guts to beg forgiveness, to ask her to give me a second chance to be a better mother to her? Would I be able to ask her what she needed from me and give her that unreservedly, not letting my own fractured ego interfere? Would I be able to say, I love you, Jenny, my beautiful daughter, my first and only child? Would I?

Or would I let my anger surface, hurl accusations, force her to see the damage she's done to this family? Hurt her like she's hurt Johnny and me? Blame her for this awful estrangement and try to salvage what scraps of self-respect I could? Blame her, so the guilt for this private tragedy wouldn't lie on my conscience alone? Make her feel the pain that I've been holding at bay all these years? Pain, that I fear, in my darker moments, would destroy me if I let it in.

More likely, I'd be cold. Frozen like an ice carving, unable to react with more than a distant politeness. Like a stranger, like the strangers we've become to one another. A protection. If I don't acknowledge her feelings, I can save myself from the pain of mine. I could end all hope with my frozenness. It would be that cold lack of emotion that would infuriate Jenny the most, confirm her convictions about me, a cold-hearted, uncaring woman who never should have had children, let alone a sensitive girl like Jenny. It would be the way to end this wondering, this half hoping, half fearing of a future confrontation with her. It would be so simple, so much in character for me, so easy. I'm horrified at the thought that I might just freeze up and be unable to express anything toward my daughter, and thus lose her for good. But it scares me worse when I acknowledge how tempting it would be to let the iceberg between us grow into an unstoppable glacier.

Almost as if they were disembodied, I watched my hands rip the card and envelope in two and throw the pieces into the waste basket. But I retrieved them instantly and went into the living room, grabbing my lighter as I ran. I threw the remnants of the card into the cold, unused hearth. Then I lit them with my lighter and watched them burn, the red-hot ashes drifting up the chimney into the night.

CHAPTER 39

MADISON, WISCONSIN

DECEMBER 1985

JENNY

It was as if they had evaporated, Chuck, Lena, and the rest of them. Gone. Gone to some vapory place in the back of my mind where dreams are kept. Only a few days after they'd left it had already seemed doubtful that they'd ever existed at all. It was easy for me to imagine I'd invented them — Jenny with friends, a boyfriend, and all those good times we had had. That I'd experienced any of it seemed laughable now. Most pitiful of all was the realization that my recent past, which in my mind closely resembled paradise, was everyone else's idea of normal, everyday life. But to me, normalcy was a dream I'd half grasped for a couple of months. Now it had receded to the realm of the impossible.

The vestiges of my old life reappeared with no problem at all. I had gotten to the point of making excuses to Al, the doughy pharmacist, those last few weeks with Chuck. I knew

I was treading dangerous waters when I'd pleaded illness to Al a couple of weeks running, and then finals, and begged out of seeing him. But with Chuck there, it had even seemed possible to live life without downers. Of course, I hadn't gotten around to trying that yet, but I was cutting back. The supply Al had given me the last time I'd seen him was lasting longer than it had in quite some time. I'd begun to feel bad about holding out on Chuck about something so major, the drugs, and what I'd done to get them. I couldn't face the idea of telling him, but figured, if at least I quit doing it, I wouldn't feel so bad about not telling him. I'd let my "job" at the Esquire Inn slide too, and just showed up sporadically when I was broke or had to get some pills to Lou. The way things had been going, I would have been done with the Esquire Inn in no time.

But all those noble dreams went up in smoke just like Chuck and Lena. I found myself taking more Valiums, more often, so I wouldn't think about them or the recent past so much. I told myself it was temporary, but I got used to taking a fairly scary number a day and couldn't seem to hold off when I wanted to. So, of course, I went back to Al's pronto, rolling around in that lumpy bed he kept in his storeroom so I could snag a nice allotment of those little yellow pills. With nothing better to do with my evenings, cruising the Esquire for some easy money also came right back into my repertoire. At first, I kidded myself into thinking I was just trying to get some money together for when Nick and I drove down to Atlanta. But that was a crock, and I couldn't fool myself into believing it for long. The old pent-up feeling of desire mixed inextricably with shame came back stronger than ever after Chuck no longer was caressing my body. That perverse urge became one of the few feelings that managed to fight its way through the thick Valium fog I had started living in again. So, I dug my sleazy "work" dresses out of the back of the closet and sought out seedy relations with the ever-abundant supply of traveling businessmen that passed through the Esquire Inn. Lou was still there of course, tending bar just as he always had. Somehow, my mind had telescoped my short interlude in the Eden of Chuck and Lena's company and made it seem years instead of the paltry weeks it had actually been. It seemed odd that nothing at the hotel or anything else in the world of my past had changed. It was all part of the time warp I'd been in to think that things should have changed. But one thing had, I noticed, when my old life rose back up to meet me. Me.

It was like being let out of prison for a few days when you'd spent most of your life there. Now, when the walls closed in around you again, you realized you had changed. I was no longer coasting, not really satisfied, never happy, but then, not expecting to be. Before, I'd had no expectations, no experiences of what life could be like to compare mine to. Oh sure, I knew how the rest of the world lived, with families, friends, good times surrounding them, but their lives weren't applicable to mine. I was tarnished, different. I knew those things were beyond my reach. My short life as an independent adult hadn't been happy, fun, or even very satisfying, but I hadn't expected it to be. I hadn't thought about wanting more than I'd had. More. That was for other people. But now, through some cruel stroke of fate or ill luck, I'd experienced how people lived on the other side of the hazy but irrevocably real barrier that existed between me and the normal world. Worse, I'd seen how I could live there permanently. Oh, not the real me, not the honest version of the fatally corrupted Jenny, but a reasonable facsimile, an acted-out Jen that wasn't too different a role to keep up. And what payoffs Jen had gotten me, the real Jenny. Friends, a life, a boyfriend, a crack at the real McCoy — love. Now, in a way neither the acted-out Jen nor the real me underneath could control, the barred doors had swung shut again, trapping us both in the life before. The acted-out Jen, the one who played at being a normal college girl, was fading fast, leaving only me, the forever-flawed Jenny, to pick up the pieces of my old life. The life that was not working, not worth it anymore.

I'd drunk more than normal that night at the Esquire. Usually, I left right after my second john had finished with me that night. (Was it just two weeks since they'd left? It seemed a lifetime.) But this night, I'd come back down to the bar to have a nightcap or two and talk to Lou awhile. I guess I was lonely. No. I was lonely, desperately so, for Chuck, even more for Lena. I couldn't face going back to that half-empty dorm room that didn't seem to have a shred of warmth in it anymore.

So, I sat at the bar and had a couple of gimlets, which was the only drink I ever had with Lou, and made small talk about movies, music, and drugs. Talking to Lou like this used to be the big social event for me. Now it seemed like such a flat substitute for friends and conversation. Ignorance is bliss, I mumbled under my breath. I guess I was getting loaded.

"What did you say?" Lou looked over at me. "Hey, how many of those did I give you? I think you're drunk, kid." He hadn't really given me that many, maybe three, but I'd taken a few Valiums before "work" too and that wasn't helping my control, though it did a hell of a job on my nerves. I felt completely numb and glad of it. "You better get home. It's getting late." Lou helped me on with my coat and walked me to the door. "You can make it to the bus stop okay, can't you? I'd walk you over there, but I can't leave the bar."

"Hey, no problem," I said a bit too loudly. "I'm an independent-type girl. I can get where I'm going all by myself." My tongue seemed a bit thick in my mouth.

"If you're sure you can make it ..."

"Bye, Lou." I gave him a peck on the cheek, something I'd never done before. Then I pulled open the heavy wooden door and let myself out into the frigid December night.

I tried to wrap my red wool scarf around my neck. The cold was really getting to me, even with the insulating effects of the booze. Fortunately, at that time of night, there wasn't much traffic cuz I sure didn't pay any attention to it as I made my unsteady way across the street. I was concentrating on holding on to my scarf, which was flapping behind me like some live thing.

I waited at the bus stop a few minutes in the biting cold before I heard the familiar rumble of the West Towne bus. I shoved some change into the slot and sat down in the front of the nearly empty bus, hoping I didn't look as wasted as I felt. Oh, what the hell, who cared how I looked anyways?

I must have dozed off because the next thing I remember was noticing the bus was turning the corner onto Lake Street. I hit the call button and stumbled down the bus steps into the arctic wind coming from the lake. I made my way past the library and the empty fountain out front over to the Union just in time to catch the last campus bus, which took me practically to my door. It took a couple of minutes of fumbling before I got together the right keys to open the outside door, which was locked after midnight, and the one to the room. It looked dark, foreign, and empty, this room I'd once shared with Lena, and I didn't want to go in. I did, though, and shut the door behind me without turning on any lights. It looked so wrong in the gloom, only the hall light filtering in under the door. Lena's bed was stripped bare, her closet door was open and nothing but a black hole stared back at me. All that was left of Lena was the poster of Lena Horne above the empty bed, mocking me from across the room. I sat down heavily on my own bed.

I don't know how long I sat like that, just staring at that dumb poster that somehow said it all. It made me think of how Lena left me behind to go chase her dream. Lena was done with just looking at her poster, trying to get up the nerve to go out there and get what she wanted. She was there, making it all come true for herself. And I was here, abandoned, my paltry dreams swept away by the force of Lena and Chuck's so much bigger ones. Their dreams were important to them. And how could I compare to the allure of their dreams? I wasn't even in the running, compared to that, in either of their lives. I was merely human, a dubious example of a friend. I had no spellbinding power compared to that of a dream.

It wasn't as though I wanted them to choose me instead of their dream, or even that I felt betrayed because they had left. I knew my place in the pantheon. It's just that their friendship had been my dream. It had proved a dream over which I had no control. They had pulled it out from under me without even realizing what they'd done. It had been a pitiful, insubstantial dream to begin with, a dream both too humble and too illusive. All I'd wanted was to have friends, to be normal. And all I was left with was Lena Horne staring over at me like some wicked fairy godmother who made everyone else's dreams come true. Like mine had been worthy only of contempt.

I was so lost in these morbid midnight thoughts, the phone ringing in the middle of the night didn't even surprise me. I answered it automatically like I expected it to be for Lena, how it always had been.

"Jen, it's Nick," Nick was talking loudly above the din of the bar crowd. "Sorry to call so late but I couldn't get away to call you until now. This place has been crazy tonight."

"Hi, Nick," I said with false cheerfulness. There was a pause while Nick collected his thoughts.

"I really hate to tell you this, but the deal about driving to Atlanta in my folks' car has fallen through. They've been waiting all this time to go down for the winter because my aunt, my dad's sister, has been sick and they're both real close to her. They found out she has cancer now. They've decided to stay up in Wisconsin this winter so they can be with her. They won't need the car down there and they do need it up here. So, we don't have wheels."

"I'm sorry about your aunt, Nick," I said, automatically turning on my Southern sense of manners.

"Thanks. I'm real sorry about this. I know how much you wanted to go — hell, I did too. Chuck's my best buddy. I wanted to see him make it big." Nick paused, waiting for me to say something, but I couldn't think of anything to say.

"I've been wracking my brains, trying to think of another way to get there, but short of hitching, I can't come up with anything I can afford. But Jen, maybe you could fly down."

"Nah, I don't think so. I don't have that kind of money, either." I lied. Probably, I did. Or I could get it in a few nights on my back.

"Well, listen, I'm going up to my folks' for the holidays and you're welcome to come with me if you don't have any other plans."

"Thanks. That's real nice of you to ask me." I had put myself on automatic now. "But I think I'll call my folks up and see if they'll send me some dough to go down and spend the holidays with them. No way would they send me money to go to Atlanta. They're very strict about that sort of thing," I improvised as I went along. "But they'll probably send me money to come and see them. So, I'll spend Christmas in Texas this year." I tried to sound bright and cheery, like that wasn't such a bad alternative to spending the holidays with Chuck and Lena. In reality, home to Texas is the last place on the globe I'd go. "Really, it's all right. Don't feel bad. It's not your fault. It's just one of those things." My Southern accent was taking over. "Now you wish your aunt well for me and don't feel bad about it. After all, they'll be back in just a couple of weeks." I was really laying it on thick now.

"Thanks Jen, you're being a real sport about this," Nick said gratefully. "When I get back from up North, we'll all get together over at my place and hear the whole story of the band's adventure, okay?"

"Sounds great. Have yourself a Merry Christmas and best wishes for the same to your whole family. Bye now." I hung up before adding y'all to my passel of lies, the fake belle smile that went with the words sliding off my face as I put the phone back on the hook.

It hadn't surprised me, finding out we weren't going. I had never really expected to. When Chuck and Lena had said goodbye that early Wednesday morning, I hadn't expected to ever see them again. This call was just reality confirming my intuition.

Chuck and Lena were gone from my life like they had never been there at all. I got up in the near dark, just a slice of hall light entering from under the door. I shrugged off my clothes and let them drop to the floor and put on the long T-shirt I wore to bed. All the while, these stupid memories of the things we'd done together, Lena and me, me and Chuck, kept going through my brain like some jump-cut MTV song you can't turn off. I saw the whole gang of us sitting at the bar where the band played, talking, and laughing after the night's show. Me and Lena decorating our room for Halloween with tacky pumpkins and black cats we'd drawn and cut out of construction paper like little kids. I saw Chuck and me renting a canoe out on Lake Mendota on one of the last good days of autumn, him improvising the words to Hiawatha while he paddled, both of us giggling. On and on, the scenes raced through my head, and I couldn't get them out. All memories now. All gone forever. I got up to take a couple of Valiums to try and make these thoughts fade away. I poured a glass of water from the jug we kept in our small refrigerator and opened the plastic bottle that held this week's supply from Al. I poured out a couple and swallowed them with a mouthful of water. Then I just stared at the bottle, my one reliable friend through all of this. "Through thick and thin," I toasted myself and the pill bottle, and poured out a small handful, maybe ten, maybe fifteen, I couldn't really see too well. Maybe some of the Percocets that I hadn't passed on to Lou yet were mixed with them. In the dark, I couldn't really tell. I swallowed them ceremoniously. I looked over at Lena's side of the room. Dammit, Lena Horne kept staring down at me, this contemptible look on her face, making fun of me, Jenny, the abandoned fraud. Without a thought, I hurled the glass over at her and watched as it crashed in slow motion against her face on the wall. Things were beginning to get a bit out of proportion, so I sat down on my bed, or maybe I laid down. I don't know if I was there for one minute or fifteen. The room swirled around me, mixed together with images of Chuck and Lena, Nick, the other band members, the grotesque faces of the innumerable johns I had allowed to fuck me at the Esquire, all melded together. And the huge face of Lena Horne, looking down from the wall, laughing at me.

All of a sudden, I felt an overwhelming nausea come over me. I knew I was about to vomit, something I hate more than just about anything. I sure wasn't going to do it in our room — we didn't even have a sink, and in my half-delirious state, the trash can never occurred to me. No, I had to get to the bathroom. How I got from my bed to the toilet down the hall, I'll never know. In fact, I can't remember anything from that moment until twenty-four hours after I reeled toward the john down the hall from my room.

The next thing I remember is the peculiar smell of rubbing alcohol, mixed with the sour smell of illness. Or was it the odor of death?

CHAPTER 40

PINE HILL STATION, TEXAS

DECEMBER 1985

MADDIE

I took Roz in my arms and held on tight, her head on my chest, my arms enveloping her lovely, trembling Roz body. She didn't resist — I don't think she had the strength to, despite whatever self-loathing she was feeling. With one hand, I petted her rain-softened hair and murmured comforting syllables into the top of her head.

I was stilled with shock. Intellectually, I knew that slave owners had regularly raped the women they held in bondage. I had already assumed that my love was a descendant of such loathsome couplings. But the recent doings of the despicable Wharton family slammed me with an utterly new level of appalling. I worked with the man! I saw Mama's rapist every damn week! In a world where Roz and I could have had the kind of relationship we would have had if we were straight, Johnny Wharton, a vile rapist, would be the biological equivalent of my father-in-law!

Could this be why Roz had ended our relationship? The last words she spoke to me before this evening had been, "You can't change being white." Had she known some of this horrific personal history when she'd said that to me? Now was not the time to ask. Maddie, squash that thought. Roz's quivering was subsiding. She sat up but remained next to me on the sofa. Sam and Frieda appeared out of nowhere. Now that they realized it was Roz who had entered the house, and that Roz was upset, they were rubbing up against her legs and trying to get her to pay attention to them. After a time, she did reach out a tentative hand and petted Frieda's head. Frieda purred loudly and Roz actually smiled at her.

As if in response to my unvoiced speculation, Roz said softly, "That's not why I ran. Not entirely, at least." She leaned her head on my shoulder. "At first, I only knew what Jerry told me, that the Whartons had kept my ancestors in bondage and that George Henry probably wasn't our blood relation. It was Chrissie, the woman sold with him who was our foremother and that the first Johnny Wharton — there have been five of them — probably was the father of Fanny and maybe of Addy too. It wasn't hard to verify, given that they had the exact same name, that the man you worked with was a direct descendant of that first one. Part of me thought it would be unfair to you to tell you about my real family history given you had to work with a Wharton. But that was only part." Roz turned to look at me with her sad and swollen face. "The other part of me felt you wouldn't, you couldn't understand. Being white and all. Your people coming here as regular immigrants. How could you know what it felt like to find out you were the product of multiple rapes? I already knew that, of course. Because of this." Roz pointed to her arm and its coloring, which was several shades lighter than her African ancestors probably had been. "But still, suspecting it, and seeing the evidence in writing, in black and white, as it were," Roz made what was supposed to be an ironic smile, but it came out as a grimace, "was a gut punch. A gut punch that you couldn't understand, and one that would burden you, too. You were right to think that part of why I left was that I didn't want to come out to folks on campus. Hard enough being one of the few Black faculty members without being a dyke, too. So, I ran home to Mama."

Roz looked so sorrowful. My heart melted in my chest when she said, "I mistreated you something awful."

I hugged her to me as tightly as I could. "It's okay," I started to say, but Roz disentangled herself from me.

"No, it is *not* okay," she said forcefully. "I didn't even know the horrific part then. It took me pestering Mama until the day before yesterday to get her to tell me the rest of my sorry story. Why couldn't I leave well enough alone? I could have wound up with this coloring with only the Fanny and Addy part of the story." She looked at me hopelessly. "And then, when I find out the worst possible thing about me, about the hideous criminal you work with, what do I do? I come running here for comfort and burden you with all these specters of my past. It is unconscionable. It is not your water to carry. It is mine, and Mama's, of course." The tears were seeping from Roz's eyes again and I reached over and gave her the box of Kleenex for her nose.

Then I took her by the shoulders and gently put a hand under her chin and encouraged it upward, so she'd be forced to look at me. "You're right. It is probably not possible for me to understand your history the way you do. You feel it. It's in you. It *is* you. But that doesn't mean I can't love you, can't respect you all the more because you have to struggle with this awful news. Couldn't that help more than hurt?" I could hear the desperate desire in my voice, but could do nothing to change it.

"I thought it would be easier for you and for me if I went away," Roz said miserably, "but when Mama told me what she told me, I thought I might die. I *wanted* to die. And maybe this is selfish of me, Maddie, but I didn't want to die without seeing your face one more time," Roz said between sobs. Then she took a couple of deep breaths and spoke again.

"My mama and daddy raised me to respect myself, to be confident in my God-given talents, and to use them to better my people by doing something useful. And up until recently, I was living up to their expectations for me. A PhD in a useful field. My research. My book. Tenure. My teaching. But this news made me feel repulsive to myself. Like I was a poster child for all the evil that my people have suffered since we were brought here. This is my history, Maddie, my story, and I don't want to live it. I don't want to be the walking, talking embodiment of all this vile history. It is too much!"

"Don't you know how proud your family is of you? How proud I am of you? That history, none of it is your fault, Roz. You rose above, that's all that matters. And don't worry about me, I can handle the news. If you want me to, I'll even beat up that Johnny Wharton for you. I never liked him before all this. Now I hate him!" I wasn't sure my little joke would work but Roz must have imagined my 106 pounds flailing uselessly against Johnny's 180 because she smiled a tiny bit, a wan, tired smile, but still ...

"I want to kill him for what he did to Mama. You want to help with that?"

"Whither thou goest ..." At that moment, I meant it.

Roz gave me a squeeze. "If I thought it would make her happy, I would, and never mind the consequences. But she told me she had to find acceptance, find forgiveness even long ago or she couldn't have gone on. And she had to go on, she said, because she had me to raise. Mama made it very, very clear that I needed to follow her example, hard though that might be. 'I didn't go through all my struggles to do right by you, Rosalyn, just to have you go throw it all away for something that's dead and done and needs to be kept that way.' Dead history, she called it. She's a rock, my mama, a rock."

Then she turned to me. "*You* are a tonic, my Maddie, you know that?" She said, and the word "my" perhaps inadvertently inserted into that sentence, thrilled me to the core.

"Mama's got it right. Here's what the white lady historian has to add. History is just a collective memory of events. Yes, they happened, and you can't change that they happened. But you can change what you think about what happened and you can try to tell a more truthful story about what happened. You can try to tell the *whole* story. You taught me that, Roz. *You* did."

"Even if the whole story includes *this*?" She indicated her beautiful Roz body, a body I adored and one whose unsavory origins mattered not at all to me.

"Think of what your mama went through to give life to you and raise you and care for you despite that she knew how you came to be. Think of how she loved you and still loves you. If she can get over the history of your origins, surely you can. You are who you are now, and no new birth story can undo all you have become. No new birth story can undo what you mean to me," I said recklessly.

"You think so?" Her voice was a child's voice full of fear and hope. "You think I can keep going after this? You think *we* can keep going?"

"Please, let's try. As maybe I've mentioned before, you are the love of my life. I don't care who contributed the sperm that made you. I know the people who made you, you, who raised you right and loved you fiercely. They were the ones responsible for the wonderful woman I fell in love with. You, Roz."

I kissed her salty face then, a long, slow kiss that I had

imagined a hundred times since the day she left me. And gradually, Roz kissed me back. But we both knew this new chapter of our lives was just beginning.

CHAPTER 41

HUTTON, IOWA

DECEMBER 1985

JANE

Going home for Christmas had been like surgery to remove a cancerous organ — painful and scary. A patient mourns the body part cut away; it is of the self, even if malignant.

All the bus ride home, I had looked out at the flat, drab landscape of northern Texas, warm rain drizzling against the window, and let my mind's eye see our farmhouse set in the gently rolling cornfields in a grove of fruit and oak trees. I imagined it in winter, white frame house against white snow, the dark squares of windows and black ribbon tree trunks defining the outline of the scene. Half hidden in the brown blanket of oaks that kept their leaves through the winter stood the ramshackle barn, unpainted, rough wood with a few fading streaks of traditional red. The house, Ma made sure, had a fresh coat of paint. It was small for a farmhouse. Upstairs, one large bedroom and a smaller room under the eaves that was my room, a bathroom with an old pedestal sink and matching claw-footed tub. Downstairs, a large kitchen lined with white painted cabinets and aging appliances; the floor's cracked linoleum a pattern I'd known all my life. Faded flowered wallpaper enclosed the small living room, faded green curtains framed the two windows. A wooden staircase, dark with old varnish, led upstairs in one corner of the room and scuffed and scarred narrow oak floorboards, without a rug to hide them, emphasized how old and humble the house was. The potbellied stove in another corner was the house's only heat. Tending it had interrupted my night's sleep on many a winter's night. Both Ma and I are handy with an axe and have the strong arms that go with splitting wood, though. The one improvement made to the house during my lifetime was the installation of a smallish picture window so that Ma could better see the birds who came to the feeder she had hung from a tree branch in front of the house. The window had been a castoff from the neighbor who had bought our farmland. Ma told me installing that window was the only gift he'd given her since they'd wed. A small back porch that faced the corn fields and led into the kitchen was where we stacked firewood in the heating season.

Our family had acquired the farm when it went up for auction at the death of the widow who'd lived there alone and rented out the land for twenty years after her husband's death. Her two grown children had settled comfortably into city life and had wanted no part of the rural Iowa they had hated as children. The deal had included the house, barn, and chicken coop, eighty acres of farmland, and the small cluster of trees surrounding the house. The widow had left her furniture behind, so we hadn't had to buy beds, dressers, or the burgundy horsehair sofa framed in dark wood with oak leaves and acorns carved into it. There was a matching small carved table with a lamp that looked like an oil lamp on the table. Ma and I had hardly ever sat in the living room until after he was gone. The first thing we did was drag the La-Z-Boy he had bought himself out to the barn. We didn't want to look at it anymore. Ma found the frame of the horsehair sofa's matching chair in the barn, refinished the carved frame, and re-upholstered it herself in a contrasting velvet fabric.

I'd take a walk through the frozen corn stubble fields in my old work boots when I got back. I'd build a snowman in front of the house if the snow was the right kind.

Christmas Eve morning in Cedar Rapids, there was Ma waving frantically from the terminal window as my bus discharged its weary passengers. We both shed a few happy tears of reunion as we exchanged bear hugs and exclamations about how great the other looked.

Big wet flakes spattered and melted on the windshield as Ma guided the car out of town and onto the country roads towards home. The snow was already plentiful and covered all but the tallest stems of dead roadside weeds. With the new blanket that the graying sky promised, it would be a picture postcard Christmas. Instead of talking, Ma and I sang Christmas carols in a wavering duet as the seven-year-old brown Dodge gripped the sanded and salted roads and rolled us toward home in comfort, if not style.

The farm matched my imaginings, icicles hanging from the eaves and white sparkling snow scarred only by the driveway. Smoke from the brick chimney drifted off into the snow-laden sky and left its homey fragrance in the crisp air. On the Formica table, baked sugar cookies greeted me. Ma and I would decorate them with frosting and colored sugar, as we'd done every year. She had gotten a small spruce tree and set it up in one corner of the living room. Boxes of ornaments ready to hang were scattered under it, mixed in with a few presents wrapped in red and gold paper.

I scurried upstairs to wrap gifts for Ma and drop the small

suitcase in my pink and girlish room. Downstairs, I could hear the clap of spoon on bowl as Ma made cookie frosting. First, we'd decorate the star and angel, reindeer, and snowman cutout sugar cookies. Then, we'd prepare the baked ham and the sweet potato casserole, Brussels sprouts, and cranberry sauce. After dinner and kitchen clean-up, we would decorate the tree and sing carols. We would drink Tom and Jerries with the Christmas cookies as we opened our small pile of gifts one at a time. Later, we'd take a nighttime walk in the snow, repeating a ritual evening we'd invented since he died.

Ma had put some Christmas music on our small portable record player, an old Johnny Mathis album we both loved. Sequestered in my room, I cut paper, tape, and ribbon, and wrapped my gifts for Ma: a painted Mexican pottery dish, a colorful shawl I'd bought at a roadside stand near the campus, and a pair of small turquoise and silver stud earrings. She'd written she'd had her ears pierced in October. She seemed happy, but preoccupied, as if waiting for the right moment to ask or tell me something.

The perfect evening ended with the two of us warm, drowsy, and smiling as we dried our pants and warmed our wool-stockinged feet by the stove after our winter's night walk.

It was in that timeless neverland, the days between Christmas and the new year, that I discovered what my mother wanted to tell me.

CHAPTER 42

MADISON, WISCONSIN

DECEMBER 1985

JENNY

I wasn't really trying to off myself. I'm not that stupid. Had I wanted to do it, I would have tried a more effective approach, hung myself from the pipe that runs along the ceiling of the dorm room or taken a flying leap from the ninth floor of the Van Hise building like that politician's son did a few years ago. They say he did it because he got a C in Spanish. At least I've got better reasons than that.

A handful of pills. A pitiful, bloodless, half-hearted suicide attempt — the proverbial cry for help. I've become disgustingly transparent, easily analyzed, and characterized by a graduate of Psych 101. I resent myself for letting a surreal night's experience of haunting memories and a mocking face on a poster turn me into a public display. Unfortunately, I'd gone so far as to pass out in the middle of our floor's communal bathroom, where all-conference hurdle champ, deans-listed, sorority-rushed Wendy Howard found me after a late night at the library. In the sane light of day, I never would have considered advertising my desperation to the whole floor.

But here I am, a caricature of a suicidal young adult, strapped to a bed in a building enveloped by the frightening odor of sterility mixed with death. I knew where I was even before I opened my eyes. I hated hospitals with a passion reserved for things that unnerved me, that terrified me with their reflection of the workings of my own soul. I know the order, the efficiency, the starched white sheets, and the beeping, blinking machines of the hospital are only the thinnest veneer covering the uncontrollable chaos of death and disease. To stop the struggle, to let blur the illusion of control for even a moment meant the overwhelming forces of disorder, of insanity would hold sway. Finding myself here meant I had lost my own battle for control. It was a realization that filled me with dread. Here, locked up in this depressing room, I had not even the power to take my own life. I had no control over it at all. I had never been so frightened.

I lay here in this beige-painted room with its barred window and bed with tie in straps for almost two days before any of the psych people got anything out of me. The other bed remained empty. Maybe most wackos went home for the holidays. I guess they'd pumped my stomach cuz it and my throat were sore. But I hadn't asked the nurse who came in to plump the pillows and bring the slime they called food. I hadn't spoken to her — or anyone — at all. I didn't care about anything or anyone enough to ask. An overwhelming lethargy descended on me. It was all I could do to find the motivation to drink, eat, and pee when the nurse took me to the toilet.

Otherwise, I slept the most profound sleep of my life, totally dreamless. My subconscious seemed to be walled up in some inaccessible fortress deep in my brain. That was okay with me. I was sick of thinking. Sick of caring. Sick of feeling hopeless. I just wanted to turn it off like some bad rerun on TV. Then this young, good-looking guy with this 'I understand and care about you' attitude about him came into my room and pulled a chair up to my bedside.

He went through the doctor's bedside manner rap of what had happened to me and how was I now. I sat through it, saying nothing, until he ran out of things to say.

"We'd like to contact your parents, Miss Wharton. I'm sure they are concerned and would want to know what's happened."

I snorted at that one, first, because I knew how they'd take the news. HE would probably go off the deep end in self-pity because he'd figure it was him who'd caused it. SHE would be annoyed at the interruption of her placid routine. His comment made me glad though, too, because it was obvious that the fake name and address I had filled out on the school forms had thrown them for a loop. It would take them a while to track HIM down. Which was fine with me.

"You don't want us to notify your parents?"

"Brilliant deduction," I croaked, my throat still sore from whatever tube they'd stuck down it.

"May I ask why?" The shrink seemed a bit nervous, and I realized he was probably just an intern. Talking to me was probably a big deal — maybe one of the first times he got to do a patient interview all by himself. I had too many problems of my own to think about to dredge up any sympathy for him, though. Or to make it easier.

"You may ask any questions you want to," I said in a sweet Southern accent. Then I just stopped talking and turned my face to the wall. None of his business why.

"Were you planning to spend the holidays with your folks?"

"Obviously, I was planning to spend the holidays dead," I retorted nastily. But inside, I was quaking. Had I been, and not even realized it?

My shock tactic was effective. The guy temporarily shut up, trying to find another line of questioning, I suppose.

"Well," he said, standing up to leave, "I'm sure our staff has tracked down your parents by now and we'll give them a call this morning to see what they have to say about all this." He started out the door.

Though half of me realized he was making a tactical maneuver, the other half thought they probably could track down my parents and maybe would call them. And that scared me out of my uncooperative mood.

"Okay, Doc, what's the deal?" I used the most belligerent tone I could muster. It sounded more like a whine than a growl.

"What do you mean?" He turned and walked back over to me.

"I mean, what do I have to do or sign to stop you from contacting them?"

"That's better, Miss Wharton." He sat down again. "It helps if you trust us a bit." When I looked incredulous, he added, "and cooperate a bit."

"Okay, I'm cooperating." I looked down at my sheets. "So, tell me, what's the deal?"

"We'd like to have you stay here while the dorms are closed for the holidays and talk with one of our psychiatrists about what's happening with you."

"And if I don't?"

"We'll have to call your parents. As close relatives, they could sign papers, if necessary, that would legally confine you here."

"Commit me, you mean?" I laughed bitterly. "Great."

"We don't want to have to do it that way, but given what's happened, we feel you might be a danger to yourself right now. We'd like to keep you here for observation — and try to help you feel better about what's troubling you."

"Fat chance."

"Well, we'd like you to try it for a few weeks. Just talking with one of our staff. You get room and board, and we don't call your parents. That's not such a bad deal. What do you think?"

"Sign me up," I sighed. Anything to stop that phone call. "I feel like I'm being blackmailed — you can make a note of that in my file, Doctor," I spat out and grimaced cynically.

"That's fair. You are. Sometimes, that's what it takes." He walked out of the room to report his success to the other jerks in the shrinks' lounge.

And left me alone to think, something I did not relish at all. As usual, when the thoughts that started crowding my brain got too much for me, I felt like getting high. But sleep was the only escape I was going to get around here and I had this feeling I wasn't going to be too successful at doing that for a while. I figured the first gut spilling I'd better do is admit my proclivity for Valium. I'd read about withdrawing from it, how tough it was, when I'd thought about giving it up for Chuck's sake, so he could go out with somebody straight for a change. That seemed a million years ago now. Like it happened to somebody else. I could hardly remember what he looked like and half wondered if I'd dreamed the whole thing.

If I tell them, they won't let me go cold turkey. Maybe I could get that feeling back for a few days while they gradually decreased the dosage. It was worth a try. I pressed the buzzer, and the nurse came real fast. She was probably surprised I'd taken an interest in myself again to the point of actually asking for something.

"What can I get for you, Jennifer?" she said in a business-like voice. Funny how she called me by name. I suppose it was one of the things they did for people who tried to off them-selves. They probably thought it made it seem like somebody cared about them. Huh. I'm not that easily fooled. She was a middle-aged lady, this nurse, with strong arms that looked like they could lift me right out of bed, no problem. I wondered how my request would sound to her. Shocking? No, I figured anyone who'd worked in this ward was probably immune to that.

"Listen, Nurse." I was a bit nervous, never having admitted my little habit to anyone before. "Could I get some Valium? I can't sleep." When she looked unconvinced, I came out with it. "Look, I've uh, got this habit — and well, I don't look forward to going through withdrawal. I thought maybe you could, like, ease me off it."

"The doctors thought you might have been — let us say — familiar with the drug." She looked down at me sternly. "Otherwise, the amount you took, plus the alcohol you drank could have killed you." How tactless, I thought. I felt a shiver run up my spine.

"Well, can I have some?"

"Oh, you'll probably continue to get some sedatives for a while — by injection."

"Lovely," I replied, my hoarse voice dripping with sarcasm. But maybe withdrawal wouldn't be so bad?

"I'll tell the doctors what you've requested though, don't worry about that." She smiled one of those fake motherly smiles. "Now, are you ready for lunch?"

After the hospital lunchtime routine was over — they watched me eat with nothing but plastic forks and spoons, in case I decided to slit my wrists — I was left alone with my thoughts again. Therapy. What a joke. To me, it seemed like some phony religious ritual — I get to spill my guts while they — the priests and priestesses posing as doctors of the psyche — stand over me dissecting and prophesying from the pattern my innards fall into. It seemed so utterly useless. As if time and exposure to Gestalt vapors or whatever might somehow produce a cure and render me an improved product. But there is no cure for memories, no way to erase them short of shock therapy, which I didn't think they used anymore. And anyways, doesn't a "cure" depend ultimately on the victim's wanting it?

I don't seek cure. No. I seek erasure. I just want it to stop, all these noises from the past, all this false hoping that the future might make me forget it. I am flawed, irreparably so, and like a badly cut gem, there's no cure for that. The thing becomes worthless, a throwaway. And in my own stupid, inept sort of way, I had been trying to erase it all. If I had regrets, it was about my methods. I didn't want to commit suicide. No, that's too dramatic of a death. I would prefer a statistical death, a car accident after a drunken Friday night, a flood victim where mine would have been one of hundreds of names. I've had enough drama for any one person already, lived a play of secretive, repetitive acts directed by my self-styled Polanski of a father, tacitly patronized by my malingerer mother.

How well I've kept your secret! All to spill it to some inattentive psychoanalyst. The irony should make you grimace, dear father. To keep you out of my life, I betray your deepest secret to academia, your God.

In that insipid birthday card SHE sent, she tried to entice me with a beach vacation in Florida for Christmas. But my holiday plans have already been made for me, dear parents. I'm spending Christmas vacation in 4 North, the psych ward of University Hospital.

CHAPTER 43

PINE HILL STATION AND HOUSTON, TEXAS

DECEMBER 1985

MADDIE

That night, the night Roz came back to me, back to me to tell me the dreadful story of the brave women and rapists who made her, she stayed. For a while, we talked of other things, of all the little inconsequential events of our lives that we would have shared day by day had we been together these past awful months. She'd had a paper published. I'd gotten a contract for a book on Eleanor Roosevelt's role in shaping the American Century, which I hadn't had the motivation to do anything for but a bit of light reading. A woman in Roz's department was pregnant, a man hired the year after me was getting tenure in mine. All the little nothings of the days and weeks and months. Mama was deteriorating, Roz admitted mournfully. She was finding it harder to find the time to take care of her and do decent work at the university. The commute here from Houston on top of it all was weighing her down.

Then Roz said another surprising thing, on top of all the others on that horrible, wonderful night.

"I think it's coming to be the time to tell Mama I'm gay," she said. "Not right now. We both need to calm down about what she just told me. But soon. She told me her biggest secret, and it is way past time to tell her mine." She frowned. "Well, my *other* big secret," she finished. "Besides being a child of white on Black rape."

I reached out to comfort her, to tell her it was of no consequence, but she stopped my arm.

"No, Maddie. I need to get used to just saying the fact of it and going on anyway. So, I'm practicing with you, if that's okay."

"I love you, brave woman. You tell me whatever, however."

Then she changed tack. "You want to come over for Christmas dinner? Jerry's going to be home."

Christmas. I hadn't even thought of it. Had no plans whatsoever, or if I had, they were the vague imaginings of the moping, sighing, and crying I would probably do at home alone on a holiday I used to celebrate with the love of my life. "I'd love to have Christmas dinner at your mama's." I felt something like astonishment over what a turn my life had made in these past few hours.

"I have one more favor to ask on top of all the other stuff I've put on you tonight."

"What? Sure. Anything. Just ask," I said, a bit too quickly.

Roz looked at me, her big brown eyes registering both fear and longing. "Can I stay with you tonight, Maddie? Can I hold you? Can we start over?"

Then I was the one who broke into sobs. I couldn't help myself. All this pent-up, useless love I'd had to stifle all these months. All this grief. I did remember to nod while I was bawling my eyes out on Roz's shoulder, though.

The lovemaking we shared a short time later was the most intense physical and emotional experience I'd ever had. Until the next morning, when we did it all over again.

We awoke to sunshine. The clouds were breaking up and for a few hours, at least, we'd have springlike weather. The air was fresh, and the garden sparkled with reflected raindrops. I walked with Roz down the stone path that went through the backyard flower garden. I kissed her gently, tenderly, and she got into her red car to make the drive back to Houston and relieve the neighbor she'd gotten to look in on Mama last night. As I turned to go back into the house, the poor white rose bush in the very back corner of the garden caught my eye. I'd have to pull it up one of these days and replace its dried-out sticks with something new. I wandered over to it, wondering what I would plant there instead. Then, I saw it. Out of the base of one of the dead branches was a tiny new shoot.

The next days were a blur of final exams and paper grading, punctuated by a bit of Christmas shopping for Mama, Jerry, and Roz. Then it was Christmas Day, and I was on my way to Mama's house in my little car in the rain. Texan weather was decidedly not the swirling wonder of a December snowfall as it had been during this season in the Wisconsin of my youth, the whiteness of the snow on the fields setting the evergreens and dark-trunk trees into stark relief. Instead, all was an indistinguishable muddy brown under a dreary gray sky.

By this time, Mama knew I was a "close friend" of Roz's and "had no people here in Texas," so it was only right that I should be invited to Christmas dinner. Grace Gaines, who insisted I call her Mama like Roz and Jerry did, was a gracious and kindly host. I'd been to Christmas dinner every year since we had taken jobs in this godforsaken part of the world. For that, I was grateful. I would be the last to the small party, as Jerry had arrived yesterday afternoon in time for the Christmas Eve festivities. Roz and Jerry had been to Christmas services with Mama this morning, Jerry pushing the wheelchair and Roz running alongside with a big cherry red umbrella. They'd invited me to attend church, too. I had in other years and been welcomed with open arms and enjoyed it thoroughly, despite being the lone white person in the pews. But this year, with all this news to process, I thought it best to let Jerry, Roz, and Mama have time to themselves. Dusk was beginning to make itself known as I pulled into the driveway of the modest ranch house and parked behind Roz's car.

"Welcome, honey, come on in and a Merry Christmas to you," Mama said after Jerry had opened the door to my knock and given me a long, brotherly hug. Though it had only been a bit more than six months since I'd seen her, Mama had deteriorated markedly. She looked small and sinewy in her wheelchair, though she was still dressed in her holiday finest. Roz had gotten her a corsage of white carnations and red berries, I noticed, and remarked on how nice the flowers looked against the evergreen dress she was wearing. I also couldn't help but comment on the delicious odors emanating from the little kitchen, with its original cabinetry and flooring from when the house was built in the 1950s. The oven was modern, though, an upgrade Jerry and Roz had made to the house so Mama could continue to make her delicious recipes in style. These days, Roz had told me, Mama mostly sat in the corner in her chair and told Roz what to do, though she occasionally had good days when she could still do the cooking herself.

We sat at the table in the dining room, with the Christmas red, round tablecloth and white napkins and the holly-wreathed Christmas candle in the middle. Jerry was full of news, and Roz and I were relieved that he kept the conversation on neutral topics and not family history. Mama had not been told that I knew, and I was fine with that decision, at least for now. Why ruin Christmas? So, we had roast ham, cornbread stuffing, collard greens, and a new favorite of mine since moving to this part of the country, fried okra. After a leisurely meal hearing about Jerry's exciting work and his busy social life, it was time for Mama's delicious sweet potato pie

Innocently, I asked, "Mama, has this recipe been in your family for long?" As soon as the words were out of my mouth, I regretted them. Weren't we supposed to be *not* talking about family history? Good going, Maddie.

"Well, Maddie, that particular recipe is from my Aunt Suzy, who toyed with it until it had some secret ingredients that only a few of us ever learned. I was close with her daughter, Patty, back when we both were young, and Aunt Suzy gave us both the recipe when we were girls. A man-catcher pie, she always said." Mama smiled in reminiscence when she related this bit of family lore. She was looking only in my direction. It was a good thing, too, because Roz and Jerry were staring at each other in surprise, verging on alarm. I remembered Roz telling me how they never heard about Mama's side of the family nor ever visited them when they were kids. I decided to risk one more question.

"Oh, does Patty still make this recipe too?"

"I don't rightly know because we lost touch many years ago. We used to play with this boy named Elton, who was a neighbor of Patty's and that's the man she married, I believe. Elton, Elton Rambles, that's right. So, I suppose it's Patty Rambles now. We were tight as ticks when we were girls, playing dolls and make-believe the way girls do. And currying and riding those horses they had out in the country ..." She trailed off.

"Wait, Mama — you rode horses when you were a girl?" Jerry couldn't help asking.

"Yes, I did, and I was a good rider and stable girl, too. That was long ago, long ago and it's all water under the bridge now," Mama concluded, and then she was done with talking about the past. "Jerry, now you unstack the table and Roz, you get the dishes going. Maddie is going to help settle me in the living room by the tree and get the tree lights lit."

And that was it. I wheeled Mama into the living room, plugged in the tree and got the sherry and the set of tiny glasses she kept with it out of the cabinet in the living room. Roz and Jerry retreated to the kitchen to do the dishes. I knew Mama wouldn't let "the company" help, so I didn't even ask.

Later, after they had opened the gifts I had brought and I opened those that had been wrapped for me, after we drank our sherry and ate our frosted molasses cookies, Mama declared it was time for her to "retire" as she put it.

Jerry insisted on helping Mama to bed and Roz let him.

At last, Roz and I were alone in the living room. We looked toward the bedroom and saw that Mama's door was shut. Then we looked at each other with excitement and hope, all mixed up with dread. Together we repeated the precious clue that Mama had left us, "Patty Rambles."

CHAPTER 44

MADISON, WISCONSIN

DECEMBER 1985

JENNY

"Because she's a bitch!" I half-screamed the words. In the awkward silence that followed, I mumbled a half-contrite "sorry" to the scrawny, white-coated psychiatrist they've assigned to my "case." That's all I am now, a "case," numbered, filed, and discussed at grad seminar 000: "Symptomatology of Psychotic Southern Belles." After I told the jerk they'd originally picked out for me, a patronizing, balding sixty-year-old, just what he could do with certain appendages peculiar to his sex, they exchanged him for this glassy-eyed prune. Aside from her slightly less repulsive sex, not much of an improvement. She stinks of the same sort of self-important professionalism that distinguishes every academic my parents ever had over for dinner. This old bag cares about me just as far as she can use my case history to advance her career. She's hoping I'm really wacko, so she'll have something exciting to report at hospital staff meetings. I'll be a "real learning experience" for her worshipping grad students.

But why fight it? I do get some pleasure out of telling my tale, imagining his face when it all comes back to him some day. So last week, I started telling my shrink and her grad student a couple of juicy details to fill out their case history with. Like for starters, how my Southern gentleman professor father — one of their own kind — had been screwing his daughter regularly for five years until I managed to put some geography between us by enrolling here in Iceberg U. As I'd suspected, they were interested in all the lurid details. When it started. Age thirteen. How often. Two nights a week when she was doing her dog walking thing. Did anyone else in the family know, like siblings? Don't have none of those, Doctor. My mother? Of course. She knew. Did I discuss it with her? Are you kidding? Well, how did I know she knew about it? She knew. It was her husband, after all, wasn't it? She just didn't give a damn. Ignored it. Probably was glad so he wouldn't be at her all the time. She didn't like sex. He was desperate. That's what he told me at the beginning. I was just a kid. A stupid, naïve kid. I believed him. And to keep still. That's what he said to me each and every time. What did I know? What choice did I have? I was trying to survive. I really can't remember why now, but at the time, it seemed important to survive. Survival: it's a normal human instinct, isn't it? No. I don't feel like that anymore. Because I'm not a normal human being. Well, you can't change the past, can you?

Today, my mother was the topic. How did I feel about my mother? Well now, are you ready to write this down? It's a classic response, probably useful in your seminar, Ms. Roberts, and no doubt, you'll be nodding in agreement, Dr. Kurtz. Yes, I can see your anticipation. Don't worry, I won't disappoint. I hate her. Detest her. Loathe her. You want to know why? Annoying question. It's obvious, isn't it? Because she's a bitch! Sorry. I forgot myself for a moment. No, I won't scream anymore. My mother seems to be a sensitive topic for me? Well, you're the doctor, you should know. Do I want to go into why I hate my mother? No, I guess you two can figure that out for yourselves. What? You're ending today's session because I'm not being cooperative? Well, I'm insulted. Here I've told you everything and this is the thanks I get. Ladies. You should show more dedication to your jobs. I'm in here for a cure and you're not helping one bit.

They left early, disappointed in me. They think I'm not taking this seriously enough. They're wrong; it's just that I can't start dishing up my feelings like mashed potatoes just to fill out some journal articles.

I know perfectly well why I hate my mother. Like the lamb would hate the Judas goat if only it realized it was being led to slaughter. But it doesn't, you see. The poor thing's only interested in trusting someone who knows the way and can lead it to safety. Suddenly, all that's left is a dead carcass on a butcher's meat hook, ready to be bought, cut up, and devoured. That's what she did to me, my mother. Left me to HIM, let him use me as her substitute. Abandoned me to do other people's taxes and then abandoned me again to that dog kennel, just when I needed her most. How could any daughter not hate a mother like that?

So yes, goddammit, I hate her. And I'm not about to change my mind. It was her fault in the first place for not giving him what he wanted in bed. For not being the wife he needed. So, he tried to find a better one in me, a little thirteen-year-old dumbbell. Yeah, that was abnormal of him, but still, she could have stopped it and didn't. To me, that was the worse crime.

It showed that she was just as much a pervert as he was. Or at least a wimp. But whatever she was, she wasn't a mother. I'll never forgive her for that. Because she let him do it, I've got this nothing life and this nothing future. That's what

I got out of your complicity, Mother. What a joke of a word. She was no mother to me.

I know it's supposed to help to articulate all these feelings to the shrink. I suppose I will do it, given time. Maybe something will come of it, though I doubt it. But I couldn't today. Couldn't tell them why I detest her. I suppose they've seen this symptom before. They no doubt know where it's coming from. But it's hard to say something so personal in front of strangers. Funny, but it's harder for me to say why I hate my mother than to tell them the slimy things my father said and did to me. Maybe what he did doesn't seem so unusual, so hard to believe to me. What she did was so much worse, so unmotherly. Such an absolute perversion of everything it means to be a mother. But what does being a father mean, really? Paying the bills and making the rules. Controlling the lives you support. Showing an interest in your family and maybe protecting them from the outside world. All of which he did right through the years of our "affair." What better protection could I have gotten from the advances of teenaged boys? And no one could accuse him of not taking sufficient interest in me. He supported me in grand style once I got smart enough to ask for stuff to keep quiet.

But mothers were supposed to take care of you. Put your needs before their own. Want what's best for you. Watch out for your best interests. Keep you safe and secure. Sure, it's all stereotypes and not many real parents live up to them. In a way, that's good. But isn't that what kids expect from their folks? A superhuman stereotype? The providing, protector father and the all-giving, all-sacrificing, all-loving mother?

In my thirteen-year-old brain, I was just beginning to realize that maybe my parents weren't all that perfect when my whole way of thinking got knocked wide open by his action and her reaction — nothing. No matter how many times I go over it, I can't help feeling like it was mostly her fault. Aren't women the civilizing influences on men? Wasn't she supposed to be delivering the services he came to me for? Wasn't she supposed to be watching out for my best interests? She was a failure as a wife and mother, and I paid the price for her failings.

Up here, in the hospital room, with little to divert me but my own thoughts, the past comes rushing back on me, vague clouds of feelings and happenings, half-memories. So much of my past seems to have faded into the misty, undefinable background of my mind, the details so blurry, my memories seem more like dreams than reality. Like nightmares. I don't like thinking about my past. There's not much of my teenage years that I can think about without the picture of him looming over me, telling me what a good girl I was, how much I meant to him. Saying all those words of love and then telling me to "Keep still!" while he did it to me quietly at 8:00 p.m. every Tuesday and Thursday. For five years, he did this, fully aware of the crimes he was committing against me, against everything it means to be a family.

I can't think about earlier memories without a queasy feeling starting in the pit of my stomach. The times he took me fishing or horseback riding at Old Johnny's or that long driving trip we took to Disney World when I was eight. Was he thinking lurid thoughts about me even then? Did he feel the rush of unnatural desire every time I ran up to kiss him or sat on his lap? Was he already plotting the way to do it, trying to get up the nerve? Even when I was ten? Eight? Even five? The knowledge of what he'd become later wiped out any good memories of him, of what I felt for him. I had loved some sort of actor in a play called "Normal Family" all those years, a charlatan impersonating a normal, caring father. I had fallen for the act, and it was so horrible a shock when the real, perverse sub-human came out from behind the genial persona he'd created for himself that I think I'm only now starting to come out of it. I'm only beginning to know why I've been so pissed off at the world all these years. Funny, I'm so out of control of my life here and yet this is the first time I feel safe enough to start thinking about all this stuff. I guess the good doctor has had some effect on me after all. Even with all her ulterior motives, somehow, I know she won't let me go off the deep end.

But it's Mother she wants me to think about for tomorrow's session. I guess I know the word the doctor wants me to come up with. The one word that describes what my mother did to me and why I hate her. Betrayal. As deep and sharp a feeling as a knife blade across the jugular. How easy it would have been to stop my life's blood from flowing away. Just a word from her, an acknowledgement that she loved me, that she'd stop him. But all I ever got from her was nothing. And giving nothing to your own child is the worst crime a mother could commit.

CHAPTER 45

PINE HILL STATION AND WHARTON, TEXAS

DECEMBER 27, 1985

MADDIE

She had to go on December 27th, Roz told me, because that's Kujichagulia, the day when self-determination is celebrated during Kwanzaa. And of course, she had to go alone. "Patty is definitely not going to open up with a white lady there," she said to me. "Sorry, Maddie, but you know I'm right about that." I did. This would be delicate enough without some additional stranger butting in, particularly a white one. On the day after Christmas, or the first day of Kwanzaa, the day of Umoja or unity, we had driven to Wharton together and found a phone booth with an intact local phone book in it. Now that we knew where to look and who to look for, it hadn't taken but a minute to find a phone number and address in the Wharton phonebook for an Elton Rambles, the childhood friend Mama had mentioned who, she thought, had married her cousin Patty. Elton and Patty, if they had indeed married and were still married, lived outside of Wharton, at 3 Live Oak Lane. She had to see where what had happened to Mama had happened. She had to finally meet some kin on her mother's side. Roz decided to present herself at their house. "Harder to slam the door in my face than it is to hang up the phone," she said. For Roz's sake, I hoped that was true.

At my, or our, house the evening before she went, we made two sweet potato pies, using Aunt Suzy's recipe. One, we'd keep for our own celebration, the other, Roz would deliver to Patty and her kin, as a way of remembering and honoring the long-ago severed bond between Mama Grace and Patty. It felt like old times, almost, making pies together in my, or our, house again. Had it only been last May when we'd cooked together, eaten together, shared drinks and laughter and love together in this house? It seemed a lifetime of grief and pain had been lived since then. It was both awkward and a complete joy, Roz and I, in the kitchen together again. As usual, I played the sous chef, fetching ingredients, peeling sweet potatoes, digging out the bourbon from the back of the liquor cabinet — for that was one of Aunt Suzy's secret ingredients. In the middle of the pie making, when Roz had flour in her hair from rolling out the dough and my arm was tired from beating eggs for the filling, Roz had stopped, reached for me, and enveloped me in a bear hug. I hadn't realized she'd started weeping until my shoulder started getting wet. "Oh Maddie," she sighed, "I never thought I would be in this kitchen making something delicious with you ever again." She held on tighter.

"We're pretty damn excellent at delicious," I said softly, breathing in her sweet Roz smell as she pressed me against her. Then I tilted my face upward so she could kiss me deliciously, which she did, tenderly and passionately.

The pies were magnificent replicas of Mama's best efforts. Six months of living under Mama's tutelage had improved Roz's culinary techniques until they were almost at the level of her mother's. In my book, too high a price to pay for the new confidence in the kitchen Roz demonstrated, but I certainly couldn't object to the results. The next morning, on self-determination day, Roz and I put the pie carefully in a basket we had used for similar gifts in those dimly remembered days when we used to go to dinner at a friend's house. She placed the pie basket on the passenger seat of her little red car and off she went to reclaim her lost cousin and learn the full story of her ancestors. She was gone until darkness had settled in for the night and it was way past dinner time.

When she entered the back door without knocking, like she had a million times before, like the house belonged to her again, my heart skipped a beat. I kissed her like we used to do and offered a glass of red wine, like we used to drink.

"Come sit by the fire, my sweet, and tell me all about it." I looked at her, trying to discern whether it was comfort or congratulations that would be required of me, but I could not read her expression.

At first, it was as if she'd been on an anthropology expedition. "Maddie, you would not believe what it's like out there. It's a different world, a different century, almost," she started. "There are fields, all barren at this time of year of course, but once, it was a huge cotton plantation running as far in every direction as I could see. Live Oak Lane is a dead-end road that once had been the very long driveway to the plantation. There were live oaks lining each side and when I came out of the trees and the road turned, it was like I had been transported to the set of *Gone with the Wind*," she said with sarcasm. "Big white house with a columned veranda, a smallish bare-wood barn a way off from the house, and gardens and grounds you could tell were impeccably kept, even though it's winter. I didn't know what to do or where to go. I was sitting in the car, wondering if I should go knock on the 'big house' door, when I saw a big, broad-shouldered man come out of the barn. I honked my horn and scared the hell out of him, but he came over towards the car and I got out. You'll never believe the first words out of his mouth."

"What, what? What did he say?"

"He said, 'You couldn't be Grace, so you must be her daughter!' Can you believe it? He recognized the family resemblance before I had spoken a single word. So, I said, 'Are you Mr. Rambles, sir? Are you Cousin Elton?' And with that, he broke into a huge grin and gave me a big hug! Then he looked me over from head to toe. 'Except for your height, you favor Grace, chile, and that's the truth of it. How is my near-to-little-sister after all this time gone by? Is she well?'

"So, I had to tell him about Mama having MS and being in a wheelchair most of the time and he said, 'I'm right sorry to hear that about Miss Grace. I didn't catch your name, daughter of Grace. What'd she call you?' I told him I was Rosalyn Eleanor Gaines, and he said what a right pretty name that is and how he wasn't surprised by my middle name given that Grace was always a big admirer of the first lady when they were growing up.

"'Aunt Suzy was always telling us young ones about the first lady, how she was for us colored folks, how she saw, like few white people in them days, that we were all God's children and should all be treated with dignity. Aunt Suzy was always talking about Mrs. Roosevelt that way.' Then, I said that speaking of Aunt Suzy, I had brought a sweet potato pie along that my Mama told me was Aunt Suzy's 'man-catcher pie.' Elton laughed at that and said that Patty had used that very recipe to catch him when they were courting, a long time ago. Then I said — and oh, Maddie — I was so scared of the answer, 'Does Cousin Patty still live here?'

"But Elton said, 'Why, of course she does. Where else would she be? Me, Patty, and our son Marvin live in the cottages out back,' he said, indicating some place behind the mansion that I couldn't see. I said, 'Mr. Rambles, sir, I would be much obliged if you could let Mrs. Rambles know I'm here. I would very much like to talk with her.'

"'Now, Miz Rosalyn, I can't do that at this time,' he said. 'She's with Old Mr. Wharton, feeding him and cleaning up after his breakfast and such and the old man does not like his habits disrupted for the likes of us.' I guess he meant Black folks, but I wasn't sure. My disappointment must have been written all over my face, though, because then he said, 'Now don't you worry none, Miz Rosalyn, Old Mr. Wharton goes down for his daily repose at four o'clock and he wakes for dinner at 5:45 p.m. So Patty has some time to herself right then, which she usually uses to make me and Marvin dinner, saintly woman that she is. I'm thinking I will take this pie from you now, cuz I'm going to need some proof to show Patty that I wasn't just dreaming this whole thing up. And you come back for dinner with the three of us. Come a bit after four, so I have a moment to get Patty used to the idea. But she'll want to see you, on that you can rely. She prays for Grace every day and I know she holds her close to her heart, even if she don't speak about her much. Grace's grown daughter? Now, that's a sight she'll want to see. She don't have to do any cooking today neither, cuz we have leftovers aplenty from our Christmas ham and such. Meanwhile, come see my girls, Babe and Beauty. And then you can take yourself to a nice diner on Main Street in Wharton for a spell. They have the best coffee in these parts, that I can tell you.'

"He took me to the barn, pie, and all, and we looked at the two horses, which you could tell were his pride and joy. Elton had carrots in his pocket and we each fed them to one of the horses.

"'This here is Beauty and this 'ol one is Babe, who I reckon is about the same age as you, Miz Rosalyn, thirty-four or there about. Old Mr. Wharton keeps 'em for his grandson and grandson's wife and they only come out to ride once in a while, so me and Marvin get to take 'em out most days. Do you ride, Miz Rosalyn?'

"'I have never been on a horse in my life,' I told him. 'But you never know.' He smiled at that, and I wondered how he knew my age. Oh Maddie, did I find out why he knew that!

"We chatted about the horses and the property for a while — he and his son do the work on the magnificent gardens around the mansion. Then, I gave him the pie and left for Wharton, where I walked around a bit and ate lunch at that diner. They did have great coffee. It was a good thing I had that stack of journals in the car, because I had a few hours on my hands and there was only so much walking up and down the Main Street of Wharton that a person could do. So, I sat in my car and tried to read. And think. Oh, Maddie, I had such second thoughts about going back. Who was I to disrupt their lives like this? But they were expecting me. So, I resolved to just make it a social call to say hi after all this time and give them Mama's regards."

"Roz, you didn't keep all your questions to yourself. Tell me you didn't do that!" I couldn't believe how long she was stringing out this story, only to tell me she didn't ask anything about what had happened to her mama that horrific night.

"Hang on, let me tell you what happened when I went back to the place later in the day. I returned a bit after four, like Elton said to, and when I got out of the car, all three of them came out to meet me. Marvin's a small wiry guy in his late twenties. Elton told me he rode Babe. Because of her age, Babe can't take a lot of weight anymore and Marvin's about the size of a jockey. Patty is tall like me but broad-hipped, and she's got a little weight on her, and edema around her ankles. Next time I'm out — and there will be a next time — I'll see if I can do a little informal health interview. Maybe she's got diabetes or some sort of kidney or liver disease. Anyways, they were all so welcoming and Patty kept looking at me and saying, 'You're the spitting image of Grace, just the spitting image. Except Grace was a tiny thing. I was always about a foot taller than her all the while we were growing up.'

"They live in two cottages, Marvin in one and Elton and Patty in the other, right next to each other out a way from Wharton Hall. You can tell they were nothing but shacks at one point, but Elton and Marvin, Patty said, fixed them up over the years. 'We didn't get 'lectricity or in-house water until 1972,' Patty told me. That's when the wife of you-know-who — what's her name?"

"Liz?" I asked.

"Yes, Liz demanded that Old Man Wharton, the man that Patty takes care of, install it. Liz had to stop at the cottages once and noticed the pump in the front yard and the kerosene lamp on the table in the yard. She asked them about it, Patty said. And then, about a month later, they had men out at the house digging a water pipe and stringing wires from the mansion."

"Did you ask them about your mama?" I said, with some agitation.

"After we each had a piece of the pie we made — that was just the perfect gift — you could see Patty was honored that we had used her Mama's recipe — she said, 'Has your mama ever mentioned why she don't come out here anymore?'

"I told them that Mama never talked about her side of the family when I was growing up and it wasn't until Jerry had done research that we even knew that our family had lived out here. But that just a few weeks ago, Mama had told me what had happened here. Patty shook her head sadly. 'Well, I'm not surprised she never tole you about us, after the way we let her down.'

"'*You* let her down? You were not at fault!' I told them. I couldn't help myself, Maddie.

"At that point, Elton interjected. 'We were all out in the barn watching Babe's mama, Belle, who was in the middle of a breach birth until Patty's dad turned the foal. So, Babe was born that very night and we were all attending to those goings on. And when we thought to look up, Grace was gone.'

"'And it was too late,' Patty added. 'We know she ran away from her folks' house a few months later.' I was nodding, so Patty knew that I knew this. 'But then we lost track of her. And she never contacted us again. Because we let her down,' Patty repeated.

"'Please, Cousin Patty, it is not your fault that Johnny Wharton would do something so evil,' I said.

"'There's more to the story than you know,' Patty replied. Elton nodded his agreement. But Patty was looking sideways toward the door as if Old Mr. Wharton might be listening. They both got quiet then.

"'Miz Rosalyn, we are so happy that you came here today. It is a sight for sore eyes to see Grace's girl chile.'

"'And see what a beauty she is!' Elton said.

"'We hope you come back to see us real soon,' Patty said. 'And please give Grace our deep regards.'

"And then she got up and it was clear to me that it was time to go, even though I had so many more questions!"

"Oh Roz, I'm sorry. I know how much you wanted to learn about everything that happened."

"I had some time to think it over on the drive back. I decided I'm not going to be disappointed. Mama is going to love to hear about them tomorrow. I have an idea what the place looked like the night it happened. They were too scared to say more, Maddie. They work for his — I guess it must be his grandfather. So, this is going to be a process. A little while ago, I didn't know that they existed. Now, I have cousins on my mama's side. It's a process and I will have to be patient."

Roz had more patience about this than I did. I wanted to know exactly what that hideous colleague of mine had done to Roz's mama that night, and I wanted to know it now. Damn, I hated him.

CHAPTER 46

HUTTON, IOWA

JANUARY 1986

JANE

My mother is growing away from me. That sounds peculiar. The daughter, by rights, should grow away from her mother. Not so in our little family where my attractive mother — an attractiveness I hadn't noticed, and which perhaps did not exist until he died — now goes to bars with her lady friends and on dates with one of her several "beaus," as she calls them. They take her out dancing and bowling and they aren't half as old as she made them out to be in her letter. She has become the whimsical adolescent and I the stodgy old woman, severe and unsmiling in my widow's weeds. I feel so old, so old, as if forty years had passed since August.

For six years, my mother had played the chaste young widow, bearing her loss with dignity, raising her only child as well as a widow could. She showed no interest in men in other than strictly neighborly terms. All this had dramatically changed in my short absence. She flirted, she laughed, she was busy and happier than I'd ever seen her. I'm not sure she knew what her feelings had been for my father. She did grieve for him for a time after he died, I suppose, though our mutual Midwestern reticence about all things emotional precluded ever talking about it. But grief does not usually last six years, nor does a heavy schedule of dating immediately follow its abatement. I realized at once she had forgone a social life previously in deference to her only daughter, who had none. Now that she had finally gotten her reluctant fledgling on her way to independence, she felt free to create a new life for herself. She had coddled and kept me throughout my college years without resentment for her missed chances. Ma was not the type to hide malice, nor martyr herself for an insecure child. She had extended my childhood because she saw my need, though she never guessed the source of my failure to adjust and I never for a moment considered telling her, even after he died. She did it out of love for me.

How, then, could I not let her go? I was newly twenty-three; she had given me four more years of her undivided attention than most children received. I kept locked up in my heart and out of Ma's gaze the despair that crept into my bones with long icy fingers as I realized my mother was no longer with me in the way I had grown to expect. She looked at me with eyes that begged approval, eyes that said, "Please let this be okay for you, Jane. Please say it's okay for me to have this fun." So, I smiled through the evenings as night after frigid January night her lovers and friends called for her, exclaiming how they couldn't believe she had a grown daughter already, she looked so young. I declined polite, insincere invitations to country and western bars and bowling alleys with the excuse I had to study. I accepted those dinner invitations she insisted I go on to check out this or that prospective next husband. For Ma's sake, I tried to be warm to these strangers. Alone with her, I generated enthusiasm for her new lifestyle and told her what she wanted to hear about her men. If she liked them, I did; if she thought they were taking her for a ride, so did I. She beamed at my declarations; my heart sank lower and lower. By this time next year, she'd have a new husband, and I'd be a stranger in their lives. I was losing my mother.

She told me I seemed happier. Was that merely a reflection cast by her own radiance? Did she want to believe it so as not to feel guilty? Or was I happier? It didn't seem so at the moment, with my mother disloyal and emotionally disinheriting me. As much as I wished for her happiness, I couldn't avoid moments of self-pity. I was being abandoned.

I was able to keep these feelings to myself and talk to her instead of general matters, fielding her questions about school and Texas. Ma, as always, was completely uncritical and satisfied with whatever I said.

"How's school, honey?"

"Great, Ma. All A's this semester." It was true. Aside from Johnny's visits, I had little to occupy my time but study.

"That's wonderful, dear, but then, you always were bright. What are your teachers like?"

"The two I like best are Professor Haystead and Joh ... Professor Wharton. Professor Haystead teaches historical methods, and she's very nice to me outside of class, always giving me extra things to read and asking me how I'm doing. She even had me over for dinner once. Professor Wharton (how odd to call him that) is an intelligent man and interesting to talk to. I'm taking Early Roman Christianity from him."

"Married though, I suppose."

"Oh yes, very." It would never occur to Ma to think I'd even consider having an affair, if that's what I was having, with an older, married man. So, though I lied by omission, I considered it kinder than the truth. Ma was a modern woman, but she wouldn't have liked the idea of her daughter involved with a married professor, not one bit.

"I'm his research assistant," I added, "so he talks to me quite a bit about the projects he's working on, all sorts of interesting stuff." I could see her attention flagging and breathed a silent sigh of relief. It was hard lying to Ma. Again.

"Hey, Ma," I said, abruptly changing the subject, "this sweater you gave me for Christmas is beautiful and so soft. Where did you find it?" I admired myself in the sky-blue pullover in the walnut-framed full-length mirror hung on the inside door of our tiny coat closet. Another indication of Mom's new life — we'd never had a full-length mirror in the house before. The sweater did flatter my pale complexion and my wheat-colored hair seemed to take on more golden highlights. I vowed to take more pains with my appearance next term. My Southern classmates seemed to think college required a wardrobe of color-coordinated outfits. My faded jeans and flannel shirts with a T-shirt underneath looked sadly out of place. I had a few items of dress clothes, most left over from high school, that I could take back with me on the bus. I had never wanted to draw attention to myself and had chosen my wardrobe accordingly. Maybe it was time to change that.

During the last few days Ma and I spent together before I headed south for the spring semester, a glimmer of hope started to rise in me despite the impending dissolution of our tiny family. If Ma could carve out a new life after the nightmare of my father was over, and after another six years of virtual nun-hood while she waited for her reluctant daughter to launch into adulthood, I might be able to shed my own cocoon and fly away too. Unlike Ma, who seemed to have legions of friends now, I had precious little to start with. I had Johnny, that was all. Johnny, with his wife, with his consuming career that left little time for me. Yet he made time. He wanted to be with me. Our connection was as wispy as spider gossamer. But I would try to make it more substantial. I would reach out to him with that silent, secret self that still somehow lurked inside me, watching and waiting for when it was safe. I would make it safe with Johnny, I resolved.

I left for Texas three days earlier than I had to, leaving Ma to pursue her busy social life, a life with which I had suddenly lost patience. I decided to plead study requiring the university's library before the screaming scene occurred where I accused my mother of that most horrible of maternal crimes, self-interest. Intellectually, I told myself I was glad she had an exciting, full life, but the child in me felt cast adrift. I had begun a new life in the alien South without realizing the finality of my decision. Home had altered beyond recognition, or perhaps the distance had changed my perspective. For better or worse, I had thrown myself into the indifferent embrace of a second-rate college in a dreary Texan town. Though I could visit Ma and the farm, I could never go home anymore. Home had disappeared.

CHAPTER 47

MADISON, WISCONSIN

JANUARY 1986

JENNY

It was my first night back in the dorm. School started next week but they had allowed me to move in a bit before the others. Doc had said she thought I would be fine on my own now, but they did have a daily check-in they wanted me to do, among the other appointments. So here I sat, on my dorm bed, looking at Lena's bare mattress, wondering if I would ever hear from her again. Wondering at all the stuff that had taken over my life in the six weeks since she'd left. Thinking, most of all, about my stolen girlhood.

Funny how little I hold HIM responsible for all this. Sure, when I think about it intellectually, I know it's all his doing. If he hadn't had perverse ideas about me in the first place, we'd be a different family now, and I might be that lively, fun person I think I would have been otherwise. My gut doesn't blame him, though. SHE could have stopped it and didn't. I blame her. She was the other adult involved in this. I was only a dumb, powerless kid, a victim. But I blame myself, too, a blame that therapy and thinking about it with any sense of detachment tells me is stupid — I was only a kid. But why didn't I fight him off, or tell somebody else if SHE didn't want to help me? In some secret self too shameful to think about, did I really mind what he did to me, did I even like it? Did I cause it to happen in the first place, trying out my flirting techniques on the best-looking man I knew, my father? Didn't I dress up sometimes, largely so he'd compliment me? God, how I had lived for his praise. I suppose, if I had thought about it at all — and there were large gaps in my memory of those years, so I wasn't sure — I thought he'd love me more, he'd approve of me more, if I let him have this biggest of gifts. In the strange way that young teenage girls have of fantasizing, I was sure I'd make him a better wife than SHE was. I was his equal, while she was a neurotic, cold-hearted woman who escaped her family to do other people's taxes and take care of dogs. Who didn't treat him as he deserved. In my thirteen-year-old romantic mind, I thought I could do it better. Not consciously. But somewhere in my fantasies about being grown up I saw myself surpassing my mother in her role as the wife. In a perverse way, his attentions were a victory for me, proving he loved me more than her. She couldn't even service him as well as I could, and I was just a beginner at being a woman. Maybe, in a distorted way, I was proud of my degradation. For, by enduring HIS attentions, I both imagined I'd replaced my mother in his eyes and gained maturity, adulthood.

I don't know what I thought. A lot of it is so foggy that the shapes moving in the mist of my memories are hard to claim as mine. Even when I do remember, it's like thinking about someone else's thoughts. The feelings seem once removed, not really mine, like an intense movie where you cry in the theater, but once the lights go on you take up your life and walk away. I do remember the terror at first, though, and the pain. Sometimes I pretended — I played house, and this was my husband. I wore the white silky slip he liked me to wear and made me take off afterwards so he could hide it somewhere. But what he made me do, I never enjoyed. I cried at first at the pain and from the fear of thinking what terrible things that stiff appendage was doing to my insides.

After the first few months, when I saw how the cards were arranged, the deck stacked against me, I stopped crying. I stopped imagining I was playing house. I lay there as he wished with the passion of the mannequin I was. He was hooked by then, I suppose, and never seemed to notice my change in attitude. Those days, I saw it as a matter of survival and as a way to ruin HER. Even though she never said anything about it, certainly, I thought, his fucking me must make her feel old, unattractive, and a bad mother. Nice mothers, after all, didn't let this sordid activity go on in their own homes. If I was to be degraded, I would take HER down with me. She deserved it, after all, for not being good enough for HIM. By not being as good to him as she should have been.

By sixteen, I was mercenary about it. I sold my services, and if I was going to keep quiet about it as he demanded I do, I was going to get something in return. I extorted huge allowances, a stereo, a color TV for my room — everything I could think of. But that got old fast. When I left, I left all of it behind.

By eighteen, I knew there was a way out. College. I remember that lovely, scary feeling of knowing I could, I would, soon be able to run from all of it. HIM and his half-smug, half-guilty encounters with me. HER, in her cold-eyed disdain, her aloofness from the sick attentions being foisted on her own daughter by her husband. Funny how I'd convinced myself that if I could just get away, I'd be all right. I could start over, start living the normal life I'd been denied for five years. I was ecstatic when I saw the ad for a summer job working at a Girl Scout camp in Wisconsin, not too far from Madison. It was kitchen and maintenance work, real grunt stuff, but I happily took their offer of room, board, and laughable pay just to get away, to start over as soon as I could.

I was incredulous at first when I realized nothing had changed. Oh, there was the relief of not having to endure his unsavory attentions any longer. I slept better at camp than I'd slept in years. Yes, the act of it had stopped and for that, I was grateful enough. But that was all. The me I had been there in that house of private horrors didn't stay there as I imagined she would. Instead, she came right along to camp, and I found myself as reclusive and snotty as ever, playing the same sarcastic leave-me-alone bitch that I'd acted out all through high school. That other she, the one that I'd developed to protect myself with, had taken over. I couldn't seem to control her, much less get rid of her and let the real me come through. It was then that I began to realize I was doomed. I would drag this load around with me forever, I'd never be free of it, and that real girl, the nice one that I thought lurked down deep somewhere in the bottom of my soul, would never come out. I was tainted now, scarred no less obviously than Hester, the wearer of the scarlet letter.

What naivete to have thought otherwise. But I had. Through those years, I had cherished the hope that once away, I could find the normalcy I craved. To find out the truth of it — that I could never wash the stain away — had been more of a blow than anything I'd endured at HIS hands. But once realized, in my typical fashion, I buried the thought and pretended everything would be okay. I ignored the certainty that I could never be like other girls, never be the girl I was meant to be. I went on with my act. And then came Lena and Chuck, claiming they liked me, fanning that tiny flame of hope that must have somehow survived despite my thinking it couldn't. And when they left, so did my last hope — I can see that now. I can see that's why I downed those pills. I suppose part of me did really want to die. But which one? The act that was tired, so tired of her practiced aloofness? Or the real girl shoved down in the shadows with no hope of living out a life of her own? I didn't know, and maybe I never would.

So why can't I summon up some healthy hatred for the man who put me through all this? Why can't I get angry at him in therapy the way they say would be good for me? I've looked inside. I've tried to find some of those feelings that my brain tells me must be there, but I can't find them, can't find them anywhere. Instead, this huge weight descends on me, smothering any feelings I might have had when I think of my father and what he did to me. It feels like the weight of death closing in on me. Still, I can't hate him. I feel empty, nothing else.

CHAPTER 48

PINE HILL STATION, TEXAS

FEBRUARY 1986

JANE

As suddenly as Johnny had disappeared from my life when we'd said goodbye in December, he reappeared in his role as my professor the first Monday of the new term. I had not expected to see him before school geared up for spring semester, as he'd told me it would have been difficult to come up with a plausible story to tell his wife. I wondered about his wife, Elizabeth Wharton. I wondered if she was a nice woman, if we would like each other if we'd met in different circumstances, if she liked being Johnny's wife, if she suspected he was having an affair. Johnny spoke of her only seldomly and never in detail. From his vague references, I had the impression she was cold and high-strung. He had once categorized her as a good candidate for a nervous breakdown. Another time, he insisted she was as cold and calculating as a computer. Yet he seemed to have some affection for her of a comradely sort. I suspected he was loyal in a fashion, too, and in some chivalrous way would revile anyone who dared call her character into question. I had only seen her once from a distance, on Johnny's arm on the way to what I presumed was the faculty Christmas party. She was very petite, I noticed, and slim, too. Although graduate students were invited, Johnny had asked me not to come, a request I found easy to accede to. I found parties terrifying, with their forced socialization and confusing rhythms. Johnny took pains to keep us from ever meeting, his wife and me, even though he knew I would present myself as nothing more than one of his graduate students. I concluded from this, and from the way he conducted our physical relationship, that he felt extreme guilt over the connection he was pursuing with me.

Six weeks apart had not dampened his ardor. His face looked almost anguished when he confessed he couldn't see me until the next evening, something I already knew because he had told me that she worked at the dog shelter on Tuesdays and Thursdays. We had made a date quietly after I'd asked him to explain a difficult passage in one of the theory readings he'd assigned while he packed away his lecture notes after class. He complimented me on the blue sweater and the gray wool pants I'd dug out of the cedar chest at home and brought back here. At his acknowledgement of my new look, I flushed with pleasure — and a little fear. What he thought of me mattered.

With scenes of Ma's busy social life buzzing in my brain, I told him I'd try to be less serious and more fun to be with this year.

"It's a New Year's resolution," I smiled up at him. He was taller than I remembered.

He said something odd then. "Don't worry about it, Janey, I know who you are."

He said he knew me. The words were threatening and very wrong, but they had been said with warmth, so I supposed he'd meant it as a comfort. He was saying I could be whoever I wanted to be with him, I told myself. That sounded like just what I needed to hear.

Tuesday evening gave me a chance to practice my new happier, more open self with him. I decided to experiment with my new persona by telling him about my trip home and practiced enchanting descriptions of the farm in winter to myself as I stirred a pot of chili over the hot plate waiting for him to show up. Soon, I heard the squish of wet shoes on the stairs and his brisk step. The second of February and it was raining sheets of ice water, muddying up sidewalks, painting doorsteps in muck footprints. The ground was unable to absorb the torrent pouring down on it, and the excess ran along the streets, filling the inadequate sewers and overflowing to create shallow ponds of dirt-tinged water.

Winters in Texas had no reason to them. The temperatures dipped into the forties, with bone-chilling wet winds and rain pelting down without end. It sometimes reached freezing and there were balmy days too, when I, with my tough Iowa blood, wore only a sweater while the Texans huddled in their heavy jackets. Here, winter did not build momentum from the snap of September frosts and proceed over the next months to swirling, white-frenzied blizzards that threatened survival and therefore made all feel more alive. Winter here was a haphazard collection of warm and chilly days and rains that ran wasted through the streets.

Inspired by these thoughts, I went excitedly to the door. I would make Johnny understand the importance of winter in my life.

Johnny was puzzled by my exuberance as he handed me his umbrella and coat to deposit in the bathroom where they could drip into the tub from a hanger on the shower head. He left his mud-stained shoes on the mat by the door and looked up at me.

"Janey, you're lit up like a Christmas tree. What are you so excited about?"

"Oh, ah, winter and Christmas ..." My voice trailed off doubtfully. Talking to him about what I felt was going to be more difficult than I'd thought.

"Did you have a good Christmas vacation with your mother?"

"Yeah, it was great," I lied. "Just like when I was a kid, with snow and presents, sugar cookies, and Johnny Mathis singing carols."

"Glad it didn't snow in Florida." That's where he had taken his wife for a January vacation combined with a history conference. "I can't stand the stuff."

"Snow? Even for the holidays?"

"Especially then. Everybody gets so damn sentimental about it. I suppose if I was a skier, I'd like it more. At least then it would be useful. But I suppose you love what you're raised with."

I canceled my plans to tell him about Christmas at the farm.

Feeling, I guess, that he'd exhausted the subjects of snow and holidays, he asked, "What classes are you taking this semester? I hope you signed up for that advanced methodology class I suggested. Johnson's a real pain in the posterior to sit on a committee with, but he knows his stuff."

I told him that I had signed up for it and Haystead's class on "Forgotten Voices" in addition to his, as I poured him a glass of red Californian wine that I kept on hand just for his visits. I don't like drinking alone.

"Sounds like you have a full semester ahead," Johnny pronounced. "Janey," he continued, "when I was snoozing on the Florida beach, this idea came to me for securing that foundation grant. Let me try it out on you and see what you think."

And off he went, describing his latest brainstorm. All through the simple meal he talked on. I only half listened, keeping the stream of his words flowing steadily with nods and encouraging comments. My mind raced through my small repertoire of appropriate subjects for conversation. I sought something to say that Johnny would find interesting, an anecdote or piece of familial history. I wanted to share something of myself with him, some bit of information that would make me seem more alive to him. But what was there in my cloistered existence that would be of interest to a man who is a star historian, a man who tells me he had the best paper at the entire history conference? He had already dismissed winter and holidays; certainly, snow-covered corn-fields would hold little attraction for him. The memories I cherished were a patchwork of nostalgic moments, and Johnny was a man who disliked the sentimental. The curious histories of a few of the folks Ma took care of at the old people's home, stories we'd shared over evening dinners, would hold little intrigue for Johnny. The lives of aunts and uncles that had fascinated me as a child seemed uniformly dull and predictable as I reviewed them quickly to myself as Johnny droned on. Of my own life, there seemed little to add to what I'd told him in our first conversation five months ago.

The more I thought about it, the more I resigned myself to continuing the pattern our relationship had slipped into from the start. For some reason unfathomable to me, Johnny seemed to enjoy my company. A natural teacher, I could tell he enjoyed my willingness to listen to him; I was his inex-haustible audience. He slept with me, I supposed, to reclaim some of his lost youth. He was of the age when men commonly felt the pull of their years and slept with younger women to forget. Were these the reasons he kept coming back, with clock-like regularity, two times each week since September? It seemed an inadequate explanation.

"Johnny, why do you keep coming back here?" The question passed my lips before I realized I was speaking aloud.

"Huh?" he said, blinking. I'd interrupted him. Then, as he belatedly comprehended what I'd said, his expression transformed. His eyes grew soft, and he crossed the room and took both my hands in his.

"Janey," he said with a soft intensity, "you mean more to me than you'll ever know."

"What?" I said, feebly. "I don't understand what I could mean to you."

"Janey, Janey," he whispered into my hair. "You must know how much I love you."

Love me? You don't even know me! I half wanted to scream. The other part of me was gratefully accepting his caresses and his words. I had little enough of love in my life, a voice inside me whispered, why should I turn away his gift? I meant much to him in some way I couldn't understand. I could see it in his eyes.

"I've been so lonely," he murmured, his lips against my nape. "And then my Janey came home to me. I need you, Janey." He kissed me briefly.

I was sorry then for wondering, though I had no answer to my question. Maybe this was the way men loved, loving what they'd decided you were with no need to know what was under the façade they'd given you. I had so little experience with men. How could I know what they were, what they wanted?

He had pulled me down on his lap on the big gray chair now and held me, stroking my hair. I leaned into him, happy for the warmth that was not explicitly sexual for once. All too soon, he lifted me in his arms as he stood up and placed me back in the chair. He crossed the room and pulled the bed down from the wall, then turned off the lights, leaving only the harsh white light of a streetlight to pierce the shadows.

He led me to the bed and took off my shirt while I unzipped my jeans and stepped out of them and into the white silk slip he always wanted me to wear. He laid me on the bed and loosened his belt and trousers. He always left his clothes on during our hurried lovemaking. I lay still as he liked me to do while he felt my small, skinny girl breasts as he sat on the edge of the bed. Suddenly, he rolled on top of me, and I raised my arms and crossed my wrists above my head as he had instructed me to do many months ago. "Keep still!" he whispered, in what by now had become an expected part of the ritual. In a single, well-practiced motion, his left hand held my wrists in place while his right parted my thighs and then he entered me with hard, jabbing thrusts. I clenched my teeth and sucked in my breath against the pain that his entering caused. I was out of practice. It took perhaps two minutes of rapid, deep thrusting that seemed to press uncomfortably against my kidneys until he came with an all but silent sigh. "Thank you, Janey," he whispered and got up quickly to tuck in his shirt and zip his pants. I heard him groping for his coat and umbrella in the dark bathroom and the squish as he slipped on his still-wet shoes. The door opened and closed softly. And then he was gone.

I felt nothing during or after these sessions. Only the sore, chafed feeling between my legs, never any sense of pleasure or release. What had happened to me during my teenaged years had no doubt ruined those possibilities for me. But Johnny seemed satisfied with the limited young woman he'd gotten involved with. I seemed to be enough for him as I was. He had said he loved me and if I tried, maybe I could accept that. He was my lifeline now, the link between me and this strange new landscape I'd chosen to live in. He cared for me. I could trust that. I'd seen it in his eyes, and it was real.

Later, when I went to sit in the gray chair and do a bit of history reading for tomorrow's class, I noticed Johnny's black leather billfold half shoved in between the seat and back cushions of the chair. It must have fallen out when he'd taken me on his lap earlier. I'd give it back to him after class tomorrow.

I threw the wallet over towards the kitchen table, where I would notice it tomorrow when I left for school. I overshot my target though, and the wallet grazed the tiny white creamer with its blue morning glories, toppling it onto the floor where it smashed against a corner and broke into a thousand fragments.

I shed tears for the broken creamer that I've never shed for myself.

CHAPTER 49

MADISON, WISCONSIN

MARCH 1986

JENNY

"Isn't it possible your mother never knew?" Martha Roberts, the graduate student, asked me casually. It was Monday afternoon and I sat in Dr. Kurtz's office at the hospital for one of my twice-a-week sessions. The room was comfortable, homey even, and I liked the big green chair I got to sit in. Sometimes, I even curled my legs under me when I first sat down, more like I was getting prepared for a long gossip session than a talk about my most personal feelings and fears. Martha sat at an angle from me in a matching chair while Dr. Kurtz sat at her beautiful mahogany desk and sometimes took a few notes. I had a view of the street from where I sat and I looked down at the people hurrying along University Avenue, the wind whipping their long winter coats or blowing back the hoods of their parkas. There was a sofa in the room too, but Doc, as I called her now, had told me I only had to lie down on it if I felt like it. I was relieved to find out going to a shrink didn't mean lying down on a couch had to come into the deal. I pretended Martha and Doc were my friends and we were just getting together for a little talk. It's just that the conversation always happened to be about me. I suppose I didn't feel so threatened when I thought of it like that. Or so crazy. It made it easier, if I took away some of their power in my mind and brought them down to my level. But it didn't always work. Not when they started things rolling with a question like that.

"Isn't it possible?" Martha repeated, as I hadn't said anything.

"Martha, my mother is not stupid, whatever else she is. How could she not know how her husband was spending his evenings?" This line of questioning irritated me. It seemed pointless. I was sick of imagining her in my mind, knowing and not stopping it. Coming home from her dog shelter and getting into bed with the degenerate who'd just gotten out of her daughter's.

"But Jenny, didn't you say she was gone most evenings, first to prepare taxes and then working at the dog shelter?"

"SO?" I said, a little too loudly.

"Listen, Jenny, I don't want to get your hopes up. Lots of women do know what's going on between their daughters and husbands, or suspect it, anyways. But because they're scared or feel helpless, they don't do anything about it. Your mom needs help too, Jenny. And we both think you're ready to deal with her in person."

"Just what are you getting at?" I replied in a voice that betrayed my agitation. I felt my guts sinking as the doctor answered.

"Jenny, I know this will be hard for you," put in Dr. Kurtz, "but I think you should contact your mother. Maybe you could ask her to spend a weekend here with you."

"Why? What good would that do? I don't need her now.

She was never there when I did and now it's too late. Besides, I doubt she'd come." I knew that was my big fear as soon as the words left my lips. She'd be too busy to come, she wouldn't care enough to bother. She'd desert me now like she did then.

"Jenny, your mom ignoring what went on between you and your father is a big issue for you. You need to set it to rest, and the only way to do that is to find out the truth." Doc leaned forward in her chair.

"So, you want me to dial her number and say, 'Hi Mom. Did you know I was fucking your husband more than you were?'" I said sarcastically, stalling for time. I thought over what they wanted me to do. No, I wasn't willing to believe she might not have known. Like Martha said, I didn't want to get my hopes up. She probably does need help, but why should I feel responsible for that? On the other hand, there was this persistent question tugging at my brain ever since I started talking and thinking about all this. Why did my mother let him do that to me? Why didn't she protect me from him? I'd thought about it a lot and no matter how many answers I'd come up with, they weren't enough. They didn't satisfy me. They were right. I did need to hear it from her, and I had to know before I got any further along in this business of reconstructing my life. But what if she never answered my letter or told me on the phone that she didn't care what happened to me and never had? It would be impossible to bear, hearing words like that from your mother, worse than any other reason she could come up with. "I knew, but I was afraid of him." "I knew, but I thought he'd leave me if I said anything." I tried out the sound of what she might say. I didn't think I could forgive her for what she had done, but maybe I could understand why, and that might help me get over this snag I got into every time a picture of her got stuck in my mind. But what if she just said, "I didn't care?" Could I survive hearing that from her? Or hearing nothing, which meant the same thing? Doc and Martha must think I'm strong enough to handle even that, or they wouldn't have suggested confronting her. Well, if they thought so, maybe I could do it. Maybe I was strong enough.

"Jenny," Martha said as these thoughts ran through my mind, "you don't have to call her. Write a letter if that would be easier."

"I know it will be painful, Jenny," Doc continued, "but in the long run, it will help you to come to terms with that part of your life."

"Okay, I'll write and invite her for a weekend," I sighed and gave in.

They were right, and I knew it. Getting it out in the open with her was something I needed to do before I could go on with my life.

Funny, a few months ago, I didn't think I wanted to go on with it.

I guess that's what I felt. I don't seem to remember feeling much of anything. At the time, getting on with my life seemed like going through the motions of living, nothing more. When I thought about it, and I had thought about it a lot while I was at the hospital and since I moved back to my dorm room, too, I couldn't remember feeling much of anything for years except this vague anger. I was always pissed off at everything, the way you get when you have a headache you can't get rid of or somebody's bugging you and won't stop. It was like an irritating, nagging noise, a hammering on the inside of my brain. But aside from that, I didn't seem to have many emotions. It had started to worry me, sitting in my bed in the hospital. I was becoming an emotional hypochondriac almost, wondering if it meant I was on my way to insanity. If you don't feel anything, what's to stop you from doing something really terrible like murder? Come to think of it, I had done some not so nice things already, though mostly I had just hurt myself.

So, I asked Doc about it one session, afraid she'd tell me I had some horrible mental illness. I did, as it turned out. But it was curable. Doc told me when you're depressed for a long time, your emotional life just sort of shuts down and nothing gets through to you anymore, not good emotions or bad. Pretty soon, you start thinking that kind of zombie existence is normal, and you just go right on, not even able to tell that there's something really wrong in your life. I didn't believe her explanation applied to me at first. I didn't feel depressed. But after a while, I got to see what she meant. I couldn't see it in myself, but I recognized it in someone else.

Doc and Martha got me into this group for incest victims. I sure fought going for a while, but once they finally got me there, I knew it was where I belonged. It was like I recognized all these people from somewhere but couldn't exactly remember where. Their stories, their faces were that familiar. It was like looking in the mirror. It amazed me how much better I felt, just finding I belonged somewhere, even if it was in a group for women who've been raped by their relatives. There were a couple of women in the group who were just like Doc had described, wooden, afraid to feel anything. Afraid that if they allowed themselves to feel all the pain and hurt, they'd just die of it or go crazy. Finally, I had to admit, I wasn't far from that way of thinking myself. That's when I started to understand what Doc and Martha were getting at. As I heard them talking together over the weeks, I saw that some women had survived. They were so brave: picking up the pieces after what had been done to them and getting on with their lives. I said that in one of the first meetings I went to and one of the older ones, she's about thirty-five, told me, "But Jenny, you're just as brave as we are. You joined the group. That's making a choice to pick up your pieces and put your life back together." I started crying then, right in front of everyone. It was such a release and, somehow, I didn't feel ashamed of letting go in front of them. They were all just like me.

After that, it was easier for me. I saw those women and something inside me said, "Well, if they can do it, if they can learn to feel again and learn to feel better, why can't you?" I felt almost obligated to do it, just to show them that they were doing something important for me, being good examples. That's when I felt like I was getting somewhere. And I guess I am, because now Doc and Martha want me to look my past in the face and ask why. Well, if those women in the group got through it, I can too. Even if the worst happens, I know I won't be completely deserted. I've got Doc and Martha and the group to give me a hand. I think I might just make it through this after all.

CHAPTER 50

PINE HILL STATION, TEXAS

MARCH 1986

JANE

A month of the new semester had come and gone, but nothing had changed. I still spoke to almost no one outside of class and my attempts at dressing a bit more formally like the other graduate students here went mostly unnoticed. Maddie continued to try to start conversations with me on occasion and twice she had tried to introduce me to graduate students who were further along with whom she thought I might have something in common. Twice, I'd had pleasant-enough conversations with them and then we'd gone our separate ways. They, probably because they already had all the friends they needed in the department, me, because I had no idea how to make friends. It had been so long since I'd had any. Childhood, really.

Johnny remained a constant Tuesday and Thursday visitor, and our ritual had settled in for the semester in its unvarying way. I didn't know what to think of it, of him, so I mostly tried not to and just reverted to my usual immersion in my studies. So it was that I was sitting curled up in my gray chair on a Thursday night after he'd left, reading some early Roman history, when I dropped my highlighter pen into the crack between the chair cushion and its arm. As I shoved my hand into the chair's upholstery to retrieve it, my fingers grazed some other foreign plastic object that had somehow also found its way there. It was one of those plastic inserts for wallets that usually held family photos. In a flash, I remembered that I had found Johnny's wallet wedged in this chair almost a month ago. The wallet insert must be his, a fact that was confirmed when I glanced at the top photo and saw a professional photo of Johnny and a woman who must be Elizabeth from a few years ago. There were only two other photos in the insert. One was of an elderly but distinguished looking man.

When I saw the other one, back-to-back with the photo of Johnny and his wife, I instinctively drew it out of its plastic sleeve and turned it over, already knowing what it would say on the back. I wasn't shocked at finding it or even surprised. All my half-trusted intuitive powers knew there was something more than his flimsy assertions of love that explained his near obsession with me. I had so desperately wanted to trust him. I had tried so hard to believe in what happened on the surface of our interactions. But the scarred places inside me could not push down the nagging doubts that plagued my dreams and late-night thoughts. Now, here was the evidence, looking solemnly out of a high school class photo with almost my eyes.

I turned the photo over once more, studying the large backhand inscription in red: "To Daddy, your Jenny." I'd hardly needed the words that confirmed what I'd known the moment I saw the photo. In this picture of Johnny's daughter,

I could see the family resemblance that I could not when comparing my face with Johnny's because I'd never suspected we looked so much like father and daughter. It was an uncanny resemblance, I thought, comparing my twenty-three-year-old face in the mirror with Jenny's eighteen-year-old one in the picture. She even wore a sky-blue sweater not unlike the one Ma had given me for Christmas. "Class of 1984" was diagonally inscribed in small gold script in the right-hand corner of the picture. So, Jenny was twenty now, three years younger than me. Yet, we looked more than sisters. We were doubles, close enough in looks to be identical twins.

No wonder Johnny hadn't wanted me to meet his wife! She would have made a fuss over my resemblance to her daughter. I wondered if anyone in his department noticed the resemblance, but perhaps his daughter was not living at home anymore. At twenty, she'd probably be in college somewhere. Or perhaps she was even dead. It was possible no one he worked with knew her that well and would remember how much she looked like me.

Johnny had always discouraged me from attending faculty parties, not that I needed much discouragement. Parties were always painful ordeals for me. But he'd always made sure I'd skip them. It made sense now; probably colleagues outside of the history department that did know his daughter attended these gatherings. I could be identified, word could get around that I'd been seen in Johnny's company, ugly rumors could be started, and Johnny discredited.

What a dirty little secret I am in Johnny's life. Not only is his student his mistress, not only am I young enough to be his daughter. I nearly *am* his daughter. I want to feel humiliation at this knowledge, but in my life, it is a word with no meaning. For I am a woman with half a lifetime spent living in secret shame. I have no reserve of self-respect to draw on now. And what is humiliation if not a breach of self-respect?

Instead, this photograph is more a symbolic confirmation of self. My self has been forged by the failure of men to have what they wanted, my father, a secure livelihood, Johnny, his daughter. Unwittingly, I have played the cowering dog, kicked and abused in pitiful compensation for its master's powerlessness. I hold this role to me like a familiar possession, comforting me in a moment of fear or indecision. It is one of the few elements of my existence that is uniquely mine. So right that I hold a picture of another me in my hand, the one of substance, the one that is desired. She is real, I, only a mannequin. I am the substitute for unfulfilled desires.

It had grown late while I sat in the gray chair staring at the photo of almost-me. The rain pounded down onto the gutters above my windows, overflowing in sheets of water that ran down the windows into the muddy yard below.

Finally, I roused myself from my thoughts and undressed for bed, pulling my flannel nightgown out of the closet and over my head. I methodically washed and brushed my teeth and then decided to lean Jenny's picture up against the small stack of books on the bedside table. I stared into the face a little longer, wondering where Jenny was now. I had a conviction that she was somewhere alive, and as I conjectured, I started thinking of her as a real person instead of the two-dimensional representation of my failed life. It was comforting to think that there was someone living out in the world who was my physical twin. Maybe she shared some of my thoughts and feelings, too. I drifted off into an uneasy sleep with this thought, only to awaken like a shot a couple of hours later at the sound of a scream I knew, after a few confusing moments, had been my own.

Frantically, I fumbled for the light, to find myself staring into the substance of my nightmare in Jenny's face. I had dreamed of eyes, large blue eyes, staring at me out of a black background. My own eyes, Jenny's eyes, interchangeable, staring with the same expression. Upon waking, I knew the dream's meaning. I knew why those eyes, the same in each of us, had made me scream in the dark. One look at the picture confirmed it. We had the same eyes, the same hunted, shameful, secret-holding eyes. More than eyes, more than faces, we were identical in our defilement. A defilement Johnny was now reliving through me.

Had I sensed this parallel between my life and Johnny's somehow? Was that the source of my initial discomfort with him? Was that the source of my *attraction* to him? Could my body recognize somehow the familial predator in him — my years of hideous tutelage under my own father making Johnny a sickly compelling type to me? I quaked violently at these dreadful thoughts.

I resolved at that moment not to see Johnny again. I would drop his class, avoid the department, leave when the semester was over and finish up somewhere else. I could not waste the money already spent on this semester; I had no idea where any more would come from. I'd use the time I now spent seeing Johnny to find a new school for myself for next year and a summer job to tide me over until then. I was proud of my rational solution.

The next day, I skipped his class and dropped it after I'd finished going to my other classes. He would wonder if I were ill, but he wouldn't think to come over until next Tuesday, four days from now, on his usual night, and I wouldn't be home. I'd plan to see a movie.

I kept the picture of Jenny propped up on the night table. I would no longer participate in making a mockery of Jenny's life. What resolve I could not find from the saving of my own dignity, I could acquire from the knowledge that, in a small way, I was helping to end her legacy of pain.

CHAPTER 51

PINE HILL STATION, TEXAS

MARCH 1986

LIZ

As I opened the door to our darkened house, I was still feeling the love from helping to feed, wash, and cuddle a litter of five-week-old hound-mix puppies that had been anonymously left in a box on the doorstep of the shelter earlier that morning. The pups had been removed from their mother's care and left to survive on their own too early, a problem we were well-equipped to deal with at the shelter. Because they were products of an unintentional mating, they were not worth any money at all and thus they'd been abandoned. We'd look for people to adopt them when they were cleaned up and a bit more independent. I was confident we could find people to love them, mixed breeds though they were.

Johnny wasn't home yet, which was not too unusual on a Tuesday. I'd been so busy at my accounting job today — we were well into tax season — that I'd completely forgotten to bring in the mail during the brief time I'd stopped home to eat a salad before heading out to the shelter. I went to the black metal mailbox attached to the wall on the porch right next to the front door and retrieved the usual stack of bills and magazines and other junk mail. I went through it quickly, sorting through what I needed to keep from what could be quickly tossed when I came upon a small envelope addressed in red in that unmistakable backhand. Addressed to me.

"Jenny," I whispered in disbelief, in hope, in fear that she was sick or in trouble. The letter was short and dry, but it made my heart beat wildly with hope.

> *Mother —*
> *I am writing to ask you if it is possible for you to fly up here for a weekend soon. I have something I would like to discuss with you alone.*
> *Your daughter,*
> *Jenny*

I read the letter again and again, trying to glean some hint of what it was she wanted to discuss with me. Finally, I realized I didn't care. She wanted to talk with me, and the subject didn't matter, though visions of felony, unwanted pregnancy, or surgery pulsated in my brain like an ambulance light. I sank weakly into my desk chair as it dawned on me that tonight my ritual phone call might be answered. I looked her number up in my address book, suddenly forgetting the digits I'd been dialing every week for over five months. Jenny had put her phone number at the end of the letter, and now that I looked at what was in my address book, I realized the two were different by a couple of digits. I'd been calling the wrong number all these weeks, assuming that she just wasn't answering her phone when in fact it hadn't even been her I'd been calling. Thinking that perhaps, if I'd had the right number, she might have answered my calls these past weeks gave me the courage to dial the number at the bottom of her note. My hand trembled violently, but I resisted the impulse to light up one of Johnny's cigarettes. Instead, I fumbled through the numbers, dialing one after the other slowly, carefully, before I lost my nerve.

It was ringing. Someone was picking up.

"Hello?" Her voice cut through the distance.

"Jenny? Ah ... This is ... ah ... your mother." I stupidly stumbled over the words.

"Oh. Hello." A note of surprise hid behind her carefully tempered tones.

"Um ... I got your letter. Would this weekend be okay?" I asked, too soon in the conversation.

"What?" The voice registered shock. "You're coming?"

"Of course, I am. Jenny, you don't know how ..." I trailed off, afraid that my emotions would turn her from me.

"There's no hurry. I mean, if it's any trouble ..."

"No, no trouble at all. I'd like to get away from all this rain for a few days," I said, too cheerfully. "Ah ... I don't know when the flight arrives, I haven't had time to check. But I'll take Friday off and be up there as soon as I can. I'm sure there are flights to Chicago from Houston every day and I can drive from there ..."

"This Friday?" she asked incredulously.

"Well, if that's all right with you." Maybe she's changed her mind, I thought frantically.

"Yes, ah ... sure. I'll make a reservation for you at the Capitol Inn. I can meet you there if you let me know when you arrive."

"Jenny, is everything okay up there? Are you in some sort of trouble?" I knew I was treading on dangerous ground, but I had to ask.

"Trouble?" she sounded puzzled. Then, as if she'd suddenly imagined what I might be thinking, she added, "Oh, no, nothing like that."

"Well, I'm glad. I guess I'll see you Friday then." I said, half hoping she'd tell me what it was she wanted to talk about.

"Yeah ... Oh, you are coming alone, aren't you?"

"Yes, if that's what you want." Maybe it had something to do with Johnny?

"Yes, alone, please."

"Okay, see you Friday. I'll call from the Capitol Inn when I arrive. Goodbye, Jenny." The phone clicked at her end without another word.

Two days. Two more days to live through and I'll see my daughter again. A daughter who wants me up there because she wants to talk with me. I shivered in the half-dark house. Who was my daughter after all these years? Why did she want to talk with me now, after all this time? Had she grown up finally, come to regret her coldness towards me? Did she want to make amends or confront me with well-worded accusations of my failures as a mother?

I made up my mind at that moment to accept any blame, admit to any wrongdoing, anything that might help resurrect a relationship with my daughter. Jenny. I was going to see my Jenny again. She would give me a chance to be a mother to her now. She had to. I couldn't bear to lose her twice.

CHAPTER 52

PINE HILL STATION, TEXAS

MARCH 1986

MADDIE

"Maddie, what do you think?" The department chairman's words jolted me out of my revenge fantasy, in which I had imagined Johnny surrounded by a coven of my most dyky friends, who were taunting him in rhyming couplets, proposing to correct his offensive anatomy. It was probably a good thing I'd been called back to reality by my chairman's gravelly voice.

It was the worst meeting of my academic career. The February meeting had been canceled due to a pathetic amount of sleet that had fallen and frozen on streets ill-prepared for ice and drivers even less prepared to drive on it. So, this was the first department meeting I'd had to attend since I'd known what my colleague was and had done and had created. I had waited until he'd taken a seat before selecting one as far away from him as possible around the conference table. It was not close to being far enough. Fortunately, I had done my homework the evening before regarding the proposed change to the graduate program we were discussing and could answer the chairman's question with sufficient detail to make my colleagues think I knew what I was talking about — and cared.

When I surreptitiously glanced at Johnny early on in this excruciating exercise, I noticed he was looking rough. Dark circles under those cold, gray eyes of his suggested he was sleeping poorly. His attire looked somewhat wrinkled. He seemed to have forgotten to shave this morning, an utter breach of his impeccable grooming habits. My first thought was that his affair with Jane had foundered. Good, if that were true. She deserved better than this two-timing criminal.

Roz had not found out much more about that fateful night than she had learned when Mama had originally revealed it and the few details Patty and Elton had added during her Kwanzaa visit to them. She'd been back once since then, but they hadn't wanted to speak of it again. "All in good time, Maddie," Roz had told me. "And really, why do I need to know more details? The important ones have been confirmed." She seemed strangely at peace with her origin story. I was the one, historian to the last, who wanted to interview Elton, Patty, and Grace in minute detail until every last element of that horrible night was revealed. Of course, that was not going to happen.

Roz had instead decided to make it her mission to reunite the trio: Patty, Elton, and Mama Grace. Mama had been reluctant. "It may be best to let sleeping dogs lie, Rosalyn," she replied when Roz had told her of her visit and the possibility of reconnecting with her childhood playmates. Tears were streaming down her face, though, at the news that Patty and Elton were still among the living and living at Wharton Hall. "Thank you, Jesus," she kept repeating, interspersed with, "Thank you, daughter, for this news. Thank you kindly."

Roz had been incredulous at Mama's reluctance to see

them again. "Mama, they want to see you! I'd be happy to drive you out to visit. Let's do it this weekend!" Roz had encouraged Mama a few weeks ago when we'd spent an evening there.

But Mama said, "Best not to churn up what's been long put to rest, Rosalyn." At first, that was all Mama would say on the matter.

The next time I was at Mama's, Roz had pushed her again. "Mama, I know Patty would love to see you again, and Elton too," she said out of the blue after we'd cleared up the dinner dishes. Mama even let me help dry them, which Roz and I took as an indication that I was transitioning to the status of "family member." Roz had been inviting me over to Mama's more frequently recently, in preparation for coming out to her and telling her we were a couple, something Roz was now committed to doing. She had hoped to reunite the old friends and then tell Mama she was a lesbian and we were a couple. And hope for the best.

This time, Mama was more forthcoming. "I've had a think on it, Rosalyn," she said, "and I just cannot go out to that place. Ever again."

Roz got it, and I got it, immediately. What had we been thinking? Of course, she wouldn't want to return to the scene of her life's most traumatic minutes. "I'm sorry, Mama," Roz said, flushing. "I should have thought about that. Of course, you would not want to go out there again. But we could have them here. I could make them dinner from the old recipes," Roz continued, thinking of the recipes that Mama had said she'd learned as a child from Aunt Suzy and perhaps her own mother too, though she didn't say so. Mama's shame over her pregnancy had resulted in a permanent estrangement from her parents. Roz had recently learned that Mama had run away from home when her belly had started to show, feeling that she had shamed the family. She had sworn the minister who had taken her in to silence and his cousin, who had given her the waitress job, too. Once she and Harold had married, they'd moved across town and even the minister hadn't known what had become of her. Her self-imposed disappearance had lasted until Jerry was born, almost six years later. When she finally had tried to reconnect with her parents, it had been too late. They had moved North, a neighbor had told her when she'd driven out to their house with baby Jerry to find it occupied by strangers, but no one knew exactly where.

At the mention of the old recipes, Mama burst into tears, something Roz had seen only once before. "Oh, chile," she said between sobs, "just look at what's become of me! I don't want them to see me like this! I rode horses with those people. Now I can't even get to the toilet by myself, hardly."

Roz got up from her place on the sofa, knelt next to the wheelchair and hugged her mama tight. "Mama," Roz said softly, "don't you think Patty and Elton have changed since those days, too? Sure, they have. They want to visit Grace's heart and soul; they don't care what's become of her body."

Mama had grown still at that and hugged her daughter back. A time passed. "You think so, truly? Truly?" It was the only time I had heard doubt in this incredibly courageous woman's voice.

"If I told them of your worries, Mama, I know just what they'd do," Roz said, the picture of confidence. "They'd laugh. They'd say, 'We're no spring chickens ourselves, Rosalyn Eleanor.' That's what they call me, Mama. Because they were charmed when I told them my middle name because of how much Aunt Suzy was always speaking well of the first lady back in the day," Roz continued. She was trying mightily to convince her mama of the rightness of the reunion. She was making headway.

"Well, maybe we could do a spring cleaning of the place, Rosalyn." Mama's voice was returning to its usual steadiness. "Maybe we could start talking about a menu. I'd like to meet their son — Marvin, did you say his name was? Maybe the six of us could have a dinner here at the end of the month, if my health holds," she relented.

My head jerked up. Had she just invited me to this momentous occasion? Roz stole a glance my way that confirmed that she had heard that too. Roz said, just to be sure, "Jerry won't be able to come home for that, Mama," she said. "He's got that big case coming up."

Mama replied, "I am not talking about your brother, Rosalyn Eleanor," she said using the name she called her daughter when she was scolding her. "I'm talking about your girlfriend, Maddie here," she said waving a hand in my direction. "Don't think I don't got eyes in my head enough to see lovebirds when they're flying right in front of me. I suspected as much when I first laid eyes on you, Maddie," Mama said, looking over at me. "I thought my daughter would tell me at some point," she continued in a scolding voice, "but I guess she thought I couldn't handle it, you being white and all." Mama had a definite twinkle in her eye. "I know what it says in the Bible and that lots of folk think it will damn you straight to hell. But Lord Almighty, don't I know from Mr. Gaines," she said, referring to her departed husband formally, as she always had, "that love comes the way it comes, no matter if the girl is an unwed mother with a mixed-blood child and the man a war hero, no matter if its two professors, both of 'em women and one white to boot." Mama was smiling now. "You *ever* planning on saying something, Rosalyn Eleanor?" She leaned out of the hug and looked at Roz. But she had a grin on her face.

Roz was in shock; I could see from my perch across the room. Hadn't seen this one coming, nor this reception either. Oh, how we had underestimated this woman Roz was lucky enough to be related to.

Roz stood up and came over to me. She took my hand and

crossed the room, so we were both standing in front of Mama. "I have loved Maddie since I first laid eyes on her in 1974, Mama. She's my soulmate," she said simply. "I couldn't bear the thought that you might reject us, like Maddie's folks rejected her," she continued. I could feel myself welling up at this simple declaration. Soulmate. I could feast on that word for a lifetime. "But I should have known better, Mama. And I guess I did, at least after you told me about my beginnings. I thought maybe it might be okay with you. Maddie and me, I mean. Thank you, Mama, for your understanding." Roz was getting weepy, too.

"Maddie, you are welcome in this family, always. Just take care of my only girl-child here, that's all I ask." She looked at our clasped hands. "You don't have to hide your true selves around here no more. I wish I had said that a space of time earlier, I do. But know it now. Maddie, why don't you pour us a bit of sherry? We'll toast to all our new and old-new family members, Elton, Patty, Marvin, and Maddie, here. Then let's get planning the spring housecleaning and this party."

"Maddie, your vote?" It was Johnny who had spoken, abruptly pulling me away from those lovely memories. I couldn't look at him. "I concur," I said, glancing at the folder of documents I had brought for just this purpose. "The changes are good ones." I had been half listening enough to know that the rest of the department members were also in favor of the changes.

Johnny. I hated him for what he had done to my sort of mother-in-law, one of the bravest and most long-suffering women I've ever known. But he had helped create, however accidentally, my beautiful Roz. I wanted to kill him. I wanted to thank him. I wished he'd disappear, so I never had to think about any of this ever again.

CHAPTER 53

MADISON, WISCONSIN

MARCH 1986

JENNY

I stood staring at the phone, not quite believing it had been my mother's voice on the other end. I almost hadn't answered it. I'd been back in this half-empty room for almost four weeks now and I had gotten some phone calls. But I hadn't had the courage to answer the phone. It might have been someone for Lena, which would have just made me think about her again. Or maybe, as I not-so-secretly hoped, it was Lena or Chuck calling. I didn't know what to say to them. I didn't want them to feel guilty for leaving or make them think I literally couldn't live without them. Yet how could I explain why I took those pills and where I'd been all those weeks? How could I tell them that in real life I was a completely different person from the one they thought I was? I didn't want to make up some ridiculous story to tell them either. They deserved better than that. It was all too complicated. So, I'd just let it ring. Sometimes it rang for twenty, thirty rings before whoever it was on the other end would give up.

Tonight though, I'd answered it. I had sent my letter to Mother four days ago and it was possible she'd already received it. Since I'd given her my actual phone number and I'd promised Doc I'd go through with this meeting with Mother, I thought I'd better pick up the phone. I hadn't thought it would be her calling, though. I guess I hadn't expected her to call at all.

It had been an odd conversation we'd had, full of unasked questions and half-finished sentences. I had expected her, if she called at all, to be cold and businesslike, maybe demanding to know why I'd interrupted her routine life with this letter and asking if it really was necessary to come up to see me. Instead, her voice had quavered with emotion. She had sounded worried and maybe even afraid. And she had called so soon after getting my letter, as if she thought it was important. As if she had been waiting for me to contact her ... No, just wishful thinking. I'd imagined the emotion in her voice. She was just nervous talking to me after all this time or she suspected what it was I wanted to talk about and that made her nervous. Or she had talked all day and her voice was tired. It was tax season, after all. There were a hundred explanations besides the one I wanted to believe.

But she was coming. That was the main thing. And I'd have to confront her with her failure. Me. And ask her why she let herself make such a mess of taking care of me. I had no idea what she'd say or how she'd react. I realized, even though I lived with her for most of my life, I didn't know my mother very well. I remember being proud to have her for a mom when I was a little girl. She was so pretty and petite; I remembered how her long hair was the color of honey. And she was nice, I thought then. She gave me birthday parties and bought me pretty dresses and lots of toys. She used to let my friends come over after school and she would make us Kool-Aid in whatever flavor we wanted. She took me riding regularly at Old Johnny's and at night she read me stories out of the little library of books that lined the bottom part of my night table. All those memories have become obscured by the more recent past. Now I thought of her only as cold, distant, unfriendly. I suppose ignoring me made it easier to deal with. But how could a mother act that way to her own daughter? No matter what she said, no matter how many times Doc and Martha explain it to me, I'll never understand that.

My reverie was interrupted by a knock on the door.

I was so caught up in thinking about my mother I didn't stop to process who might be on the other side. I just got up to open it. I was wearing a red and black plaid knee-length nightshirt with my typical black leggings underneath. My hair hadn't been styled or even combed, since I'd gotten home from school hours ago. I flashed momentarily on my tawdry appearance, decided I couldn't care less, and opened the door.

It was Chuck.

"Hi there, remember me?" he asked, standing in the doorway with a smile and his blue scarf around his neck. His hair was sprinkled with a few snowflakes that hadn't melted yet, and he looked absolutely gorgeous. I just stared at him, my mouth hanging open.

"Chuck," I finally managed to whisper.

"Well, are you going to invite me in? That is, if you don't have company."

Something about that last remark brought me around. Had he been calling and thinking my failure to answer the phone was because I'd taken up with somebody else?

"Sorry, come on in. God, I look like a wreck and so does the room." I started throwing some things I had piled on Lena's bare mattress into the closet, so he'd have room to sit down. He just stood there though, looking at me.

"I think you look beautiful," he said quietly and very, very seriously.

I stopped cleaning up and looked at him. He was so handsome standing there. I just wanted to go over and hold him. But he'd probably find it disgusting once he knew who I really was, I reminded myself. It was time to tell him the truth, some of it, at least. I owed him that.

"Chuck, a lot has happened to me since you left, and I feel I have to tell you about it."

"I knew it," Chuck said, sinking onto to Lena's now bare mattress. "I knew as soon as I heard from Nick that you two weren't coming that something was up. I've been trying to call you for weeks, you know. I even sent Nick over here to find out what was up. But you were never home," he sighed. "My own damn fault. I should have never left without you. Okay, let's hear it. Who is this new guy?" Chuck looked really upset, like it mattered where I'd been these past two months.

"There's no new guy, nothing like that," I said, touching his hand for emphasis, as I sat down beside him, not too closely. There seemed to be an electric current running between us. It felt so good, I felt so alive to touch him, that I withdrew my hand quickly. In the end, it would just hurt more losing him.

"What then? Tell me." Chuck leaned toward me and twisted a bit so he could see me better on the bare mattress where we sat, where Lena used to sleep.

"Well, I sort of had an accident." I fumbled for a way to start this impossible explanation.

"What? A car accident? What do you mean? Were you hurt?" Chuck looked at me like he expected to see bandages or scars.

"No, not that kind of accident. I guess it wasn't even really an accident, it was more kind of accidentally on purpose." I was really making a mess of this, and Chuck looked more stricken by the minute. "Oh hell, Chuck," I finally blurted out. "One night, about two weeks after you left, I went out and drank a lot of booze and came home and swallowed a handful of Valiums and a few Percocets. They didn't go so well together."

"Jen." Chuck grabbed my wrists and made me look him in the eyes, something I'd been avoiding since he arrived. "Just what are you trying to say?"

I broke away and walked to the other side of the small room. "Okay. I'm sorry. It's not so easy to tell you." I heard my voice beginning to quake. "I never said it out loud before," I said, more to myself than Chuck. Then I went over and looked at him sitting on the edge of the mattress. "I tried to kill myself, Chuck. Guess I wasn't all that good at it though, huh?" I shut up quickly before I lost it completely and started sobbing.

I gazed downward at my hands and sat again on Lena's bed, my eyes blurring with the tears I was trying to control. Chuck moved closer to me, put his arm around me, and stroked my back with his hand, and I couldn't help it anymore. I started sobbing quietly into his shoulder. He held me for what seemed like a long time, until I finally was able to get control of myself. He got a Kleenex from Lena's desktop and wiped my nose for me just like I was a little girl. Something about that kindness gave me the courage to tell him the rest.

"Oh Jen. Why?" Chuck asked when I had finished getting myself back together. There was real anguish in his voice and his eyes glistened in a way I'd never seen before. There were tears there. I got up and walked over to the window again, as far away from him as I could get in the small room. Telling Chuck about me was the bravest thing I'd ever tried, and I was scared.

"It's really hard for me to talk about it to you because I don't think you'll like me very much once you know." I surprised myself with my newfound candor. But he was too nice a guy to keep lying to. "I guess Nick calling and saying we weren't going to Atlanta after all was kind of the last straw, but it wasn't the reason I did it, not really. I came back here that night I got drunk, and I saw this poster of Lena Horne." I pointed to where it was standing, rolled up and leaning against the corner. "You know, the one Lena used to have hanging on the wall." He nodded and I went on, "Well, it got me to thinking about dreams and how you and Lena had some and I didn't, I couldn't, not those kinds of dreams. You know, like being a success, being a singer, a recording artist. Or anything like that. All I could dream about was being normal, trying to live like a regular twenty-year-old-girl. And I couldn't even accomplish that because I am so abnormal."

Chuck looked really confused but I just kept on, hoping he'd understand. "You know what my dreams were? I dreamed I could have a friend like Lena and a boyfriend like you, Chuck. But that person Lena liked, the one who you went out with, it wasn't really me. I couldn't let the real me show through because she was too damned messed up. She was somebody nobody would like, an oddball, a freak." Chuck was shaking his head in disagreement or disbelief, about to say something, but I motioned him to stay quiet. "I'm telling you how I felt that night, Chuck, how I felt a lot of my life until just a few weeks ago. I felt it was hopeless and I wanted to go away from myself. I guess I wanted to die right then. But I drank so much that I got sick and somehow made it to the bathroom. A girl found me in there, passed out. They told me getting sick saved my life. The downers didn't have time to work too well. I wound up at University Hospital." I paused before saying the infamous floor, the one everybody joked about going to. "On 4 North. I was there for six weeks because I didn't have anywhere else to go and they were afraid I'd try it again if I got the chance. Maybe I would have, I don't know. Now I'm seeing a shrink and she's helping me understand why I wanted to die, why I've felt this way for so many years."

I paused for breath and dared to look over at Chuck. He had been looking down at the floor, but looked up at me when I stopped speaking. His eyes begged me to go on with my explanation, to start making sense, to tell him why.

"You're the first person, besides my shrink and her grad student, that I've ever told this to. But I want you to know because ... well, because I just can't keep lying to people I care about." My voice started quavering again. "Oh Jesus, I'm so afraid to tell you. What I am, it's so terrible, so perverse and what I've done since, that's just as bad. Doc was wrong. It doesn't help one bit to understand the reasons, not when you have to tell somebody else. I can't expect you to understand." I grabbed for a Kleenex to try and control the sobs that were welling up inside me again. I had to get through this first. There would be plenty of time to cry later. Plenty of time.

While I'd been blowing my nose, staring into the window reflection of myself, a red-faced, tear-stained, horrible-looking vision, Chuck quietly came over and stood behind me.

"Jen, there's no reason to be so afraid to tell me," he said gently. "Why do you think I came back here, tried to call you all those times? I care about you." He turned me to face him. "And I'm not going to stop just because you've had some rotten times in the past or done some things you weren't so proud of." He tried to kiss me then, but I pulled away.

"You don't know, that's how you can say those things. You don't know me, not really. You just think you do. I don't know who you think I am, but it's just a lie, an act I was trying to get away with so somebody, somebody would like me." I was totally losing it now, almost hysterical, and stupidly angry at Chuck for being so goddamned nice to me, when all I deserved was his contempt. Well, I'd have it soon enough. The anger helped me control my tears. I wanted to get it out, tell him everything, so he'd hate me. I wanted him to. I deserved it and he wasn't going to cheat me out of it.

"Remember how weird I was about sex, Chuck?" I hardly knew what I was saying now, and it didn't matter. "You probably thought I was a virgin or something." I laughed cruelly. "Well, far from it. I've slept with dozens of guys, fat old farts in their fifties. And they paid me for it, too." I hurled the words at him, daring him to be nice to someone like me. "One guy I slept with just to get pills. I'm a drug addict too, or at least I was. Most of the time you knew me, I was high on downers, Valiums. A prostitute drug addict. I bet you didn't know you had a junkie whore for a girlfriend, did you, Chuck?" I didn't dare look at him now. I didn't want to see his face and see his look of disgust, of contempt as my last memory of Chuck. "And that's not the worst of it, not by a long shot." The words were coming out in an ugly hiss now. But what the hell did I care how I said it? The results would be the same anyways. "I started having sex before you hardly even knew what it was, I bet. At thirteen. I became a prostitute at thirteen. And guess who my john was? Guess who paid me to do it with him? My john was Johnny, my own goddamn father! Twice a week, just like clockwork, every time that bitch of a wife of his, my mother, went out of the house for the evening. Me and Daddy." I spat the word in an exaggerated Southern accent. "Did it in my bed. Well, he did it, I just got it. Got the pain, got the shame, got ruined for life. Yeah, I got it all right. I'll be getting it the rest of my goddamn life, which I had hoped would be mercifully short." I was just raving now, past sense, past caring. The therapy sessions had meant nothing after all. I still felt just as rotten. My life was just as hopeless. There was no cure for this. They'd all lied to me, the Doc, Martha, the women in the incest group. There was no way out but the way I'd botched at Christmas. My past was my reality. There was no escape.

I put my head in my hands as these thoughts came to me.

The room was quiet. I thought maybe Chuck had somehow left while I wasn't paying attention. It was like I was in a dream, nothing seemed to be quite real. I looked up and there was Chuck, looking at me, his face quiet, inscrutable.

"Well, now you know. So why don't you just leave? Let's make this short and sweet, okay? It was nice knowing you, Chuck," I spat. "Now just get out of here and leave me alone." I turned and went over to the window again.

But Chuck wasn't about to leave. Instead, he came over to me, forced me to face him and said in an angry voice, "Just cut it out, will ya? I know what you're trying to pull and you're not going to get away with it. Come over here, sit down, blow your nose and let's talk about this like two adults." He took my arm and led me over to Lena's bare mattress, sat me down and put the box of tissues next to me.

"Chuck, I'm telling you the truth." I thought he must not believe what I'd said. "It's not some BS story I made up just to get rid of you. With a life as rotten as mine, who needs to make up stories? So, just give it up, okay? It's all true, all true. So just go before I ..."

He cut me off. "Will you cut out the martyr shit? I'll go when we've talked this all out and not before, and unless you can say something that's gonna help this situation, I'll do all the talking. You just shut up and listen." He was pissed off at me, something I'd never seen in him before. I wasn't sure what was going on, but seeing Chuck so mad scared me back into some semblance of reality. I sat there, trying to get a grip on myself, and waited for him to talk. He was quiet for a minute.

Then he said, "Just how dumb do you think I am? I knew there was something with you right from the start. You were so angry and afraid at the same time. But you had a lot of spunk too, and I liked that. Maybe I liked you cuz you were a challenge. You weren't a normal girl, you're right about that. But normal girls are boring, and you weren't. You were smart, pretty, and real feisty. That's why I liked you." I tried to protest but he waved my words away.

"I'm a musician, remember? I've been around stoned people ever since I was in high school. And just because all I do is smoke a little grass now and then and do a few lines of coke a couple times a year, doesn't mean I don't know somebody on downers when I see them. I knew you were doing something all along. And that night when I had you over and we had a fire in the fireplace and everything ... well, when I picked up your coat to hang it up in the closet, your pill box fell out of the pocket, and I opened it and saw it was Valium you were on. I just thought I'd wait for a while to talk to you about it, but then this Atlanta thing came up ..." He trailed off and shook his head sadly. "If I'd only known how dangerous it was for you to have them ..."

A silent minute went by. I didn't know what to think, what to say, so I said nothing and tried not to think. Then Chuck started speaking again. "I'm not trying to insult you or anything, but I never thought you were a virgin, even before we made love," Chuck said, quietly. "I knew something had happened to you that made you afraid. I thought maybe you'd been raped. I guess I wasn't so far off the mark, either." He looked at me, but I looked away. I didn't want to start crying again. "Having something like that happen to you when you were just a kid must really mess up what you think about yourself. Make you do all sorts of things that you wouldn't ordinarily think of doing." He drew a deep breath, then let it out. "I'd be a liar if I said I didn't mind about you selling yourself like that. I mind a lot. It makes me feel terrible to think you did that to yourself. And I guess it hurts my pride, too, to think my girl would do that. I'm sorry, but I can't help feeling that way. I can understand why you did it, though. I bet it made you feel real lousy about yourself, just the way you wanted to feel. Just the way your old man made you feel. God,

I'd like to kill that son of a bitch." His voice was filled with quiet fury. I looked up at him in surprise. That was probably the last thing I'd expected him to say. I thought he might want to kill me, for lying to him, for shaming him by my actions, for involving him with a fraudulent girlfriend. But instead, he wanted to kill the guy who made me this way.

"Jen, we haven't known each other for that long and in a way, I suppose, it wouldn't be that hard for me to say, hey, this lady's got problems, why don't I shove off while I can." Here it comes, I thought. He just had a weird way of doing it. "But Jen," he took one of my hands in both of his, "I really missed you when I was in Atlanta. It wasn't just being with a girl I missed. There were girls down there I could have gone out with. But I didn't want to. I wanted you to be there. I was bummed when I found out you weren't coming. Then when I couldn't get you on the phone either ... What I am trying to say is, I care about you. And I want you to know that's why I want to still be there for you, and not out of sympathy. So, don't think that. You're gonna make it through this, I can feel it. And I want to be there watching it happen. Is that okay with you or what?" Chuck looked over at me, waiting for an answer.

I thought about it for a minute. All the things I wanted to say, how I wasn't worthy of these feelings, how he was too nice for me, how I couldn't handle it, somebody caring about me, the real me with no secrets hidden away. But maybe the therapy was working a little. Cuz Doc's words came back to me. "You're not a bad person just because of what was done to you, Jenny, and our goal is to get you to believe that." Well, here was someone who apparently thought that way already, who could be my role model for my feelings towards myself. A friend. God, how I needed one of those right now. The therapy was working. I knew it when I didn't say any of those things that had first come into my head. I just said, "It's okay with me," and then I leaned over and kissed Chuck on the lips.

And the one kiss turned into many, many more. We made love then, sweetly, and slowly, and it felt good and right like it never really had before. And afterwards, we just lay there in each other's arms, Chuck burying his face in my hair and telling me about Atlanta.

The guy who owned the nightclub had liked them, liked them a lot, Chuck told me, and he'd made quite a few tapes of their live performances at the club. He said he wanted to release an album of theirs. He was a good guy, Chuck said, a political man who thought the most important thing Blacks could do for themselves was get a good education. He was a family man and his kids, he said, were going to go to college, no matter what. When he found out that Lena hadn't enrolled for spring semester because of the opportunity he had given her, he got really upset, especially when Harry told him how well she was doing and what she was studying. He made her call that professor friend of hers in the Linguistics Department that very day, Chuck went on, and he — Ed Coleson's his name — got on the phone to Lena's professor himself and personally asked him if Lena Campbell could somehow be registered for classes this semester and that he'd have her up there as soon as he could. It ended up that the linguistics professor signed Lena up for two courses of his and an independent study and he talked another professor friend of his into enrolling her in his class too, so she'd be a full-time student. "We'll go back down there at Easter to finish cutting the album. Harry, Rupert, and I all got in touch with Prof. Davis, and he took our case to the grad music department. So, we're good."

"Lena's here?" I asked, incredulously. I had sort of wondered why they hadn't stuck me with a new roommate.

"Yeah. We all got back a few hours ago. She's over at Harry's. She insisted she'd be in the way tonight and she wanted us to have the room to ourselves. She'll stop by tomorrow and move back in this weekend if that's okay with you."

"Okay?" I said, half delirious with all my good fortune. "It's fantastic!"

I woke up at dawn, Chuck asleep next to me, and sprang out of the bed.

"What's wrong?" Chuck put his head up, startled.

"I just thought of something. I've got to get that poster of Lena Horne back up before Lena gets here. Oh, I hope it didn't get too wrinkled. Where the hell did I put the tape?"

"You sure it won't make you think about ..." Chuck asked.

"No, it will be okay, now," I answered him. And it was true.

CHAPTER 54

PINE HILL STATION, TEXAS

MARCH 1986

LIZ

I dreaded telling Johnny that Jenny had written me. I supposed I wanted to protect him from the knowledge that Jenny had specifically asked that only I come to see her. Jenny's coldness those last few months she was with us had hurt him so deeply, and now, after more than a year of trying to adjust to her absence, he would face rejection all over again. Poor Johnny.

But I was wrong, dead wrong about his reaction.

By Thursday evening, I'd arranged to take a day off from work, despite being in the middle of tax season. I'd bought a round-trip flight from Houston to Chicago, and I'd rented a car to drive from there. I would leave my car at the Houston airport; no need to interrupt Johnny's schedule more than I would by my absence.

Thursday night he came home around eleven, as he had all month and last semester. Apparently, the grant writing was still not finished, or he'd found something else to do those evenings. I wondered if he found extra things to do at the university just to avoid coming home and spending time with me. But I never said anything to him about his late hours, for fear he'd criticize mine. Our relationship had deteriorated to perfunctory exchanges about the running of the household, and I hadn't even noticed. Or, if I was honest with myself, minded all that much. My life now was about work and the dogs and the new friends I was making at the shelter. Ever since Jenny left, Johnny had also retreated into his work, adding nights, weekend conferences, long hours to his schedule with abandon. No wonder I was nervous approaching him about this. We hadn't really talked in a couple of weeks.

Johnny came home looking tired and almost depressed. But when I asked him how his day had gone, he answered, "Fine, just fine," and gave me a little smile. He was tired, and if he was too tired to complain to me about university office politics, he was undoubtedly too tired to hear disturbing news. Yet, I had to tell him tonight since I was leaving early tomorrow morning.

I brought him a couple of fingers of bourbon, neat the way he liked it, and we sat in the matching armchairs in the living room. Johnny looked at me a bit surprised when I set the end table between our chairs with our ritual, his bourbon, my sherry. Lately, we'd gone to bed when our separate nights had ended, hardly even bothering to acknowledge each other. Johnny didn't protest tonight though when he saw me pour the measure of bourbon. He disappeared upstairs into the bathroom for his nightly shower. He came down when he'd finished, sat down heavily in his armchair, and sipped his drink in silence for a few minutes. I nervously swished the liquid in my glass and wished I had a cigarette. But I didn't want to admit to Johnny that I had started again, and I hadn't, not really. It was just during stressful moments that I craved one.

"Well, Liz, what's up?" Johnny finally opened our conversation.

"What made you think something was up?" The false lightness in my voice hit a sour note.

"The way you're fidgeting over there, I figured you had something on your mind. So out with it, Lizzie. I'm tired and I want to catch some sleep before I have to get up and go do it again."

I said nothing, suddenly struck dumb with indecisiveness. How could I tell him what had happened, how hopeful I felt about it, when he, by request, was being left out of the whole thing?

"Well? You've taken on more hours at that mutt shelter? Another evening's dinner you won't be making for us?"

I took a deep breath. Here goes. "Jenny called." I finally managed, just as Johnny was about to launch into a tirade about my extra-familial activities.

"What?"

"She called me Tuesday night," I continued with a lie. She had written, not called. I had called her, not the other way around. But I didn't want to get into all those details.

"Tuesday? So why am I hearing about it only now? What is going on here?"

"Well, Johnny," I scrambled for an excuse, "you came home so late on Tuesday and Wednesday, I got home late from our board meeting at the shelter and there just didn't seem to be enough time ..." Johnny glowered at me, and I gave in. "Well, truthfully, I was afraid of how you'd take it."

"Take what?"

"Well ... ah ... Jenny called to ask me to come up to Madison for the weekend."

"What? Just like that? After how she's treated us? Then she just calls up and asks you to come up for a social visit, huh? She certainly has cheek, that girl does." I looked at him in disbelief. This was the last response to my news I'd expected. "Why, that ungrateful little bitch ... you didn't tell her you'd come, I hope?"

"Johnny, don't you ever call our daughter a name like that. She's our daughter, Johnny, our only child. Of course, I'm going. I'm leaving tomorrow morning, in fact."

"Tomorrow! That's it, Liz, just knuckle under to her every selfish whim. She doesn't speak to us for over a year, and you let her get away with this flip little gambit. What did she say she wanted, anyways? More money, I suppose. That's all we've been good for to her. So, what does she want you up there for? Did she say?"

"She said she wanted to talk to me about something, Johnny," I said, half in shock and not fully able to digest his violent reaction to my news. "She sounded scared. I'm worried about her, Johnny. She could be in trouble up there. It was hard for her to ask, Johnny. I think she really needs me."

"In trouble, I bet that's just what it is. Screwing some college boy who doesn't have the money to buy her an abortion."

"You shut up, Johnny," I said viciously, appalled at how he could talk this way about her. It was the first time in our marriage I had ever said such a thing to him. "Don't you dare say that about our daughter. I don't care how much she's hurt you. You don't have any right to talk that way about her. No right at all." I felt as if I'd been plucked out of the grip of reality and suddenly set down in some horrible nightmare. Why was Johnny talking like this?

"I'll say whatever I damn well please about that crafty brat. What she needs is a good talking to by someone who isn't going to fall for the scams she's cooked up. I'm coming with you."

"Oh no, you're not, Johnny. Not after the attitude you revealed to me about her tonight. I had no idea you were capable of saying such hateful things about her. And here I was afraid to tell you about her call because I was afraid to hurt your feelings. I can't believe what I just heard. I can't believe it." I was close to tears, but I fought to control myself. I needed to have the upper hand in this and if tears got in the way, I immediately forfeited all pretense of control. Johnny hated women who cried when they were angry.

"You were afraid to hurt my feelings? Why? Wasn't I invited?"

"No," I said, a dead, cold, calm descending on me, "as a matter of fact, you weren't. She asked specifically that I come alone."

"Well, you're not going and that's that. If she doesn't want to make amends to both of us, then she's not going to have the chance to see either of us." Suddenly, Johnny bolted from his chair, crossed to mine, and put his hand under my chin to make me look at him. "Don't you see what she's trying to do, Liz? Divide and conquer. That's the scheme she's thought up now. Don't forget, Liz, I knew her a lot better than you these last few years. She talked to me right up until a few months before she left for Wisconsin that summer. She's a little liar. She'll say anything to turn one of us against the other. She hates us both — I don't know why. She's just a bad kid, Lizzie, maybe even a nut case. But she's trying to turn you against me, I know it. I just know that's what she's trying to do." His voice took on a desperate note, and he retreated into his chair and sat there staring at the bottle of bourbon. Then he refilled his glass for the third time. Johnny never drank more than a single drink before bed, or much more than that any other time. I watched him down his third bourbon in one swallow as I tried to think what to do.

"Johnny, I'm sorry that this upsets you so much. I had no idea. I guess I just assumed that you felt the same way about Jenny as I did. She's a troubled girl, I agree, but that's no reason to hate her. She needs us, maybe now more than ever, and I have to go to her. Can't you see that?" I tried to keep my voice calm, reasonable.

"Liz," Johnny whispered my name hoarsely, "you choose. You go up there without me tomorrow and you can forget about this marriage, forget about the life we've built for ourselves. That's my ultimatum," he said thickly, with an intensity I'd never seen in him before.

He got up, grabbed my wrists, pulled me to my feet and stared down at me. His steel-gray eyes had never looked so cold or so full of hate. "Now, you go ahead and pick. But if you choose to cave into the wishes of that manipulating, selfish little beast, you can forget about coming back here to this house. Ever." He hissed into my face. "You hear me? Now, you think about that, Liz." He wheeled on his heel, grabbed the half-empty bottle of bourbon, and walked out of the room and up the stairs to our bedroom on the second floor.

When he was out of sight, I collapsed onto the sofa, too mortified to even cry. Where had this stranger come from, a man the total opposite of the controlled, rational man who had been my husband for more than twenty-three years? He had looked odd when he'd come home tonight, I reflected. Maybe something had happened at the college? But he was a tenured professor. I couldn't imagine anything devastating enough to cause such an out-of-character reaction from him. Maybe it was Jenny herself. Had she written him hate letters I didn't know about? Tried to get more money from him? Had she done something I didn't know about to him that had caused this rupture in his feelings for her? I thought back over Jenny's senior year, her last year home with us. When she'd turned on Johnny in those last few months before she left us, it had broken his heart. No, I wasn't wrong about that. Something had happened since then that I didn't know about. That was the only plausible explanation.

He hadn't meant what he'd said about choosing between Jenny and him. He couldn't have meant it. He was a bit drunk and something about my trip there had set him off. Maybe it was just disappointment that he had not been asked to go, made all the worse by the excessive amount of bourbon he'd had tonight. I shook my head, wishing I could clear this horrible evening's memories out of it. Maybe he was calmer now. Maybe I could talk to him, find out what was wrong, find some clue that would begin to explain his violent reaction to my plan to visit Jenny.

I must have sat cogitating for an hour before I got up, climbed the stairs, and went into the bedroom, telling myself to be calm, to try to understand. Surely, there was an explanation, a hurt he'd suffered I knew nothing about ... something that explained why he said those terrible words about our daughter. I poked my head cautiously into the bedroom. Johnny was lying on the still-made-up bed, his bathrobe wrapped tightly around him. The bottle of bourbon lay on the floor, empty. He was asleep or passed out, I couldn't tell. In any case, there would be no talking to him tonight. To catch my early flight from Houston tomorrow, I'd have to leave before dawn, before Johnny usually awoke, even when he hadn't been drinking. That was it, then. There would be no talking about it before I left. And I had to go. I had to keep the appointment I'd made with Jenny. She needed me there. I could feel it. And I could not let some ridiculous half-drunken threat keep me from her. Johnny would be angry with me, but he'd see in the sober light of day how foolish he'd been. And if I could start to bring Jenny back to us, if I could begin to make her part of our family again by this visit, in the end, Johnny would be grateful to me for ignoring his "ultimatum" tonight.

For the first time in our marriage, I went to sleep, or tried to, in the bed down the hall, Jenny's bed, which I had stupidly kept made up and ready for her all these many months. I talked to myself silently most of the night, telling myself how worthwhile this trip would be, how Johnny hadn't meant what he'd said, all sorts of calming little half-truths. But my stomach quaked in fear that I had started a loose stone rolling that would soon turn into an uncontrollable avalanche.

Still, what choice did I have? First and foremost, I was a mother and there was no escaping it. Oh, I had tried when I'd seen how I had failed Jenny. I had tried to deny how much my life was defined by my relationship — or lack of relationship — with my daughter. But I'd only been deluding myself. Now, by some miracle, I was being given a second chance. I had to take it. I had to try. Surely, Johnny would see that.

He was still sound asleep when I got up to go, taking my little overnight bag from the closet where I had put it after packing the night before. I looked at him long and hard for a second, then took my bag and quietly closed the bedroom door. Downstairs, I wrote Johnny an innocent, loving little note, pretending in it that last night hadn't occurred at all and hoping, as I wrote it, he would forget about it, too. I left it on his armchair, where he'd sit and read the paper for a few minutes with his second cup of coffee before leaving for the university.

Then, I put on my coat, made sure I had the tickets in my purse, grabbed my car keys from where they hung next to the back door and left the house for my car. And I wondered as I drove away from our house if I had closed a door on the life I had shared with Johnny.

CHAPTER 55

MADISON, WISCONSIN

MARCH 1986

JENNY

Awake for hours, my head swimming from the coffee I'd been pouring down my throat all morning, I was in no shape to calmly greet anyone, particularly my mother. I walked the icy sidewalks of State Street up to Capitol Square where I'd booked my mother a room at the Capitol Inn across the street from the huge, white-domed marble building, trying not to slip on my ass, trying not to start smoking again, trying to breathe properly like they'd showed me to keep from hyperventilating. I spent most of the mile walk silently cursing Doc, Martha, and myself for talking me into this ridiculous confrontation. What, after all, did I have to say to her? Why couldn't I forget I had a family and try to get on with it?

I had no idea what I'd even call her. Mother sounded so formal, Mom, too falsely friendly, Liz stuck in my mouth like old chewing gum. Oh God, here I was at the Capitol Inn, pulling on the heavy brass art deco door to the hotel, the bone-chilling damp wind following me in when I finally managed to pry it open.

I recognized her right away, sitting on a black leather chair in the lobby in her mid-calf coat in an odd shade of lavender that somehow looked becoming on her. For an instant, I could see her objectively; a gracefully aging, petite forty-six-year-old, slim to the point of boniness, shoulder-length hair an attractive silvery blond. A good-looking woman. She looked nice, too, a little shy and nervous, but the type you could count on. For a moment, she looked like that to me.

Then, the memories flooded in, transforming her into an evil, uncaring bitch who abandoned her daughter to the perverted attentions of her husband. But the other impression lingered, too. She was vulnerable here, like me, afraid of getting hurt. I hadn't thought I'd be able to be civil to her, much less friendly. But now, seeing her, my grim determination to expose to her the depths of her betrayal and my hatred wavered. Up close, she looked scared and very tired, not at all the monster of my imagination. And after all, I had the upper hand here. I was on my turf; she was here on my terms. I took a deep breath and went over to her.

"Jenny." She smiled gratefully, probably a little worried that I wouldn't show up. She stood and her arms went up for a moment as if she wanted to hug me, but fell to her sides again when I made no effort to step into them. It made me mad, her trying to force me into a public display of affection. Who was she trying to convince that this was a normal greeting between a mother and a daughter who hadn't seen one another for a while? Strangers in the lobby who couldn't care less? Was she trying to fool herself so she could shove aside the facts — that our family was nothing but a bunch of play-acting perverts? Or was she trying to put one over on me, fool me into thinking she cared? Fat chance of that.

But I couldn't stand there, two feet in front of her, my mouth hanging open, saying nothing. So, I said, "How was the drive up here from Chicago? Was your flight from Houston okay?"

She was shaking, I noticed, cold in her thin lavender coat. Or maybe she was nervous.

"It was fine, just fine. Everyone was so helpful at the airline and at the car rental place. Wisconsin is cold this time of year!" she said, a little too enthusiastically. Then she noticed her gloved hands were trembling and self-consciously stuck them in her pockets.

"How are you, Jenny?" I saw fear in her eyes, a fear I didn't understand.

"Okay, you get used to it after a while — the cold, I mean." I wasn't paying attention to this conversation. I couldn't concentrate. It seemed to be going on far away from me, muffled by the distance. I felt like I do in dreams when I'm so frightened that I'm paralyzed. Even though I know death is just a heartbeat away, I can't seem to move to save myself. What the hell was I doing here with her?

"You said something about showing me where you live on campus?" she was saying from a million miles away.

"Uh ... there are taxis right outside. We can get one to campus. It's impossible to find parking, so better to leave your rental car here at the hotel." I somehow managed to make my lips move. Now that she was right next to me and it was too late to run, I was terrified. My heart was bouncing against my chest like it would break a hole in it, and I was sweating profusely and shivering at the same time. I thought I might be sick. It's only your mother; it's only your mother. Get a hold of yourself, you idiot.

I pointed out the sights as they flashed by, Lake Monona, the Park Street high-rise dorms, the huge and ugly Humanities Building, where Chuck, Rupert and Harry spent all their time, the ancient red science building that had turrets that made it look like a haunted house, the Union and on up the steep hill of Observatory Drive past the Commerce and Social Sciences buildings to my dorm, Liz Waters. She insisted on paying the cab driver and I let her. She exclaimed at the dorm's location, overlooking the biggest of Madison's four lakes, Lake Mendota. I pointed out the cafeteria and we made our way up the stairs to Room 207, my and Lena's room. Lena had put fresh sheets on her bed, "just in case," she'd said, thinking my mother might want to stay over. I thought it would be more likely she'd book the next flight out of here once we had our little talk. Though I'd never felt this way when Lena was here, a wave of claustrophobia passed over me as I shut the door, locking us in the same room together.

Lena. Lena had come by, just to talk. She wanted to make sure it was okay for her to move back in. She knew something was up with me. Like always, she could read me on some gut level, but like always, she didn't ask questions. I loved her for that. I told her a lot had happened to me and that I'd tell her about it after she moved back in. Then I asked her if it was all right to wait until Sunday night to move back in because my mother was coming for the weekend. Lena looked surprised at my announcement. I had hardly mentioned my mother to her before, and she probably could tell from my face that I wasn't exactly excited about this visit. But she agreed and told me if I needed to ease the tension, I should give her a call and she'd have lunch with us or something.

Chuck, too, had been understanding about my mother's coming, though he'd been disappointed that we wouldn't be able to spend the weekend together. I told him why I had invited her, and he told me to come over to his place if I needed a shoulder or anything. I thought about Lena and Chuck, the ghosts of their presence hovering over me like a protective shield. No matter what happened when I had my little talk with her, they would still be there. That knowledge gave me the courage to face her.

"Would you like some coffee?" I offered to break the ice. We both loved the stuff, maybe one of the few things we had in common. Other than sleeping with HIM, that is.

"That would be great, Jenny. I'm afraid I didn't get much sleep last night. That's nice," she continued, indicating the Mr. Coffee Harry had given Lena this fall for us to use. "You can make it right in the room."

"It's my roommate's."

"Oh, I didn't know you had one," she said, even though there were obviously two made-up beds in the room. "I hope I didn't inconvenience her ..."

"It's okay. She's staying at her boyfriend's place for the weekend. She's been gone, anyways. She just got back from Atlanta. She's cutting a jazz album down there." I didn't know why I felt I had to brag up Lena to my mother. What did she care who my friends were?

"Well, she sounds interesting. Are you friends?" she asked, hesitantly, like maybe it was none of her business.

"Yeah, she's the best friend I got." I was getting kind of choked up thinking about that. Or maybe it was because my own mother knew so little about me. A long silence followed, punctuated only by the drip, drip, drip of Mr. Coffee.

"What a nice room you have," she exclaimed at my cluster of junk and dorm-issue furniture. "And you certainly couldn't ask for a nicer view to wake up to every morning." She looked out at the frozen expanse fronted by bare tree trunks that was Lake Mendota at the end of this endless winter.

I sucked in my breath. It was now or never. I couldn't stand another minute of this strained small talk.

"Well, I haven't been waking up to the view lately. I just got out of the hospital a few days ago," I said defiantly. Actually, I had been out for weeks, since school had started up for the semester and the dorm had re-opened. "They kept me in the hospital 'for observation' when they discovered I had nowhere to go for Christmas vacation."

"Oh my God." She sank on to Lena's mattress. "I knew there was something wrong. I knew it." Her face looked ashen. "What is it? Are you going to be all right?" There was real anguish in her voice, as if she suspected the worst, like terminal cancer.

I lost some of my defiance, then. She really was worried about me.

"No, no, nothing so tragic as what you're thinking," I lied. "I was up in 4 North." At her blank stare, I added, "The psych ward. I took a bunch of pills and they stuck me in there to make sure I didn't off myself." My flip manner didn't quite come off the way I wanted it to. I found my chin was quivering.

"Oh Jenny, oh honey. I knew something was wrong, I knew it," she repeated, more to herself than to me. "I've been trying to call you all fall ... but I had the wrong number. And here, something like this ... why didn't the university call us? You'd think they'd try to contact the parents ..." Her face wore a strange expression, something I didn't quite recognize. Maybe her concern was all an act, I thought.

"Oh, they wanted to call you," I answered, about the University Hospital, "but I made them a deal. I said I'd go to a shrink if they would leave you two out of it." I wanted this news to hurt her, and it looked like I'd hit home.

The coffee had finished dripping and I poured her a cup. She took it black, I remembered. Like me. She thanked me when I handed her the cup, but looked at it strangely like it had fallen from the sky. She was upset, I could tell. Well, good, I thought. She should be.

"Jenny," she said softly, after a few more seconds of silence had passed, "are you okay now? I mean ... Why did you ...?" She paused, her voice unsteady.

That question broke through to the anger I'd been trying to control since I started this impossible morning. I reeled around from the window where I'd been staring out at the silent, icy lake. "That should be pretty obvious to you, shouldn't it?" I hissed at her.

"Jenny, I tried to be a good mother to you. I know I've made mistakes. I wanted to be closer to you ..." She was crying now, tears streaming down her cheeks. They seemed real enough. But who was she crying for? Maybe she had begun to feel a bit of shame for how she'd acted. "I don't know how I failed you." She sucked in a breath and wiped her nose with a Kleenex she'd taken from her pocket. "I know you never forgave me for that time I worked evenings ..."

I didn't let her finish. I couldn't believe what she was saying. "What do you mean, you don't know how you failed me?" I spat the words at her. "How can you say that? You don't give a damn about me, do you? Don't you even remember what you put me through all those years?"

"What, Jenny? What? Just tell me ... please. I'll try and make it up to you. I know I didn't give you enough of my time ..." She broke off in a sob.

I looked at her incredulously. "Time? Who cares about time? Why didn't you make him keep his grimy hands off me? All those years! All those years you were off at your god-damned dog shelter, not giving a damn what he did to me!" I was screaming at her now, my fist slamming down on the windowsill.

Suddenly, she was up and across the room, grabbing me by the shoulders and forcing me to look at her.

"Jenny," she said, in a voice grown deadly calm. "Jenny, look at me. Look at me! What are you saying? What are you saying?" she whispered in a voice filled with so much horror that I knew without a doubt Martha had been right. She didn't know.

She didn't know. The knowledge broke through me like a dam opening, washing away her role in the horrible past I had thought we shared. Instead, I saw her standing there on some distant shore named Family, calling out to me that I'd make it there, just swim for it and she would be there to dry me off and warm me. All I had to do was swim for it.

I looked at her face then and the fear I saw there started the tears trickling down my own face. Her fear was for me.

"Mom," I said, suddenly finding it easy to use the word. "Mom, sit down."

Like a child, she retreated and stumbled back onto Lena's bed. I stood across from her, over her. "You don't know," I whispered, looking into her frightened eyes. "You don't, do you? All those years and you never knew." I looked at her, but it wasn't an accusation. I'd never told her, after all. At first, I'd been too confused, and he made me promise. Later, I suspected she knew and was glad so she wouldn't have to service him herself, another story he had planted in my brain.

"What did Johnny do to you?" she asked in a choked whisper, taking my hands in hers. "What did he do to my poor Jenny?" That's when I knew she was on my side. But the words stuck in my throat. I couldn't tell her. I only looked at her, my eyes overflowing, and hoped that she'd understand without the words.

"Did he ...?" She couldn't say it either. It was too hideous a thing to talk about, an act that violated us both to the very core of our existence. Now I could see how much pain this would cause her. Mine seemed so easy to bear by comparison, an old, almost friendly kind of pain, so familiar to me it was. But this would turn her whole life upside down, make her rethink everything she'd lived for the past twenty-some years. She would need my help now, more than I needed hers. But she hadn't thought about herself in all this yet. Her whole attention was on me.

"Did he ... do ... everything to you?" She finally managed. I nodded dumbly and the next moment felt her arms come around me.

"Oh my God, oh Jesus, my poor baby, my poor Jenny." She rocked me back and forth and stroked my hair. "My poor little girl, so alone all these years."

As it struck me how right she was, how alone I've been all these years, I sobbed like I've never cried in my whole life. Mom was there holding me all the while, comforting me with little girl words like, "Everything's all right now, don't worry, I'm here, honey, everything's going to be okay ..." on and on, in just the voice I needed until it was all gone, all that awful loneliness.

"Mom, I missed you." I managed to sputter between gasps because I wanted her to know.

CHAPTER 56

PINE HILL STATION, TEXAS

MARCH 1986

JANE

There was blood on the sleeve of my sky-blue sweater, I noticed, after taking off my raincoat and huddling for a moment in the gray chair that I dragged closer to the gas space heater. Not a lot, but it would leave a small oblong stain on the cuff. It was dried now, no use washing it off. Friday night, and the rain was pelting against the windows, a rain that would never let up. My socks were drenched. I took them off and hung them on the kitchen chair closest to the heater.

Two weeks had passed since I'd found the picture of Jenny in the insert that had gotten left in my gray chair cushion. I'd seen too many movies in those weeks, spending Tuesday and Thursday evenings in dark theaters sitting through two full shows, just to make sure he'd have given up looking for me. Daytimes I'd carefully walk out of my classes with groups of grad students who knew him, or the class's professor. I knew he wouldn't risk coming up to me in front of people he knew. I'd received letters from him. I had disposed of them unopened in anonymous trash containers all over campus. But it had been a strain avoiding him and I'd known there'd be a confrontation. Sooner or later, my luck would run out.

What I hadn't counted on was Jenny's accidental interference in my plan to starve Johnny out. She had invited her mother to visit for the weekend in Madison, Wisconsin, where I'd found out a little while ago from Johnny, she was a sophomore. With his wife gone for the weekend, he'd had a lot of time on his hands to pursue me, an ambition he hadn't given up on after half a month. He had staked out my house and when I'd come out to do some early evening grocery shopping, he stepped out of a dark corner and grabbed my hand, his features contorted in pain. Lost in a second's sympathy for that suffering human face, my resolve had wavered. He pleaded for an explanation, whining like a whipped dog.

"Couldn't we go inside and talk awhile?" he begged, adding that he couldn't go on without at least knowing why I didn't want to see him any longer. I glanced up at my room in the old house from the street corner where we stood under a deserted covered bus stop to get out of the rain. I could not have him in my room, with its memories of our intimate rituals hanging in the air like ghosts, daring me to give in to him as I had on innumerable Tuesdays and Thursdays in the recent past. I would meet him in a couple of hours, I told him, at 8:00 p.m., at his office in the history building. It would be deserted on a Friday night; we'd have privacy, and we could talk.

He agreed too quickly, a pitiful, bedraggled figure, his drenched hair matted against his head. There was no trace of the cool, self-possessed man who'd seemed so attractive to me just a few months before. A wave of contempt washed over me, a cold, nauseating feeling that welled up into my throat and stuck there. I felt I was going to scream, but for what reason, I couldn't quite fathom. Then.

"See you at eight," I mumbled, instead and took off at a trot towards the grocery store a couple of soggy blocks down the street. I didn't look back to see if he was watching me go.

It was still on the bedside table, the photo with a face not quite my own, staring at me with those haunted eyes, as I woodenly put my few groceries away. I crossed the room and picked up the picture to look into that face once more. "I won't betray you," I whispered, maybe to both of us. I slipped the photo into the pocket of the dripping raincoat I still wore and closed the door softly behind me.

In the ten-minute walk to Johnny's office in rain that spattered against my plastic raincoat like machine-gun bullets, I found an anger for what had been done to Jenny that I had never felt for myself. A molten ball of fury lodged in my chest, ready to explode in a burst of cutting words. I found myself muttering words, camouflaged by the rain, designed to strip Johnny of every shred of the false dignity he dared to pretend, all the while making his daughter's life a mockery.

As Jenny's stand-in, I had the power of allure, a power I could now use to speak the words that Jenny, I believed, had never spoken. Johnny, in his perverse attraction to me, would listen. I would make Jenny's father understand what price he had extracted from his daughter, I resolved, the heat of anger bringing a flush to my face the rain could not cool. I would tell him exactly how despicable he was.

But rage was an alien emotion in my repertoire, and by the time I had reached the steps of the old history building, it had burned through me, replaced by a quaking fear. I stood in terror of an unbidden return of this emotion I could not control. I wanted to bury that fury so deep it could never surface to rule me again. I had lived my life in unconscious slavery to an anger I feared, once unleashed, would destroy my tenuous grip on a near normal life. More than anything, I feared Johnny's power to make the beast within me surface. I drew in my breath sharply, feeling I was in the bowels of a horrible nightmare, and braced myself to confront him. For Jenny. For Jenny, I could do this, I coached myself harshly.

He was, as I had expected, already there, pacing the room anxiously. I suppose he feared I wouldn't come, and, as an icy finger of fear gripped my spine at the sight of him, I wished I hadn't. I swallowed hard and entered the room.

"Janey," he called in distress from across the room. I noticed how, in his Southern-accented voice, the word was almost indistinguishable from his daughter's name. Instinctively, I felt for Jenny's picture and touched it like a protecting talisman.

"Janey, Janey," he said, crossing the room and grabbing me by both shoulders. "Where have you been? What is it? What's the matter?" Pain seared his voice. "Jesus, I thought I'd lost you." He looked into my eyes, and I saw his cloud with doubt. I'd been standing there limp and motionless, my brain and heart dulled with fear.

"What is it, Janey? You've got to tell me." At my continued lack of response, he shook me a little. "Janey, talk to me. What's wrong with you?" His voice was half concerned, half riddled with irritation. Wordlessly, I reached into my pocket and pulled out the photo, backing out of his grasp as I held it out to him.

His head snapped up in shock as he recognized the picture, and he grabbed it from me and quickly threw it down on the top of his desk as if it were in flames.

"Where'd you get ... I know what you're thinking Janey ... ah ... Jane ... but give me a chance to explain." He turned and walked over to the window, trying to think of a good story, no doubt. I gratefully leaned up against the desk, sending a pair of red-handled scissors scuttling across the desktop and onto the floor. I picked them up and set them back on the desk next to the photo of Jenny looking up at me with those eyes full of pain.

Johnny turned and came toward me. "Jane," he said softly, dropping a syllable from the name he'd given me, "I'd be a liar if I didn't admit I saw your resemblance to Jenny. She's my daughter. She's twenty and she's a sophomore at the University of Wisconsin in Madison. Her mother's up visiting her this weekend. That's why I could get away from the house tonight," he explained in a calm voice. As if his words could soothe me. She's alive then, I thought, and she has a mother who loves her. Knowing it made me feel better. Jenny was safe from him then, at least for now.

"It's quite a striking similarity. You two look even more alike than this photo shows," he said in a voice that contained a hint of pride.

"Sure, when I first saw you, I noticed it. Of course, I did." He spoke faster now. "And what middle-aged man doesn't secretly want to make it with his beautiful daughter? Okay, so I admit, I was curious. Here's a chance to do the forbidden thing, you know, legally, two consenting adults and all that." He was stumbling now, his usual eloquence failing him as he tried to lie his way out.

"The first time it was curiosity. And, of course, it was exciting. You're a beautiful girl and I'm an aging professor. A real ego boost. But Jane, listen to me. That was the first time. After that, it was you I kept coming to see. It's you I love," he ended, unconvincingly, looking into my eyes to see if I believed him.

"Yes, I should have told you about Jenny, about having a daughter. But I was afraid of what you might think. Jesus, I'm sorry, Jane. But it has nothing to do with us. Can't you just forget it now? Please, Jane, I love you so much," he murmured as he drew nearer, stroking my hair and putting his arms around me.

I looked at the floor, still silent, unable to find one word to start to describe what he was to me, what we were. The horrible, perverse thing we'd done. I was afraid a word spoken now would start the process that would unravel my sanity, my very life. How could words describe these feelings, feelings that would be wasted on this brute who dared to continue to desecrate his daughter to my face with his lies?

Thinking my downcast eyes were a sign of tears, forgiveness, or some sort of feminine demureness, Johnny grabbed a handful of hair from the back of my head, making my face rise to his. Then with a hard, bruising, almost vicious motion, he brought his mouth down on mine. There was fear, too, in the way he gripped me to him. He was afraid that I would spoil what he so carefully had pursued, so conscientiously maintained. From Jenny to Janey, a subtle evolution, yet one that freed him from guilt or fear of reprisal from his wife, the courts, or Jenny herself. He'd had the perfect solution to his unnatural longings and now, that solution was threatening to withdraw.

He held me in a one-armed vise grip while his other hand fumbled with his pants zipper. "Janey, Janey," he whispered hoarsely into my ear, forgetting his new distinction between Jenny and me in his desperation. Perhaps he'd even said, "Jenny, Jenny." It was so difficult to tell the difference. I could feel our hearts beating against one another as he gripped me to him. He pressed me against the desk, rubbing his genitals against me as he tried to undo the zipper of my jeans. My one free hand felt behind me for the picture of Jenny. Yes, I could feel it, there where he had left it on the desk. In my mind, I could see her eyes, that haunted, wounded blue staring out of the depths of her. Those eyes, pleading, begging, as they had every night of her life for so many years. Stop it, stop it! Blue eyes crying silently, terror ringing them with bottomless darkness. Those eyes I could not tell from my own. Blue haunted eyes dividing into two identical pairs, blending back into one, piercing my soul with their anguish. Eyes that would never light with laughter or love. Jenny's eyes filled my mind until I could not see but for their terrified gaze.

It was Jenny's hand that reached for the red-handled scissors next to the picture, Jenny who had the courage to start what fear of my own rage held back. But it was my hand and my strong arm that swung the scissors around Johnny's hard, groping grasp. It was my rage that plunged the scissors into his back. It was Fate herself who saw that the blade went straight into his heart.

Johnny knew whose hand had begun what mine had finished. In the moment before he crumpled to the floor, he looked up at me, his eyes wide with surprise. "Jenny," he gasped, looking straight into my face and there was no mistaking the name that time. As he fell, his arm brushed the desk and sent Jenny's picture fluttering to the floor.

I was calm as I picked the photo up from the floor and slipped it back into my raincoat pocket, calm as I took the five ancient coins from their case on his bookshelf, calm as I removed the small perfume bottle of ancient glass from its stand, calm as I zipped up his zipper with a tissue from my pocket. I looked at his dead face, frozen in a surprised grimace. Just like my father's death mask. I had prayed for Father's death. This time, for Jenny, I had acted. She was safe.

I didn't look back as I turned out the light, gently shut the door, walked back down the hall, down the stairs outside the building and headed back home in the pouring rain.

My socks were almost dry on the gas space heater. I put my them back on and went over to the window. The rain poured down relentlessly in the dark. I shut the heavy curtains, reducing the noise to a muffled throbbing. Then, I carefully blew out the flame in the heater.

It seemed the only possibility now. As the sulfur smell of propane began to permeate the room, I settled down in my bed under the quilt I'd had since I was a girl and shut my eyes. There was Jenny's face smiling at me as I dozed off.

It couldn't have been more than a minute or two when I awoke with a start. Jenny's thankful smile in my vision had metamorphosed into a scream, a scream that told me that I must get up, I must go, I must go now. I jumped out of my bed. I turned off the gas, I opened the window. I dug into the bottom of the desk drawer and pocketed the $300 in cash I had stashed there to pay the rent. In my backpack, I put my toothbrush and comb, some underwear and socks, some T-shirts, and another pair of jeans. My sandals. Some books to read. My wallet with a bit more money and my driver's license. Sunglasses and a baseball hat. The Roman coins and the tiny ancient glass vial stayed in my raincoat pocket.

The Greyhound station was just three blocks from my house. There were night buses going south across the border. I hurried out into the rain.

CHAPTER 57

WHARTON HALL, TEXAS

APRIL 1986

LIZ

Old Johnny had a massive stroke two days after he heard the news about Johnny's death. The old man didn't last long; within the week he joined his grandson in the great beyond. Now, thanks to the near-barren wife of the last Johnny Wharton (me), there would be no other Johnny Whartons. That suited me just fine. But someone had to take care of burial arrangements and such for the old man, and as Jenny and I were his only relations still living, I was tasked with the unpleasantness. In the will that Johnny had written for him, Old Johnny had donated his house to the Texas State Historical Society to be turned into a tourist destination, complete with all the antique furnishings in the house. Old Johnny, I now noticed gratefully, had not been overly acquisitive for a man of his class and mostly, I had to go through old clothes and business papers and a few trunks in the attic.

The rest of the property, the barn and the horses, Babe and Beauty, and the two small cottages had been left to Johnny "to dispose of as he would." For Patty, Elton, and their son Marvin, he had left $1,000 each — an astonishingly paltry sum for their many years of service. Fortunately, the cottages, the horses and barn and all the financial assets of Wharton Hall except the house and grounds around it were now, as the surviving spouse, mine to dispose of as I would. And I had some ideas about that.

Patty, uncomplainingly and quietly, helped me pack up Old Johnny's things. "If you've no use for the clothing, Miz Wharton," she ventured, "my church would be glad to have it to give to our less well-off elders."

"That would be a relief, Patty. Yes, we'll bag up everything for your church. My, but the man had a lot of shoes, didn't he?" I responded, as we worked our way through the bureaus and armoires. The old place had no closets whatsoever, a small feature to be thankful for, now that we had to go through all the places where Old Johnny might have stored personal items.

Patty and I worked away the first hours of the morning, putting most everything on the pile for the church. As we sorted through the ancient trunks in the attic and came across one with a relatively new combination lock on it, I had a flashback about that day a decade ago when Johnny had erupted in anger because our nine-year-old daughter had put on a cowboy hat she'd found in the very locked trunk I was now staring at. In a flash, I remembered something I hadn't thought about in a long time.

"Patty, can we take a tea break? I'd like to talk with you about something."

"I'll go put the kettle on, Miz Wharton. Should I call Elton from the barn?"

I supposed she was thinking it was now time to tell them

about their future. But I had something else I had to ask first. It was now or never.

"Patty, we'll talk about the cottages and such in a little while and when we do, Elton will be at the table, too. But first, I need to ask you about something that has been on my mind for a long time."

Patty made us tea in the kitchen and we both sat down at the huge oak table that had been where the house servants took their meals way back when. It was gleaming with wood polish, in impeccable shape for being 150 years old. Patty was a meticulous housekeeper.

She put two cups and saucers from the old china set that would soon be part of the historical society's collection on the table. She took a wooden kitchen chair from its location next to the old open fireplace and placed at the end of the table. Patty sat on the end of one of the long benches that lined each side of the table. She had set my cup of tea in front of the chair, and I took the indicated seat.

I decided to get right to the point before I lost my nerve. "Patty, all my married life, I wanted to know about Johnny's father — Reverend Johnny — and how he died. Johnny would never tell me. But your people were here then. Maybe you know something?" I realized that holding back on the terms of the will was a small sort of blackmail that I was using on Patty. But it felt like the only tool I had to pry the truth from this reticent woman and this house full of secrets that would soon pass from my life. So, I used it.

Patty looked surprised at my request. "You don't know about the Reverend's passing?" she asked.

"No, no one ever told me about it. It was off limits even to bring him up to my husband. I tried to get some information from Old Johnny once but talking about his son seemed to anger him so. And he made it clear that he was not going to talk to me about him."

Patty nodded. "I remember that evening when you had dinner with him on the veranda, Miz Wharton. I don't like to talk unkindly about the dead, ma'am, that's a fact. But seeing how they never told you nothing about him and seeing how Old Mr. Wharton has passed on now and Professor Wharton too, I suppose there's no harm in it." It was the longest speech I'd ever heard Patty make.

"He was a good boy at heart. That's what my mama Suzy said about Reverend Johnny when he was a boy. But when the time came, they made him do it, just like every Wharton man before him. It was kind of a ritual like thing, among the Whartons, I heard tell once. When Professor Wharton — around here, we called him Young Johnny — was visiting with Old Mr. Wharton once upon an evening ... well, I heard things over the years. Old Mr. Wharton liked to talk to Young Johnny about what it was like around here in the old days, when he was young, and tell stories his father and grandfather, the original Mr. Wharton, told him. He said it was what men of the planter class did and should do, so we 'darkies' — he called us — would know our place. All the men of the planter class did it, Old Mr. Wharton said. It was better than a whuppin' and more fun too, that's what he said. And Professor Wharton, he laughed. I remember that distinctly."

"I don't understand. What tradition? What's better than a whipping?"

"Back when my people was slaves here, Miz Wharton, that's what I'm talking about. You didn't pick fast enough, you got yourself a whuppin'. You sleep too long or fall off too early, you got yourself a whuppin'. You sass the Massa, you got yourself a bad whuppin'. And even after Mr. Lincoln freed us, my people were still working cotton for several generations as 'croppers.'"

"Yes, I did hear that cotton was grown by sharecroppers here after the war until about the Depression, I believe."

"Yes, ma'am, that's right. And during the 'cropper era, my people still got a whuppin' if they did something Mr. Wharton didn't like."

"So, are you saying Reverend Johnny was told to whip your people if they misbehaved?" I was totally confused.

"Maybe, ma'am, I don't rightly know about that part. But there was another thing done around here to keep my people down. A much worse thing than a whuppin'. That'd be the ritual Old Mr. Wharton was talking about ..." Patty trailed off and looked down at her tea.

"Patty, what are you trying to tell me? Please go on."

"I don't rightly like to talk about this, Miz Wharton, because they come for my mama when she was a girl and there was a sadness about her ever since," Patty said quietly.

"Patty, are you talking about ..." I could barely get the word out, "... rape?" I said, my voice reduced to a whisper.

"Yes, ma'am, that was the ritual Old Mr. Wharton talked about to the professor that time I overheard. But, of course, I already knew all about that cuz my mama told me when I was a girl, so I'd take care to stay out of the way of Mr. Wharton when the time came."

"The time came? What time?" I could hear a note of hysteria in my voice now. I wanted to run. The implications were clear. But I had pried the lid off this silence and now I was going to get more than I bargained for.

Patty stoically continued, her voice a quiet monotone. "When a Wharton man come of age, he was to take one of us young girls and ... have his way with her, that's what Old Mr. Wharton said. Only he didn't use them words. He said that it kept discipline among the darkies, that's what he said, knowing that their girls could be taken by the Massa at any moment. That's how it was done back in slavery days, Old Mr. Wharton said to his grandson Young Johnny, and that's how it was done during the 'cropping times, too. Any complaints and you were thrown off the land, that's what he said. And this tradition should continue, Old Mr. Wharton said, so that my people would know their place and the Whartons would know theirs — which was over us. That's what he said to Professor Wharton and, as my mama said, that's what he had tole Reverend Johnny, too. So Old Mr. Wharton got my mama to come up to the big house when she was just thirteen years old and he told his son, Reverend Johnny, that he would never be a man unless he had his way with my mama. She hadn't even come of age yet. She was just a girlchile at the time this happened. And she and Reverend Johnny had played together when they was kids."

Patty sat quietly for a moment and then continued. "Reverend Johnny did what he was tole, but it didn't sit well with him. He even tole my mama he was sorry he done it, right sorry. And then he and Old Mr. Wharton had a big falling out and Reverend Johnny run off and that's when he took himself to the seminary. I believe he took off to ask forgiveness from God for what he done. People around here said he was never right in his head after what he'd done to my mama and she being just a little girl yet. He took to wandering the world, not hardly working, not hardly living. When she was serving Old Mr. Wharton a time or two, my mama heard him talking about 'my son, that damn crazy bum' to his friend Mr. Johnson. And he never set foot at Wharton Hall again until it was time for his son, the son that Old Mr. Wharton raised, cuz the Reverend was never right in his head ..." Patty stopped talking and looked up at me with alarm. "Oh, Miz Wharton, you don't want to hear the rest of this story, really, you don't."

"Please, Patty, don't worry about me. Please, I must know the rest. How did Reverend Johnny die?" My own voice was shaky, but it was too late to continue my years of ignorance now. After what I had learned a couple of weeks ago during my visit with Jenny, and after what had happened to my husband, I was beyond shock forever.

"Well, when Young Johnny come of age, Old Mr. Wharton wanted him to go through the ritual too. It was to be on a Wharton man's fourteenth birthday, that's what we heard. But that night when Young Johnny come of age, we weren't watching properly cuz of the mare Belle. She was giving birth in the barn. We were all there watching because the foal was turned, and my daddy had to help turn her right while she was still inside Belle. So, there was a lot of excitement, and no one noticed that Grace ..." Here, Patty broke suddenly into sobs. I went around the table and put my arm around her. And though I knew, I knew what was coming, I felt nothing, nothing at all. As I awkwardly put my arm around her heaving shoulders, I realized that in all the quarter century we had known one another, I had never touched Patty until this minute.

"Who is Grace, Patty?" I asked after a while, when Patty had calmed herself a bit.

"She was my second cousin, as close to me as any sister." Patty's voice was full of regret, and she shook her head sadly as she said this. "Her people had once lived at Wharton Hall too, but they moved to Houston back in the twenties. Her mama and my mama were like sisters though, so we visited as often as we could. Grace and I were like twins, we were, not in looks, but in here." Patty tapped her heart with her closed hand. "She visited for a couple of weeks near every summer when we were girls and we learned to ride the horses. Elton played with us too, those summers. That evening, as I was saying, Grace left us to go to the outhouse, but nobody noticed because of Belle giving birth. Then, after Babe was born and we all knew Belle would be okay too, and mother and daughter were all settled in for the night, that's when we looked around and noticed Grace was missing. My mama had a bad feeling about it right from the start. Old Mr. Wharton, he'd been there for the horse birth, but Young Johnny — he wasn't in the barn. We weren't allowed in Wharton Hall in the evening unless we were called to service. So, to this day, I don't know what he was doing right then. We called and called and looked and looked and finally we found Grace, huddled in the corner of an old tool shed. She was crying and bleeding and shaking something terrible. I was just a girl myself, so I didn't completely understand what had happened, but my mama did. She knew right away. She never forgave herself for not watching Grace more careful that night, though it was true we weren't exactly sure when Young Johnny's birthday was."

"Patty, are you telling me that my husband raped your cousin, Grace?" I said this calmly and without emotion. I felt nothing, could feel nothing.

"I tole you, Miz Wharton, some things are better left in the dark. But yes, ma'am, that's the God-honest truth of the matter. Elton, though he was but sixteen at the time, said, 'Grace, why didn't you scream out? We woulda come after you.' And Grace said, 'Cuz Young Johnny said, 'Keep still! If you scream, you die, and all your darkie relations will be out on the street.' Only he used that other word, not darkie. I will never forget those words as long as I live, Miz Wharton. That's what he said."

Keep still? Keep still! The very words that had defined every act of sex for me for more than twenty years. And then I had a worse thought.

"Patty, could you tell me what Grace looked like then? Was she small and thin?"

Patty looked up from stirring her now-cold tea with her spoon, making little scraping noises against the old china. "Yes ma'am. In that way, we weren't alike at all. She was a little mite, small and thin as a rail. She was just fourteen at the time it happened. But let me finish telling you about that awful night because I ain't tole you about Reverend Johnny yet. A little after we found Grace in the tool shed and Mama was in the cottage cleaning her up and trying to find her some clean panties and such, we hear tires on the dirt road and see headlights. Nobody came here hardly, so we didn't know what to think. So, Elton — who was as upset as I've ever seen him — he wanted to find Young Johnny and give *him* a whuppin' — said he was going out to the front of the house to see who could be coming at this time of night. It was after dark and all. Mama tole me to go with him and don't let him touch Young Johnny, that's what she said. So, the two of us crept around the front of the barn, which was in deep shadow that time of night, and from there we could see the big house veranda. Of course, we had never seen Reverend Johnny, but we knew right away it was him cuz he come out of the car like he was being chased by the devil and he was yelling, 'Where is my son? Where is my son?' Real loud. Old Mr. Wharton and Young Johnny both came out of the house onto the veranda then, and Old Mr. Wharton had his shotgun pointing at his own flesh and blood. He said, 'You get off my property this instant or I will shoot you dead, kin or not. It is done. Your son is a Wharton man. You are too late. Ha! And he enjoyed it too, didn't you my boy?' Then Young Johnny stepped up. 'How dare you come here trying to disrupt my birthday? You're no father to me!'

"And then Reverend Johnny said, 'You will burn in hell for your sins, the two of you! You will burn in hell!' And Young Johnny said — excuse me ma'am, I don't swear like this but to tell it right I have to say what Young Johnny said — and he said, 'Fuck you, Father!' He said 'father' real mean like. Then he said, 'Old Johnny's right, I enjoyed it, quite a bit. It just might become a habit. I'm nothing like you — I am a Wharton man and you're just a crazy loser, no man at all!' Remember, Miz Wharton, Young Johnny was just fourteen at the time and he was under the thumb of Old Mr. Wharton but still, that's no way to talk to your daddy, regardless.

"Reverend Johnny said to his son, 'I came to save you from this scourge, from him,' he said, pointing at Old Mr. Wharton. 'But I came too late and now you, too, are damned. You are doomed. You will burn in hell, the both of you. And I will burn right next to you.' Then he got into his car and drove away. And the next day, they found him drowned in the river, right in his car." Patty went back to stirring her tea. "So that's the all of it, Miz Wharton. I wish I hadn't a tole you, but you asked."

A long moment passed in silence. And then I asked, "Patty, after all this happened, why did you and Elton stay on? When you knew what he was? Why didn't you leave?" Old Johnny was a monster, I saw now. I thought about what I had half-overheard on my wedding day. A monster. And my own husband ... all I could hear reverberating in my head was, 'Keep still! Keep still!'

Patty looked up, her face a mask of sorrow. "I have asked myself that over and over. I think it was my penance."

"Penance? What for? You were just a girl yourself when this happened. You couldn't have protected Grace from Johnny. You were just a girl yourself."

"No ma'am, I know that. I know I couldn't have protected Grace. No, I believe I have been doing penance for all these years for not *being* Grace. For not being the one that got it. My best friend, my cousin, my near to twin, she got it instead. That was just not right. I wished I could take that pain away from her and just bear a little bit of it instead. You know, I never saw Grace again after that night. Next morning, my daddy took her to the bus station and put her on the bus back to Houston. And her folks cut all ties to my folks. My mama near to died over that cuz she loved Aunt Daisy and she felt she had let her down. I ain't never seen Grace again to this very day. But I do believe my penance for not being Grace that night has finally been paid, finally paid. Cuz I lived long enough to see the good that came of that horrible night."

"The good, Patty? What good could there possibly be?"

"The daughter born of that night, Miz Wharton. She looked us up and came out here. She come to see me and Elton not three months ago. She's a spitting image of Grace, she is. And she brought news of Grace, who met a good man who married Grace and adopted her little girl. Grace's girl's name is Rosalyn Eleanor Gaines. Gave her the first lady's middle name, Grace did."

Later, we called Elton and Marvin in and the four of us discussed the future. The historical society would hire them, I'd been told, Patty to keep up Wharton Hall for tourists, Elton and Marvin to take care of the grounds. They were happy when I conveyed the terms to them. I told them about the $10,000 they would each get from the estate for their loyal service.

"What about Babe and Beauty?" Elton asked. He loved those horses; I'd known that for years.

"They're yours, along with the barn and the cottages, Elton and Patty. I'm the widow, I inherited the buildings and horses, and I will sign the papers to make sure they're all yours now. On one condition. You let me come ride on occasion."

We shook on it, and I loaded the couple of boxes, mostly of old photos, I took from Old Johnny's house. As I drove away, my mind reverberated with three words: Rosalyn Eleanor Gaines.

EPILOGUE

MADDIE

She was staring into a shop window, a few stores down and across the street from The Soap Opera, where Roz and I had just emerged with our small bags filled with soaps, lotions, and oils in sandalwood, rose and patchouli. We always stopped at the iconic Madison store the day before our flight back to Texas and the start of another semester. It had been a wonderful break to return to the city where we'd met, the city where we still had so many friends. And to return together, something I had thought would never happen again, was more precious to me than Roz will ever know.

I blinked and looked up again, but she had disappeared into the shop. It couldn't be. It was implausible in the extreme. But it was. It was Jane.

I squeezed Roz's hand, the small act of love something I would have never dared in our Texan college town. Here, it was uneventful. "Follow me," I whispered and wove through the throngs enjoying the perfect blue-sky summer morning and "Maxwell Street Days" — the end of August sidewalk sales, when restaurants put out tables, chairs and umbrellas on the streets and stores set their wares on outside tables or racks and discounted them heavily. We were half hidden behind a rack of Indian-print dresses across the street from where the apparition had disappeared into a clothing store.

"Maddie, what are we doing?" Roz asked reasonably.

"I thought I saw Jane," I breathed.

"Wow." Roz was aware of my theory that Johnny had been murdered, not by some random thief out to steal antiquities from a poorly secured professor's office, but by Jane Meyer, my former graduate student. The fact that she had disappeared shortly after his murder had added to my suspicions. And the police were looking for her too, I'd heard from our department secretary, though without success, so far. I even thought of half a motive, an insight I'd had at the funeral that I'd never been able to shake. Jane had found out, I was certain, that she looked exactly like Johnny's daughter. Just why would a man want to have sex with a woman who was a body double for his own daughter? The possibilities were unsavory or worse. Given Johnny's criminal behavior toward Mama and my suspicions about more recent events, I was inclined to say, "Atta girl, Jane," rather than go to the police with my theory of motive. Johnny had gotten the karmic justice he so deserved.

These reflections made me realize that it had probably been Johnny's daughter I'd seen and not Jane, after all. As if in confirmation, my ghost came out of the store just then, followed by her mother, Liz Wharton. They looked happy together, Liz and her daughter, smiling and sharing some little joke between them. Liz seemed fully recovered from whatever she'd felt over Johnny's death. She smiled easily, I noticed, and even laughed at what her daughter had said. I wasn't sure she was living in Pine Hill Station any longer.

All these thoughts going through my mind had made me forget that I was supposed to be hiding from view, and, between the passersby and my own inattentiveness, I found myself in front of the rack of clothing instead of behind it. I heard my name being called.

"Maddie? Maddie Haystead?" Liz had seen me from across the street and was heading my way, daughter in tow. Jenny, the daughter, still made me start a bit. She was such a dead ringer, as it were, for Jane. Nothing for it now. I'd been seen. I didn't stop to think that Roz and I were wearing matching Women's Transit Authority T-shirts, the one with the raised fist inscribed in the symbol for female. In Madison, this was uncontroversial. But what would Liz think of this overt display of our feminist politics? And had she seen us holding hands not two minutes ago?

I walked toward her and met her in the middle of the closed-off street. Close up, I saw she looked relaxed and tan. We were of a type, I noticed, both slim and petite. Roz, looking gorgeous in her new, close-cropped Afro, had followed me. No stopping this now.

"Hi Liz, good to see you looking so well," I said, truthfully enough, as I shook her hand. The last time I had seen her close up was when I had murmured the conventional "so sorry for your loss" at Johnny's funeral. "Vacationing in Wisconsin?" I continued, not knowing what else to say.

"Sort of. My daughter goes to school at the UW here. She'll be a junior this fall. Jenny, you probably don't remember Professor Haystead, but she was in the same department as your ... father. Maddie, this is my daughter, Jenny."

"Hi, Jenny," I said and shook her hand as well. She was like a hyperreal Jane, much more alive and vivacious. A happy version of Jane. Still, the resemblance was eerie. I thought it likely that neither of them had met or even knew about Jane. "This is my friend, Rosalyn Gaines," I said, indicating Roz, who had drawn up next to me. "She's a professor of epidemiology at our university."

I suddenly realized that Roz was looking at her half-sister, a petite, blond girl, a dozen years her junior. But Roz had assumed neither woman knew of their relation, I could tell. She approached her sister with curiosity, putting her hand out to shake. Jenny took it politely and said, "Hi Dr. Gaines."

But Liz looked like she had seen a ghost.

"Did you say Rosalyn Gaines?" she asked, faintly. Her nicely tanned face seemed drained of blood. She looked at Roz with deadly seriousness. "Would you happen to know Patty and Elton Rambles?"

Roz hadn't been ready for this either, I could see. We both had thought it unlikely that Liz knew of the connection between her late husband and my love. But Liz's reaction and her question suggested that she had talked to Patty and Elton. Roz hesitated for a moment, then, I could see that she had made up her mind to be honest.

"They are my cousins," Roz said quietly.

Liz was doing some quick thinking, too. "Rosalyn," she said, looking at her full in the face and putting out her hand to take Roz's. But she didn't shake it. Instead, she dropped the bag she'd been carrying onto the street and took Roz's hand in both of hers. There were tears in her eyes and her voice quavered. But she asked, "Do you have time to have a drink with Jenny and me? We could sit at the Union Terrace, overlooking Lake Mendota. You too, of course, Maddie." The way she looked at me, I could see she had correctly assessed the nature of our "friendship."

"I think we have some family matters to discuss."

#

ACKNOWLEDGMENTS

Many people deserve thanks for supporting my quest to become a novelist. Two that deserve special mention, and my enduring gratitude, are my always-encouraging writing group leader, reader, and mentor, Maggie Shopen Thompson, and my talented editor and reader Miciah Bay Gault. For their insights and advice, I also thank other early readers of this novel, including Sandy Bogard, Maya Carter, Kayla S. Dunigan, Judith Hinds, Antoinette D. Jones-Houser, Annulla Linders, Therese Mageau, Julia Ostrov, Kristen Plylar-Moore, John Waldo, and Mary Welz. For their inspiration and motivation, I thank my writers' group, North Branch Writers. For her long-ago-help with my efforts, I thank Judith Siegel Flatt.

For their belief in my work and willingness to take me through this project, I thank the good folks at Atmosphere Press: Kyle McCord, Alex Kale, Erin Stalcup, Ronaldo Alves, Erin Larson, Cameron Finch, and the many other people who contributed to making this manuscript a published novel.

Thanks also to my assistant with all things technical, Amy LaFrance.

For his spot-on advice and for being my unwavering brace, backing me up in all my endeavors, I thank my best friend and love, Michael Strebe.

ABOUT ATMOSPHERE PRESS

Atmosphere Press is an independent, full-service publisher for excellent books in all genres and for all audiences. Learn more about what we do at atmospherepress.com.

We encourage you to check out some of Atmosphere's latest releases, which are available at Amazon.com and via order from your local bookstore:

Dancing with David, a novel by Siegfried Johnson

The Friendship Quilts, a novel by June Calender

My Significant Nobody, a novel by Stevie D. Parker

Nine Days, a novel by Judy Lannon

Shining New Testament: The Cloning of Jay Christ, a novel by Cliff Williamson

Shadows of Robyst, a novel by K. E. Maroudas

Home Within a Landscape, a novel by Alexey L. Kovalev

Motherhood, a novel by Siamak Vakili

Death, The Pharmacist, a novel by D. Ike Horst

Mystery of the Lost Years, a novel by Bobby J. Bixler

Bone Deep Bonds, a novel by B. G. Arnold

Terriers in the Jungle, a novel by Georja Umano

Into the Emerald Dream, a novel by Autumn Allen

His Name Was Ellis, a novel by Joseph Libonati

The Cup, a novel by D. P. Hardwick

The Empathy Academy, a novel by Dustin Grinnell

Tholocco's Wake, a novel by W. W. VanOverbeke

Dying to Live, a novel by Barbara Macpherson Reyelts

Looking for Lawson, a novel by Mark Kirby

Yosef's Path: Lessons from my Father, a novel by Jane Leclere Doyle

Surrogate Colony, a novel by Boshra Rasti

About the Author

Cynthia J. Bogard has reinvented herself as a novelist after a successful career as a Professor of Sociology and Women's Studies at Hofstra University in New York. Born and raised in rural Wisconsin, she's lived in Kuwait, Greece, Mexico, New York, Texas, Vermont, and in Madison, Wisconsin.

World traveler, longtime feminist and environmentalist, Greece, mid-20th century jazz, and Mother Nature are all close to her heart. These days, Cynthia lives with her spouse and two rescue dogs in Montpelier, Vermont.

Visit www.CynthiaJBogard.com for news and other writings by Cynthia.

CPSIA information can be obtained
at www.ICGtesting.com
Printed in the USA
BVHW032210140223
658497BV00001B/2

9 781639 886338